D0712004

Shop 'til Yule Drop

ALESIA HOLLIDAY
NAOMI NEALE
STEPHANIE ROWE

LOVE SPELL NEW YORK CITY

LOVE SPELL®

October 2004

Published by

Dorchester Publishing Co., Inc.
200 Madison Avenue
New York, NY 10016

ISBN 0-505-52607-7

Visit us on the web at www.dorchesterpub.com.

Shop 'til Yule Drop

TABLE OF CONTENTS

A Publicist
and a Pear Tree

by Alesia Holliday

For Leah Hultenschmidt, who does a difficult job with enthusiasm and grace. Thanks for letting me borrow your name!

Acknowledgments

As always, to my editor Kate Seaver, who is to editing what
Tiffany's is to jewelry. Thanks for your insights.

To the Bus Stop Ladies, who listened to me whine about
writing a Christmas story when it was sunny and eighty degrees outside. And to Lisa Wangerin, who kept saying Isn't
it August yet?

And to my family, who understands Scary Deadline Face,
but loves me anyway.

Twelve Shopping Days Left

From: KatieC@Today.msn.com
To: LeahD@M&MPublishing.com
Sub: Author publicity
Date: December 13, 2004

Leah,

You're terrific!! I'm just dashing off a note to say that we got your packages on the M&M authors, and they're fabulous!! We're going to highlight a different one of your December release authors on each of the remaining days until Christmas here on the *Today* show. I'll trade off interviews with Matt and Ann. You should come to the set with your authors—we'll do lunch.

And I know NBC is always looking for talented publicists, so if I can coax you away from that corner office at M&M . . .

Later!

Katie

From: TheRipster@RegisandKelly.com
To: LeahD@M&MPublishing.com
Sub: books 'n stuff
Date: December 13, 2004

Leah—I simply *must* have a science fiction book discussion on my show! It's hot—it's sexy—just like me! Let's take your three lead authors and focus a special Christmas Reading on Other Planets with Ripa Book Club around them. How does Monday look?

Call me!

Kelly

From: sue.b.marcus@nytimes.com
To: LeahD@M&MPublishing.com
Sub: The List
Date: December 13, 2004

Leah,

You did it again! All top fifteen slots on the Friday fiction bestsellers list will be filled with M&M authors! How do you do it? That's seventeen weeks in a row!

Sue

From: JimBishop@publishersweekly.com
To: LeahD@M&MPublishing.com
Sub: interview
Date: December 13, 2004

Leah,

We'd like to interview you for an article on the Top Ten Publicists in Publishing Today for the January issue. (You're number one, of course!)

We want to capture the flavor of the exotic books you promote, so we're going to fly you to Tuscany for a week in a villa for the photo shoot. (On our dime, naturally.)

Call me—let's schedule.

And congrats!

Jim

"Leah? Leah? LEAH!"

"Wha' . . . Wha' happened? When? Did Katie call?" I snapped to attention, if you could call yanking my head up off my desk and discovering that drool had plastered three phone messages to my face "snapping."

"Katie who? Were you asleep? At your desk? Really, Leah, I'd hope I could expect more of you."

The Bitch Queen (or BQ, as I not-so-fondly called her) who was, sadly, my boss and M&M's vice president of publicity, stood glaring at me, tapping her ridiculously pointy shoe. Since the pointy toe came back in style, Selena Evans— fashionista wannabe—had looked more and more like her idol, the Wicked Witch of the West. (I wonder if she got all teary-eyed when she went to see *Wicked* on Broadway.)

"Leah? Did you hear me?" Oh, oh. She was PO'd now.

"I'm sorry, Selena," I said, peeling Post-it notes off my woefully inadequate cheekbones. (I look exactly like Claudia Schiffer, except for her cheekbones. And her extra seven inches in height. And her blond hair.)

"I wasn't sleeping. I was thinking about the plans for the marketing tie-ins for the fall line." It was almost true, even. I'd been dreaming about the Jimmy Choo pink-and-crystal stilettos I planned to buy with the enormous raise I'd get for having fifteen authors on the *New York Times* list.

And shopping is kind of like marketing, right?

"I need those PR plans for the June books on my desk by five o'clock tomorrow, Leah. I don't care about the marketing tie-ins, yet. Anyway, you know perfectly well that marketing and merchandising tie-ins are *my* exclusive purview."

She turned on her three-inch heels and brushed an imaginary speck off of her size-two skirt, then marched off to wherever she stored her Prada broomstick, no doubt.

I briefly contemplated shooting a rubber band at the back

of her pointed head and was just reaching for my stash when she stopped in mid-stride and looked back at me over her shoulder.

"Just because we worked a little late last night is no excuse to slack off today, Leah. If this job is too much for you, I have the résumés of at least one hundred girls on my desk. I'm sure one of *them* would be able to stay awake at her desk."

Parting shot delivered with consummate Cruella de Vil malice, she finally stalked off.

I stared blearily around at my "corner office." Ha. Third cube on the left was more like it. A four-by-six beige-on-beige space where the bulk of our authors' vastly over-inflated hopes for national TV spots, European book tours, and full-page ads in *USA Today* came crashing down to Earth—or, to be specific, to my mud-colored carpet with the double-espresso stain in the corner.

Well, at least if I had to fall asleep at my desk after working until two in the morning on a Sunday night and then hoofing it back here at eight A.M., I had *great* dreams.

I looked at the piles of paper threatening to collapse my desk under their weight and sighed. Twelve shopping days 'til Christmas. That meant only nine business days until our ten-day holiday break. Or—reality check—only nine days in which to do a month's worth of work.

Coffee. I had to have caffeine to deal with this. A nice gingerbread latte from Starbucks might help, plus it would be festive. I grabbed my new Chanel clutch (well, new to *me*—thank God and Santa Claus for eBay) and headed for the elevator.

Luckily, Selena wasn't lurking around playing hall monitor, as she loved to do. As the elevator doors started to close behind me, I heaved a sigh of relief.

Escape.

"Hold the elevator!" A slender hand and arm weighted

down with bracelets dripping Swarovski crystals stopped the motion of the elevator doors, and Gillian and Devon pushed their way into the elevator with me.

If there were anything harder to stomach pre-caffeine than assistant editors, I hoped never to see it. These two were among the worst we'd ever had during my three-year tenure at M&M. Gillian had recently graduated from Harvard and managed to work that fact into all conversations approximately once every ten minutes. Devon (and Jenny in HR told me that Devon's real name is Donna; talk about pretentious) had so many trust funds she couldn't keep them all straight.

Of course, that was a much better way to be able to afford to work in New York publishing than my route—the "live on coffee and Ramen noodles diet in order to be able to afford a tiny apartment you share with three other girls" plan.

Devon lived on Central Park West with her parents, naturally. Not a lot of Ramen noodles there.

My envy-induced sulking didn't preclude me from listening in on their conversation, natch.

"Can you *believe* these authors? I'm raking in the loot!" Devon rubbed her hands together and chortled.

"I got six boxes of Godiva just this morning. I *love* the holidays. Who needs to shop for gifts when you've got authors?"

They snickered, and Gillian's eyes widened in an exaggerated expression of shock and dismay. "What? You *recycle*?"

Devon brushed her fake blond hair off one Armani-clad shoulder. "Recycle? Please. I have recycling down to an art form. I've got a stack of name tags in my desk already made out to friends and family. Usually I don't even have to rewrap. As if I'd ever eat all that chocolate. Can you imagine the hours of Pilates I'd be forced to endure?"   •

The elevator doors stopped, and the doors opened about a half-second before my hands could reach her throat. Probably a good thing, since murdering editors tends to give you a bad rep in the very, very small world of New York publishing. The Deadly Duo was headed to Starbucks, too, so I paused to let them get ahead of me.

Way ahead.

Gillian glanced back at me and stopped dead. "Leah, why on earth do you have writing all over your face?"

My mouth fell open. *The message slips. Great. "Her face was an open book" takes on a whole new meaning.*

I grabbed a tissue out of my purse and scrubbed at my cheek, which was probably the color of Santa's suit by then. Gillian and Devon walked on toward the lobby Starbucks, cackling loudly.

I dumped the tissue in the nearest of the wastebaskets discreetly placed at the edge of the lobby's marble floor. One Publisher's Square, as everybody called our building, was all about tasteful displays of power and money. The pianist serenading us with a Muzak-ized version of "The Twelve Days of Christmas" grinned at me as I passed. I could feel my face get even hotter, so I started power breathing. Relaxation exercises never worked for me, but they were at least a distraction.

The festive joy of the holiday decorations that festooned the lobby mocked my Grinchy mood. I sneered at the tinsel and poinsettias, feeling my heart shrink three or maybe even four sizes smaller on the spot.

A friendly voice broke into my scowling thoughts. "Tired of hearing about how people at Harvard celebrate Christmas?"

I smiled up at the welcome sight of Sarah Mitchell, my favorite editor and best friend, who'd clearly encountered the evil twins. "No, this time it was how the rude and inconsiderate authors were burying them under an avalanche of expensive chocolate gifts, which they were then forced to recycle as presents for unsuspecting relatives."

I may have sounded just the teensiest bit bitter, because Sarah started laughing as we entered my favorite house of caffeine. "Not much chocolate on publicity row this year?"

"Ha! Three cards. That's it. And two of *those* were e-cards. Can you believe it? Nothing says Happy Holidays like the supreme effort of sending an e-card." I snorted in disgust and realized we'd reached the front of the line of crazed caffeine addicts.

"Tall gingerbread latte, please."

The barrista was used to my ten A.M. fixes. "No whip?"

"Today I want whip. No, *extra* whip. And cinnamon. In fact, give me a chocolate croissant."

Pete recoiled in mock horror as he rang up two days' worth of calories on his tinsel and lights–decked register. "What's the occasion, Leah? Big celebration? Did you finally land a national TV spot for one of your science fictoids?"

I bared my teeth, but before I could actually bite him, Sarah cut in. "Leah's got the Grinchies, Pete. She's drowning her crabbiness in cinnamon whip."

After Sarah paid for her tall Americano, we headed back to the elevators.

"Hey, this might cheer you up, Leah. My brother's in town for two weeks, and I'm having a little party Friday. Can you make it?"

"Party. Paaarty. Gee, the word sounds familiar, but I can't quite grasp the concept. The BQ has me working so many hours, my social life died a slow and hideous death along with my ficus. Can you elaborate?"

"Food. Drinks. Music. Be there. Eight o'clock. And I

heard that Howard isn't all that happy with the BQ, so maybe she's piling on the work to try to impress him."

The elevators opened on our floor, and I trudged off, waving at Sarah as she headed for the editorial side of the floor. "I'll try to make the party, but don't count on it."

Interesting about what she said, though. Howard was the president, CEO, and king-on-throne of M&M Publishing. If he so much as slanted an eyebrow in Selena's direction, she'd have me jumping through hoops from now till the Fourth of July.

Back in cube sweet cube, I slumped in my chair, sipping latte. *OK, can't put it off any longer.* I touched my mouse and morosely watched my Josh Duhamel screensaver dissolve into a list of my new e-mails. Josh's pixels were the closest I'd been to a man's bare chest in a long, long time, if you don't count the hairy guy at the gym who always flashes his paunch at any woman within a ten-foot radius. (And that's just sick and wrong.)

It's eleven, Leah. We've come to the conclusion of the e-mail avoidance portion of our entertainment.

"All right, already," I muttered, responding to my own thoughts, thus cementing my title as Nut Job of the Season. I scanned my . . . OH MY GOD! *Three hundred and sixty-seven new e-mail messages? Since* two o'clock *in the morning?*

That's averaging four thousand e-mails per week, which means I should be dead before I'm thirty.

Way before.

Also: Don't these people have lives?

I slumped farther in my chair, until my face was practically level with my keyboard. No messages from Katie, Kelly, or any other morning talk divas, I noticed, as I did a quick scan. I reviewed the list of senders and felt my forehead getting scrunchier and scrunchier. Could twenty-six-year-olds get Botox?

Seventeen new messages from Glenwood E. Hamilton III, our newest author. The ink on his contract wasn't yet dry, but he was already demanding a conference call and a written report of my publicity plans for his book. He thought *Good Morning America* would be the perfect spot for his book tour kickoff.

Great. Perfect.

Except for the part about *Good Morning America*. Or the part about a book tour.

First, Diane Sawyer at *GMA* wasn't really known for reviewing science fiction mass-market originals with titles like *Head-Banging Artichoke Babes from Outer Space*. (Not that I—a mere PR slut—would ever presume to question editorial's brilliant choice of book titles, of course. But, *please*.)

Second, M&M didn't send first-time authors on book tours. These days, we rarely sent any authors on book tours, unless they were *New York Times* bestsellers. Book tours cost a lot to put together and were spectacularly ineffective for authors who weren't "names." The horror stories I'd heard from our authors who'd set up their own tours were scarier than a one-armed bikini waxer. These poor authors, drunk on the euphoria of a first published book, would hit all of their local bookstores on a series of weekends. They reported hours of isolation, broken only by the thrill of directing people to the bathroom.

So, Glenwood III was in for a big letdown. As usual, it fell on my shoulders (or typing fingers, to be precise) to toss a little reality his way. Authors rarely complained to their editors about anything, and Selena considered herself to be entirely too far up the food chain to talk to writers. I once heard her brag that she hadn't spoken to an author in three years.

My phone rang, and I glared at it but picked up anyway.

"Leah speaking."

"Hello, darling. It's Mom. We are so excited to come visit New York at Christmas! Are you excited? Do you have our reservations confirmed? Daddy wanted to call, but I told him that our big girl living in the big city could take care of things all by herself. We're just so proud of you, dear. Do you carry that pepper spray we gave you for your birthday?"

Mom paused for a breath, and I felt the smile spread all over my face. It may be totally uncool to have Midwesterners for family, but I adored my parents and was *so* looking forward to spending the holidays with them here, for the first time ever. Since September 11, Mom and Dad thought New York was the center of all evil in the country, and that my daily commute was an obstacle course of muggers, terrorists, and flashers. I'd tried to explain that security was in place, and New York was as safe as good old Columbus, Ohio. They clung to their view of "The Big Apple," as Dad insisted on calling it, though, and nothing was going to convince them any differently. The pepper spray was stuffed in my desk drawer somewhere, because I'd been afraid I'd spray it in my own eyes if I ever tried to use it.

"Yes, Mom. I'm very safe. Your hotel is set; I just quadruple-checked your reservations this morning. I'm sorry you can't stay with me, but my roommates haven't decided yet if they're going out of town or not for the holidays."

My three roommates had been friends in college and spent most of their time making me feel like an outsider. They were nice enough, but every other sentence was an inside joke or gossip about some person I'd never met. I would have minded more if we ever saw one another, but they were all serious party girls and my 24/7 workaholic lifestyle meant I generally left for work around the time they got home. They all worked as bartenders in various oddly named clubs, like Puce and Redundancy. I'd found them through a roommate-wanted ad. The rent was reasonable enough, and none of them were terrible slobs, so it was good enough for now. Someday, though . . .

I sighed.

"What's the matter, dear? Would you rather come home for the holidays? I can fix up your room for you." Mom wouldn't hesitate to bail on plane tickets and reservations if she thought she could get me back to Ohio for some TLC.

That's tender love and claustrophobia, in case you don't have an overprotective mother. Speaking of which, *claus*-trophobia fits me in so many ways. Is there a *Santa Claus*–trophobia?

I shook my head and laughed. "No, Mom, I am not homesick, and I don't want to come home to Ohio. I was thinking about my roommates. They're a little tiring sometimes."

"What's wrong? Are they dopers? Are they crack addicts?" My mother saying the word *dopers* has to be one of the funniest things in the world. This is a woman who thinks you can overdose on Vitamin C and get high. We mainlined orange juice in Ohio.

"Yes, Mom. It's a problem when I keep tripping over their used needles in the morning."

"What?" Now she was hyperventilating.

"Mom, Mom. Calm down. I was kidding. They're perfectly nice and definitely *not* dopers. They just tend to leave decisions till the last minute. I'll probably find out on Christmas Eve whether they're leaving town for the holidays."

I took a sip of rapidly cooling latte. "What about you? Are you packed? Are you excited?" Getting Mom talking about packing was a surefire way to distract her from the phantom drug dealers in my neighborhood.

"I'm almost packed! I just need an evening gown—you know, just in case we decide to go to a ball while we're there. Did your sister call you?"

"Ball? What ball? Mom, I told you we would just be casual and hang out. You definitely do not need an evening gown. And, no, what's up with Mindy?"

My sister was about eight months pregnant, due in late January, so there was no problem with my parents coming to visit at the holidays. Well, no problem if you don't count my brother's wife, Trina, who was about seven months pregnant with twins. Mindy and Trina had been playing a game of Whose Pregnancy Symptoms Are the Worst? for the past few months that was driving everyone else in the family insane.

Dad said he'd actually left the dinner table during a discussion of whose Braxton-Hicks contractions were more painful. (I don't know, something about fake contractions that make you think you're having the baby, but you're not. They start tossing around phrases like *cervical dilation* and *uterus* and I tune out. I mean, yuck.)

"Mindy's having contractions. The doctor said not to worry, they're just those Haxton-Bricks again. Whatever those are. I tell you, when I had you kids, there wasn't all of this silliness. You just went in, got drugged up, and pushed the baby out."

My mom snorted. "Can you imagine your father participating in a hot tub birth? That's Trina's latest notion. Your brother said he threw up watching the video. No wonder, if you ask me."

Mom wasn't a big fan of natural childbirth. Me, neither, if it ever came to that. Do they have pregnancy tests that come packaged with the epidural?

"Mom, is everything OK?"

She sighed. "Yes, dear. It was just a little vomit. Even your big baby of a brother can—"

"No, Mom. Not Josh. Is everything OK with Mindy?"

"Oh. Yes, she's fine. Everything is on track for January twenty-second. You better believe I'll be camping out in the hospital with her. It's going to be fun to be awake for an actual birth—I missed all of my own."

The New Message counter on my screen flashed in my eyes. . . . 368, 369, 370 . . . "Mom, I love you, but I have to get to work. I have a kajillion e-mails to answer. I'll call you soon, and we'll confirm the details again. I can't wait to see you and Dad! Love to Mindy and Trina and the babies."

"Bye, honey. See you soon."

As I replaced the phone in its cradle, I grinned and shook my head. My family is the least dysfunctional family I know. No divorces, no drinking problems, no adultery, no nothing. You'd think I had to be in denial, but we're like some weird throwback to the fifties. None of my friends could believe I'd never been in therapy. I almost felt left out enough to go find a shrink, until I calculated how many pairs of shoes I could buy with the cost of weekly couch sessions. Trust me, I can lie down on my own couch and talk about my childhood, while I admire my well-shod feet.

I looked at the screen again. No magical elves had cleared out my e-mail in box while I talked to Mom. I sighed again and glanced at my watch.

Hey, almost lunch time. I need to do my Christmas shopping.

I logged off my computer, guilt seeping out of my pores,

and snagged my bag from my desk drawer. I still hadn't found gifts for Mom and Dad, and they'd be here in ten days.

As I lurked in front of the elevator doors, sneaking glances down the hall toward Selena's office, I thought about what to get Mom that would scream *I Heart NY* and be fun for her to show off to all her friends. She adored kitschy stuff, but I'd already splurged on the three-foot tall neon-orange lava lamp shaped like the Statue of Liberty for her birthday. How could I top that?

"Leah! Where are you going this time? It's harder and harder to find you at your desk these days!" Selena had snuck up on me from behind. *What was she doing on that side of the hallway?*

"Um, I . . . er, my parents are coming for the holidays, and I thought I'd take an early lunch to do some shopping. I *was* here until two this morning working on the PR plans, Selena. It's not really fair to—"

She cut me off with a look. "Again, Leah, any time you think you can't handle this job, please let me know. I'm sure I can find a *qualified* candidate."

Just then, Howard's secretary rushed into sight and hurried toward us. "Selena, Selena. Howard's been trying to reach you about Alexis Day and her PR opportunity at the hospital. He needs to see you in his office right now."

Saved by the CEO. Whew.

Selena speared me with a glance. "Don't think this conversation is over. I'll catch up to you later. If you can be bothered to make it back to work after lunch."

She stalked off down the hall toward Howard's secretary just as the *ding* heralding the arrival of the elevator sounded. *Oh, fine.* Now *it finally gets here.*

* * *

I put my feet on automatic pilot and took off down Madison Avenue. I planned on turning off toward Tiffany's but had to fight my way out of the surging crowd of holiday shoppers. One woman wearing a full-length fur and a rabid expression actually snapped at me when I crossed in front of her. I started humming "Tis the Season to be Greedy" and kept walking.

In spite of my earnest words to Selena earlier—and they were the truth, I *was* woefully behind on my to-buy list—I had to visit my necklace before I could even think of shopping. I slowed my steps in front of the blue and white–draped window and sighed.

There it was, in all of its sparkling glory. It wasn't the most expensive piece in the store—not by a long shot. It wasn't even the most beautiful. But there was something about the tiny gold star, with a single diamond suspended in its center, that drew me hypnotically to the display window again and again. Surrounded by bigger, bolder, and brasher pieces, my necklace was the Charlie Brown Christmas tree of jewelry. A gossamer-light chain laced through the pendant, fragile as moonlight on Christmas Eve snow. Fragile as hope; ephemeral as dreams.

I shook my head, impatient with my flight of poetic stupidity. Dreams weren't ephemeral, they were idiotic. And I'd seen how well hopes worked out the last time I'd hoped for jewelry at Christmas. I could still envision the shock on Mickey's face when I mentioned the diamond ring I was so sure he'd gotten me for Christmas.

Ring? But, but, we're just having a bit of fun here, aren't we? I mean, the sex is fine and all, but it's not like we want to settle down and make babies. We're not even thirty yet!

The sex is fine and all—what could ever top those immortal words of holiday cheer?

As I slumped farther inside my coat, trying to pretend

my ears weren't going to freeze and fall off any second in the December chill, a lightbulb flashed in my head.

Sadly, it wasn't a euphemism for a magnificent epiphany about the nature of love and loss. It was an actual lightbulb.

A huge one.

A flashbulb, to be exact. On an enormous camera. Right in my face.

Blinking through the giant purple and red spots obscuring my vision, I said, "What?"

I kept blinking, eyes watering, and one of the giant spots started to look like a man.

It figures.

As my poor retinas struggled to focus, the photographer's features came into view. He leaned against the window, still holding the evil camera, and grinned at me.

"Sorry. I didn't mean to blind you. Got caught up in the moment and forgot I had the super-sized flash on—to use technical photographer's jargon. It's for the inside shots but, well, I saw you through the window and had to come outside and capture you."

I blinked again, but this time from his words. *Did he just say he had to capture me?*

Thoughts of raiding space pirates danced through my head, as I gave him the quick no-I'm-not-really-checking-you-out once-over.

Holy Artichoke babes, the man is totally hot.

(OK, I really needed to quit thinking in phrases parodying my current books, but it was a hazard of the trade.)

From his tousled, sun-streaked dark hair (and trust me, with the fortune I pay at the hairdresser's, I know the difference between real sun and the bottle—this guy was no Miss Clairol) to the tips of his scuffed boots, the man was a total yumfest. He stared at me with green eyes the exact color of the emerald half-moon earrings I'd coveted last Christmas.

He pushed away from the wall and stepped nearer. "Miss, are you OK? Again, sorry about the flash. But I really need to ask your permission to use you."

Use me, oh, please use me. My thoughts circled madly around the ways I'd love for him to do just that and— *WHAM!*—my nipples got hard.

OK, so eight months without sex has turned me into a shameless nympho. Any minute now I'll be humping his leg like a crazed poodle.

I made some kind of weird gargling noise and pretended I was coughing. "Er, um, I mean, who are you, and what are you talking about?"

The Mad Flasher/User reached a hand out toward me, and I backed away fast, desperately rummaging around in my bag.

"Look, buddy, I warn you that I'm a native New Yorker, and I know how to use this." Triumphant, I closed my fingers around my weapon, whipped it out of my bag, and brandished it in front of his face.

There was a small silence as we both looked at my spare bottle of deodorant.

He grinned again. "I'm glad to know that. I'd hate to have taken the picture of a stinky subject. You smell pretty good from here, though."

I shoved the Extra-Strength Super Dry back in my bag, feeling my cheeks blaze to the color of Santa's suit. "I was going for the pepper spray, but it's actually back in my office drawer. Anyway, you're not going to accost me right here on the street, are you? And what are you talking about with capturing and using?"

I glared at him when his grin widened. Damn if he didn't fill out those faded jeans really, really well too. (OK, I wasn't *only* looking at his grin. So sue me.)

"I was talking about your permission to use your photograph in a shoot I'm doing for the store. Christmas at Tiffany's and all that hoopla. But I like the way you put it better. Not the accosting part, but the capturing and using sounds . . . intriguing."

He shifted his camera to his left hand and held out his right. "Luke Mitchell. Photographer. Rude and insensitive flash-shooter-offer. All-around nice guy. And you are?"

"Annoyed. Perhaps you could give someone warning before you take her picture? What if I'd had some kind of heart condition, and that hideous flash caused me to have an infarction and die right here on the street?" I folded my arms across my chest and glared at him. Not that I really knew what an infarction was, but it sounded bad.

Anyway, I had no time for this, no matter how gorgeous he was. It's not like he could be in serious contention as a dating prospect, either. The timing was all off. There were only twelve days until Christmas; not nearly enough time for him to date me and dump me on Christmas Eve. Then it would be another entire year until next Christmas, way too much time for us to stay together so he could dump me by Christmas Eve.

Like every guy I'd ever dated had done.

Not that I'm bitter.

Luke broke into my calendar-centric musings. "Well, you look pretty good for somebody who's in imminent danger of infarcting, um . . . I didn't catch your name?"

"No, you didn't, because I didn't give it. I don't want to be part of your book or your hoopla, or whatever. I'm a publicist; the last thing I need is to be part of somebody else's publicity. Sorry to be rude, but I have to go." I almost hated to cause the smile to fade from his lovely face, but I had to get back to reality. I still hadn't done any shopping, and Selena was undoubtedly sitting outside of my cubicle with her stopwatch.

As I turned away, he touched my arm. "Look, I know I was rude, but I . . . I saw you staring at that necklace with a look of sadness on your face, and I felt it clear through to my gut. That's how I know when I capture the truth in a shot—I feel it in the pit of my stomach."

"So, I'm like nausea?" I tried to stop the smile twitching at the edges of my lips, but he saw it and muttered something. (I could have sworn it was *No, more like heartburn*, but I might be wrong.)

"Look, miss, um . . ."

"It's Leah, OK? Just Leah."

"Look, Just Leah, the expression of longing on your face perfectly captures the essence of holiday shopping. Or what holiday gift-giving *ought* to be about. An Audrey Hepburnesque innocence and wistfulness."

"*What?*" He had to be kidding. Talk about PR Speak— *Hepburnesque?*

He rolled his eyes. "Hell, I don't know what that means, either. It was in the catalog copy, and I thought I'd give it a try. My sister says women love that flowery stuff."

I laughed. "Nice try, but I'm afraid I can't. Good luck with your shoot."

"At least take my card. I'm in town for two weeks for this shoot and to visit my sister. If you change your mind, or if you'd like to have a drink or dinner and talk about old Hepburn movies or something, give me a call." He pulled a crumpled card out of the pocket of his faded leather jacket and pressed it into my hand.

I shook my head and opened my mouth to refuse, but he pressed his finger against my lips, then jerked it away, eyes widening as a tiny spark of static jumped between us. It fireballed into a sizzling current of electricity that shot through my body all the way to my toes. Every nerve ending on my body stood at attention. All from one touch.

Just think if we were naked, said the wanton seductress who lived deep inside my brain.

Yeah, I live too *deep inside your over-active brain. Why don't you let me out to play now? I'll bet this guy is off the charts on the Orgasmotron,* Seductress Leah said.

I felt heat shooting to my cheeks this time. Luke still stood as if frozen in place, and then he slowly brought his finger to his mouth and pressed it against his own lips, as if he were tasting my mouth with his own. The sensuality of it sparked the heat racing down to an area approximately in the center of my new silk panties.

Gotta go, gotta go, my rational side said.

Wanna come, wanna come, the rest of me said.

I stuffed Luke's card in my coat pocket and took off, almost running, down the sidewalk. I definitely didn't have time to get flustered over a case of the lusts for some guy who was only in town for two weeks.

What could it hurt, though, really? my rational side said.

"Traitor," I muttered as I shoved my way through the crowds and considered my worthless lunch hour. I hadn't bought any presents, and now I was going to be late for the afternoon staff meeting.

Deck the freakin' halls.

Eleven (Hundred) E-mails

The Ghost of Christmas Present must have been looking out for me, because when I shot into the conference room fifteen minutes past the appointed start of the weekly staff meeting, there was nobody there. As I glanced around, clutching the doorknob, Gillian walked by in the hall and started laughing.

"Didn't you get the message? Selena has a big powwow in Howard's office. No meeting today."

She cast a critical gaze down my rumpled appearance. "You know, one doesn't have to attend Harvard to have heard of the invention of the iron, Leah. You're never going to get anywhere in life if you always dress like the cleaning lady."

I gritted my teeth together to keep from replying with a truly withering put-down.

I even tried to think of one.

Somehow, "Oh, yeah?" didn't seem to have the cachet I was going for.

As Gillian swept on down the hall, no doubt to recycle yet more expensive chocolate, I felt the magnetic lure of my computer sucking me back to my cubicle. It was time.

Time for the Annual E-mail Purge.

Every year, just before the holidays, I purged my in box of all of the accumulated e-mails I'd opened, skipped over, or just tried to ignore altogether. By the time I returned to work after our weeklong holiday break, there were always new ones waiting for me, but at least I had the satisfaction—for one brief, shining, cyber-moment—of seeing the e-mail counter register a big, fat zero.

I pulled my chair up to my desk and rolled up my sleeves. I was determined. I was dedicated. I was dying to get it over with.

I opened four temporary folders under the in box umbrella and labeled them according to their status as per my snap executive decisionmaking and the planned final resolution of their soon-to-be contents:

1. Totally Ridiculous Requests
2. Never Gonna Happen
3. Maybe, If You're Astonishingly Lucky, and
4. You Just Might Get What You Want (aka Merry Christmas)

Then I took a deep breath and a long swallow of the Diet Coke I'd snagged from the vending room, and got to work. (I wasn't really ignoring BQ's edicts about the PR plans for the June books; she'd said she wanted them on her desk by five o'clock tomorrow, so if I worked half the night, it wouldn't be a problem. *Much.*)

Plus, this way I could be a Rebel Without a Claus for a while.

I looked at my list and—out of nowhere—the annoying photographer's face flashed in front of me. Except, he really hadn't been all *that* annoying. I put my hand in my coat pocket to see if his card was still in there. *Yep.*

LUKE MITCHELL, PHOTOGRAPHER. That was the entire card. Well, that and his cell phone number and e-mail address. He must really move around a lot, if he didn't even have a P.O. Box listed on his business card. I sighed and wondered what his neck would taste like. *I wonder how he gets his mail?*

Mail . . . oh, *mail! Snap out of it, Leah, and get going on the e-mail.*

Sighing, I clicked open the first message.

Two hours and a slight case of carpal tunnel later, I'd at least sorted all of my messages into the four new folders (and discarded outright about three hundred of them). My tally:

1. Totally Ridiculous Requests = 570
2. Never Gonna Happen = 412
3. Maybe, If You're Astonishingly Lucky = 101
4. You Just Might Get What You Want (aka Merry Christmas) = 17

Fresh from a bathroom break and a quest for another cold soda, I tackled the TRRs.

To: Leah
From: Glenwood E. Hamilton III

Leah, I know you're very busy, but I fail to understand why you have failed to respond to my last twelve messages. It has been three entire days, and I consider this lack of attention to be quite a failing on your part.

Three "fails" in two sentences? How did this guy get published?

I watched *Good Morning America* this morning and noticed that the author who discussed her current book was writing some kind of non-sense called "chick lit." What is this? Books about poultry? Why are books about fowl being considered for national news shows, but I have not yet been booked for my insightful space epic, *Head-Banging Artichoke Babes from Outer Space*?

Please respond at your earliest convenience.

Very truly yours,

Glenwood E. Hamilton III

P.S. Per your use of the nickname "Glen" in your prior correspondence, please be advised that I find nicknames to be a failing of the proper use of the English language. Glenwood or Mr. Hamilton will do. Thank you.

Another "fail," Glennie? How's that for *proper use*? So, writing back at my "earliest convenience" means approximately the day that the Earth is sucked into a huge hole in the sun and explodes, Glennie. Aaarghhhhh.

I took a deep breath and searched for calm professionalism.

To: Glenwood
From: Leah

Glenwood, as I've explained before, *GMA* rarely books first-time authors of mass-market paperbacks. In fact, *never* would probably be the correct use of the qualifier in this case. Furthermore, we don't start pitching books to the media so far out—in this case, eleven months before your book will actually be released.

Please enjoy the holidays and know that we at M&M are working hard to make your book a success. Also, feel free to contact Selena if you have any further questions.

Happy Holidays!

Leah

I stabbed the Send button and felt a maniacal grin trying to surface. Merry Christmas, Selena! You can have Glenwood all wrapped up and tied with a pretty ribbon.

My smile faded a little as I realized I had 569 more TRRs to go, but I cut and pasted the final paragraph of my e-mail to Glennie at the bottom of very brief notes for the next hour and finally worked my way through them all. One folder down, three to go.

I opened the Never Gonna Happen folder and sighed.

To: Leah
From: Selma

Our 17th annual Science Fiction Conference (Theme: **BUST THE STEREOTYPE—WE DON'T LIVE IN OUR PARENTS' BASEMENTS**) will be held in late January in Buffalo, New York. We'd like to invite you to give a talk about new trends in publishing. Dressing up as your favorite X-Men character is optional (but we highly recommend it; the editor who wore a vinyl bustier to talk about series characters in fiction was very popular).

To: Selma
From: Leah

Although I am honored to be asked, my schedule is unfortunately booked solid for winter conferences.

(And I'd stab myself with a rusty ski pole before I'd go to Buffalo in January; *great* planning.)

I wish you all success with your conference. Please do ask me again.

(I'll see if I can't get my vinyl bustier out of the cleaners by then. Or maybe my Klingon costume.)

The phone rang as I contemplated my non-existent cleavage and wondered how much mileage in cup-size terms I might get out of a vinyl bustier. (Note to self: check fetish stores; can't hurt to look.) *Wonder if Luke likes vinyl bustiers?*

Whoa. Where did that *come from? Must quit thinking about nomadic photographer. He's probably the kind of guy with a girl in every one-hour developer.*

"Leah speaking."

"Leah? Are you finally back? Where are those plans?" It was Selena, and she sounded hysterical. *Maybe she's finally cracking under the burden of all that nastiness.*

"Selena, you said by five tomorrow. I am just trying to get a few other urgent tasks out of the way so I can devote my full attention to the plans." I made a face at the phone, realizing my career was doomed if we ever got videoconferencing.

"Tomorrow? Tomorrow? I'm sure I said today. Howard wants to see those plans ASAP, Leah. And I need to call some . . . *authors*."

She said *authors* with the inflection most people would use to say *toenail fungus*. Why did this woman work in publishing, again?

"So send me some names and phone numbers. I want four or five of the . . . least needy ones. And definitely *not* that annoying Hamilton person. He's e-mailed me a thousand times in the past week. I had to get a nail repaired from hitting the delete key so often." She made a weird, shuddery noise, as if the thought of it horrified her. For once, Selena and I were in complete agreement. Just think—it took Glenwood E. Hamilton III, to make it happen.

"I'll send you the authors, Selena, but I won't have the plans until tomorrow, as you originally requested. We want them to be really good, don't we?"

This was kind of a no-win question for her. She couldn't really say, *No, we want them to be total crap.*

She blew out a sigh with explosive force. "Fine, Leah. But we really have to talk about your subpar job performance. I think we'll move your annual review up to early January, shall we?"

After dropping that bomb, she hung up on me. I stared at the phone in disbelief. Three years of working my butt off to climb M&M's corporate ladder, in spite of my secret suspicion that somebody had slicked Vaseline on the rungs, and my job performance is subpar? I unclenched my fingers from the phone, resisting the urge to slam it against my forehead.

After I sent off the names of five of the "least needy" authors I could find in my Contacts. I glared at my computer screen. Good thing I'd already sorted all my e-mail messages, or they'd all end up in a No Freakin' Way folder, now.

I took a deep breath, tried to shake off BQ's corrosive influence, and opened the next NGH message while mentally categorizing take-out dinner possibilities. It was looking like another late night.

If I were Cinderella, my Metro Card would have just turned back into a big rat. My bleary eyes watered as I opened the very last e-mail in the Just Might Get What You Want folder. At least I'd saved the best for last. Alexis Day was one of my favorite authors. This e-mail actually had only hit my in box late this afternoon. I always made responding to our authors a priority, even when they asked for the moon, the stars, and an appearance on *David Letterman*. But Alexis was one of my special favorites. She was a *New York Times* best-selling author and one of the most gracious people I'd ever met. None of her amazing success had turned her into a diva. Everybody at M&M loved her.

I scanned her message. She sounded pretty abrupt, which was unusual.

To: **Leah**
From: **Alexis**

I've tried for weeks to get through to Selena about this, since Howard's e-mail about me working directly with her from now on. (Which I don't agree with—I love working with you, but I can address that with Howard.) In any event, she won't return my calls. I haven't spoken to her one single time. And my e-mails all bounce back with some stupid out-of-office-I'll-get-right-back message.

She hasn't.

I'm trying to set up a reading event at a local children's hospital for a charity drive for their cancer-patient wing, and I need some help with publicity so we can bring in some serious dollars. So far, I've gotten nothing from M&M. First, I was simply embarrassed. Now I'm angry.

I'm attaching a file with the details. I want a response within twenty-four hours with specific points addressed, or my next call is to Howard. Believe me, I can find another publisher that doesn't treat its authors like this.

Sorry to dump this on you right before the holidays, Leah. I hope your mom and dad are well.

Best,
Lexi

Holy cow. If we lost Alexis Day to another house, Selena would find a way to blame it on me. I'd never work in publishing again. I shoved everything else out of my mind and sent her file to print. As I pushed my chair back to go in search of an IV bottle of Diet Coke, I glanced at the clock again.

I won't get home till after two A.M. again. Am I a party girl or what?

Ten Outraged Authors

I arranged my naked body, draped in ice-blue satin, on the display counter.

"That's perfect, beautiful. Just one more like that, and we'll still be on time for our reservations at the Four Seasons. And then later I'd love to see you wearing nothing but drops of champagne back at my place for dessert." Luke's green eyes gleamed with unconcealed desire, and the way his jaw clenched told me I wasn't the only one having a hard time keeping my mind on the photo shoot.

I smiled my most enticing you-know-you-want-me, I-am-a-sex-goddess smile. "Anytime, darling. But only if you let me have *my* dessert first." I slid my tongue across my bottom lip and watched his hands tighten on the camera.

"Leah, I must have you. You are the sexiest, most desirable woman I have ever met. Promise me you will be mine forever." He strode over to me and captured me in his manly arms and

My alarm went off.

Bleary eyed, I gazed at the clock in the pre-dawn December dark. What kind of idiot gets up at six when she only went to bed three hours ago?

And, *"Manly arms"? "Mine forever"? Is Glennie III writing the dialogue for my dreams now? Aarghh.*

I dragged my protesting bones out of bed and found the last clean thing in my closet. Unfortunately, it was a blue suede mini.

"Record low temperatures, New Yorkers! Better bundle up nice and warm!" The perpetually perky radio announcer sounded like he was laughing at me. Any minute now he'd say something about idiots who wear miniskirts in December.

I turned the radio off and headed for the bathroom. Time to do something with the hair. *Is it bad to wear a ponytail to work every day for five weeks?*

Only eight A.M., and there I was in my cubicle again. Other than slush-stained boots, and frozen legs, the commute hadn't been as bad as usual. I turned on my computer, smiling in anticipation of my empty in box. At least I'd finished *that* onerous task last night, before getting to work on Lexi's event.

"You have two hundred and twenty-nine new messages."

I stared at the screen in disbelief. I'd been down to zero at two A.M. and now—barely six hours later—I was completely overloaded again? What were these people *doing*, staking out their computers for an e-mail from me, so they could pounce on it and reply immediately?

I pondered sending out a mass e-mail to all of M&M's authors: Go to Bed. Go Directly to Bed. Do Not Pass Go. Do Not Collect Royalty Dollars.

Scrolling down the screen, I discovered that eighteen messages were from Glennie. My finger hovered over the delete key as I wished fervently for Selena's power to ignore anything she didn't want to deal with. Then I noticed a message from Selena on the bottom of my screen. As I scrolled down, I found another message from her.

And another.

And another.

Twenty-six e-mail messages from Selena? I should have stayed in bed.

My stomach clenched in a gastrospastic knot, I opened the earliest one. It was a forwarded message from one of our authors. The author had responded to Selena about my e-mail to him yesterday. (Yes, he was a Never Gonna Happen.)

I scanned his message rapidly. *Unprofessional . . . expect more from you . . . lack of publicity . . . take my next contract elsewhere . . .*

Great. I was so fired. Which was totally unfair, because it wasn't like anyone was going to take him up on his Science Fiction Train Ride Across America venture, at the tune of six grand a pop.

I thought longingly of my dream. I could use some manly arms right about now. I wouldn't turn down the champagne-licking part of the evening, either.

The vicious shrilling of the phone interrupted my slightly pornographic thoughts.

"Leah sp—"

"Leah, where the *hell* have you been? And what were you thinking, to tell all those authors to call me? Do you know that I had one hundred and eleven voice mail messages? In case you're interested, one hundred and eleven is the exact number that fills up our system capacity. Not one hundred and twelve. Not one hundred and ten. One hundred and eleven whining, moaning, complaining voice mail messages. *Are you hearing me?*"

I heard her. She sounded a little hysterical, if you asked me.

"Yes, I hear you, Selena. One hundred and eleven. Actually, message capacity is probably a matter of minutes, don't you think? I mean, the number of messages is probably irrelevant. Who would program—"

"Shut up! I don't care! I don't want to hear about voice mail capacity! I want to know why you told all these people to call me. Are you *asking* me to fire you? Do you *want* to be unemployed and go back to Nowheresville, Idaho, and milk cows? Do you??" She was definitely hysterical.

"It was Ohio, actually. And we didn't have cows. Well, anyway, you told me you wanted to be more in touch with the authors, Selena. I just—"

"Five authors! I wanted to be more in touch with *five* authors. Five *important* authors. Not the rank-and-file of every idiot we've ever published!" She stopped, breathing heavily.

Something snapped in my mind, and I quit being afraid and started being angry. "Selena, we don't publish idiots. We publish writers who have finally achieved their life's dream of becoming a published author. I think you should treat them with a little more respect."

There was total silence on the line. In three long years, I'd never stood up to Selena. She was probably picking herself up off the floor, so she could start reviewing résumés for my job.

A throat-clearing noise from behind me almost made me fall off my own chair. I spun around.

Oh, Holy CEO. Howard.

Howard smiled at me. "Well said, Leah. Well said. When you're done with your phone call, please stop by my office. I want to talk about the plans for Alexis Day's hospital appearance. It looks like Britney Simpson or Jessica Spears or some pop star person may be attending too. Huge media event. See you in ten."

Leaving me gaping after him like a suffocating carp, Howard strode off, silver hair gleaming under the fluorescent lights. *What a man.*

"Squawk, squawk, squaaaaaaaaawk!"

What? Oh, Selena. I looked at the phone I'd dropped in my lap when Howard was talking. *He'd complimented me.* I smiled.

"Selena?" This time I interrupted *her* mid-sentence. "Howard just stopped by and asked me to his office for a meeting. We'll have to continue this discussion later. Thanks for calling." I gently placed the phone in its cradle and stood, trying to ignore the way my knees were shaking.

I'd finally stood up to Selena and her petty tyranny. The repercussions were bound to be sure and swift. Selena was totally an "off with their heads" kind of manager. As I walked down the hall toward Howard's office, I realized my neck hurt already.

Do they have actual guillotines in Human Resources?

The lunchtime elevator lurched its way down to the lobby, bearing a dozen hungry businesspeople and one happy publicist. I caught sight of myself in the mirrored doors and couldn't believe my grin. Laughing in the face of destruction, probably, but for a single hour I refused to let Selena get to me. Howard and I'd had a great meeting, with Lexi on speakerphone for much of it. The plans for her appearance were well under way. Howard in action was a pretty impressive sight. The man could work a phone. We had network news covering the event now. (Of course, having a famous pop star attending didn't hurt.) I was actually humming as I made my way off the elevator.

"Hey, Audrey!"

That voice sounded familiar. Where . . . ?

"Hey, Leah! Over here!"

I whipped my head (luckily, still attached to my neck) around to find the owner of the sexy voice, most recently heard starring in my all-time favorite dream.

It *was* him. And he was walking over to me. *Serious* hot attack.

"Luke? What are you doing here?"

He smiled down at me and reached over to flick a strand of hair out of my face, then laughed and held both hands up in front of him. "Whoa. Don't want you to have to use that deodorant you're packing again."

I grinned, feeling my face pinking up. "Sure, remind a girl of her most embarrassing moment at the very beginning of a conversation. That's the way to her heart."

"Is that something I should know? The way to your heart?" He said it lightly, but his gorgeous emerald eyes gleamed with something very like the heat I'd seen in them in my fantasy . . . er . . . dream.

"Oh, the way to my heart is a long and torturous path, barred by briars, brambles, and a rusted-out fifty-seven Chevy. What are you doing here in One Publisher's Square?"

A new elevator car full of people rushed out and swarmed past us, bumping my arm. Luke put his hand on my shoulder and gently steered me off to the side.

"I'm here to find you." He grinned at me again, and I heard a teensy crackling sound.

Oops, was that the ice castle around my feelings cracking?

"Riiiiight. You just happened to wander into the one building in New York where I work, without so much as knowing my last name?"

"Who needs names? A picture's worth a thousand names." He pulled something out of his jacket pocket and handed it to me.

It was me. Only not me. It *was* me, only more than. More beautiful, more alive, more fragile than I really am or have ever been. I looked incandescent in the photo, gazing with longing at my necklace in the window. Somehow, through some photographer's magic, the necklace appeared to be dusted with light. It glowed more brightly than any of the other pieces, disdaining carat or size comparisons.

"So, how'd you do it?" My voice sounded a little trembly.

"Do what?" He tilted his head, and the curls at the back of his neck almost scraped his shoulder. His hair was a little too long, his clothes were a little too worn, and there was no way this guy would ever be called pretty. He was all long, lean, dangerous man, and his presence pushed at me in a way I'd never felt before. All at once, I got what Mom loved so much about Harrison Ford playing Indiana Jones.

He smiled and almost absently twirled a strand of my hair in his fingers. "Do what, Leah?"

I stared at his hand in my hair, transfixed. *What would those hands feel like on my body?*

I had to snap out of the haze of hormone overload. "Do, um, what? I mean, right. Do. What did you do to the picture to make me look like that?"

He looked disappointed and let my hair slip from his fingers. "You don't like it?"

"I love it. I mean, it's beautiful. But I'm not. Beautiful, I mean. I've never looked like that. Some high-tech kind of photo retouching or something?"

He leaned down until his lips were almost touching my ear. "You look exactly like that right now, Leah."

As his breath feathered across my ear, my knees suddenly felt all wobbly again.

"You're dangerous." *Did I say that out loud?* I groaned.

Luke straightened and started laughing. "Well, I've been called worse."

"Hey, butthead!"

Startled, I turned to see Sarah bearing down on us, arms flung open. Was she going to hit me? *Hey, butthead?* Had Selena turned her to the Dark Side?

I opened my mouth to respond, when Luke made a loud whooping noise.

"Angel face!" He laughed and flung his own arms open just as a delighted Sarah jumped up and into them.

Oh, Holy Bad Girlfriends. Was I just flirting with my best friend's new guy? There's a special room in hell for people like me.

I tried to become invisible and slink off, but Luke's hand shot out and grasped my arm in a very firm grip. We all started talking at once.

"Luke, I—"

"Sarah, I—"

"Leah, I was just—"

We each stopped mid-sentence and cracked up. Luke put one arm around Sarah's shoulder and the other around mine. I squirmed away and looked at Sarah, trying not to look like the kind of shameless hussy who would have sexual dreams about her best friend's man.

"Leah, what is that weird expression on your face? Selena give you indigestion again? And when did you meet my brother?"

Nine Press Releases

Finally. All nine breaking-news press releases for the January books done and ready to go to Selena. Amazing what a little lust-inspired adrenaline rush can do for the energy level. Better than coffee, any day.

I tried again to banish all thoughts of Luke from my mind, sending up yet another silent prayer of thanks that he wasn't Sarah's boyfriend. Somehow, I'd wound up promising that I'd make it to the party Friday in order to get out of joining them for lunch. I didn't think I could have made it through lunch without jumping on Sarah's brother, which is *not* recommended by the *Good Friend Etiquette Manual*.

To force my misbehaving libido back toward work and away from Luke, I grabbed the stack of press releases off the printer and settled in to proofread.

FOR IMMEDIATE RELEASE
DEBUT AUTHOR SAPPHYRE SUNBURST (and

why can't they ever make up pen names that sound reasonable? This woman is Doris Jones in real life) RADIATES ON TO THE SCENE (yeah, yeah, I know. Radiates. But you try to come up with something that goes with Sapphyre Sunburst) WITH HER IMPRESSIVE FIRST NOVEL: *STYROFOAM WINDS OF SHA'KALAR* (just how is a wind Styrofoam? I mean, come on). CALLED "THE FRESHEST NEW TALENT IN SCIENCE FICTION IN A DECADE," (no need to tell them that it was the *Dubuque Daily Prophet,* owned by Doris's Uncle Elmer, who said it) SUNBURST BUILDS A WORLD WHERE EVIL WARLORDS BATTLE NUBILE AMAZONLIKE WARRIORS IN A FIGHT TO SAVE THE UNIVERSE (and certainly *that's* an original plot. Only, oh, a half-million or so male-fantasy novels and comic books that are exactly the same).

Hey, I only had to plug it—I didn't have to like it.

FOR IMMEDIATE RELEASE
    NEW YORK TIMES BEST-SELLING AUTHOR CONNOR EMISH SHOOTS FOR THE STARS WITH THE SIXTEENTH IN HIS CRITICALLY ACCLAIMED SPHERICALS SERIES.

OK, this guy I actually liked. His books were fantastic too. He had a fan base only slightly less loyal than the average J.R.R. Tolkien reader, which made publicity pretty easy.

I'd written a few paragraphs about the plot of his latest,

added a couple of reviewer blurbs and sales information, and this one was good to go.

FOR IMMEDIATE RELEASE

DEBUT AUTHOR GLENWOOD E. HAMILTON III SHINES THE LIGHT OF HUMOR ON INTER-STELLAR HIP-HOP IN HIS FIRST NOVEL: *HEAD-BANGING ARTICHOKE BABES FROM OUTER SPACE.* (How somebody with a board as far up his butt as Glennie III could write about hip-hop music, I had no clue.) *SAN FRANCISCO GAZETTE* CALLS THIS BOOK "A BREAK-OUT TOUR DE FORCE." (Glennie must have naked pictures of the *Gazette* reviewer with a farm animal. Not to be cynical, but that particular reviewer hated *everything.*)

The phone rang again, jolting me out of my memory of Glennie's turgid prose. He was into alien babes, so there were a lot of green and scaly bosoms heaving.

And that was just the first chapter.

"Leah speaking."

"Leah! I can't believe I finally caught you."

"Glennie, er, Glenwood. I was just thinking about you." I rolled my eyes and cursed Alexander Graham Bell for about the fifteenth time that week.

"You were? Well, how *unusual* for you, given the quantity and quality of your correspondence and communication with me." He paused, no doubt to let his snide little remark sink in.

"I've tried several times to reach Ms. Evans, but she is apparently out of the country on urgent promotional matters." He sounded impressed.

It was part of my job to cover for Selena.

"No, I just talked to her this morning, Glenwood. She's in the office."

Oops.

Buoyed by my petty rebellion, I smiled and decided to share my newfound holiday spirit. "I'm just finishing your press release, Glenwood. It's far too early to send it out, given your release date, but I thought you'd like to spend some time reviewing it and offer any suggestions."

"I, well, really? I'd love to. Thank you so much, Leah. That is, um, actually, that is only appropriate in this circumstance. I'll be expecting it at your earliest convenience."

For a moment there, he'd almost sounded human. Then Robot Glennie'd kicked back in. Too bad.

"OK, then. I'll e-mail it off to you today. Happy Holidays, Glenwood."

"Well, yes. Um, Happy Holidays to you, too, Leah."

I replaced the phone, using the full power of any mental or psychic abilities I might have to command it to quit ringing.

It rang immediately.

I sighed and picked it back up. "Leah speaking."

"Hello, Leah Speaking. I'd like to speak to Just Leah, the Woman Who Will Not Be Photographed."

At the first sound of Luke's deep voice, tendrils of heat started to unfurl in my nerve endings. *Holy cow. Was a fling in order? Get him out of my system that way?*

I looked at the piles of work threatening to crush my desk from sheer stress overload. When would I have the time for a fling with someone who was leaving town in two weeks?

"Leah? Are you there?"

"Sorry. Just considering and rejecting options." My voice sounded dejected, even to me.

Luke picked up on it. "What's wrong? Am I interrupting something? Sarah gave me your number, and I was just calling to invite you to dinner. Are you free tonight?"

I started laughing. "Boy, do you move fast. Is this how you keep up your girl-in-every-country-of-assignment quota?"

"Hey! Ouch! Plus, I didn't exactly go on dates in Iraq during the past ten months." His teasing tone turned serious. "I'd just like to get to know you. Sarah told me about you during lunch, and she thinks you're fantastic, so that definitely authorizes me to skip some of the 'get to know you' chitchat and go right to dinner, right?"

I caught myself twirling my hair and stopped immediately. *No, no, no. Not the hair twirl.*

"Well, I don't know. There's a whole Date Event Calculator we women use, you know. Coffee equals five points. Lunch equals ten points. Taking someone's picture without her permission is probably a minus twelve. You'd be on the negative side of the scale, if you weren't Sarah's brother. I guess that counts for a point or two." A grin stretched my cheeks. Even my hair follicles tingled.

Watch out, Leah! Danger, danger: Bad Boy Ahead.

"Well, if you let me take you to dinner, I'll at least get out of the negative range, right? Seems only fair to let a good friend's brother redeem himself." I could hear the laughter in his voice, and that tipped the scales to Yes.

"Dinner would be great, actually. But I can't do it tonight—I'm swamped. How about tomorrow?"

Bad idea, bad idea, my mind said.

I don't care, I don't care, my body said, yearning to jingle some bells of its own for a change.

"Tomorrow would be great. Call me when you're free, and I'll meet you at your office. Until tomorrow, Leah. I'll be looking forward to it." His voice was a little husky, and

I heard warning bells go off in my mind. This man could be dangerous to my self-imposed work first, fun later philosophy.

Warning bells, jingle bells, who cares? 'Tis the season.

Realizing I was still holding the phone and staring off into space with a stupid grin on my face, I shook my head to clear it of lustful fantasies that may or may not have involved new and improved uses for eggnog and spiced rum. An image of Luke's face smiling down at me popped into my mind.

Oh, Leah. You've got it bad.

Humming something that sounded suspiciously like "Joy to the World," I picked my press releases back up and glanced at the clock. Oh, no. It was already mid-afternoon, and I still had to get PR plans to Selena by five.

The stress slammed back into place; my neck suddenly ached under the weight of my head. There had to be easier ways to make a living.

So much for joy.

Eight Compromises

Christmas Gifts to Buy:

1. *Mom*—Nightgown? Sexy from Zygogo Boutique? Euwww! This is *Mom*! No sexy—no sex. I was a true stork-brought baby. Nice, Momly nightgown from Macy's. Also find something for her tacky-mania obsession. Empire State snowglobe? Nah, too common.
2. *Dad*—Tools always good. Where to buy tools? Ask John in mailroom. He looks like a tools guy. (Could ask Luke. No, sounds like a weird come-on—"Tell me about your tool, big guy." *So* not happening.)
3. *Sarah*—lovely, very thoughtful writing-related gift so she can pursue her own writing that she never has time to do. Leather-bound journal? Exotic pen set?

4. *Mindy*—beautiful nursing gown with matching nightgown for baby.

5. *Josh*—Book about being a dad? Book about twins? Book about having time to read books when you are father of twins?

6. *Trina*—same as Mindy, or hurt feelings. Except need bigger nightgown (body of woman who just had twins) and two matching nightgowns. (Do boy babies wear nightgowns? Will cause gender identity crisis in perhaps boy newborn? Ask Mom.)

7. *Babies*—nightgowns or gender-specific night apparel. Mindy having girl; Trina and Josh want to be "surprised." (Isn't the fact that not one but two babies can come out of opening size of quarter surprise enough?) Remember to decline invitation to attend births. No desire to know sister or sister-in-law *that* well. Yuck.

8. *Luke???*—Can't give him present now; would seem like mad stalker or woman channeling Glenn Close and likely to boil his bunny. What if he's still around at Christmas? Will have to run out on C. Eve and buy last-minute something when no stores open. Will end up in Chinese deli with gift-wrapped chopsticks. Will Luke like chopsticks? Will I seem like Chinese food–obsessed woman with eating disorder to give new b. friend chopsticks? B. Friend?? Where did THAT come from? One dinner and you're buying him kitchen utensils? Why not just show up with your blender and toothbrush and announce you're moving in? Does he even have an "in" to move in *to?* Remember to ask Sarah where he lives when

he's not moving around. Maybe he only has a
P.O. Box because he has no permanent resi-
dence. Oh, great, now am hung up on man
with no address. Will marry homeless man
and live in box on street and have much hot
sex but no hot water.

Somehow I made it through a hellish day, and even got
Selena her PR plans before six. I was all set to offer profuse
apologies for not delivering them by five—I'd even prac-
ticed my apologetic tone on the way to her office—but her
secretary said, "Oh, Selena left at four for her weekly facial. She won't be back until tomorrow."

I was bizarrely proud of myself for not throwing a kick-
ing and screaming tantrum right there on the floor.

Of course, just because Selena was gone didn't mean any
of my to-do list had magically cleared itself, so I'd trudged
back to my desk, sighing at the thought of the dinner with
Luke I'd passed up to do Selena's job for her yet again.

This morning, I was determined to attitude-adjust myself
all day long, if that's what it took. I'd smiled at everyone
and said hello as I walked in the building (which only
gained me suspicious stares—New Yorkers are not interested in morning cheer, even around the holidays; We're
Grumpy but We Rock is kind of our motto). I'd even tried
not to cringe when the Muzak-ized version of "White
Christmas" assaulted my ears in the elevator. Then I'd
worked my butt off (oh, I only wish *that* were a literal
phrase) all morning. I was especially pleased at the way the
plans for Lexi's reading at the hospital were shaping up.
The fund-raiser just had to be success. I almost felt like I
was raising money for the children's hospital as a gift to
myself. Sort of a *take that* to all the people who thought my
job was unimportant.

My planned reward for all this good cheer? A luxurious, leisurely lunch hour of shopping, which just might include a little something new to wear tonight. Not that I was considering this a date or anything. It was just taking the poor, lonely brother of a friend out for dinner, so he wouldn't have to eat alone around the holidays.

Yeah, right. Like a guy who looks like that *would have to worry about eating alone. It's a date, and you know it.*

Changing my self-talk channel back to All Positive All the Time, I opened e-mail for the first time all morning. There was a message dated last night around midnight right up top, and the e-mail addy looked vaguely familiar.

To: **Leah**
From: **Luke**

Don't forget to call me about dinner. Or, which seems more likely, don't talk yourself out of calling me.

(**Oops. How did he know?**)

Sarah and I watched *It's a Wonderful Life* tonight. It's our annual tradition, and we haven't missed a year since she was about five. For some reason, I kept thinking about you. I've always thought Jimmy Stewart was nuts for giving up on his dreams and staying in one place all his life. But tonight, the look on your face in front of that store window kept popping into my mind. And how a man would do almost anything to bring a smile to your face.

Man, I've had too much rum punch. Better go before I ruin my tough-guy image forever.

Call me.—Luke

I stared at the screen, mouth hanging open, hand clenching my computer mouse so hard I might break it. *Oh, wow.*

Oh, wow. I . . . he . . . oh, wow. If he's this potent over e-mail, I'm in big trouble.

"Leah, you're in huge trouble." Selena's voice over my shoulder sleeted ice water on my emotion/hormone overload.

"These PR plans are crap. Worthless crap. Total, ineffective garbage. You have us doing the same thing we've done a hundred times before. Do you have a spark of imagination in your lumpy body?"

She dumped my neatly organized file folders on the floor. Papers spilled everywhere; the result of all of my careful work devastated by her chilling condescension.

'Tis the season to be an evil bi—

"Leah! Did you hear me? Do you have anything to say for yourself?" The BQ was looming over me in my chair.

I *so* hate to be loomed. My hands clenched into fists.

But I also hate to be unemployed. My hands unclenched.

"Selena, I was acting on your explicit instructions that we use your detailed PR plan template for every single author, adding in components depending on the author's status in the publishing hierarchy. Lead authors get—"

"I know what the system is! I invented it, for God's sake. But that doesn't mean you can't show a little creativity for once in your useless life. We are going to have to seriously rethink your job description after the holidays. I just can't take any more of cleaning up after you. Now, please, please try to redo these and use a little imagination and initiative this time, will you? We have a meeting with Howard at four-thirty. Plan to be there with the new plans. In the meantime, I have to go lie down and take my migraine medicine."

She swiveled on her heel and stalked off, leaving me surrounded by the detritus of hours and hours of hard work, demolished. I could feel the tears threatening, but wouldn't give her the satisfaction of crying at my desk.

So I bolted for the bathroom.

"Leah? Leah? Gillian said you were in here. Are you all right?"

Sarah's voice was filled with concern, which brought on a fresh round of tears. I looked up at the door to the bathroom stall, behind which I was trying to disprove all marketing claims of waterproof mascara manufacturers.

I had cause for a class action lawsuit, if the black staining my fingers counted as evidence.

"Leah, I know those are your shoes. I was with you when you bought them, so open the door. Come on. I'm worried. Even Gillian was concerned."

I blew my nose, sounding like a Christmas goose with a bad cold.

Honk!

"Yeah, right. *Gillian* was concerned. What did she say? She's probably spreading the story all over the building by now."

Sarah tried the door, and it rattled on its hinges. "Leah, open the door. Gillian, um . . . Well, you know how she is. But forget about her. What's wrong with you?"

"Oh, nothing. Just everything. Just I hate my job, and I hate my boss, and I hate my life, and I haven't had a date in seven months, and I haven't had sex in so long I think I'm an honorary virgin again, and the first guy I want to jump on in a long time is—"

Stop there!

"Is what? The first guy you want to jump is what? Leah?" She pounded on the door. "Leah, open this door right now. I'm really getting worried about you."

"No. Go away." I snuffled into what looked like the last

of the second roll of bathroom tissue I'd drenched since I ran in there.

"Fine. If you won't come to me, I'll come to you."

I heard the door of the stall next to me slam open, and the next thing I saw was Sarah's head peering at me over the top of the ugly avocado-green partition between us.

"Now will you tell me what's wrong?"

I sighed. Getting Sarah to give up once she had her mind made up to do something was about as likely as convincing *Good Morning America* to interview Glennie. I stood and opened the door.

"All right, all right. Don't get your panties in a twist. Here's what happened." I told her everything, except for the part about Luke.

"Oh, Leah. I'm so sorry. She really is a psychopath. I don't know why Howard puts up with her."

She watched me in the mirror as I tried to repair my ravaged face. "Aren't you having dinner with Luke tonight? That should at least be fun, and he—oh, no. Oh, Leah. Luke isn't the one you want to jump, is he?"

I forced out a laugh. "The look of abject distress on your face isn't exactly flattering, Sarah. If you don't want me to go out with your brother, just say so. It's no big deal."

She was shaking her head before I even finished my sentence. "No, it's not that, you idiot. I love you. I just wish I had a different brother for you to go out with. Luke is . . . well, Luke is a wanderer. He's never stayed in the same place for longer than a few months. His job puts him in danger and . . . he always said he'd never settle down."

I finished putting a fresh coat of mascara on my lashes and examined my face for traces of crying. Looked great, if you didn't count the redness or the puffiness. I sighed and turned around to face Sarah.

"Look, I'm not looking for a commitment. Or even a

date. But he asked me to dinner, and I thought I'd be nice to your brother. That's all. Sure, he's totally great looking, and I might have felt the slightest tiny bit of attraction, but it's no big deal. I'll cancel dinner, if you want." I shrugged and tried to pretend that I wasn't holding my breath for her answer.

She smiled. "No, I don't want you to cancel. Just promise to never, *ever* tell me any of the details if you two hook up. There are some things a baby sister doesn't want to know. Now get your purse. We're going out for some retail therapy."

"But, I have to get the new plans ready for Selena and—"

"Screw her. She can't treat my friend like that. We'll take an hour, and you'll still have almost three hours to revise the plans. Howard's going to be in that meeting, and she'd never dare act like a BQ in front of him."

I trailed along behind Sarah as we left the bathroom, thinking glumly that Howard wouldn't always be around to protect me. *Whatever. I still have shopping that needs to be done, and I need to get out of here for an hour. I'll worry about it later.*

Famous last words, as they say.

Christmas Gifts Bought:
1. *Mom*—Slippers. Empire State snowglobe. Will make up for boring gifts by wonderful tour of NY over holidays.
2. *Dad*—Tool not good. Cannot take large hammer or saw on airplane for return trip. Tape measure not usable as weapon? Can go in checked bag? (Reminder: avoid John in mailroom for at least a month. Apparently all guys think *tell me about tools* a come-on).
3. *Sarah*—Subscription to writing magazine??

(Who knew that leather-bound journals cost $200? What are they made out of—mink hide?? Euww. Exotic pen set $500. Would be afraid to write.)

4. *Mindy*—Cotton v. pretty nursing gown; Sarah said silk bad idea—baby spit-up. Matching baby blanket.

5. *Josh*—Book about joy of fatherhood. (Say good-bye to your free time, bro. Mwah ha ha.)

6. *Trina*—see #4; two blankets. Yellow blanket cannot cause gender identity crisis in newborn.

7. *Babies*—Receiving blankets. (Wonder what they "receive." Is it because most people receive them at baby showers? Reminder: forgot to mail baby shower gifts to Mindy and Trina. Did not in fact purchase baby shower gifts. Can card do double-duty: M. Christmas/ Happy B. Shower? Maybe too tacky. Buy/ Mail b. shower gifts.)

8. *Luke* Gift-wrapped chopsticks. Am doomed.

Seven Plans a-Sinking

My voice mail light was blinking when we got back from our retail therapy. (Cost: four hundred and twelve dollars. Compromises on gift selection: eight. Being out of the office for an hour: Priceless.)

I wanted to ignore it, but I'd called and left a message for Mindy the night before to be sure she was doing all right.

"You have four new messages."

Message one: "Leah, it's Selena. It's twelve-thirty. Where are you? Where are my plans? I hope you're not at lunch at a time like this. It's not like you really need to be eating, anyway. You're about to bust out of those pants as it is."

I hit delete with my middle finger, just for the symbolism of it all. Then I glanced down at my size-ten black pants. I was *not* busting out of them.

Gritting my teeth, I pressed three to continue.

Message two: "Leah, it's Mom. We are so excited, honey. I swear, your father has repacked his shaving kit three times. He's worse than I am. I made five pounds of peanut butter fudge to bring to you, but the girls were over. You know how pregnant women are. There's at least a half-pound left, though. Only a little more than a week 'til we see you, but maybe I'll make a fresh five pounds for you next week."

Remember to call Mom and thank her for being the best mother in the universe.

Message three: "It's Lexi. I talked with the hospital administrator, and she is so excited with the plans you and Howard put in motion. I can't thank you enough, Leah. I'll be in touch soon."

I adore her. Why can't all authors be like Lexi?

Message four: "Leah, it's Luke. I'll pick you up at work at seven. Be hungry."

Oh, I don't think hungry is going to be a problem, Luke.

He probably meant hungry for food, though. Which wouldn't be a problem, either, since I shopped through lunch. Maybe we could talk about the various uses of champagne . . .

I stopped myself in mid-daydream. PR plans. Meeting at four-thirty. End of life and career as I know it.

Back to work.

As I stepped into the inner sanctum—Howard's private conference room—at four-thirty on the dot, Selena gave me the evil eye. She jumped out of her chair and rushed over to me.

"You can just give me those papers and go, Leah. You've caused enough strife for one day." She snatched the reports out of my hand, and I was too stunned to protest.

Sarah walked in the door just then. She must have heard Selena, because she said, "Oh, I know that Howard wants

Leah in on the meeting so we can discuss Lexi's plans." She flashed a brilliant smile in Selena's direction and put her hand on my arm to steer me over to the conference table. As Lexi's editor, Sarah wielded a lot of power at M&M. Alexis Day added quite a bit to the bottom line of the company, and she'd been very vocal about her loyalty to Sarah.

Selena glared at me and—if looks really could kill—I'd have been a puddle of blood and gingerbread latte on the floor. "Fine. Just keep your mouth shut unless somebody asks you a question." She sat back in the chair directly to the right of the head of the table and scanned my documents.

Sarah rolled her eyes and took a seat halfway down the table, motioning me to sit next to her. Over the course of the next ten minutes or so, a few other editors showed up. My shocked expression amused Sarah.

"Leah, what is it?"

"I can't believe these people are late for a meeting with Howard."

Sarah laughed. "You said Howard like most people would say *Queen Elizabeth.* And you'll notice that he's not even here yet."

"Well, nothing against Her Majesty, but she's not the mastermind behind seven divisions of the largest publisher in the world." Even after three years, I still occasionally flashed on how unbelievably awesome it was to be part of M&M and the books read by people in twenty-seven countries.

Sarah started to respond, but just then Howard made his entrance, flanked by his secretary and two assistant editors. I noticed Gillian was one of them. And she was talking.

More like sucking up, actually.

"Oh, Howard, it is such an honor to be invited to sit in on one of your meetings. I'm so delighted to—"

"Right, right, Jan. Take a seat over there in the corner." He waved Jan, er, Gillian over to a seat by the fake potted palm. I tried to stifle a smug look. I was sitting by Sarah, at the actual conference table, after all.

"*Leah!* Great to see you here. Lexi is delighted with the progress you've made on her event. Always a good idea to keep our best-selling authors happy. Good work." Howard smiled at me, and I eloquently and professionally responded.

"Your . . . thanks . . . hospital . . . great. Um, great. Thanks." *OK, maybe not all that eloquently. Aarghh!*

Howard just smiled at me and turned his attention to the group. "All right. What have we got? Selena, plans for PR on our upcoming books?"

Selena smiled and pulled my reports closer. *My* reports. The plans I'd sweated over to make them original, fresh, and powerful. The plans I hoped would garner more publicity for the books included than any plans we'd done before. *My* plans.

"Howard, I'm so glad you asked." Selena stretched out one hand with its scarlet-tipped fingers and patted Howard's arm.

"As you know, I've been working 24/7 to try to come up with a brand-new strategy for our books. That tired hierarchy system that my staff keeps trying to promote just isn't doing us any good. I mean, it *will* be 2005 next year. We need to be open to new ways of doing business."

My mouth dropped open. *New ways? Tired hierarchy system her staff keeps trying to promote? More like the hierarchy she force-feeds down our throats, while threatening us with death and destruction if we ever deviate the slightest inch from her rigid path.*

Selena's viperlike voice slithered its way into my consciousness. ". . . and new ways to promote debut authors, with special concentration on . . ."

She stole it. She stole my entire plan that I'd worked so hard on, and she was claiming it as her own. I listened, growing more and more appalled with every word, as my hideous boss outlined my entire new and creative PR plans as her very own brainstorm.

I yanked my gaze away from Selena's lying mouth and looked at Howard.

He was buying every dishonest, lying, deceitful, false, untruthful, corrupt, devious, cheating, mendacious, disingenuous word. (Hey, I may not be an editor, but my parents didn't pay for four years of college for nothing.)

That witch. I had to make this right. I was going to tell Howard the truth, and to hell with the consequences. I opened my mouth to speak.

Howard beat me to it. "Selena, this is excellent work. Your best yet. Leah, you can learn a lot from Selena. Stick with her, and you'll go far in this company."

He rose to leave. "I have a drinks appointment, so gotta run. We'll catch up on the rest later. Good work, Selena."

And then he was gone. Sarah and the other editors jumped up to follow him out, with Gillian trying to catch his attention. "Oh, Howard, do you think . . ."

As the sound of a gaggle of editors faded off down the hall, Selena rose and stretched. "It's such a good feeling—a job well done. Isn't it, Leah? Oh, well, you'll feel it someday, I'm sure. I'm holding out hope."

The smile she shot at me was pure malice frosted with triumph. It said, *Don't mess with me—ever. You won't just lose; I'll crush you.*

And then she was gone.

I sat there, alone, staring at the door.

"Oh yeah?" I said to the empty room.

Great comeback, Leah. Selena would have been shaking in her kitten-heeled boots over that one.

At quarter 'til seven, I turned off my computer. Total times I'd reread Luke's e-mail for courage and emotional support: thirty-four. If he stood me up after the day I'd just had, I'd cheerfully hunt him down and beat him into a green-eyed pulp, cheekbones or no cheekbones. I peered around the edge of my cube. The coast was clear. If I made a dash for it—

"Leah! Are you leaving? So early?" Gillian was standing in the hall, making a big show of looking at her watch with an exaggerated expression of shock plastered on her snarky face.

I took a deep breath, stabbed the elevator button, then turned to look at her. "Look, *Jan.* I have had what you might call a bad day. In fact, it was a hideous, vicious, stinking cesspool of a day. So you don't want to mess with me right now. Do you get me?"

If ever in my entire life I had a scary expression on my face, that was the moment. Gillian actually backed up a step. For a brief moment, I felt powerful.

Then I just felt tired.

"Good night, Gillian." I stepped into the elevator and thought that I'd never felt so uninterested in going out on a date in my life. Maybe Luke had gotten cold feet. The bell for the lobby dinged, and I braced myself, unsure which I hoped for more: that he was there or that he wasn't.

He was.

"Hey, Leah. I was worried you might stand me up." Luke smiled; a slow smile that did a lot to dispel the fury still blasting shock waves through my nerve endings. He wore a pair of black pants with a black sweater, and his long hair brushed against the impressive shoulders inside his dressy black leather jacket. He looked good enough to eat, with maybe a little whipped cream. Or chocolate syrup. Or both.

Low-carb diets were so overrated.

"Hungry?"

"Desperately." I licked my lips, then realized what I was doing and snapped my shameless tongue back inside my mouth. Honestly, I'd be doing a cheerleader hair toss any minute.

Luke's gaze was fixed on my mouth. "I, uh, let's go, then." His voice was husky, and he clenched his jaw a little too.

OK, maybe I'm not the only one who's hungry.

I smiled and shoved all my work problems to the back of my mind (repression is a good thing), and tilted my head. "Lead on, Mitchell. I'm all yours."

He held out his hand for mine. "I like the sound of that."

I trudge through the snow and slush on the streets of New York every night, but somehow—with Luke—I saw things through his photographer's eyes. He pointed out the splash of bright red of a scarf wrapped around a child's head and neck, the sparkle of icicles reflecting the glow of a traffic light, and the contrast of a theatergoer's full-length fur with her goat-herder boots. We laughed at the awestruck tourists who kept bumping into people as they looked up, up, up at the buildings; frantically shooting photographs to show the people back home what Christmas in the big city looked like.

"Do you like Mexican?" he asked, pausing to tuck one of my curls behind my ear.

The touch of his fingers as they brushed my face blew rational thought out of my mind.

"I, what?"

He smiled. *What green eyes you have.*

"Do you have colored contacts?" As soon as I said it, I groaned.

He roared out a laugh. "No, I have the Mitchell eyes. All the men in my family have them. Sarah and Mom both have brown eyes and were always moaning about how unfair it was that the guys got the green eyes."

"Oh. Well, I'm sure you've heard this a lot, but they're really, um, beautiful."

The smile faded from his face, and a look of intensity replaced the humor. "Somehow, hearing it from you sounds different. I prefer blue eyes, myself. And slightly curly brown hair. With freckles. And a personality that seems way too big for such a tiny person."

Since he'd just described me exactly, it was kind of hard to get bent out of shape by the "tiny person" part. Although . . .

"Hey! I'm five feet, four inches. That's the national average, I'll have you know." I pulled myself up to my full height.

He laughed again. "I'm betting there's nothing average about you, Leah. How about Mexican?"

"What?"

"Do you like it? For dinner?"

I looked around for the first time and noticed we were stopped in front of Dos Caminos. The man could really make you forget your surroundings. At the same time, I realized my fingers were frozen.

"Brrr! I'm suddenly freezing! And, yes, I adore Mexican. This place is great—they make amazing guacamole right at your table! Let's go in."

He put his arm around me, and we stepped inside to the fragrant aromas of *queso* and salsa and *frijoles*. Mexican food and a totally hot guy—life was good.

As we waited for our table, a shrill voice penetrated the first good mood I'd had in weeks.

"Leah. Leah! Is that you? Will you stop over here, please?" It was Selena. No other voice could stab an ice pick through my skull quite like hers.

I clenched my eyes shut, hoping it was a nightmare that would go away. There must be seven million restaurants in New York. It was a bad B-movie cliché that she would be in this one.

"Friend of yours?" Luke sounded amused.

"No, she's about as far from being a friend as you can get. Will you excuse me for a minute?" I resisted the urge to pull him along for moral support and dragged my feet over to where Selena was sitting at a table in the bar.

"Yes, what's up, Selena? We were just about to be seated, so if this can wait . . ."

"No, it cannot wait. I'm sure your friend can find a table without you, Leah. Carleton, this is that staff person I told you about. Leah, this is Carleton Dunstan IV."

We nodded at each other. Another number. Now I have Glennie III and Carleton IV. I wondered what Carleton One through Three looked like, because this guy was pretty unprepossessing. Must have been fishing in the shallow end of the gene pool by the time they got to him. Receding hair, receding chin, bulbous eyes—it sure wasn't his looks she was after. As he limply shook my hand, I noticed the high-end Rolex on his arm. *Now I see the attraction.*

"Carleton and I are going to spend the holidays in Aruba at his private chalet, and I've just decided to take vacation the first week of January, so I need a rush on the PR plans for the July and August books. You may want to get your dinner to go, because you're going to be a little busy at work for a change over the next several days." The BQ smirked at me.

She actually smirked. I felt a dark and desperate desire to stab her eyes out with a tortilla chip.

"Well, Selena, I—"

"Run along, Leah. We're having a conversation here." She waved her hand at me as though brushing away a fly and returned to her animated conversation on the difficulty of finding good native help in Aruba.

Do they have native uprisings in Aruba? Is there any remote possibility she'll be caught and forced into slavery?

The thought of Selena forced to cook and clean some native chieftain's hut while wearing a burlap sack brought a grim smile to my face as I crossed the bar to return to Luke. Suddenly, I didn't have much of an appetite, though.

"Our table is ready, Leah. Hey, are you OK?" He caught my chin in his hand and looked down into my eyes. The warm concern I saw there almost opened the floodgates again.

"I'm fine. I just . . . would you mind if we go somewhere else for dinner? Anywhere else? I'm suddenly not in the mood for guacamole."

He narrowed his eyes and looked over at Selena. "Is it her? Did she give you a hard time about something?"

"I don't want to talk about it, really. Would you mind if we just go?"

He stepped over to the hostess desk and murmured something to the brightly dressed woman and handed her some cash. Then he crossed back over to me and helped me put my coat back on, and we left the restaurant. I never glanced back at Selena once, as much as I wanted to do it. I wouldn't give her the satisfaction.

* * *

Although Luke and I had dinner at one of New York's awesome delis after escaping Selena, I never recaptured my festive spirit. *From festive to festering in one easy step.* I hated to let her ruin my evening—it felt like letting her win some intangible prize in her quest to ruin my life—but I couldn't escape the sensation of a vise gripping the sides of my brain and inexorably squeezing all creativity out.

I told Luke a little about it, but (typical guy) he wanted to offer suggestions as to how to handle it. I snapped that I could handle my own career issues, thank you very much, and that pretty much slammed the door on the evening. We were pretty quiet as he flagged down a taxi to take me home. I mumbled a good night as he opened the cab door.

"Good night, Leah. I'm sorry I tried to jump in with both feet and tell you how to solve your problems. Sarah has yelled at me about that before. But I'm a guy. I think we're just wired that way." He smiled in a way that told me his words and his apology were sincere.

I tried to summon up a smile, but exhaustion was crushing me. "Good night, Luke. Thanks for the panini."

I pulled the door shut and gave the driver my address, then looked out the window as we pulled away from the curb. Luke stood there, hands shoved in his pockets. He watched, unsmiling, as I lifted a hand in a wave.

He didn't wave back.

So much for getting my bells jingled this year. I'd just blown it with the first real prospect in a long, long time.

I slouched down in my seat, wondering where the one-horse open sleighs were when you needed one.

Six Hours Talking

Thursday morning dawned as gray and cloudy as my mood. Alone in bed, as usual, I closed my eyes and wondered what my night might have been like if I'd brought Luke home with me. The thought of his hands and the things he might be able to do with them shot a delicious shiver through my body.

Then I threw back the covers and stepped out of bed and shivered for real.

"More record low temperatures, New Yorkers! Happy almost holidays!! Better bundle up nice and warm!" The radio announcer had to be a coke fiend. No way was somebody that cheerful all the time. Either that or somebody'd spiked his eggnog.

My cell phone rang. "Leah speak—I mean, hello."

"Hey, Leah. It's Mindy. I figured you'd be up."

I flopped back down on the bed and pulled the comforter around my knees. "Hey, big sister. And I mean that literally. You must be huge."

"Nice. Really nice. Maybe I should call somebody at that

fancy publishing house and let them in on your nickname, Stinkerbelle." I could hear the smile in her voice, but my sister sounded tired.

"Mindy, are you OK? Mom said there had been some issues with your pregnancy, and . . ."

"No, I'm fine. Just a little tired all the time. I guess I'm anemic and they're worried about pre-eclampsia." She sighed.

She definitely didn't sound fine to me. "What's pre-eclampsia? And if you start talking about placentas or something gross, be advised I will hang up."

Mindy laughed again. "No placentas. It's really nothing. I just have to keep my feet up and basically let everybody wait on me like I'm a big, fat, gestating cow. I hate it."

My sister was a trial lawyer at a legal aid clinic, and her case load usually ran in the triple digits. Sitting still with her feet up had to be the toughest challenge she'd ever faced. She was probably driving her husband nuts.

"How's Brad enjoying the chance to spoil you?"

"He likes it too much. I warned him not to get used to it. They've almost completed construction on a day care facility at the courthouse, and I'll be bringing Baby Natalie there when she's about three months old, I think, since I get honorary courthouse employee status."

"It's Natalie this week? I thought you were settled on Chloe." Ever since Mindy found out she was having a girl, she'd been trying out different names every week. I was just glad we were past the classic goddess names. The baby had been Artemis, Aphrodite, Hera, and Persephone for a month. I finally had to tell Mindy that Persephone creeped me out—who wants her niece being dragged off to the underworld for half a year at a time? That ended the goddess phase.

"I guess Trina and Josh settled on Chloe for their girl about a month ago, but I hadn't heard about it. Mom confirmed it, though, so it wasn't just Trina trying to pull a fast one." She sounded rueful, and I had to laugh. Trina and Mindy had been locked in a weird pregnancy competition, but they were as close as Mindy and I were. Josh got married after I moved out here, so I didn't know Trina as well yet.

"Did they find out what flavor the second twin is yet?"

"No, the ultrasound tech still can't get a legs-open shot of twin number two. So Dad may or may not have a grandson to teach everything about the Buckeyes. Not that the mystery has stopped him from buying three tiny Buckeye softball gloves, three tiny Buckeye footballs, and so on and so forth."

My dad was a rabid fan of all things Ohio State Buckeyes, and of course all three of us ended up in college there. Now he was trying to get the indoctrination started early with the next generation.

I glanced at the clock. Crap. I was going to be late again.

"Mindy, are you sure you're OK? Because it's getting late, but if you need to talk, I can call in to the office and—"

"No, no. You go to work. I just wanted to call and tell you I'm fine and not to worry. Mom and Dad are so excited to come out and see you. You'd better be coming home to see me in a month when the baby's born too."

"Um, yeah. About that . . ."

Mindy started laughing again. "Don't worry, Leah. You don't have to be in the delivery room. I'm thinking it's going to be just Brad and me. I promise—no placentas."

"I love you, Mindy. Talk to you soon."

"Love you, too, Stinkerbelle."

I closed my phone, relieved that everything was fine in baby land. Mindy might have been a bossy older sister, but she was also the one who beat up the neighborhood bully when he'd picked on me. He'd plowed his fist into her face, causing a major-league black eye before she got him trapped on the ground, but when she was done with him he'd never bothered me again.

Sometimes I wish Mindy were here to beat up Selena.

Oh, crap. Selena. If I didn't get going on those PR plans, I'd be the only one in New York working all day on Christmas.

To: **Selena**
From: **Leah**

It's one A.M. Thursday night (or I guess it's Friday morning), and I'm finally finished with the plans for the July and August books, other than certain items I need from the authors who have yet to respond. I based these plans on my templates that were so successful in our meeting with Howard the other day. (Take *that*, O Evil One.)

Please let me know tomorrow (today?) if you have any comments, so I can incorporate any revisions over the weekend. (Yet another weekend shot in the butt; it's not like I need to do any shopping or cleaning to get ready for my parents' visit. Thanks loads, Selena.)

—Leah

To: **Sarah**
From: **Leah**

It's Friday at four-thirty, and still no word from BQ on those plans she so desperately had to have. In fact, I heard that she was out for a three-hour lunch, shopping. But, hey, really, who needs sleep? I read somewhere that many of the world's famous geniuses survived on only two or three hours of sleep. I think I'll go mainline some more caffeine in case she gets here by five and dumps another month's worth of work on me that has to be done before we close for the holidays next Thursday.

To: **Leah**
From: **Sarah**

You're still coming to the party, aren't you? I'm not trying to pry, but Luke has been in a foul mood ever since you two went out the other night. Turned him down, didn't you? The Lofty Gorgeous One isn't used to that. Women usually fall all over him.

You *have* to come to the party. I have a great new neighbor I want you to meet. He's an accountant, but not at all boring. We had the best talk about music the other night. He's totally right for you.

To: Sarah
From: Leah

If your accountant is that great, why don't you go out with him? I've sworn off men forever. Plus, I'm soon to be unemployed at this rate, and men find the whole poverty thing to so unattractive. No, there was no "turning down" with Luke. There was nothing to turn down. Just two acquaintances sharing a friendly dinner. I don't think I can make it to the party, though. BQ is bound to turn up any minute.

To: Leah
From: Sarah

It's seven o'clock on Friday night. You're coming with me if I have to drag you. Too bad for her if she can't get back to you by now. People are allowed to have lives, you know. By the way, I spoke with Lexi today. She's so happy with the work you're doing for her on that charity event. Thanks so much for that.

She was right. What normal person hung around the office on a Friday night, just waiting to be tortured? I shut off my computer with a snap and grabbed my purse and coat. If Selena couldn't get back to me in a reasonable amount of time, too bad for her. I ran down the hall to intercept Sarah at the elevator, thinking that maybe a really good bottle of wine would help me make the apology I knew Luke deserved for my attitude the other night.

"Oh, Leah! I'm so glad to finally find you. Will you stop by my office, please? Now?"

It was her. The hideous banshee of death in her pointy shoes. I sighed and my whole body drooped. So that was it.

No wine.

No apology.

No making up with Luke.

No making out.

I had to get a new job.

I had to get a new life.

Sarah rounded the corner just then and flashed me a huge smile. "Great! I knew you'd see the wisdom in listening to me."

"Yeah, I listened. Only it didn't do me any good. Selena caught me. Have a great time. Say hi to Luke for me and . . . Sarah? Tell him I'm sorry. He'll know why." I turned away, trying to swallow past the huge lump that had suddenly formed in my throat. Sarah caught my arm.

"Listen to me, Leah. If it's getting too bad, you need to tell Howard. I know she stole your plans at that meeting, and I was going to tell Howard about it, but I knew you wouldn't want me fighting your battles. And no matter how late you get out of here, please come over. My roommate's gone for the holidays, so you can crash at my place, and we'll sleep in till noon and go out for pancakes."

She gave me a quick hug and then stepped on the elevator, giving me the thumbs-up sign. I smiled weakly back and then trudged down the hall to Selena's office. It was going to be a black Christmas.

Only thirty minutes past midnight. That's not bad. I fidgeted with my watch for the third time in front of the door to Sarah's apartment. The beat of reggae Christmas carols and the sparkle of lively conversation pulled me in at the same time the thought of facing Luke pushed me away. I raised my hand toward the doorbell and then lowered it, bell unrung.

Also for the third time.

"If I only had my camera now."

I closed my eyes, feeling my face go hot. I'd recognize that sensual drawl anywhere. But why did it have to be in the hallway where I was making a fool out of myself?

Luke stepped up behind me and put his hands on my shoulders. I could feel his breath stirring my hair. "Deep-seated aversion to the islands sound of 'Rudolph the Red-Nosed Ganja Man'? Or is it just that you didn't want to see me?"

A terrifying urge to lean back into the heat of his body and wrap myself in his arms swept through me. Clearly, it was part of that Needs to Get a Life thing.

I twisted out from under his hands and turned to face him, conjuring up a smile from somewhere. "Neither. I'm just exhausted from another sixteen-hour day and wondering if I'm really up for a party. Once I go in, Sarah won't let me get away, so . . ."

"So you were considering getting out while the getting is good?" He tilted his head and looked into my eyes, searching for something.

I broke eye contact. "Something like that. Plus, I forgot to bring any wine, and—"

"You know Sarah. She has enough booze for three parties. Come on. I'll protect you from the drunkards." He tucked me under his arm and opened the door to the party.

As I breathed in the fragrance of warm man, tinged with the slightest hint of a woodsy cologne, I wondered: *But who will protect me from you? Or from myself?*

I took a deep breath and put on Leah's Party Face Number 217, good for all festive occasions. "OK, let's do this."

* * *

Sarah hugged the last of the guests as they pulled their coats on and waved good-bye. As she closed the door behind them, she collapsed back against it and smiled. "Well, it's only three in the morning. That's kind of early for one of my parties. I must be turning into a grown-up."

Luke, who sat next to me on the couch, our feet side by side on the maple coffee table, laughed. "I don't think you'll ever grow up, baby girl. And just who was that guy making the moves on you in the kitchen earlier? Is he somebody I need to beat up?"

Sarah blushed. "That was my neighbor, the accountant I was planning to set Leah up with tonight."

I felt Luke's body tense next to me. "I don't think Leah needs to be set up with anybody, Sarah."

I struggled to gain enough energy to be indignant. "Hey, you two. I'm right here, if you don't mind. Can we not talk about Leah as if Leah's not in the room? But Leah doesn't . . . oh, geez. Now you have me doing it. *I* don't need to be set up, thank you very much. And it looked like your accountant had *your* figure on his mind tonight."

Luke groaned. "That was a lame pun if I've ever heard one. Are you sure you work in publishing?"

"Yes, but I'm just a 'PR slut.' We don't actually have any talent, or hadn't you heard?" I winced at the bitterness in my voice, but then yawned so huge that my jaw felt like it was cracking. Tiredness won out over introspection.

"Lame pun or no lame pun, yes, I think my adorable new neighbor is interested in me a little. And he's nice *and* straight *and* doesn't live with his mother. We're going to have dinner tomorrow." Sarah tossed her head and struck a triumphant pose.

"So now I'm going to bed to get some beauty sleep for

my date. Leah, I made up my roommate's bed with fresh linens for you. Luke, you're on the couch again. Good night, kiddies. We'll clean up the rest of this mess in the morning."

Luke and I looked around at Sarah's "mess" and burst out laughing. She was such a neat freak, she'd cleaned up all night during the party—not in an obnoxious way; just unobtrusively picking up a dish here and a glass there. The only thing left to do was wash a couple of trays that had held chips and veggies.

I yawned again. The week of no sleep and huge stress had finally caught up with me.

"Sounds like you'd better get some sleep," Luke said.

"Yes, I think I should," I said.

I didn't move.

"OK, I'm going now," I said. "Right this minute."

I still didn't move.

"Oh, to hell with it. I have to know." I put my arms around his neck and pulled his head down to mine. "I have to know what you taste like."

I touched my lips to his, lightly at first, just a whisper of a touch. I kissed the edge of his mouth and then his bottom lip, ever so gently, just a thought—barely a promise. He held himself utterly still, and for a moment I felt my insides shrivel up.

Did I read the signs wrong? Is he hating this? Is he completely uninterested?

I started to pull away, and my movement seemed to break through his reserve and shatter his control. His hands shot up and captured my arms, keeping them firmly around his neck for a moment. Then he tunneled his fingers through my hair and caught my head in his hand, holding it firmly so I couldn't back away.

"Oh no. Please don't start something like that and just stop. We're under the mistletoe, beautiful."

I blinked and looked up.

"That's a cobweb."

"Close enough." Then he slanted his mouth over mine and claimed my lips in a kiss that seared clear through to my toes. Where my lips had gently roamed over his, his were firm and possessive as he kissed me in a way that brought new meaning to the word. At the first touch of his tongue, my whole body almost melted into his, as if to say hold me, touch me, love me.

This time I moaned, and the sound seemed to incite him. He dragged me closer, until I was sitting on his lap, and I could feel his hardness against the side of my hip. I moaned again because I wanted to get closer and closer, and I felt my nipples hardening and my thighs loosening and suddenly I needed to feel his skin. I yanked frantically at his sweater, desperate to feel the smooth skin of his belly, and was rewarded when my fingers touched warm, smooth skin over hard muscles. The feel of my hand touching his skin made Luke's kisses evermore urgent, and he shifted until he was lying half on top of me on the couch, and all I could think was *naked. I need to be naked. It's been so long*.

"Hey, guys, I thought I'd just wash those last trays tonight, so . . . oh! Oh, crap! I'm so sorry . . . I didn't, oh, man, I . . . you . . . Good night."

At Sarah's first words, I'd whipped my hands out from under Luke's sweater and dragged my mouth away from his. As she fled back into her bedroom, I shoved at Luke's shoulders and pulled my own shirt, which had somehow become partially unbuttoned, back together.

I couldn't look him in the eyes. I'd practically jumped the poor man on his sister's couch. How low-rent is that?

Of course, he was jumping right back, a voice in my mind said silkily.

Sure he jumped right back. He was a normal man who'd

had a woman throw herself at him. We barely knew each other, yet I was playing the starring role in *Sex-Crazed Nympho Does Christmas*.

Luke shifted a little to give me room to sit up. He lifted my chin so he could look in my eyes. "Hey. I hear that brain going full-bore. Want to tell me what you're thinking?"

I jerked my chin out of his hand and jumped up off the couch. "Nothing. I mean, we just got carried away. I mean, I hardly know you and you hardly know me, and I don't know what you think, but I don't usually crash right into touchy-feely with a guy I just met. I'm no blushing virgin—don't get me wrong—but sex is about emotional intimacy for me and we don't . . . I mean we won't . . . I mean . . . I'm just going to wash those veggie trays." I grabbed the nearest tray and nearly spilled ranch dip all over the carpet. My hands were shaking as much as my knees.

Luke stood and took the tray out of my hands. "Slow down. I don't jump in the sack with a woman I just met, either. There's some chemistry between us that is making me a little crazy, though. Plus, you've been my sister's best friend for the past few years, so can't we at least move a little past the first date phase? I promise to slow down if you'll let me take you to dinner this weekend. A real dinner. Not a quick panini when your boss has ruined your mood."

I stared at him, unsure of who scared me most. Him or me.

"I can't. I mean, I'm going to have to work all weekend. You . . . you're leaving right after Christmas and then you'll probably be gone for months, Sarah told me. I don't want to get involved with somebody who's going to leave before we ever even have a chance to see what might happen."

"Leah, that's not fair." He set the tray down on the kitchen counter with enough force to make the carrots jump, then shoved his hand through his hair.

I folded my arms and glared at him. "What's not fair? Is

it true or not that you're going to leave, probably for several months, and that you never know when your schedule might bring you to New York?"

"Yes, it's true. Leah, what I do is important. Besides doing photo shoots for places like Tiffany's, I put a human face on the amorphous concept of war. I turn Terrorist Strike, Film at Eleven into the image of a child holding his dead mother's hand after a suicide bomber took out her bus. It's more than what I do. It's part of me."

"I know, Luke. I know your job is important. It's not like you're just a PR slut pushing entertainment on an ever-increasing market share like me, right?"

"That's not what I meant, and you know it. Damn it, I want to—"

I smiled, trying to hold back the tears brimming in my eyes. "I know what you want, Luke. I want it too. But I'm not going to be somebody's little pre-Christmas fling. I have kind of a track record of getting dumped at Christmas. How stupid would I be to deliberately set myself up for the same thing all over again?"

"Leah, I—"

"Good night, Luke." I turned and went into Sarah's roommate's room, closing the door behind me on Luke and on the opportunity for what would probably be the most explosive sex in the history of the world.

Oh, well. Orgasms were overrated, right?

Yeah. I wasn't fooling *myself*, either.

Five Golden Dreams

After tossing and turning for the next few hours, during which I had three—*three*—separate fiery-hot dreams about Luke, I finally gave up, grabbed my shoes, and threw my clothes back on. I might as well be cranky and miserable in my own apartment. I tiptoed out of the bedroom and glanced over at the couch.

Luke had done his fair share of tossing and turning, too, if the state of the quilt tangled around his legs was any proof. He even looked dangerous in his sleep, with his un-shaven jaw and the hard muscles that were clearly defined beneath the T-shirt he'd slept in. I tortured myself for a moment with the view, and then let myself out of the apartment. *Doing laundry helps with unsatisfied lustful urges, right?*

"Leah, I can't live without you. Come with me to travel the world and do important things. I'll photograph all of life's injustices, and you can be a publicist for starving children in Africa. Please say you will, my darling." Luke swept me into his arms and into his fervor. We'd travel the world together. We'd do important things. We'd be like a sexy version of Mother Teresa and Gandhi, except if they weren't religious. Or, you know, celibate.

"Yes, Luke. Oh, yes. Take me with you. I'm yours!" As he passionately kissed me, I saw fireworks.

I heard bells.

I heard my alarm clock go off.

"Huh? Whazzat?" I blearily raised my head from the pillow, where I'd crashed in a brief nap. Just thirty minutes, I'd told myself, thirty minutes of rest before I drudged my way to the office to waste the last Saturday before Christmas working on plans for the July and August books.

I sighed. *Just as well. Do starving children in Africa really need publicists? More likely they just need food.*

I made a mental note to send money to a charity that fed needy children in Africa and reached out to smack my alarm clock into submission. The buzzing noise was even worse than the annoying radio announcer as a wake-up call. I rolled over and stared at the ceiling, which—I noticed—needed a touch-up, like so much else in my life. I covered my face with my pillow.

It wasn't really fair that I had to be tortured by the man even in my dreams.

It creeped me out to be the only one in the office. My footsteps echoed eerily on the tile in the lobby as I walked past the receptionist's desk toward my cubicle. Of course, all normal people were out doing last-minute holiday gift buying, or spending time with loved ones. But not me. Oh, no. I was here, all alone, wrapped in misery. The sole person in the universe idiotic enough to work on the last weekend before Christmas.

"Hi, Leah!"

I made a sound that was an odd cross between a squeal and a scream, and turned to see Howard looking at me as if I might be dangerous.

"Are you all right? Didn't mean to startle you. Thought I was the only one dedicated, devoted, and/or desperate enough to work on the Saturday before Christmas." He grinned at me. "House full of kids and grandkids. Needed a little peace and quiet, so I escaped. How about you? Overrun with relatives too?"

I smiled. He was so conspiratorial, like we were good buddies chatting, instead of uber-boss and lowly employee.

"Not exactly. I just have to revise some plans for Selena. She wants the July and August plans right away, since she's decided to take the first week of January off."

Howard's eyes narrowed. "She's taking the first week of January off? That's the first I've heard of it. We have a huge promotional meeting for the new Sphericals book that week with Connor. I need her to be there, and she knows it."

Half of me cheered silently that Selena might get in trouble; half of me quaked in my mental boots that she'd fry me for telling Howard her plans, and half of me didn't give a flying fart one way or the other. (Um, that's one too many halves, but you know what I mean.)

I was too tired to be diplomatic, but I tried anyway.

"Well, maybe I misunderstood. Anyway, nice seeing you. I'd better get to work."

"Right. Good seeing you, Leah. E-mail me an update on the plans for Lexi." He stood there silently as I headed down the hall to my cubicle. I would have given my last three dollars to know what he was thinking about.

Maybe he's fed up with Selena. Maybe he'll fire her and

hire somebody who will appreciate me. Maybe the new PR director will be an incredibly hot guy who will take one look at me and see the real me—the talented, brilliant, sexually imaginative woman who will impress him so much that he'll promote me and invite me to Barbados for a week.

I bumped into my cubicle and realized I'd been daydreaming again. Bad habit. Bad daydream. *Bad Leah.* With my luck, I'd get a new boss who'd invite me to Barbados all right—an enormous old guy with overactive sweat glands who would invite me to go with him on the weekend his wife took their eight kids to the Hamptons.

Sighing, I dropped into my chair and switched on my computer. At least I knew what I was doing when it came to publicity. Even Selena hadn't been able to undermine my confidence about that.

Two hundred and nineteen new e-messages.

What was I saying about confidence?

Four Good Intentions

So there you are one minute, minding your own business, doing laundry and wondering whether *hand wash only* is a rule or more like a guideline, and the next minute you're swirling figure eights beneath the branches of the Rockefeller Center Christmas tree like a tourist. Or, if you skate like me, more like figure squigglies.

Luke had timed his call to coincide with a critical period in my Sunday routine: the breakfast decision. Every week, I brought all of my analytical focus to bear on the issue of whether to: (a) go out for breakfast, thereby forcing me to take a shower, get dressed, and at least attempt to appear somewhat presentable, or (b) stay in for breakfast, forcing me to get dressed and face the prospect of one or more of my roommates' men wandering out in their underwear to stare bleary-eyed at me and ask for coffee.

Option A was a pain in the butt, but option B was a pain in the ego. Never once had one of *my* men been the one to wander out and ask for coffee. Not that anybody commented on it, but it was the kind of thing they noticed. Evelyn asked me once if I knew anybody at a new lesbian club who might help her get a job. "Hot hetero chicks get great tips, I've heard." They'd listened to my protests that I was just in between men at the moment with an air of amused indifference.

Figuring, after the weekend I'd had, that I'd hurl if I had to face another one of their half-dressed hunks smelling like sex and martinis, I was on the way out the door when Evelyn wandered into the kitchen, dressed only in a T-shirt three sizes too big that read NYPD over her left boob. I so didn't want to meet the owner of that T-shirt in his underwear and risk actually howling in frustration, so I grabbed the doorknob to make a quick escape.

"Hey, Leah. How are you? We never see you anymore. Still working so much?" She smiled at me, looking like she was still half asleep. I really liked Evelyn, but it annoyed me that she could look gorgeous first thing in the morning. Her silky blond hair wasn't even brushed yet.

Life can be so unfair.

I sighed and released the doorknob. "I'm fine, and yes, working a lot. How are you?"

"I'm great. We're all going home for the holidays, so you'll have the place to yourself. I guess we're going to carpool it out sometime tomorrow. If we don't see you again, Happy Holidays."

"Happy Holidays to you too. And tell the other girls, OK?" I smiled and made my getaway, pulling the door shut behind me before one of New York's finest could show up and start nuzzling Evelyn's neck right there in the kitchen.

I'd made it to the bottom step when my cell rang. It was Sarah.

"Hi, Sarah. I'm sorry I left so early yesterday, but I had a lot to do—"

"It's Luke. Don't hang up."

I stared at my phone, as if I suddenly had video-conference technology and would see his face. Amazing how just the sound of his voice was more energizing than a double espresso.

"I wouldn't hang up. I'm not a rude person, Luke."

He blew out a sigh. "I know you're not. Look, I'd just like to get to know you better. I haven't been this interested in a woman since . . . well, in a long time. Could we start over as friends? I'll buy you pancakes with strawberries and whipped cream."

My stomach growled really loudly, and I laughed, trying not to think about one of the dreams I'd had about Luke. The one that featured strawberries and whipped cream.

I cleared my throat. "OK. You had me at pancakes. The strawberries and whipped cream are shameless overkill."

He laughed again. "Great. I'm outside your apartment. Sarah gave me your address."

Startled, I looked up and at the glass doors of my entry-way. Sure enough, there he was. Larger than life. *Oh, boy. I'm in so much trouble. Just friends, just friends, just friends.*

I walked to the door and opened it, then leaned against it and folded my arms over my chest. "That's pretty cocky of you to be standing here. Were you really that sure of me?"

He looked sheepish and grinned a little. "Nope. But Plan B was to offer to bring coffee and croissants and the Sunday paper to your apartment, and I thought you'd find it harder to turn me down if I were already here. Also, Sarah made me promise to tell you that she only gave me your address and let me borrow her cell phone after I signed an oath in maple syrup that I'm not turning into a mad stalker and that you won't get mad at her."

I laughed. "Signed an oath, huh? Sounds like a waste of perfectly good maple syrup."

* * *

So, like I said, there I was, clutching Luke's arm and trying to remember how to ice skate, when it had been about eighteen years since the last time I skated.

"You should take pictures of the tree, Luke."

He steered me around a group of skating carolers. I sneered at them. Big deal, so they could skate and carry a tune at the same time.

"The tree? You mean, the Christmas tree? My specialty is more human-oriented, but you're right. That tree has been a holiday icon around here since 1931." He expertly avoided a wobbly child and her equally wobbly mother.

"That long ago? They were putting up trees during the Depression?" I could feel my legs gradually spreading farther and farther apart, which was *so* not a good thing when skating. Luke moved in closer to me and nudged my right leg back where it belonged. I knew I looked like a drunken camel, but I chose to pretend I was as graceful as Sarah Hughes in the Olympics. (Only taller. Maybe.)

"Yeah. I remember Sarah telling me once that Rockefeller Center was still a muddy construction site for that first tree. The Great Depression shadowed the holiday season, but the workers proudly planted their tree in the dirt. It was part of the jobs program, and they celebrated the unbreakable human spirit as much as the paychecks they received that Christmas Eve."

I looked up at him, surprised. "You're a poet in addition to a photographer, aren't you, Luke? Under that tough leather-jacket-and-boots-wearing exterior, you're a marshmallow."

He frowned in mock ferocity and growled at me. "Marshmallow? I'll show you marshmallow!"

Then he lifted me by the waist until my skates left the ice, and he kissed me. Oh, what a kiss. Somewhere in the dim recesses of my brain, I was sure the ice must be melting and soon all of Rockefeller Plaza would be a giant puddle of sizzling-hot water. Right about the time my resistance to the idea of a holiday fling was melting along with the ice, something slammed into my legs and knocked us over backward. I looked up from where I was sprawled on top of Luke and saw a small boy standing just behind us burst into tears.

"Mommeeeeeeee!"

Whew. Saved by the toddler.

I pulled myself up off the hard ice and the even-harder chest muscles I'd fallen on, and held out a hand to help Luke back on his feet. He grinned at me and stood, ignoring my outstretched hand. "No offense, Leah, but you're not exactly all that steady on your feet."

Yeah, especially when you're kissing me and sending tsunamis of need through my system.

As the boy's mom swooped in to rescue him, apologizing profusely to us, Luke grasped my hand firmly in his, tightening it when I tried to pull away. After we reassured ourselves that Little Mikey was all right, and reassured Mikey's mom that we were fine, we decided we'd had enough skating for the day.

I unlaced my skates with fingers grown stiff from the cold. "Luke, we need to talk—"

"I know, I know. I said just friends, and then I jumped on you. I'm sorry. You're just so adorable, and . . . no. No excuses. I didn't live up to my end of the deal, and you should tell me you never want to see me again." He smiled, but in a grim sort of way.

"OK, I never . . . you think I'm adorable?" I flashed my most brilliant smile at him, and suddenly he didn't look at all grim.

And the rest of my day didn't look bad, either.

Three Brand-new Babies

When the phone wakes you up out of a sound sleep in the middle of the night, it's never good news. I grabbed my cell phone. It was Mom. "What's wrong? Is Dad OK? Is it Mindy?"

"Calm down, honey." It was Mom, and she'd been crying. I could hear it in her voice. I sat up and shoved my hair out of my face, then leaned over to switch on my lamp.

"Mom, what is it? Who is it? Tell me."

"It's Mindy, honey. Well, it's Trina. No, it's Trina *and* Mindy. Oh, dear Lord help us." She started crying in earnest.

Oh no. Please, no. Please let everything be fine. Please, please, please. "Mom! Tell me. Are they OK? What about the babies?" I could hear my dad's low voice in the background, and then he was on the phone.

"Hey, baby girl. Calm down. Everybody's fine. Well, as fine as circumstances allow, I guess. Mindy went into labor last night, and they couldn't stop it. So Baby Natalie was born at 4:15 A.M. All seven pounds, six ounces of her. They say she's a thirty-six weeker and she's going to be just fine. Mindy's doing great too. Her blood pressure came down like magic."

I breathed in a lungful of air. "Thank God, Daddy. What about Trina?"

Dad hesitated a moment. "Well, her water broke in the middle of the night. Apparently there was some rupture problem or detached something or other. All I know is that the doctors felt they had to take the babies. They performed emergency surgery on Trina, and the twins were born at four-thirty."

He chuckled. "Darned if the first thing Trina said wasn't 'What time was Natalie born?' Those two and their competition."

"Are they healthy, Daddy? They're so early. Are they OK?" I couldn't stand it if something were to happen to my niece and . . .

"Daddy? Is it a boy or girl? The other twin?"

"It's two boys. Guess those ultrasound techs aren't foolproof. Now we're going to have to repaint the pink half of the nursery before the twins come home. They're doing as well as can be expected, the nurses told us. I guess thirty-one weeks isn't that young for twins, but there was a bit of a problem with lung development in Josh Junior."

I moaned. "Lung development? What does that mean? He can't breathe? What are the doctors doing? Are they good doctors?"

My father interrupted me before I let my panic get the better of me. "Shh, shh now, Leah. They have this special stuff called surfactant that magically helps the babies' lungs develop outside of the womb. Josh Junior and Cole are going to be just fine. Your mother is just crying from relief, exhaustion, and sheer overload, I think."

Thank you, thank you, thank you.

I laughed a little unsteadily. "They should have named one of them Frank."

"Frank?"

"For frankincense. Myrrh would sound funny. OK, I'm babbling. When do the babies get to come home?"

Dad sighed. "Well, Natalie and Mindy should be able to come home in two days, but Trina will be in longer because of the C-section. And the babies might be in the NICU for a while."

"Nick You?"

"The NICU. Means neonatal intensive care unit. We were able to go in one at a time, and you wouldn't believe how tiny some of those babies are. It doesn't seem possible that they could be alive. Modern medicine is pretty damn impressive. Still, seeing IVs stuck in my grandsons' heads was a bit much for me." Dad made a shuddering noise.

"Do you need me? I'll be right there. I'll have to change some things around but—oh, your trip! What about your trip?" I couldn't be selfish at a time like this, but a tiny frisson of sadness surfaced briefly. I'd looked forward to showing my parents around New York for months.

"I don't know, Leah. Honestly, both Trina and Mindy told us not to cancel our trip. We're only coming up there for a long weekend, and Mindy's in-laws are on their way now to stay with Mindy for the first week. I know your mother doesn't want to leave her first grandchildren, but she also doesn't want to miss seeing New York with you. Let me talk to her."

He must have put his hand over the phone, because I heard a muffled conversation. I dropped my head on my knees and thought that I'd really like to tell Sarah and Luke the news.

And Luke?

"Honey, it's Mom. As long as the doctors assure us that the babies and the moms are perfectly healthy, we still want to come. It's only for two and a half days, really, and Trina and the babies will still be in the hospital, surrounded by professionals. Plus Brad's family will be descending in a horde on poor Mindy, so she won't miss us."

Mom had a little competitive thing of her own going with her children's in-laws.

"Are you sure, Mom? I can cancel and try to get a flight out there . . ." Except finding a flight would probably be impossible. But I could try.

"No, let's just keep our plans as they are for now, dear. We have all those theater tickets and everything. It's just such a blessing. I can't wait for you to see their darling tiny toes. You *are* still coming for New Year's, right?"

"Wild publicity directors couldn't keep me away now, Mom. Now tell me everything. I want to hear exactly what they each look like. Does Natalie have Mindy's big nose or my little cute one?"

As I settled back on to my pillows for a long conversation about tiny fingers and toes (she'd counted them all!), I sent up another silent prayer. My praying skills were a little rusty, but I managed something that sounded like *"Amazing Grace," "Hark the Herald Angels Sing,"* and a Sarah McLachlan song all rolled up into one.

Three beautiful, healthy babies. *Now* I felt the holiday spirit.

I arrived at work in a great mood for the first time in I didn't remember how long. I'd talked to both Brad and Josh, and they were jubilant. The doctors had been cautious, but generally optimistic for early release dates for Mindy and Natalie, only a few more days for Trina, and a good prognosis for the twins. *Wow.* I couldn't quite work my mind around the idea that I was suddenly Auntie Leah three times over. I was grinning like a fool when I stepped off the elevator.

Into utter chaos. Associate editors four deep were scurrying down the hall. Half the PR staff from our sister division was clustered around the reception desk. I could hear Selena shrieking from about fifty feet down the hall, near Howard's office.

"What the heck is going on?" I asked Howard's secretary as she ran past me so closely she almost knocked me back into the elevator.

"No time. Total clusterfutz. Lexi's event. Howard's office. Now." She was panting, and I was terrified. What could have gone so terribly, hideously wrong as to cause this?

Gillian ran by just then, clutching a stack of papers. "Oh, Leah. You are *so* screwed. How could you let this happen?" She gave me a pitying look and kept going. That, more than anything, chilled me to the bone. *Gillian pitying me?* It must be worse than bad.

I dropped my coat and purse right there on the floor and ran down to Howard's office. As I skidded in, all conversation in the room stopped, and every pair of eyes turned toward me.

"Leah, how could you? I had faith in you. You have totally let Lexi down." Howard's eyebrows hunched over his glaring eyes as he yelled at me.

"What . . . what is it? What's wrong?" I didn't recognize the voice that came out of my mouth. It sounded weak and terrified.

Selena jumped in with both feet. "Leah, you moron. You complete and utter screw-up. How could you tell the press that Lexi's charity event was at seven *A.M.* today instead of seven *P.M.*?"

"What? No, I didn't . . . I remember . . ." I frantically thought back to the events of the past week. I *had* been distracted, but to make an error that huge? Not to double-check an important press release? No way. I couldn't have.

"Well, maybe if you kept your mind on your job, instead of on your social life, you would remember little details like the most important public relations event of the season for M&M Publishing." Selena almost spat the words at me.

Howard picked up the story. "The press arrived and started setting up at six-thirty this morning. Since the hospital administrator and marketing director don't arrive at work until nine, the media personnel wasted an entire hour setting up and then cooling their heels, wondering when the hell Lexi and the pop star would show. They're all so ticked off, they've refused to come back tonight. We're going to get no publicity for the event and no money for the hospital charity. Lexi is so furious with us, her agent is on the phone to six other publishers already."

"But I didn't . . . I mean, I'm sure the press releases were right. If I can just . . ." I was stammering and trying not to cry. I *knew* those press releases were correct when I wrote them and sent them to Selena for approval. Then her secretary had mailed them out . . .

I narrowed my eyes. Was it possible? Could Selena have sabotaged one of our most important authors just to get back at me? She hated Sarah too. Was this a coldly calculated play?

"Get out. Just get out. We're trying to do what we can to fix this." Howard started dialing his phone again and wouldn't even look at me. When he put his head down to dial, Selena snaked a vicious smile at me.

Oh yeah. It was possible. But I was formulating a plan.

I backed out of Howard's office and then took off at a dead heat down the hallway toward my cubicle, grabbing my coat and bag on the way. I had my cell phone open before I even sat down. "Megan? Hey, how are you? I know, only six months till our next reunion of the Buckeye Public Relations Society of America gang. Hey, is that emergency e-mail chain activated yet? Great! I need a huge favor."

Within ten minutes, Megan had activated the largest network of PR professionals in the country, via our hometown chapter. I smiled as I saw the URGENT! MEMBER NEEDS HELP! message flash into my computer in box. Then I dialed again.

"Luke? Is there a society of news photographers? A guild or something? There is? Look, I have a huge favor to ask."

Less than a half hour later, I stepped back into Howard's office and silently handed him a sheaf of hard copies of e-mail messages. As he talked urgently on the phone, he looked up at me in disgust, and then down at the top message.

"... and I need ... uh ... by tonight ... hang on a minute, Fred."

He propped the phone between his shoulder and jaw and riffled through the papers I'd handed him.

"ABC will be there . . . NBC says no problem; for a good cause . . . FOX says you get a freebie since it's the holidays . . . CNN . . . CBS . . . Holy crap, Leah. Did you pull this off?" His expression was a combination of doubt and admiration.

"Yes. Yes, I did."

Furthermore, I did not *make a mistake on those press releases.* But I wasn't not saying any more until I could prove it.

I turned to walk out of his office.

"Leah?"

I paused at the door, but didn't look back at him. "Yes?"

"Great save, kid. Great save."

I sat on the couch in my apartment, old ratty sweatshirt drawn down around my pulled-up knees, remote control clutched in my hand. I flicked channels as fast as my thoughts spun around in my head.

CNN: ". . . Alexis Day, best-selling author of . . ."

ABC: ". . . M&M Publishing's star, in a special appearance . . ."

FOX: ". . . truly a magical holiday season for the children in this hospital, as the fund-raiser starring author Alexis Day . . ."

NBC: ". . . anonymous gift makes a total of four hundred thousand dollars raised in an hour for new medical equipment . . ."

CBS: ". . . other news, Donald Trump is back . . ."

Well, four out of five ain't bad.

My cell phone rang. Caller ID said Sarah; it was probably Luke again. I answered on the second ring. "Hello? I've been waiting for you to call. How did the shoot at the store go today?"

"Leah, it's Sarah. Luke got called out of town on an emergency. A coup d'état in South America, I think. His voice was really garbled on my cell phone. He asked me to call you and tell you he'll be back in two days, so don't make any plans for Wednesday night. And hey—good save on Lexi's event. She's really happy with how it turned out and promised me she's not going to switch publishers." She blew out a sigh. "Of course, I groveled a little. What happened this morning? You don't make mistakes like that."

I narrowed my eyes. "No, I don't. I can't prove it yet, but I think Selena deliberately sabotaged the event to make me look bad and make you lose M&M's star author. She's crazy when it comes to building her personal power base. I spent the afternoon backtracking my steps and found the original press release document on the system, with the earliest chrono date/time stamp, and it was *my* press release. Then I found subsequent versions saved by Selena's secretary."

I felt my temper shooting through the roof, just at the memory of what else I'd found. "The most recent date stamp, though, was at five A.M. this morning. Selena created that document. *That* was the press release that had the wrong time on it. *That* was the one she sent out."

I paused to take a breath. "Sarah, she did it on purpose."

"That bitch. She would ruin a children's hospital event to raise money just to satisfy her own personal agenda?" Sarah wasn't quite yelling into the phone, but it was the closest I'd ever heard her get.

"It sure looks like it. I put together a file of all the documents and brought it home with me. I'm going to Howard with it tomorrow, just to make sure my butt is covered if she tries to get rid of me."

She groaned. Really loud.

"Oh no. Oh, Leah, why didn't you go to Howard today?"

"He was in conferences all afternoon, and I didn't want to interrupt him. Plus, his secretary wouldn't let me. What's wrong?" I felt my microwave-pizza dinner sink like a rock in my stomach.

"Leah, he left the country. His family usually goes to Paris for the holidays, and he's totally out of touch with the office during that time. He said he doesn't even care if the building burns down, don't bother him during family time. Selena will have free reign during the rest of the week."

It was my turn to groan. "Maybe I'll just call in sick. Except I have to get a few things done before my folks get here Thursday. Oh, I'm an idiot!! Sarah, I forgot to give you the awesome news! I'm an aunt!!"

We talked more about babies and my family, but the entire time we were on the phone, I felt the anxiety worming its way into my brain. When we said good-bye, I tried to reassure myself that Selena had done her worst—really, what else could she possibly do in three days?—but, after all, this was Selena.

Not for the first time that month, I wondered how I could get hold of a nice prescription for Valium.

Two Crushing Disappointments

Tuesday brought a blessed reprieve: Selena was out of the office all day—at "important meetings" if you believed her e-mail auto-reply, or at her cosmetic surgeon having "important touch-ups" if you believed her secretary. Either way, I didn't care as long as she wasn't around to torture me.

I spent as much time on the phone with my family as I did working that day. The doctors were planning to release Mindy and Natalie that afternoon, and the twins were doing well. I finally talked to Trina, and she sounded tired but good. She anticipated going home on Friday—Christmas Eve. The babies would stay in the NICU for at least another week or two, though, so she and Josh planned to spend most of their time at the hospital, just going home to sleep at night. They were so happy to hear that I'd be down for a few days the next weekend for New Year's that it alleviated some of my guilt at not rushing to Ohio on the next available flight.

Mom and Dad were still planning to come visit for the weekend, so I firmed up my list of the things we wanted to see and do. I knew keeping Mom really busy would be the only way to keep her from going totally nuts over the thought of not being back home with her grandbabies.

One helping of guilt down; one to go. I worked feverishly on final touch-ups for the PR plans Selena wanted to review before she left for her extended vacation. Around four-thirty, I stretched and was contemplating a late-afternoon Starbucks run when my phone rang. It was the receptionist.

"There's a Glenwood E. Hamilton III here to see you, Leah. Are you available?"

I groaned. Just what I needed. Face-to-face time with my most annoying author.

"Leah? Do you have time to see him?" The receptionist sounded impatient.

"Sure, I'll be right up." Responsibility won out over personal preference.

I stood and took a deep breath. *Remember not to call him Glennie.*

As I walked into the lobby, I glanced around, but he wasn't there. The lobby was empty except for our receptionist and a totally hot bicycle messenger. I could quit my job and become a bicycle messenger. I'd get good exercise, not be stuck in an office, and get to work with hot guys with excellent butts.

I dragged my gaze away from the messenger's behind. I really had to do something about my sex-starved situation. I glanced at my watch. Only a little over twenty-four hours until my dinner date with Luke.

Maybe I'd just have Luke for dinner and take care of my perpetual state of hormone overload. I leaned on the edge of the reception desk, waiting for Glenwood to come back from the men's room or wherever he'd gone, when the absolutely delicious messenger guy walked up to me, holding a package.

"Um, Leah?"

"Yes? Do you have a delivery for me? Where do I sign?"

He laughed nervously. "No, um, I mean, yes I have something for you, but it's not like a delivery or anything. I'm Glen, er . . . I mean, I'm Glenwood E. Hamilton III."

I looked at him, my mouth dropping open. "*You're* Glennie? I mean, Glenwood? I mean, *really*? What are you, like twelve?"

He grinned and held out his hand for me to shake. "I can see why you're in PR, with that silver tongue. Can we sit down for a minute?"

I shook his hand, and then shook my head to clear it of disbelief and foot-in-mouth-itis. "Sure. Yes. Um, this way."

As I led him to our small conference room, I kept glancing back at him. *This* was Glennie? Where did the attitude of an eighty-year-old man with hemorrhoids come from?

As we sat down, he fidgeted a little, then answered my unspoken question. "I'm only twenty-one. I guess I figured that if you thought I was older, you'd take me more seriously, so I kind of put on that 'the Third' act. But I think it backfired, and you were getting annoyed, instead. And you always seemed so nice, even when I was a total jerk, so I wanted to come clean. So, here I am."

He shoved a small package at me. "This is for you. It's just a little present for being so nice. Thanks. And it's nice to meet you. I hope it's nice to meet me. I mean, I hope it's nice for you to meet me. Well, you know what I mean."

He grinned, and I understood instantly how he'd written

such hot and realistic sex scenes. This guy probably had women chasing his bike down the street in droves.

I smiled back. "It's great to meet you, finally. The real you. And you didn't have to get me a gift, but thank you so much. It's my very first holiday present from an author this year."

"Great! Then open it."

I opened the awkwardly wrapped package to find a tiny crystal bird inside a small box.

"It's totally corny, but getting my first book published has made my dreams fly. And you're the person I've worked with the most so far, since my editor hasn't started work on my manuscript yet, and . . . Anyway, it's kind of dumb, but I hope you like it." A tinge of red tinted his cheeks.

I was surprised to feel the lump in my throat. I swallowed hard and then smiled at Glen. "I love it. I'll keep it on my desk, so I can remember what you said whenever I look at it."

We sat there for a minute in silence, grinning at each other like a couple of dolts.

"Hey! You're twenty-one? Do you know how great that is in the world of publicity? Are you really a bike messenger?"

"Yeah. It's a mindless job so I can have creative energy to write at night." He ducked his head. "I know it's stupid, but—"

"No, it's fantastic! Humble Bicycle Messenger Shoots for the Stars with Debut Novel for M&M Publishing. Have you ever delivered anything to any of the news studios? That would be a hook to get you an interview: 'And can you believe, Matt, that just last week Glen delivered a package to us at the studio, and here he is being interviewed on the *Today Show*.'"

I shot my fist in the air. "Yes! Glen, we are on our way."

We spent an hour or so planning strategies and just getting to know each other, and then I said good-bye. "Thanks for letting me meet the real you, Glen. I like this version just fine."

He smiled. "You're pretty great yourself, Leah. If you want to have coffee some time, I really like older women."

I punched him in the arm. "Watch it, buddy."

He laughed and gave me a brief hug, then sauntered over to the elevator. Twenty-one, and the world at his feet. Or at the soles of his bike shoes, anyway.

Older woman. Hmmph!

Back at my desk, there was still no sign of Selena or any messages from her, so I decided to finish my holiday shopping. Maybe I could visit my necklace, since I knew Luke was out of town. Not that I thought he'd make fun of me or anything for visiting a necklace.

Not exactly.

A new day and life was good. I'd actually gotten a full night's sleep with my roommates gone and total silence in the apartment. Plus, I had a dinner date with Luke to look forward to and I'd bought a little something to wear (emphasis on *little*) that was definitely going to make one photojournalist's temperature rise a few degrees. Not only that, but Mom and Dad would be in town tomorrow. I was even considering introducing Luke to my parents, but didn't like to think about it too much in case I jinxed myself.

As I walked down the hall toward my cube, humming "Santa Baby," I heard the one voice guaranteed to make my mood drop and my blood pressure rise.

Selena was in the house.

She caught sight of me and stormed down the hall my way. "Leah! Where have you been? Slacking off just because it's the holidays, no doubt?" She said this loudly enough to reverberate off the walls, not to mention be heard by anyone in a three-mile radius.

"No, I actually—"

"Right. Look, you may have pulled in a few favors and gotten a little press coverage Monday night, but the fact remains that your error almost cost us a *New York Times* best-selling author." She skidded to a stop about a foot in front of me but didn't lower her voice. This was clearly a command performance.

I was fed up with command performances. And I had evidence.

"Selena, I know what you did."

A look of uncertainty flashed across her face so fast I almost missed it. "What are you talking about? We're discussing what *you* did. Or, rather, failed to do. I'm sorry, Leah, but it was really the last straw. I'm tired of baby-sitting you and making excuses for your incompetence."

"*My* incompetence? Selena, how dare you? You're the one who—"

She cut me off again. "See me in my office at five. Don't be late." Then she pivoted on her heel and stalked back off down the hall.

Sarah was out of the office, and I couldn't reach her on her cell phone. Luke's phone was probably out of range, and I wasn't exactly going to call and cry on his shoulder when he was in the middle of some war or something. How pathetic would that be?

I spent most of the morning staring blindly at my computer, wondering what I could do. I had the evidence, but there was nobody there to present it to. *She wouldn't actually fire me, would she?*

At lunchtime, I escaped the building for a little while and wandered up and down streets filled with cheerful holiday shoppers. I didn't even have the energy to window shop or go visit my necklace, which was a first in my lifetime. I kept trying Sarah, but no response. Finally, I forced myself to return to my office and get some work done.

My voice mail light was blinking. *Maybe Sarah had finally called.*

It was Sarah, but the news wasn't good. "My stupid cell phone battery died, and I won't be back for hours, but I wanted to talk to you right away. Luke just called to let me know that he won't be back today. Maybe not this week at all. Something came up. Now don't get freaked or anything—he said he's fine. Just hot on the trail of some lead or other. He does this all the time. That's why I told you not to get involved. He's my brother, but he can be a pain. Hey, do you want a—*beep!*

Did I want a what? And what did "something came up" mean? A lead? A new job? He met a sexy, kick-ass rebel leader, and she seduced him? What?

Message two: "Baby, it's Dad. We've, well, we've got bad news. There's a problem. We . . ." There was a pause, and I heard the scariest noise I've ever heard in my life. It sounded like my father was crying.

"The babies had a downturn. Well, not Natalie. She and Mindy are fine and at home, thank God. But Josh Junior and Cole both had sharp glucose drops during the night. I guess a lack of glucose can cause brain damage. The doctors have glucose drips going through their IVs, but they're concerned and, well, Josh Junior is having a problem with lung development. So your mom won't leave the hospital. She's set up a vigil at the NICU and the hospital chapel, and she won't eat or sleep. We really need to be there for

Josh and Trina and the babies, Leah. I'm sorry about the trip, but we can't come now." *beep*!

I sat there rocking back and forth, tears running down my face. What kind of problem? How could I get to Ohio right away? Why didn't I have a car?

Message three: "Damn machines. Leah, it's Dad again. We need you, baby. Your mom needs you. Please come home. I know you can't get out of there today, but try to get a flight for tomorrow. Call me when you know your plans, and I'll pick you up at the airport. Love you, honey. Bye."

Flights. I had to find a flight. I scrubbed the tears off my face and went online to search for a plane ticket to Ohio.

Two hours later, I slumped in my chair, defeated. There wasn't a single airline seat to be had in the next four days. The holiday travel season was in full swing, and there was no way I would get on a plane. I'd begged, pleaded, and cried on the phone, to no avail.

"Yeah, yeah. The last woman who called said all seven of her closest relatives were dying, lady. I still got no seats." The bored and harassed-sounding worker hung up on me, the click sounding decisively in my ear.

I buried my head in my arms, and tried not to howl. *Why, oh, why didn't I ever renew my driver's license in case of emergencies?*

"Leah, are you an idiot?"

"What?" I jerked in my seat, and turned to look up at none other than Selena looming over me. "What do you want? I'm in no mood for you right now, Selena."

"I don't care about your moods. IT told me you were snooping about in the files for the press releases. I don't know what you think it is that you know, but let me tell you this—"

"Oh, shut up." I'd finally had it.

"What?" Selena couldn't have been more shocked if I'd poked her with an electric flat-iron. "How dare you?"

"Oh, I dare just fine. And right now I have more important things to worry about than your sabotage and your ultimatums. So, if you'll excuse me . . ."

"No, I definitely will not excuse you. You can consider this your notice. You're being terminated. Clear out your desk and get out. *Now*. I'll send security to escort you to the door. And don't even *think* about asking for a reference."

In slow motion, I turned to look at her. Could any human being be so deliberately evil? Suddenly, I just didn't care. All I cared about was getting to Ohio to see the babies and my family.

"Fine, Selena. You win. But I wonder how you sleep at night." I grabbed my purse and stuffed my few personal items in it, then shoved past her, noticing with satisfaction that she'd cringed away from me for a moment.

"I sleep just fine, Leah. But of course, I have a *job*." Parting shot delivered, she stood there and watched me all the way down the hall.

To my eternal triumph, I didn't start to cry until the elevator doors were completely closed.

A Publicist and a Pear Tree

I stumbled aimlessly down the sidewalks of Manhattan for a while, wondering which crisis to focus on first. When I tried to assign priorities, the order was pretty clear:

1. the babies and how could I get from New York to Ohio two days before Christmas.
2. my prospective boyfriend may or may have not have been captured by rebel forces.
3. my future as a short-order cook, now that I would be permanently blackballed from publishing.

I tried to figure out if focusing on assigning priorities had made me feel any better.

Nope.

I stopped short, realizing that I had to go to my apartment. I'd have access to my computer and a phone and could try to find a way to get home. I wiped my face and looked around, seeing my surroundings for the first time in blocks.

Somehow, I stood in front of Tiffany's, directly facing the window where my necklace was so beautifully displayed.

Except it wasn't.

It was gone.

I started laughing so hard that I had to lean against the wall, and I didn't even know when the laughter turned to tears. *Just when I'd finally decided to quit waiting for Prince Charming and give that necklace to myself, somebody else's Prince Charming swooped it up for her. Wasn't that just my luck?*

I dug in my bag for a tissue and wiped my face, then blew my nose loudly enough to startle several passersby. Then I squared my shoulders and turned toward my apartment. I would find a way to get home to my family. Even if I had to hijack a car and driver, since my maxed-out Visa sure wouldn't cover it.

Resolved and slightly less soggy, I started walking, and my cell phone rang. I pulled it out of my pocket, still walking. Private number, according to caller ID. I contemplated ignoring it, when I realized it might be the hospital. My breath caught in my throat, and I snapped my phone open.

"What? Hello? This is Leah. Are the babies OK?"

"Leah? Leah, this is Sarah. Are you all right? What about the babies? What's happening?"

"Oh, Sarah. Oh, I have so much to tell you. Where are you? I really need to—"

I heard muffled but loud laughter on her end. "Sorry, Leah. I didn't catch that. It's really loud here. Listen, I'm having lunch with Lexi, and she really wants to meet you. She said you've only communicated over phone and e-mail. I called you at your office and some really weird message was on your voice mail. What's going on?"

"It's not my office anymore, Sarah. Selena fired me." I slumped against the side of a building. "It's probably not appropriate for me to meet Lexi at this point."

"*What?* What do you mean, she fired you? We'll just see about that. You meet me in the office in twenty minutes, Leah. No, meet me downstairs in the lobby. We're going to have a little chat with Selena Evans. And I think you may be *un*fired."

"No, wait—I have to—"

"Twenty minutes, Leah. And Lexi has something for you." She hung up, leaving me staring at my phone. *What to do?*

The deciding factor was the image of Selena's gloating face. If I had just half a chance to make her pay for what she'd almost done to that children's hospital, I didn't care at all about my job or my future in publishing. Lexi, at least, was going to know the truth. I checked my bag to be sure that a certain file folder was still in there, and then I smiled.

"Hold on, babies. Auntie Leah is on the way. But first she has to kick some corporate butt."

An older couple hurried past me. "You see, Helen, I told you these New Yorkers stand around and talk to themselves on the street. Why couldn't we just stay home in Montana, where we belong?"

"Hush, now. She'll hear you."

I shouted out a laugh. *Finally*! One of my most cherished goals met—somebody took me for a native New Yorker! Then I took off running. I had a butt to kick.

Gillian and Devon were standing in the hallway, gossiping, when Lexi, Sarah, and I stepped off the elevator. Gillian smirked at me, but Devon took one look at Lexi and rushed up to us. "Oh, Miss Day, I've read all of your books. I'm such a huge fan. I'm in editorial, of course, but now that Leah is no longer with the company, I'll be glad to help in any way I can with your publicity."

Lexi didn't have much time for butt-kissers, apparently. "Yes, thank you. Except Leah isn't going anywhere unless I go with her. Now lead me to Howard's office immediately, Sarah."

She swept down the hall in the wake of a grinning Sarah, while I trailed behind her. As I passed Devon, I gave my most innocent smile. "No more gifts to recycle?"

My smile faded as I saw who stood in front of Howard's office, barring the door. "I'm sorry, Miss Day, but Howard is out of the country. I'd be glad to help you with anything you may need, and . . . *Leah!* What are you doing back here? Miss Day, I'm so sorry if this woman has been bothering you. We let her go today and—"

Lexi narrowed her eyes. "Yes, I heard all about it. Out of my way, Selena. Howard is on his way in, and he told me to wait in his office. *You* I don't need."

Selena's face turned even more white than usual. "But, he's gone to Paris. I'm sure you're mistaken."

"No, you're the one who's mistaken if you think you can get away with this crap at *my* company, Selena." Howard's voice boomed down the corridor, and we all turned to watch him barrel down the hall.

"I have put up with your nonsense and superiority act for a long time. But this is beyond evil." He stopped in front of us and waved a sheaf of papers in front of Selena's pointed nose. "Is it corporate espionage? Are you leaving and taking authors with you? What possible reason could you have for deliberately sabotaging Miss Day's event?" He was breathing so hard his face was purple.

Lexi patted his arm. "Calm down, darling. And I've told

you a hundred times to call me Lexi. This piece of garbage is not worth you getting your blood pressure up. Let *me* do it."

Lexi's tone of warm concern vanished, replaced by ice-covered steel, when she turned to face Selena. "You listen to me, you sorry excuse for a human being. Ruining one of my press events would be bad enough, but not even *I* think the world revolves around me. However, almost costing that hospital the money that they raised for new equipment by robbing them of press coverage is a hideous act. I will make it my goal in life to spread the word about you among every author and publisher I know, until I guarantee you never get a job publicizing so much as a bake sale."

Selena stepped back a foot or so, then recovered and drew herself up to her full height. "I'm sorry for whatever you think I've done, Miss Day, but I don't need a job. I'm perfectly happy here at M&M."

Howard broke in again. "Not anymore, hotshot." He nodded toward the security guards who'd just rounded the corner. "They're going to escort you to your office to clean out your desk. My secretary will accompany you to make sure you don't try to use the computer. You're finished, Selena."

"I, you can't . . . I'll . . ." Selena turned on me. "This is *your* fault!" For an instant, I thought she might actually hit me.

Instead of backing off, though, I stepped forward. "No, Selena, it's your fault. All I wanted to do was work hard and help you and learn from you, but you sabotaged me at every turn. Why? All I want to know is why?"

She glared at me and then turned to go. Suddenly, she whirled back to face me. "Because you're better at it. You're better than me. The authors like you and they hate me, the annoying bugs. I couldn't stand it."

She hung her head and continued, mumbling. "Nobody gets to be better than me. Nobody."

I stared after her in disbelief as the guards escorted her down the hall. *Better? Me?*

Sarah took my arm and pulled me inside Howard's office. "Come on, Leah. I think Howard and Lexi have a few things to say to you."

Dazed, I followed her inside and sank into a chair.

"Good job. Sorry about the grief. Good work." Howard smiled at me, and I realized that when Sarah had said "a few words," she hadn't been kidding. *No need to get gushy, Howard.* I was on the verge of hysterical laughter, so I bit the inside of my cheek to keep from losing it.

Lexi smiled wryly at Howard. "Nice speech. Good thing I'm the writer and not you, old friend."

Then she turned to me and took my hand. "First, Leah, I'm sorry for being so temperamental about this and also for ever doubting you. You've worked so hard for me for the past three years, I should have known you would never make an error of this magnitude. Second, I've had the feeling over the past several months that you were doubting the importance of your job and what you do."

I tried to protest, but she held up her hand. "No, we all go through periods of self-doubt. Do you think I've never asked myself why I'm writing about alien worlds and galaxies instead of using my talent to write about social issues and really make a difference in the world?"

She smiled and let go of my hand, then leaned forward in her chair and looked at each of us in turn. "Let me get up on my soapbox for a moment and tell you something. What we do is important. We entertain people. We take their minds off the job, and the bills, and the ex-husband or cheating girlfriend. We take them to worlds that are limited only by the powers of the author's and the reader's imagination. We dream, and they dream with us."

She reached into her pocket, and drew out a folded sheet of paper.

"And sometimes—just sometimes—we give them hope. 'Dear Miss Day,

Thank you for coming to the hospital tonight to read to us. I love all your books, but I think you need more dragons in them. Dragons are my favorite. I have leukemia, which is a bad kind of cancer that kids get sometimes. Guess I was one of the unlucky ones. I just wanted to say that when the doctors have to do bad things to me, like take my bone marrow, I pretend that I'm inside of one of your books, discovering another world, and that makes it not hurt so much.' " Lexi paused for a moment, unable to continue.

Then she took a shaky breath and finished. " 'When I grow up, I want to be a writer just like you. Yours truly, Trevor.' "

As we sat there in silence, not a dry eye among us, my heart swelled inside me until I thought it might burst. I jumped up to hug Lexi. "Thank you. Thank you so much for sharing that letter. *That's* why I do this. *That's* why I care so much. A letter like that and a tiny crystal bird. They represent more to me than any amount of money. I really needed to be reminded of that."

Howard started laughing. "That's no way to go into salary negotiations for your new job, Leah. HR will take advantage of you with an attitude like that."

I looked at him, still a little dazed with emotion. "New job? Sir? Aren't you in Paris?"

"Call me Howard. I can't have my new vice president of publicity calling me Sir. Will look bad to the staff. Make me look stuffy. No, we decided three years in Paris was enough. Staying home this year. Glad I did, too, when I got Lexi's call."

I was stuck a few lines back. "Vice president of . . . *what*? I'm getting promoted?"

I looked at Sarah. She was dancing from foot to foot. "All right, Leah!! Finally, a PR director I can get along with!"

"But, I'm . . . I mean, thanks, but . . ." No way was I ready for this job. I wanted it more than anything, but three years in the business might not be quite enough to handle it.

Howard smiled at me. "I know exactly what you mean. Great friend of mine is tired of spending his time fishing. He was the VP before Selena. He's going to come back for a year or so on a part-time basis as a consultant and train you. Make sure you don't make any huge mistakes. You seem to be pretty good at fixing mistakes, though."

He grinned again. "Now get out. All of you. Don't you have shopping to do or something?"

Lexi beamed. "Oh! Shopping! Sarah, if you'll just get that basket."

Sarah reached down behind the desk and lifted an enormous gift basket into her arms. I tried not to be envious. I did have my crystal bird, after all. Then Sarah handed the basket to me.

Lexi stood and grinned. "Merry Christmas, Leah. This is for you. And I'd better not hear about any recycling."

I stood there, almost reeling under the weight of what had to be twenty pounds of chocolate, champagne, and fruit wrapped up in a beautiful basket. "Thank you so much! I would never recycle it. I'll enjoy every bit. Thank you so much."

"You're welcome, dear. Thank *you* for saving my charity event Monday. And Merry Christmas."

Lexi reached up and hugged Howard. "See you later, Howard. I expect to see you and your beautiful wife at my

tree-trimming party tomorrow. My pilot is on his way back
to Ohio this evening, and I'm going to enjoy the next few
weeks in New York until the crush of the January book tour
starts."

I started to walk out the door, still dazed. Then it hit me.

"Did you say *Ohio? Your pilot?* Do you have a plane?"

Lexi seemed a little embarrassed. "I know it's a ridiculous luxury, but I bought a small plane when it finally
kicked in that my success wasn't a fluke. It makes touring
so much easier. My pilot lives in Ohio with his family, and
he's going to take the plane with him and go home. I don't
need him back until mid-January."

Now it was my turn to dance back and forth. "I, oh, I
know this is a huge imposition, but could I catch a ride with
him? My sister and sister-in-law both had their babies this
week, and the twins aren't doing well, and I need to get
home, and there are no flights, and I don't have a driver's license. Well, I don't have a car, either, but . . ."

Lexi was already dialing. "Let me call him right now. Of
course you can ride along. There's plenty of room in the
plane." She stepped out in the hall to talk.

I set my basket on the desk and threw my arms around
Howard in a huge hug. "Oh, and thank you so much, sir—I
mean Howard. I'll be the best vice president-in-training
you've ever had."

He patted my shoulder for a moment. "You'd better, or
I'll sic Lexi on you. She's pretty scary when she gets going."

Lexi came back in the office, looking devastated. "Oh,
Leah. Honey, I'm so sorry, but he's already gone. I asked
him if he could come back, but he said there was no way he
could get a flight plan cleared this late for the holidays. I'm
so sorry, honey. Is there anything else we could do?"

My heart plunged back down to my shoes. I'd dared to

hope that everything could work out like in one of our author's books, just for once. But Lexi had been so kind, and I didn't want her to feel badly about me. I put on my game face.

"No, no, I'm sure I'll figure something out. I'll just have to borrow a car. No worries. Thank you so much, Lexi. I have to get going, but we'll talk first thing after New Year's about the tour, all right?" I hugged her again.

Sarah touched my arm and drew me aside while Howard and Lexi said their good-byes. "Leah, I have dinner plans with Lexi, but I'll call you the minute I get back. We'll figure something out, OK? Don't be discouraged."

I smiled, but I didn't know what Sarah could do. She suffered from the same lack of car, driver's license, and disposable cash that I did. I waved good-bye, retrieved my beautiful basket, and dashed out of there.

I could figure this out. A vice president could figure this out.

About an hour and a half later, I finally made it back to my apartment. Juggling an enormous gift basket on the subway is not as much fun as you might think. I was exhausted from the hot-and-cold-running emotions of the day, and I still had to figure out a way to get to Ohio. But I had a warm feeling in my soul. *My job really did matter.* I suspected that I'd carry the words in that letter around in my heart for a long, long time.

"Nice basket. Did you rob a gift shop, or should I be worried about my competition?"

I almost yelped at the first words, then recognized Luke's voice as he stood from the shadows on my building's front steps.

"Luke! You're back! Are you OK? What happened? Were there rebels? Did they capture you? Are you hurt?" I thrust the basket at him so I could hug him, but realized it wouldn't work that way, either. He laughed and put the basket down on the step, next to an odd-looking potted plant, and swept me up in a fierce hug.

"Yes, Just Leah, I'm fine. I wasn't captured or hurt or anything bad except being lonely for you." He pulled back a little and looked in my eyes.

"When I was setting up to take the first pictures of the new general in power, which normally would have had my adrenaline pumping, all I could think of was you. That's when I discovered that running around the world all the time may have lost a little of its charm for me."

My breath caught in my throat. "What are you saying, Luke? You'd never quit your job! I've seen your work. You're too good. And what you do is as important as what I do."

He tilted his head. "Now *that's* a new tune we'll have to explore—you saying your work is important. I'm glad to hear it. But no, I'm just thinking of accepting the promotion my boss has been pushing at me for a year or so. It would mean working in the New York studio at least half the time. Think you might want to date a guy who'd be around that much?"

I started laughing. "I think I could handle it. But how would your schedule work? When would you start? What—"

Luke put his arms around me again. "Later. Let's talk later. Right now all I want to do is this."

Then he kissed me. Hard. He devoured my lips like a refugee from the Atkins diet would devour a bag of potato chips.

I devoured him right back. Right there on the street.

Then we both cracked up. "Wow! I'd better keep traveling at least a little, if my welcome home kisses are going to be like that!"

I smiled and batted my lashes. "Why, sir, I think we

should go upstairs and discuss this. And speaking of travel-ing, maybe you can help me find a way to—"

"Get to Ohio?" He swept an arm toward the curb, where the most disreputable truck I'd ever seen waited, parked halfway up on the sidewalk.

"Your chariot awaits, milady. I'm driving you to Ohio to-night. I slept on the plane all day, and I bought coffee at the deli. We should be there by tomorrow morning to see your niece and nephews."

I looked at him, dumbfounded. "What? You . . . does it even run?"

He shouted out a laugh. "Yes, it runs great. Just looks like crap. And I talked to Sarah when I was trying to find you. Your cell phone was turned off."

I grabbed my phone out of my pocket. It *was* turned off. When had I done that? I switched it back on, and the mes-sage light flashed.

"I have to check this, Luke. It might be about the babies."

He held my hand as I quickly retrieved my voice mail.

"Leah, it's Dad. Merry Christmas, honey. The twins are out of the woods!! The doctors said they've never seen ba-bies respond so quickly to treatment. The twins are doing so well, they may be able to come home in another week or so. Everybody is going to be just fine, honey. The doctors promised." Dad gave a war whoop. "Everybody's just fine!! Call us, baby. Love you and can't wait to see you."

I closed my phone and thought I might collapse with re-lief right there on the street. "The babies are fine, Luke. Everybody is doing great."

Luke hugged me tight and stroked my hair, murmuring wordlessly.

I snuffled a little and then stepped back to dazzle a smile up at him. "Luke, you're my hero. I can entertain you on the drive with the story of an evil witch queen and the valiant

PR princess who defeated her." I smiled a little mistily, thinking of Trevor. "There are even dragons in this story. But right now, let's run upstairs and I'll pack."

"Wait just a minute. I have a little present for you. I hope it's not moving too fast, but I bought it before I left and, well, not the tree part, but . . . Well, anyway. Merry Christmas." He bent down and scooped up the potted plant I'd noticed earlier, which seemed to be decorated with a few strands of tinsel, and handed it to me.

"What is it? A houseplant?" There was a tiny box at the base of the plant.

A tiny blue and white box.

It couldn't be.

I looked up at Luke, and I knew from the smile on his face. It was.

I sat down on the step right there in front of the door and opened the box. There, nestled in satin, my necklace with its tiny star shone up at me.

I remembered my thoughts the first time I'd met Luke.

Fragile as hope; ephemeral as dreams.

Except maybe hope wasn't all that fragile. Maybe dreams were made solid by our quest to achieve them.

"Do you like it?" Luke's voice was tentative, but the warmth and caring I saw in his eyes weren't tentative at all.

Maybe love was even possible.

"I love it, Luke. Will you put it on for me, please?"

"Actually, I meant do you like the pear tree," he teased. "You know, a partridge in a pear tree. Only I couldn't find any partridges, so I had to settle for that necklace."

He fastened the delicate chain around my neck and then turned me around to examine the effect. "Just about perfect, I'd say."

"Yes, it is. Wait—do you promise not to dump me on Christmas Eve, no matter what?"

"I definitely promise that."

"OK, then. Everything is perfect. Just perfect." I hugged him again.

He looked up. "Is that mistletoe?"

I looked up, too, then laughed. "No, that's an icicle."

"Close enough."

King of Orient Are

by Naomi Neale

To Craig, whose Christmas Eve trip to the hospital taught me more about the season than I would ever have learned from a thousand carols, stories, or tree decorations.

Chapter One

The next-to-last way Keely Boston expected to spend an afternoon was holding a pair of men's briefs for her best friend's critical inspection. Maintaining a faux bulge with the leftover banana from her sack lunch was the last. "Magi? As in O. Henry, Gift of the? And by the way, nice job on spoiling my dessert," she teased, glancing at her watch.

"It's not *magi*. That's plural. He's a *magus*. It's like saying, 'Hello, I'm an alumni of NYU.' Wrong! It's alumnus. Can you push out the banana some? This is C.J. I'm shopping for, not Pee-wee Herman."

"Magi, magus, whatever. And enough banana adjustment. I'm in a hurry here." Bottoms Up was certainly an appropriate name for the men's half of an underwear boutique, but Keely Boston would have felt more comfortable on the women's side of the apple green–colored wall, in the more familiar territory of Knickers Down. The fruit safely tucked back into her purse, she gaped at a pair of black boxers emblazoned with a motel sign pointing directly at the fly. The arrow's tip seemed to tease apart the pucker of cloth. OPEN 24 HOURS! proclaimed the ruddy neon. "What kind of guy wears these? Not one I'd care to know."

"C.J. already has that pair."

"C.J. would." Keely always wanted a flea dip after spending time with C.J., his mullet, and his biker's jacket. But Nadine was her friend, Keely reminded herself. Her best friend. Her only friend. Had three years of single-handedly running her own business really reduced her to this sorry state of affairs? She hadn't expected a single pair of boxer shorts to make her feel so lonely.

Bottoms Up was practically empty save for a clerk hunched over the counter, a copy of *Rolling Stone* between her elbows. Nadine rapidly riffled hangers along the racks. "No. No. No. No." She withdrew a white pair of Lycra briefs sporting charcoal-shaped spots arranged in the shape of a snowman's face. A carrot protruded from the middle. "Impractical. No. Good Lord no."

Keely peered over the seasonal rack to see what in the world Nadine thought too outrageous. It would have to be something extreme. Briefs fashioned of holly? A marzipan thong? No, it was some sort of snowflake jockstrap constructed from thick pipe cleaners woven with silver garland. "Mmmm." From a single manicured finger Nadine hung the skimpy white concoction in front of her waist, swiveling her hips as she gazed at her reflection in the mirror. "No." Flick! The snowflake skittered across the rack to join the other rejects.

"Sweetie, I have calls to make. Christmas is a personal shopper's personal hell." One-thirty, read Keely's watch—an expensive-looking designer knockoff. The manager of a discount jewelry store had added it to a stack of gift-wrapped boxes for various clients the week before. *With our compliments,* the big-bosomed manager had mouthed to her. *Merry Christmas.* Her first bonus from a merchant, thanks to a client she thought of as Tasteful Trinkets—a certain elderly Mr. A. G. Armitage of the Upper West Side, nicknamed after his request to purchase inexpensive bracelets for his office assistants and matching diamond pendants ("tasteful trinkets, but they've got to look like something!") for his five . . . what was the word? Girlfriends? Mistresses? "What are they calling women who swap sex for commodities these days?" she asked aloud.

"Clever." Nadine looked up then, obviously annoyed. "Why aren't you looking?"

"My clients would raise an eyebrow if they knew I was looking for your biker boyfriend's underpants, you know. Now, about that magus of yours. . . ."

"Forget the magus for a minute, would you? Your clients are all Botox addicts. I doubt they could move an eyebrow with a crane. You're a snob, plain and simple, but it all comes down to this—you're a personal shopper, right? C.J.'s a person. A person with tattoos. So shop!"

Keely threw up her hands. Trying to direct a conversation with Nadine was like trying single-handedly to herd Times Square tourists. Beneath her wool coat she wore her meeting-with-clients best, a smart little sweater set that in the hothouse temperatures of Bottoms Up made her neck and back itch. It was an outfit that still sometimes made her feel like a little girl dressed up for Halloween, though a conservative Halloween to be sure. "I've still got other people's lists to finish before Christmas," she said, hoping to speed things along. "For people who actually *pay* me to hit the stores."

Keely had a theory that at some point in her life Nadine had given herself an emotional Scotchguarding; other people's extreme moods simply rolled off and never at all sunk in. "I'm giving you valuable life experience," her friend replied, brandishing a black thong. "You've spent a lot of time with your nose in magazines and catalogs, but it's obvious that you have no idea how to pick out men's shorts. What if one of your rich old lady clients sends you out to buy something naughty for her zheegolo?"

"I only have one rich old lady client, and I pity the gigolo who'd hook up with her. Perfect Present is the one I ought to be shopping for right now, actually." If she worked hard enough this month, Miss Adeline Mercer could be the client who might make her enough money for a downpayment on a Lenox Hill condo. She'd dreamed about that modern, sleek condo—so beautiful, so expensive, so different from her fusty Victorian apartment building in Queens—since one of her long-term clients had made known her intentions to move in January.

Miss Mercer had been a pain since the day she'd hired Keely to find for her brother "just the perfect present . . . something one would really cherish." Keely should have had this job wrapped up weeks ago. Yet every time she visited the elderly widow, the old biddy rebuffed her offerings for Brother Warren. The tasteful items of clothing she'd picked out after combing the stores? "Just a little commonplace, dear." The retro-styled pens and watches she'd proffered? "Not *quite* the thing, I think." The books of 1940s photographs, the golf accessories, even an old autograph of a jazzman Brother Warren admired, all returned to the merchants from whom she'd procured them. Over porcelain teacups delicate as her client's spindly fingers, Miss Mercer would simply smile and assure Keely, "I'm sure you'll find just the perfect present, dear."

"Give the woman a Hammacher Schlemmer catalog already." Nadine considered a plastic mannequin, cut off at its neck and upper thighs, modeling a pair of Lycra briefs printed with smiley faces.

"Perfect Present is from an entirely different century. She doesn't look through catalogs like normal peop—what the heck are you doing?" Without warning, her friend had hefted the mannequin from atop its glass shelf and straddled its neck with her thighs. The smiley faces skidded across the shelf to land in a heap on the floor. "Stop that! You look like you're doing something perverted with a quadruple amputee!"

"Like hell." They both looked toward the clerk, still absorbed in her magazine. She blew gum bubbles in time to a sixties recording of what sounded like "Jingle Bells" crossed with the theme from *The Dating Game*. "If I like this pair, I'll buy it. Money makes the world go round, kiddo. Forty-two dollars worth of underwear will far outweigh any inconvenience that I . . . oh yeah, mama likes!" She held the dummy upright at arm's length. It now wore a thong with a pouch decorated like a tuxedo. "It looks like a miniature maître d'. Think C.J. would seat me and serve me if I really worked on his tip?"

Did her blush show? One of the disadvantages of being blonde and fair-skinned was that anyone who wasn't either blind or nearsighted could see the scarlet, enflamed skin that marked her embarrassment. Keely swept back her short hair with her fingertips. Yes, her cheeks felt warmer than usual. "Shouldn't some things be between a girl and her boyfriend?" In theory, anyway. Keely craved more in the way of practice. If only her schedule allowed her to squeeze some in!

Her friend, however, had already pushed her way through the racks to the register, plastic mannequin stuffed under her arm. "You'll want to put this back," Nadine said as she plopped the dummy onto the counter and brandished the maître d' shorts. "And I'll be taking these."

"You know." Her attention removed from the magazine, the clerk proved to have a thick and unexpected middle European accent. "There is similar pair next door. Matching pair, for woman like, mmmm, French maid?"

Biting her lip was Nadine's way of pretending to think. "Oh, really now?" Keely wasn't at all surprised when her friend shifted attention to the swinging doors in the wall separating Bottoms Up from Knickers Down. "Want to come?" she asked.

"I'll just wait," Keely suggested, crossing her arms and leaning against the counter. If she accompanied Nadine, they might wind up spending the entire afternoon underwear hunting. "Remember, in a hurry here. Clients equal money. Money equals new apartment."

"Believe me, I'll be back in a jiff."

Keely could have sooner believed in Santa. The clerk brandished her magazine and gave Keely a wary expression, as if afraid a customer might try to engage in light conversation. Keely turned her back and tried to soothe her jagged nerves with the music playing on the loudspeaker overhead. Barbra Streisand's twitchy rendition of "Jingle Bells"—apparently recorded after an injection of unadulterated caffeine into the singer's jugular—didn't relax her any.

Beneath a television hanging from a support beam, an ancient VCR whirred, playing highlights from old Christmas movies on the screen above. Keely crossed her arms and watched, smiling at Lucille Ball's Auntie Mame as she and her nephew soundlessly pleaded for a little Christmas. There was that boy from *Family Affair*—Johnnie Whitaker?—scrambling after his halo as the littlest angel. She grinned at the sight of a roly-poly Burl Ives snowman careening over a claymation landscape, and laughed outright at the sight of Ralphie and his friends panicking over Flick's tongue stuck to a frozen flagpole.

Image after image of perfect Christmases flickered over the screen, grainy and sometimes hard to see against the gray light streaming through the shop windows. Little Natalie Wood, colorized, contemplating the Macy's Santa's beard. A spiny fish skeleton of a tree drooping onto the floor, weighed down by the single ornament Charlie Brown had hung from it. Rudolph's red nose, glimmering through foglike cotton.

And there was Jimmy Stewart, his hair falling in sloppy lanks over his forehead, looking at something in the palm of his hand. "Zuzu's petals," Keely said in barely more than a whisper. The scene was so uncomplicated and pure that it made her ache for a simpler, unrushed holiday. She'd worked for weeks to give her clients and their families a happy Christmas morning. Was it fair hers was doomed to be lonely?

Christmas hammered mercilessly at her solitude. Every carol, every card, every decoration drove home the fact that she was ending another year alone. The holiday season was not for those without a family—or for the single. Its inevitable coda, New Year's Eve, seemed designed solely for the pointed purpose of highlighting the fact that she was single, hurtling toward thirty, and unlikely ever to achieve her perfect mental photograph of her future life. After each day's hustle, she couldn't ignore the fact that the only company she kept in her Queens apartment was her stacks of magazines filled with images of lives done right.

That would change soon, if she had anything to say about it, starting with where she made her home. She'd spent the last three months envisioning how she'd decorate that condo in Lenox Hill, if she got it—she'd already started a file of photos from the decorating periodicals. Starting next month, she might be able to say farewell to the timid, frizzy-haired, wooly-sweatered temp she used to be. Good-bye, shabby chic—howdy, *Architectural Digest!*

"Look!" Keely was startled to find Nadine beside her once more, brandishing a pair of black panties trimmed heavily with white lace. "Ooh la la!"

"Ve-ry subtle." Keely flicked her eyes back to the television.

"Forget subtle." Nadine twirled the French maid panties around her index finger before stuffing them into the candy-striped bag dangling from her wrist. "C.J.'s a biker. Me in these is the best present he'll get this Christmas. Men are pretty much the same, you know. Different packages, but once you take off the wrappings . . ." On the screen overhead, Jimmy Stewart and Donna Reed, their faces tear-streaked and beaming, hugged. "Your problem, Ms. Boston, is that you're too much like your Perfect Present."

All Keely could do was gape. What an unfair comparison to her least favorite client! "Not true!"

"Oh yeah. Perfect Present is sending you into fits because she's gotten into her head there's a holy grail, flawless and shining. The truth is, she'll have to make do. Maybe Brother Warren won't end up with a summer sausage, but he'll get the kind of Christmas present the rest of us get. And see, you've got this romantic notion that there's a George Bailey out there, noble and handsome and true, when the reality is . . ."

"I can see where you're going." Nadine could be like a horsefly, always buzz-buzz-buzzing. "I date. I've dated! It's tough to look for a serious relationship when you're busy trying to start a business from the ground up." Keely was dimly aware that the clerk was listening to her every word and finding them more interesting than the

Rolling Stone disc reviews. She lowered her voice. "When you talk like that, it sounds like—" She grappled for a phrase.

"Like what?"

"It sounds like you're *settling*. I don't like that." Wasn't that the worst thing a person could do, to give up? It depressed her to think that in the romance department she might have to settle for something less than perf . . . no, she hadn't almost said that word! "I don't think there's anything wrong in holding out for just the right guy. I don't care to *make do*."

Nadine shrugged. "Listen. C.J.'s fun. Is he serious marriage material? Doubtful. All I'm saying, sweetie, is that you're allowed to date for fun. You don't have to approach every guy as if he's your George Bailey. Relax a little. You're twenty-seven. You're a baby still! Have fun! See some of the *wrong* guys for a change. Just for laughs!"

"I don't seem to have time for fun."

"Take some. You're not struggling to make the rent these days." Shopping bag rustling, Nadine reached out and rubbed her friend's elbow. "Kee, I'm not criticizing. Five years ago when I was more your age, I was the same way. These days?" She shrugged. "I've learned to cope with lowered expectations. Just promise me you won't turn into the kind of unmarried woman who cuts photos from bridal magazines and pastes them into her dream wedding scrapbook. Okay?"

Was Nadine serious? Insecurity prompted her to protest, "I don't!"

"Maybe not, but I did see you leafing through a *Modern Bride* at the Barnes and Noble newsstand last week. I just thought I'd, you know, nip it in the bud. In case you had any ideas."

"It was research!" Magazines were Keely's life. She found immense comfort in her copies of *Vanity Fair* and *Jane* and whatever else she could haul home from the bookstores; it had been by studying advertisements in the upscale magazines that she'd developed her shopper's eye. It was from their articles that she'd found the courage to leave behind temping and strike out on her own.

She could get that immaculate life the magazines had promised—with its good clothing, and its spacious apartment with refined decorations. She would replace the shadowy, masculine presence waiting inside with a real guy—a catch, in fact. Visions of a new life had driven her for three years now. She *would* get it for herself, starting with the Lenox Hill apartment.

"Ah! There! See?" Nadine pointed up at the television screen, which in bright primary colors and broad lines was showing an animated manger scene. Keely adjusted her glasses and squinted to make out the figures hovering around the Baby Jesus' cradle. "Magi," crowed Nadine. So they were finally back at that topic again. "You're not sulking, are you?"

Good thing Keely was used to her best friend's . . . well, some people might call it *abrasiveness*. Nadine herself would call it *candor*, and had always claimed it had propelled her miles ahead of the other editors at *Vroom*, a magazine for motorcycle enthusiasts, despite the fact she couldn't tell a Harley Davidson 1200 XLH from a Vespa scooter. Sulking over Nadine's abundant energies would be like shaking a fist at the wind for blowing down a house of cards—it was wisest simply not to open the windows. Nadine didn't need to know how truly lonely she felt, right then. Keely peered at the frantic animated figure bopping around the screen a little more intently. "I see Magi, all right. Bugs Bunny too. Was he at the Adoration?"

Nadine suppressed a grin and made a dismissive motion. "Scoffer!"

"So we can talk about this magus now? It's just that I have a hard time believing your new guru was in Bethlehem two thousand years ago and now rents office space off East Fifty-ninth so that kooks like you—"

Her friend pretended to gasp. "Kooks like me! And he's a spiritual counselor, not a guru."

"Whatever. Since I've known you, you've been through numerology, the kabala, the Keirsey Temperament Sorter—"

"By the way, you are *so* ISTJ right now that it isn't funny." Nadine crossed her arms.

"—color wheel analysis, feng shui, Russian gypsy fortune-telling, runes—"

"You can't count runes. I stopped casting them after my niece swallowed Teiwaz."

The clerk, who had been following the conversation with interest, suddenly spoke up. "I have a Ouija board."

"Isn't that special?" Nadine let loose one of her most gracious smiles, polite but deadly. Keely cringed inside as the clerk slowly bit her lip and went back to pretending to read. "Let's get out of here."

Outside, where thick clouds of vapor streamed from the sewer grates and the sound of car horns and squealing bus brakes assaulted their ears, Keely wrapped her scarf around her neck. "You were mean to that girl."

"Oh, my heart bleeds. Anyway, Ouija boards are just stupid. Everyone knows that. So come on. Come down to East Fifty-ninth with me. We'll see my magus and then do Thai for dinner. Come on!"

"I can't." Keely gave in and looked at her watch. She'd wasted so much time! "I've got an appointment with Miss Mercer."

"Fun. I know better than to stand between a girl and her career. Just a sec." Nadine began fishing in her purse for something, at last stuffing her shopping bag between her knees so she could use both hands. "Breath freshener?"

In Nadine's palm lay a large, flat tablet, somewhere between grape and slate gray in color, speckled with dark flecks. It looked like some sort of fortified fish food. "What is that?" Keely wanted to know.

Nadine popped the pill into her mouth and crunched. "It's a garlic, sunflower seed oil, and licorice tablet. Oh, and stinging nettles. All natural! Is my tongue purple?" She shot out her tongue and pulled at the tip until it was within view. "When Perfect Present shoots you down," she said, pointing once more at Keely, "you just keep my magi in mind. I am purple, aren't I?"

Without a word more, Nadine had slung her purse over her shoulder and started walking down the street. Keely bit her tongue, trying not to laugh. "Hey!" she cried, calling out her friend's name. When Nadine turned, cupping a hand to her ear, Keely couldn't help but shout out a last word. "Not magi. *Magus!*"

Nadine lifted the thumbs and index fingers of her leather-gloved hands to form a big W. "Whatev!" she called out. "You'll be begging to see him. I guarantee it."

Chapter Two

Keely hungered for the arithmetic of the wealthy: a twenty-seventh-floor apartment multiplied by a Forty-third Street address equaled a magnificent view. From this height, Manhattan seemed almost like a sea of spiny branches dotted with patches of evergreen, with occasional spaces where geometric stone and concrete shot toward the sky. Only an occasional noise punctuated the tranquility.

"Mmmmm." Over and over in her hands, Perfect Present turned a heavy antique doorstop in the shape of a pineapple. There was no mistaking the doubt on those lips. Oh well—the doorstop had been one of Keely's second-string, just-in-case choices, and could be returned. "I'm not certain."

Hovering over clients made them nervous. Keely had found most of them needed space and leisure to make their final decisions. At the same time, she never liked wandering; it gave the client an impression of impatience and boredom. Itchy as she was to have Perfect Present choose something, anything, she anchored herself by the heavily curtained windows and pretended calm. From time to time, Keely would hear a gentle thud when the old woman set something back down on the wood. Otherwise, the apartment was quiet. "I'm positive you'll like the other gifts I've selected," Keely said in her smooth, professional voice. Did it sound a little ragged around the edges? Well, she'd had a long day. She wished the woman would hurry.

Everything about the apartment reflected Miss Mercer's thirst for perfection. The chintz of the sofa and its pillows matched the chairs, and their dark woods matched that of the coffee table and bookcases, and all of them corresponded perfectly to the carved wood paneling. Books were set into picturesque, camera-ready arrangements, interspersed with fussy porcelain sculptures in faded pastels. Next to the avocado-green telephone, an ancient but mint-condition rotary dial model, lay a leather box containing yellowed writing paper. A gold pen was at its side.

The entire living area was careful, precise, and looked as if it hadn't been altered in years. Keely was almost afraid to touch anything, lest it crumble into dust like a relic of ancient times. At what point had Perfect Present decreed that her living space had reached an acme of completeness and sealed it from the outside world and from change? Lingering here too long felt like being embalmed in one of her grandmother's fruitcakes.

Only at the last minute did Keely turn and notice Miss Mercer grappling with the largest of the boxes in front of her. One tumble, and she'd have hundreds of dollars of smashed electronics Brookstone would never allow her to return. "Let me help," she murmured, desperately propelling herself across the room.

"I don't understand. Is it a toy, dear? My grandnephews

are all grown." Keely hoisted the package into an upright position and set it on the coffee table, then sank down into the chintz upholstery beside her client. She ought to have hovered, after all.

"No, it's not . . . well, yes. It is a toy. But not for children. It's a remote-controlled Peugeot 206. See?" She pointed to a photograph on the box. "You said your brother was a car enthusiast. Well, this model has a lightweight two-speed transmission and a solid countersunk chassis. There's a pistol-grip remote control with a dual steering . . ." Miss Mercer looked absolutely blank. No amount of ad-speak would make any impact on her. "It can reach speeds of up to seventy miles per hour!" she tried to enthuse.

Perfect Present had what Keely always privately thought of as a marshmallow face; age seemingly had separated flesh from bones and set it floating on a soft layer of its own, kept covered with fine powder. No cheekbones, chin, or jaw-line interrupted the pillowy curves. Only the old woman's tiny lips moved, now; they pursed into a moue and relaxed, over and over, before releasing her dictum. "Brother Warren lives in a small rent-controlled apartment on Roosevelt Island, dear." Miss Mercer never sounded cantankerous. She merely specialized in shades of perplexity—as many as the Eskimos had words for snow. And to Keely, every single shade was like nails on chalkboard. "Where in the world would he have room for a car to run at seventy miles per hour?"

"You're right." Important client, Keely reminded herself, trying not to twitch. Important friends.

"I'm so sorry, dear," said Miss Mercer. "But it's not quite *perfect*." The five words were the woman's catchphrase, her Jimmie Walker *dy-no-mite!* or her Gary Coleman *Whatchoo talkin' 'bout, Willis?*

Deep breaths, Keely reminded herself. Miss Mercer was

moneyed, and worth working for; she had many wealthy acquaintances. Commissions from wealthy people might help her make that down payment on the Lenox Hill condo by January. Anyway, the gizmo had been another of Keely's second-tier choices. She'd been through this round of doubt and disapproval twice before with the woman—embarrassing encounters in which Miss Mercer had said no to all her proposed gifts. This time, though, Keely had done her research and covered all the bases. She wouldn't let the car's rejection shake her confidence. Something had to appeal. "I don't know where my brain was," she admitted with a feigned smile. "How silly of me."

"I do hate to be a bother. What an inconvenience for you to return it!"

"No, no, it's fine. The doorstop, though . . . didn't you tell me your brother collected them? I thought you and Brother W—I mean, I thought you and your brother might like it. It's originally from the estate of . . ."

Already Miss Mercer was making one of her faces again: a prim, unsure pout that made Keely's teeth ache. "It's so dusty. And it's not at all shiny."

"It's an antique!" Keely caught herself exclaiming in surprise. She modulated back to dull, polite tones to match her surroundings. "It's not dusty. After a century, the brass has acquired a patina and . . ." It was no use. She was as likely to sell Miss Mercer a bundle of used pornography. "Well. Let's look at the next box, okay?"

"I'm sure it's a lovely doorstop," said Miss Mercer, wringing a handkerchief. "Lovely for someone else. I *do* hate to be so much of a bother. I want to be able to recommend you to friends, dear, but I have to be able to assure them you found Brother Warren's *perfect* present."

There it was—the carrot dangled at stick's end. Frustrating as she found the woman, Keely couldn't ignore the prospect of last-minute clients during the holiday season. "I understand," Keely breathed, removing the lid of a deep Paul Stuart box. In her old life as a temp she used the same broad smiles and reassuring words to deal with maddening employers. The same techniques had worked on bad dates as well. "Now, the last time I was here you didn't like . . . that is, we decided that none of the clothing I'd picked out was quite right for your brother."

"It was simply too slipshod, dear," interjected her client. "Modern clothing has come down in tone from what it used to be. Don't you agree?"

"Certainly, certainly. Now, as you see, I've gone for a more formal look this time." Keely pulled aside the crisp tissue paper and fanned out the three shirts so that they overlapped one another. "A classic white, Chinese blue, and a pinstriped shirt, each with French cuffs. And!" Keely opened the small, velvet-covered box lying inside, feeling it snap open with a sense of satisfaction. "Aren't these gold cufflinks beautiful? I thought we could have Warren's initials carved on them, if you approved."

"What beautiful shirts!" Miss Mercer's age-speckled hands darted forward so that she could stroke and admire the material. "Truly lovely!"

Triumph at last! A glow warmed Keely's face. From the moment she'd chosen the items, ensuring each was conservative and old-school in style, she'd known they would please the most difficult client she'd encountered in almost three years. She nearly would have gambled her entire hard-won career on it, in fact. "You like the colors, then?" Keely needed to hear the old woman's approval. She'd worked hard enough for a good word, damn it!

"Oh, they would be perfect," said Miss Mercer. "It's all beautiful, dear. But . . ." The old woman's hand trembled a little as she brought a finger to her lip in thought. "I don't think Brother Warren would wear anything so—and please don't take this the wrong way, because I know how hard you've been working—but I don't think he would wear anything so *fancy*."

If her client had hopped up, pulled off a wig to reveal Norman Bates, and *Psycho*-stabbed her in the heart right there, Keely could not have been caught more off-guard. Those shirts had been a flawless selection! "I thought you liked them." Her voice had gone painfully hoarse.

"Oh, I do, dear. They're truly lovely. But they're not quite . . ."

"*Perfect*. I know, I know," Keely joined in on the chorus, trying not to grind her teeth. She wasn't quite certain what teeth-grinding was actually supposed to accomplish, but her molars certainly itched to try. An occupied jaw would at least keep her from muttering the obscenities she really wanted to spew. Maybe having one's own business was overrated. Would the temp agency take her back if she asked?

The glitter of her expensive-looking watch caught Keely's eye again. No. Hell would require one heck of a cold snap before she went back to that life again. Endless months of working anonymously at a barren desk among people who never bothered to learn her name? Eating lunches at a table by herself while reading magazines? Forget it. This business was her ticket out of a drab world where lives like those in the lunchroom magazines were out of her grasp. "We wouldn't want you to have to settle for anything less than . . . perfect."

The word felt like vinegar on her tongue.

Miss Mercer found fault with the nautical-themed wall clock ("he simply never was one for boats"), the selection of skin care products intended, as the designer label stated,

for the mature man ("Ivory soap is all Brother Warren's
ever needed!"), and the portable DVD player ("goodness,
aren't those Japanese clever, though!"). In the end, Miss
Mercer's profuse apologies all boiled down to one thing:
nothing was quite *perfect*. Keely found herself confronting
the same empty dizziness she felt immediately after giving
blood, before the obligatory orange juice. She had no more
items to show.

She had too much at stake to be out of ideas. "I was also
thinking, Miss Mercer, that you might, you know, pamper
your brother with a spa day . . ."

"Oh my, dear. Isn't that something for ladies?"

". . . or a series of massages . . ." Already Keely could
see her opponent's mouth working into a rejection, so she
spoke more quickly. "Perhaps even a magazine subscription of some sort."

"Oh, no, no, no. That won't do at all." Miss Mercer
looked hurt at the suggestion. "That's not very special, is
it? My friend Marcia Hengrove told me you found the most
creative gifts last holiday season, and here I'd hoped I
could say the same to my friends. . . ."

Marcia Hengrove was an easily pleased woman of years
who had been more than willing to pay premium prices on
gifts of gourmet food that, despite the elevated cost, probably tasted no different from the typical Harry and David
gift basket. Miss Mercer was the equivalent of physics' fa-
bled immovable object waiting for her irresistible force.

"One more idea," Keely said hastily, willing herself not
to give up yet—and hoping her most difficult of clients had
not given up on her. "I couldn't bring it along, of course,
because it's an antique, but I could show it to you on approval if you were seriously interested. You mentioned in
our initial interview that the Revolutionary War is one of

your brother's many interests." Lenox Hill, she reminded herself. She was only one gift away from the mother lode. "One of my dealers showed me something very special the other day." Did she have to specify that she meant a dealer of antiques? Was Miss Mercer likely to think the worst, and assume heroin? No, she had the woman's interest. "A small sword, worn by Commodore John Barry as commander of the *Lexington* during the war for independence. It's virtually a piece of history!"

And a pricey one, too, at that. Keely felt a twinge of guilt for even bringing the sword into their conversation, as it was intended for a certain Mr. Jarod Barry-Chyldes who resided in a much-maligned recent skyscraper on Fifty-sixth Street. Without benefit of genealogical evidence, Mr. Barry-Chyldes had decided that the commodore was a long-lost ancestor; he wanted an artifact to present to his adolescent son on Christmas Day. There would have been a larger bonus from Barry-Chyldes than from Miss Mercer, but Keely would more than make it up in fees from the old bat's rich friends. And what kind of crazy person gave his teenaged son a sharp-edged weapon for the holidays, anyway?

"How exciting," said Miss Mercer, clasping her hands together. It was an empty gesture, Keely immediately recognized—an apology for the naysay sure to follow. "But do you know, I'm afraid I'll have to hold out just a bit longer. I don't care to *make do,* you see."

The words were identical to those Keely had said aloud only a few hours earlier. She froze, suddenly terrified. Some part of her mind flashed forward forty-five years into the future, when her own face would be hidden behind a layer of extra flesh. Would her perfect Lenox Hill condo be suspended in time, like this one? Would she turn out to be another Perfect Present, unmarried and lonely because she let opportunity after opportunity pass by in favor of the ideal that never materialized? How many Christmases had Miss Mercer spent alone?

"Thanks." Keely rose and let the old woman squeeze her trembling hand. Through the soft, powdery flesh, Miss Mercer's fingers felt as fragile as hollow fish bones. It felt eerily as if she shook her own aged self's hand. She had to find that gift, just to prove it existed. If she found it, Keely would justify to herself that all this time wasted would have been worth the work. It would be like finding a perfect guy—in the end, the results would justify the wait. She *had* to find it.

Twenty-five minutes later, the box of a radio-controlled Peugeot on her lap and a carton containing her other finds on the cab seat beside her, Keely stabbed with a fingertip the 3 on her mobile phone. "I'm quitting," she announced.

"You are not," Nadine automatically replied. Without warning, her friend let out a stream of titters. "*Stop* that! Naughty boy! C.J. got his maître d' shorts a little early," she explained.

"If it weren't for the fact I am officially begging to meet this counselor of yours, I would be so hanging up on you right now. How about tomorrow morning?"

"Wait!" Nadine said, sounding for a moment as if she'd dropped the phone. "He only meets people in the evening. Meet me for an early dinner. Thai? Listen to this, C.J. keeps pronouncing *prix fixe* like . . ."

The one drawback to a tiny cell phone, Keely thought as she stuffed it back into her purse, was that punching a weensy button to end a call was nowhere near as satisfying as slamming down a receiver.

Chapter Three

By the curb, Keely stopped to investigate the bottom of her boot. Somehow, a wad of mint-green chewing gum had managed to pick up a crumpled half-pint milk carton, a cigarette butt, and a liberal peppering of street grime. "You know," she said, contemplating whether to pry off the gooey mess, "when most people say their therapist's office is across from Central Park, they mean literally across the street. Or at most a block or two away."

Nadine arrested the complaint with a single raised finger. On the world's tiniest cell phone, she barked orders at one of her magazine's flunkies—orders full of phrases like *chrome exhaust, west coast choppers,* and *max cleavage on the biker chick.* In her tight-waisted long black coat and with her long dark Bettie Page hair streaming down her back, Nadine looked more like a chic satanic makeover artist than motorcycle enthusiast. To Keely she hissed, "Don't be obstructionist. The park's right over there."

In the direction that Nadine waved her hand behind her

head, Keely saw through the twilight a vague and distant slice of green. "Why do I listen to you? If you'd been Columbus, you'd have told Isabella and Ferdinand that India was right across from the coast of Portugal."

"People who claim they were celebrities or royalty in their past lives usually have a severe case of overweening ego," said Nadine. "Don't lollygag!"

"I'm not. . . ." With a sigh of disgust, Keely scraped her sticky sole against a lamppost. "I thought you discovered in one of your past life regressions that you'd been the daughter of a Beothuk native chief."

It was with immense dignity that Nadine replied, "I would scarcely call a twenty-three-year lifespan as Ouduit, little pride of the great Beothuk father Ranamasasut, cut down in my young prime by the French conspiracy with the Mi'kmaq, as anything close to 'celebrity,' and if it was, it was more than balanced out by my existences as an indentured Egyptian scribe and as a French servant during the Hundred Years' War, thank you very much. Besides, hello? Past lives went out with Shirley MacLaine's career." They trudged into the murk, passing only business types hurrying home and a line of people patiently boarding a bus. "I just want to reiterate that my magus is not a traditional counselor, okay? You brought money, right?"

"You didn't mention money." Keely felt a moment's panic. She wasn't broke, exactly, but her checking account was on the low side, and everything in savings was either earmarked for the IRS or set aside for her condo down payment come January. How in the world was she going to shell out big bucks for a consultation? "You know, it's a tight time of year. I'm having second thoughts."

"Relax." Nadine refused to sound concerned. "I've got a spare five I can lend you."

In the middle of the sidewalk, Keely halted. Was this one of Nadine's crazy schemes? "I only need a five?"

"Sometimes I give him a ten if he's been really helpful." Was it some sort of token introductory rate? Should she ask? Was she supposed to ask? Did she really want to know? "Oh, and he likes these." Nadine passed off the world's tiniest cell phone to her other hand and reached into her right hip pocket, pulling out four identical miniature containers of Smirnoff. "You can give him two. He'll like that."

"What the hell is going on?" Keely found herself accepting the tiny bottles. She hoped no one else witnessed the exchange. Her friend was absolutely insane!

On leather-gloved fingers, Nadine rattled off a few more rules. "Don't mention anything about his clothing, don't talk too softly, and for the love of God, don't mention anything about the smell."

"Holy hells." Keely waved a hand over her face as they stepped into a gentle billow of steam from one of the street's treacherous grates. "What is this guy's deal? Is he some kind of hippie?" She had an image in her mind of an aging stoner type with a tendency to mix liquor in his coffee and who knows what in his brownies. "I'm not really comfortable—where are you going?"

Nadine disappeared into the upward cascades of steam. "Hang a sec," she called back.

It was warmer on the grating than out in the cold air by a good thirty degrees, but every breeze brought back the icy reality of the December temperature. Where were they, exactly? Even the building was dilapidated. Its ground-level display windows, deep and rectangular and sharp-edged, had long ago been covered over with Scotch-taped newspapers. Only a hand-painted legend running around all three sides of the right-hand window gave any indication of what the store used to sell, its bold letters made scarlet by the reddish bulb illuminating the side of the building. Keely mouthed to herself the words on the leftmost pane of glass:

ORIENT ARE

Orient are? As in *we three kings* and Nadine's alleged magus? For a split second a chill ran along her limbs, raising the hair on her arms. No—it had to be a coincidence. The only reason that notion had come into her head at all was because they were on the way to the magus' office. Acting on an impulse she could not name, Keely reached out and with the outside edge of her hand, wiped a long clean path in the moisture to reveal the rest of the legend.

A RUGS AND PERSIAN CARPETS

She blinked, then a moment later dissolved into relieved laughter. *Orient area rugs and Persian carpets*! Talk about letting the eerie atmosphere get the best of her!

"Hey, Nadine," she called out, turning. "You'll never guess—"

Caught off-guard, every cell in her body screamed in fright. Only inches away from her face was a homeless man. A mugger. A shambling assailant with baleful eyes and a hostile leer.

In the flash it took for Keely to take in his sudden, unwanted presence, all her humor and lung power disappeared. As her heart thudded, she tried to dredge up anything she had learned from eight Saturdays of self-defense classes in the community center with Nadine.

The mugger's lips parted, revealing a mouthful of teeth the color of old ivory. "Tiffany!" he barked at her so abruptly that she jumped. Involuntary tears formed in her eyes. His breath smelled like dead animals soaked in alcohol.

Remember as much as she could about her assailant—that's what she was supposed to do. Atop his head, stuck into the matted hair, was—something. She couldn't quite make it out. Keely backed away slowly. The man's eyes were red. There was months' worth of hair growth on his chin and cheeks, and his skin was dark, like suede—though whether from a lack of bathing, or sun, or natural coloring she couldn't tell. "I'll give you money." Her voice sounded as if she hadn't used it in years, like a rusty hinge on a deserted house. "Just keep away. I don't want any trouble."

"Tiffany," he repeated, murmuring the word like it was foreign to him. Then slowly, pitilessly, he lifted an arm in her direction, index finger outstretched.

Later, when Keely recalled the encounter from the safety of her own apartment, it amazed her how the milliseconds had slowed to a crawl. One electrical charge in her brain told her to run, to flee; another told her not to turn her back on what was very possibly a dangerous criminal. Part of her brain was still busy observing the man, registering that the odd object decorating his head was a paper crown from a Burger King kid's meal.

Overriding all these impulses, though, was the question that suddenly occurred to her: Where was Nadine? *What had he done to Nadine?* Only when her friend's name escaped her lips in a squawk did she realize she'd spoken aloud.

"What's the prob? I'm talking here." Over the strange man's shoulder, Nadine materialized from the mist, her ear once more pressed against her cell phone. "Yeah. Yeah. Yes, I said yes. Okay. Uh-huh." Keely had been about to yell out a warning when Nadine with her free hand reached into her coat pocket, fished around, and withdrew the Smirnoff. The gentle tinkling sound caught the crown-wearing vagrant's attention; he focused and he grabbed for the miniature bottles while Nadine kept talking. "Yullo! I'm taking a meeting. Later. Now, Mel," she said in a more normal voice, sliding the phone shut. "About my publisher. Important stuff. Breakfast meeting tomorrow over the cover kafuffle. What tone should I take? I was thinking aloof and maybe a little pissed off, just to keep him guessing, you know?"

The moment for flight had passed. Though Keely could still feel the adrenaline coursing through her, Nadine's matter-of-fact address to the homeless man had rooted her feet to the grate. Her mouth worked, impotently at first. When her brain began once more to combine syllables into speech, she wrangled words from her outraged throat. "You *know* this guy?"

"Keely, Melchior. Melchior, Keely." Neither of them acknowledged the introduction. Melchior, if that was his name, tipped back his head and downed the first of the vodka bottles. Even as he guzzled, Keely noticed that his eyes took in her clothes, her hair, her shoes. It felt uncomfortably as if he was passing judgment. When he lowered his arm, the motion let loose a musty odor from his layers and layers of clothing that nearly sent her reeling back. What a smell! Why in the world were they still here? How could Nadine endure standing so close to—

Wait a sec. Consider the evidence. *Don't mention the smell.* The serving sized bottles of liquor. Nadine addressing this smelly, disgusting bum as if she knew him. Even the outlandish name made sense now. "Melchior?" Keely asked. The fear she'd felt moments before had mutated into anger, pure and simple. "Of Melchior, Balthazar, and Caspar? *This* is your magus?"

The pair had the gall to stare at her as if she was the lunatic. "Of course it's not the same Melchior," Nadine assured her with derision, but belied her assurance when she asked the bum in a doubtful voice, "Are you?" When he shook his head and cracked open the other bottle of liquor, Nadine began to scold again. "Of course he isn't. Don't be ridiculous!"

"Me!" Keely nearly convulsed. "Better ridiculous than insane!" She wanted to let Nadine really have it and storm off in a huff, but she couldn't leave her friend alone with this bum. The man was filthy. He probably hadn't seen a shower in weeks. His capelike collection of multiple open coats and that stupid cardboard crown on his head made him look like a lunatic dressed up as the King of Diamonds. His teeth were rotting in their sockets, his camouflage pants had probably been scavenged from a Dumpster, and his spanking new high-top Adidas had probably been shoplifted. Something though—whether pity or just an impulse to remain politically correct—made her refuse to point out how disgusting he was.

Melchior shrugged. "The wannabe got something against Persians?"

"This isn't about racism!" Keely countered, angry. That had been below the belt. How was she even supposed to know he was Middle Eastern? His skin tone was dark, but again, it could have been weeks' worth of dirt or simply a suntan. "I've got nothing against Iranians!"

"Not Iranian! No, no, no! Persian, not Iranian . . . but it's all the same to you 'cause if it don't happen outside the pages of your *Vogue* and your *New Yorker* and your *Vanity frickin' Fair* it ain't happened at all, right?" Keely reeled back, appalled. How did he know about her magazines? Had Nadine told *all* Keely's secrets to this—this—homeless person? Or was he just ranting? Tippling again from the Smirnoff, Melchior turned in Nadine's direction so that he could continue his stream of thought, punctuated liberally with spittle. "He's not gonna be in the mood for 'tude, if you catch my drift. Best be dressed for success. If you wanna impress you better bring the zest."

Nadine sighed. "Damn it. I don't *do* zest that early."

The fake magus grabbed his groin and scratched, prompting Keely to avert her eyes and hold a hand over her face. "Fake it. Ain't led you wrong before." Suddenly the vagrant turned his head in Keely's direction, his eyes wide and wary. "In the nest of the twin red owls, on the back wall under the lady, Lady Liberty. At the plane of the eyes' gaze. You know what I'm saying?" He held up two fingers to his eyes, then extended them straight out.

He was crazy, Keely realized with pity. Not just homeless, but mental as well. "At the plane of the eyes' gaze. Your eyes, not mine. Left, left to the very end. That's where you'll find it. Wear the Dolce and Gabbana," he said, turning suddenly to Nadine. "He'll like that."

"Oo, good idea! The black, right? Not the red." Nadine clicked a button on her cell phone and murmured a memo to herself.

"Definitely not the red. Black is the new tan. The new tan."

Every few words the man's neck would jerk. The muscle tic made him blink in a confused way. Was he in pain? Keely couldn't tell, but she knew damned well how uncomfortable this entire situation was making her. "Okay, you're taking fashion advice from a . . ."

Once again, politeness forbade her from finishing a sentence she wished she hadn't started. Melchior, however, had already taken offense. "Bum?" he suggested, his words dripping with contempt. "Alcoholic? No-goodnik? Derelict, drifter, westward leading, still proceeding, gutterpup? Oh, I see, we're back to the slurs already, are we? I'm taking the hard knocks from someone who—" This particular tic seemed so bad that for a moment his entire head jerked back. Keely cringed, torn between wanting to help and wanting to run. The man slowly relaxed and again pointed a finger. "You've whittled your life down to nothing. That's what you'll be. Nothing."

Of all the insulting, obnoxious . . . and Nadine took *advice* from this guy? "You—" And yet, the accusation was so close to what she had been thinking the day before in Bottoms Up that for a moment she wondered if he had the ability to . . . but no, mind-reading was not only impossible, but ridiculous. "Nadine, let's go."

"Tiffany," the homeless man repeated, not taking his eyes from Keely. She shivered and prayed they could find a taxi quickly.

"No, she's Keely. Not Tiffany," Nadine reminded him, despite the fact that Keely didn't want the bum to know her name. Tiffany was just fine with her! "She has a client who's looking for—"

"Done and over! She won't listen. That's where he is, Tiffany. Waiting for you." There had been a change in the man's voice. He sounded tired and worn, but no less insane. "Meant for you. That's where he'll wait."

There was nothing more Keely wanted at that moment than to get away from the smelly vagabond and from this questionable block and even away from Nadine, her supposed friend who had Froot Loops for brains and all the common sense of Silly Putty. She'd had enough. She was ditching Nadine, even if it pissed her off, and escaping back to her apartment. "I'm going," she said with decision, clutching her bag and turning to walk in the direction of the park. "Are you coming or not?"

"Oh, Keely, don't make one of your fusses."

"This magus of yours needs medication, not new clients."

"Yo! Yo!" The crazy man waved his arms in the air. "Where's my frankincense? What about my goddamned fee? What about the surtax for insulting the minority sooth-sayer? We astrologer kings don't work cheap, sister! We don't work—" His neck jerked, but when it resumed its normal posture, his eyes were blazing. "For bupkis."

Against her better judgment, Keely swung around and dug into her purse for the spare five left over from dinner. "Don't spend it on liquor," she ordered. The man's living encyclopedia of bad smells made her want to retch.

"That's it?" Melchior wanted to know, obviously scorn-ful. "A lousy five bucks is all it takes to appease your nag-ging liberal guilt?"

Enough was enough. "You're on your own, Nadine!" Keely snapped over her shoulder as her shoes beat a rapid rhythm across the grate.

Stepping out of the warm steam and back into the crisp evening air felt like returning to reality from some strange dream. A cab was slowing down near the corner; she'd never been so relieved to see one in her entire life. In her hurry to trip across the pavement to its yellow safety, she didn't hear anyone behind her until a set of knuckles pounded on the cab window. Nadine, probably running af-ter her to beg forgiveness. Keely's instinct was to tell the driver to move on, but before she knew why, she'd rolled down the window a couple of inches. "Don't even—what?"

A man bent down to peer at her, his mouth positioned at the window crack. All she could really see of him was a bushy reddish goatee, white teeth, and shoulders. "Don't be alarmed," he begged through the window in a clear, reassur-ing tenor. "I just wanted to ask you if you knew that man you just talked to."

Who was this guy, anyway? And why was he harassing

her? Was he the police or something? He didn't have a uniform. "Were you listening?"

"Only a little. You gave him money. You acted like you knew him. I was just—hey, are you okay?"

"Don't be lame," Keely snapped, irritated beyond endurance. Couldn't he see she was in a hurry? "Everyone gives the homeless money."

"Listen, I'm only trying to help—"

By then she'd already told the driver to move on. Keely watched the stranger recede into the distance through the back window. He was younger than she'd originally thought, and shorter, and had bad posture. Owing to the fact, she realized to her horror, that both his wrists and hands were thrust into braces connected to metal crutches that supported his weight.

She'd insulted the homeless, plus she'd just snarled *don't be lame* to a disabled guy. Fan-freakin'-tastic. No doubt about it now—she was going to straight to hell.

Chapter Four

Some of the papers in the see-through plastic folder the antiques dealer had pushed across the table bore the unmistakable imprint of a color bubblejet. On top, though, were documents over two centuries old, so fragile and yellowed that each sheet lay within a protective clear envelope of its own. "I ordered by date, okay? You don't often find provenances as thorough as you'll find for this here item," said Mr. Shreves, his gray mustache widening as he smiled. Keely always looked forward to visiting this particular gallery. Though the exterior was forbidding, with its heavy locked door and its discreet sign informing the public at large that the proprietor saw clients by appointment only, inside was only amiable clutter, the gentle sounds of classical music over the satellite radio, and the owner's chatter. "No indeedy! This provenance is almost worth more than the sword itself. I took the liberty, hope you don't mind, of itemizing all the different documents."

"Wonderful. Thank you!" Privately, Keely doubted

whether Jarod Barry-Chyldes even knew that an antique was only as valuable as its documentation. She made a mental note, though, to give her client a phone call and tell him to put the provenance papers away in a lockbox until the Barry-Chyldes heir was old enough to appreciate the history behind it.

"My daughter taught me how to use a whatchamacallit, a shred sheet, with all the little boxes?"

"Spreadsheet?" She grinned. "Welcome to the computer age, huh?"

"That's it. So I used it to list all the documents in the provenance, from the commodore's original commission of the weapon—you don't get a lot of those, by the way—up to the paperwork when the family let it go during the Great Depression. You know, I've kept all my records by hand ever since I took over this business from my own mom and dad. My box of file cards was always good enough for me." Mr. Shreves had already wrapped the Commodore Barry sword in velvet and packed it into a flat, oversized box lined with foam rubber; he fastened the lid's seams with dark tape as he talked. "Now the girl's got me keeping inventory in the shred sheet and I've gotta say: I wish like crazy we'd had these computer things fifty years ago, because it would've let me take off a hell of a lot more time for fishing, you know?" Keely laughed at that. "How's the business going for you, anyway? How long you been doing this? Two years now?"

From her inside coat pocket, Keely's cell phone began to vibrate. She pulled it out and examined the caller ID. Nadine. Again. For the seventh time that day. "Three. This has been the craziest of all the Christmas seasons I've done but you know, crazy's good. Crazy pays the bills." Crazy also ended you up on some cul-de-sac off East Fifty-ninth for insults and possibly assault by a bum your former best friend found off his medications yet decided was a good career and fashion counselor. With her thumb, Keely sent the call to voice mail—again, for the seventh time that day. It was odd how little guilt she felt about it. "It's actually fun to get out and do the kind of shopping I don't get to do the rest of the year."

"Anyone else looking for last-minute gift ideas?" the old shopkeeper asked. In a singsong voice intended to be playful, he added, "I can get you some good deals! My girl bargained under everyone's nose for all the good lots at an estate sale last weekend. I got some nice Archibald Knox terra cotta, the real stuff. And oh man, oh man, you should see the Roycroft she picked up. You like Roycroft?" He turned and lifted a photocopy paper box onto the scarred wooden counter. From within he began to produce some metal objects; each of them had been hammered by hand until their surfaces were covered with a lovely texture that Keely wanted to reach out and touch. "She even got a pair of the Roycroft princess candlesticks—probably the rarest copper work the studio did. You like Arts and Crafts period? Yeah, everyone likes Arts and Crafts."

Keely dredged up what facts about Arts and Crafts style she could remember reading at the newsstand in *Style 1900* magazine. "They're beautiful!" Keely said quite sincerely. Considering the number of well-off clients she still had looking for last-minute gift ideas, the pieces might prove ideal for one or more of them. Truthfully, she would have loved to have been able to buy one of the dozen or more pieces merely for the handling of it. The so-called princess candlesticks, large yet graceful, were truly exquisite, as was a vase that seemed surprisingly delicate for being made of copper. "May I?" she asked at last, unable to resist. At the proprietor's happy nod, she picked up a round piece with a flat base. Careful not to smudge its patina, she rotated it so that it glistened in the light of the multiple stained-glass lamps hanging overhead. "So cute," she commented, mentally picturing it in her dream apartment, holding candles for the dinner of her dreams with the masculine, silhouetted figure she seemed doomed never to find. "It's decorated with a bird." Her phone started vibrating again. With irritation, she reached into her pocket and stabbed the voice mail button.

Mr. Shreves put on his half-glasses and peered over their tops, which struck Keely as an eccentric thing to do. "Oh yes, the owl design. Not especially rare, but not very common either. I prefer them over most of the other Roycroft bookends. In particularly fine condition, it seems." From the box he lifted out and unwrapped a matching piece. "Hoot hoot!"

Keely's phone buzzed once, reminding her that there were voice mail messages she was ignoring. "Twins," she said, setting the first bookend beside the other.

Her brain reeled in circles, though her body remained in place. Is that what déjà vu felt like? Although Keely had replayed the previous night in her head, it had only been to rebuke herself for even going along with it. She hadn't recalled any of the details, though, until that moment. *In the nest of the twin red owls . . .*

Copper was a red metal. And two twin owls stared her right in the face.

Okay. That was weird. But coincidences happened all the time. How often had she hummed a song to herself and heard it on the radio shortly afterward, or thought about someone only to have them call immediately after? Her phone started vibrating again. Cursing to herself, Keely pulled it out. She couldn't turn it off or else her clients couldn't call. Yet something had to be done. She took a few steps away from the counter before snapping the clamshell open and pressing it to her ear. "What?"

The curt syllable was rewarded with a gasp and a short silence. "You finally picked up!" said Nadine at the other end. "Does that mean I'm forgiven?"

"No."

"Okay, you sulk then. When you're ready to talk, I'm standing outside the store."

"What?" Keely's squawk was three times the volume she intended.

"No rush. I know you have business. But listen to this, I had my meeting this morning and my boss l-o-v-e-d the D&G that Mel—"

"I'm hanging up now."

"I'm just telling you, Kee, that you ought not dismiss things simply because you don't understand them. When I started seeing a homeopathic—"

Mr. Shreves didn't even bat an eyelash when Keely returned to the counter with an audibly yawping coat pocket. If Nadine wanted to talk, fine. Let her talk. Nowhere did it say that Keely had to listen. "You don't happen to have a back way out, do you?"

"Problems with the fuzz?" His tone was so deadpan it took her a moment to realize he was joking. "Give me a few minutes, then I'll show you. Okeydoke?"

Keely could live with that. Nadine sometimes had the attention span of a magpie. Maybe she'd wander off after something bright and shiny.

Though Mr. Shreves specialized in turn-of-the-twentieth-century Americana, there was enough stuffed into the narrow confines of the store to keep collectors of any era happily occupied for hours. Mentally she noted a stack of old ragtime piano music in the center of one of the tables; sometime after her accounts had been settled in the new year she'd have to return and sift through the pile for some colorful covers to frame.

Honestly! She wasn't sure which annoyed her more, the thought that Nadine was outside the store stalking her, or that a few minutes before she'd nearly been suckered into believing the magus' twaddle. Anyone could tell his synapses weren't firing on all cylinders. He hadn't even been able to get her name right! Trust Nadine to look for another easy fix to her life. Keely only wished there were such a thing.

Toward the back of the shop was an enormous player piano, its façade carved with elaborate oak leaves. A piano roll, smooth and creamy, arced from its front. From the way Mr. Shreves had displayed its shiny, complex innards, she suspected it was lovingly restored. Funny, but the human brain was a little bit like that player piano. When everything was in working order, music came out, harmonious and sweet. Even the tiniest rips in the piano roll, though, or the most minor of defects in the works, and it would produce cacophony. In a way she even felt sorry for Melchior—if that was really his name. He needed a shelter, or maybe local or state medical aid. Of course, Nadine's piano roll had a few too many holes itself. Bringing Melchior alcohol and money made it easy for him to avoid seeking help.

The store's back wall was hung with utility shelving to display smaller items. Decades-old street signs mingled with old metal lunchboxes and knickknacks. Keely felt like a kid unleashed in Toys R Us, unable to figure out what to look at first. The old mechanical penny banks, their paint so worn and rusted that the original colors had to be guessed?

The vintage dairy signs with their illustrations of perky milkmaids? The old pub sign hanging from a beam overhead, with the Statue of Liberty's silhouette advertising Fine Belgian Beer? The old cookie jars lined up in a—

Keely looked up again and blinked. The audible gulp that followed felt like swallowing a golf ball. Lady Liberty, at the back of the store. It had to be coincidence. It had to be.

At the plane of the eyes' gaze. Your eyes, not mine. Right before her, at eye level, a shelf ran the length of the wall. Her own legs carried her, hypnotized and almost against her will, to the left. Past the colorful cookie jars she floated, past the banks and jewelry boxes and old medicine chests, until she was at the shelf's end.

An old-fashioned red fire engine sat slightly apart from the rest of the display objects. Its front wheels, fashioned from the same cast iron as the rest of the figure, hung over the shelf's edge. From lifting it a few inches she could instantly tell it weighed a ton and had to be at least eighty or ninety years old—when were fire trucks first built with combustion engines? Although the paint had chipped away over the last century and the faces of the finger-sized fire men had faded from generations of children playing with it, there was something charming about the toy. It was unique. In its own playful, singular way, it was something to be displayed and admired, right down to the worn figurine of a tiny spotted dalmatian sitting on the truck's back end.

She gazed at it without breathing for long, long moments. Then she reached inside her pocket for her phone and punched a series of numbers.

"Don't you bleep your phone at me!" said Nadine, immediately.

"Have you stayed on the line all this time?" Keely gasped. She couldn't have!

"Of course I did. I knew you couldn't ignore me forever, and as weird as you're acting today, who knew when you'd pick up your phone again, so I—"

"Nadine, I'm hanging up. I have to call Miss Mercer."

"Oh, I see. I'm persona non grata now. Well, you'll be changing—" *Beep!*

Keely bit her lip in thought as she dialed her client. How many apologies would she have to make if Miss Mercer didn't like the fire engine? And yet . . . what if? The question nagged her. What if Melchior was right?

"Something wrong there?" She almost jumped out of her skin; Mr. Shreves had crept behind her unannounced. He looked at the fire engine and shook his head. "Fine piece, that."

She nodded, still stunned. "It's awfully . . . Don't you think the paint's chipped away in places? I mean, it's worn."

Mr. Shreves reached out to touch the piece. "Ms. Boston! A few scratches and dents don't make a thing bad!"

"But is it . . . ?" The words came out as a whisper, the way one might speak when in a hushed church, only she couldn't bring herself to utter the benedictory final word: *perfect*. Keely stared back up at Lady Liberty and shook her head. Somehow she almost felt affronted by the fire truck, just as she had been with the magus. Why couldn't good things come in *nice* packages?

Chapter Five

On her first two passes, Keely couldn't at all bring herself to slow down until she had nearly reached the next crosswalk. She decelerated on her third attempt, but so alarmed was she by the steam's mossy odor that she redoubled her pace until a don't-walk sign glowed red immediately opposite where she stood in the twilight.

"This is ridiculous," she told herself aloud. A young man in a business suit whooshed by, his eyebrows raised at her remark. Oh great. Now she was attracting the wrong kind of attention. "Hello! I'm not the crazy one!" she remarked to his back, instantly mortified at how insane she sounded. Of course she was the crazy one. Who else would tramp around the corner from East Fifty-ninth in the near-dark, looking for answers she knew wouldn't be here? It was a pity—the guy had been cute too. Not magazine-ad sexy, like the man of her dreams—the one she pictured greeting her with a kiss when she came home at night, or treating her to candlelit dinners and red roses. But cute. Dateable. Yet who would want to date a crazy woman? She sighed.

Pass number four. She would stop this time, she promised herself. What in the world was there to be afraid of . . . besides being mugged and murdered? Amazing how confidently her footsteps had fallen on the pavement when she walked back in the direction of the park another time, and how that confidence faltered the moment she once again heard the hollow ring of her feet against metal. *Oh, screw it,* she told herself. *Take yourself home.*

"How many times am I gonna have to listen to you clippity-clop by on those bargain-buy shoes, sweetcheeks?" From the darkness loomed a shadow, silhouetted against the light streaming down from the building. "Just because I'm down and out doesn't mean I'm deaf, and Little Miss Wannabe, you are getting on my last nerve."

If she had already been timid of simply walking by, Melchior's gruff voice jarred her into a flight-or-fight stance. He seemed even more ominous than he had the first time they'd met—tall, severe, and imposing, despite the paper crown adorning his head. His beard seemed ribboned in grease, and even from a dozen feet away she could smell the alcohol in which he'd been marinating. A moment before, though . . . well, it had been a trick of the eyes, one of those pranks the brain plays. She knew he was insane and in need of treatment, and quite possibly dangerous, but when he had stepped forward to accost her, his silhouette against the red light and fog had seemed almost regal. Like Old King Cole, only considerably less merry.

"Hola, chica," he said when she didn't speak. "You here to waste my time?"

"I don't—I didn't—that is, I didn't know if you'd remember me," she stammered out. She must be insane, but she had to ask him the question. Just the one question, then she'd leave for good and never come back. "I'm—"

"You need a shelter?" he asked, lurching forward, his arm outstretched. He sounded confused again. "Maybe you need a shelter? Maybe she needs a shelter," he said over his shoulder.

For a moment, Keely felt the same kind of abstract sympathy she felt at the sight of a dead squirrel or pigeon; Melchior was obviously talking to one of the figments of his schizophrenia. She was doubly startled when the figment spoke back in a thin tenor. "It's you who needs the shelter," it said, manifesting itself as a shorter black shape by the vagrant's side.

"I think K-k-kelly here needs the shelter more," Melchior mumbled. Keely didn't bother to correct him on her name. She wouldn't be back. "Shelter her."

"Nice to meet you again, Kelly," said the shorter man. He distracted her for a moment. Who was this guy? When the mist cleared, Keely thought for another confused moment that the second man had four legs—but no, they were crutches. It was the fellow she'd insulted from the taxi, the day before. Great. Just great. "So you do know our friend Mel."

"I . . . not really," she said. Should she explain? Should she apologize for the lame comment? What was the point? In five more minutes she'd be in a cab on her way back to Queens, where she could shut herself away behind the battered triple-locked doors of her apartment and forget the evening's irritations by basking in HGTV and this month's stack of glossy, upscale magazines. That was her real life— the only thing distinguishing this situation from a nightmare was that she still had on her clothes.

"So, you've known Mel for how long?" Keely's jaw felt

rusty from disuse. When she didn't answer, the man leaned back, lifted his arms so that he could advance the crutches that he held in his grip, and swung his legs forward to move closer to her. "Mel tells me that there are friends who give him money. And other things, too, right, Mel?" The homeless man shrugged, licked his lips, and with gloved fingers began to rub his armpits through layers and layers of clothing. "I think that if he does have friends like that, they would help convince him to get to a shelter, where the nice people there like me could help him get the proper assistance he deserves. Isn't that right, Kelly?"

His tone was condescending. The man would have been short even if he hadn't been hunched over on his crutches, Keely realized—no more than five foot seven or so. Not tall enough to cut a romantic figure in any's bride scrapbook. He was decidedly ordinary, too, with his tousled reddish-brown hair and bushy goatee. His eyes were blue and kind, but behind that kindness, his little mini-homily had carried a point intended to sting. "For your information," she informed him curtly, resenting a lecture, "I just met this man yesterday. I think he *should* be in a shelter. Take him away."

"Noooooo!" When Melchior instantly put his hands over his ears and started making distressed noises, it alarmed her for a minute. She was in way over her head here. "No, no, noooo!"

"Now see what you've done?" complained the man.

"What *I've* done!"

"No kidding, Kelly." Using his crutches as leverage, the man advanced a little closer. He had a nice smile, though at that moment Keely didn't want ever to see it again. "You can't use phrases like *take him away* in front of people like Mel. Some are paranoid enough as is without threats of incarceration—it's hard for you and me to understand what these guys fret and fantasize about. They've already lost so much. Free will is all a lot of them have left."

"Fine, so I'll keep my mouth shut." Her guilt at setting off Melchior made her sound abrupt.

He waggled a finger in the air as if he was coloring in an outline of her face. "I'm not getting the hostility, here. You and I probably both want what's best for Mel, right?"

"If I'm hostile it's because I've told you repeatedly, I barely know him. If you need to give a sermon, give it to my friend Nadine," Keely informed him. At least Mel had stopped covering his ears and pretending not to hear them; he stood there comforting himself from a much-crumpled bag of peanut M&Ms. When he extended a palm nearly black with dirt and grime to offer her one of the candies, she shook her head and tried not to shudder. "As a matter of fact, I should go."

"No, no." The man raised one of his arms and made a dismissive gesture, resting the weight of his upper body on the other crutch. "You obviously came here for some reason. Don't let me get in the way. You know, though, the ten-dollar donation you give one homeless person can, at Advent Shelter, provide food to men, women, and children who are—"

"Hell yeah! Time for gifts to the magi!" Melchior slammed a last M&M into his mouth and while chewing, stuck out his hands in Keely's direction.

Blue Eyes quirked his lips and fixed her in a *now look what you've done* expression. It only made her want to kick them both and howl with frustration. What kind of awful person was she, wanting to attack the disabled and the homeless at Christmastime? What next, stealing presents from the Toys for Tots barrel? "Here then," she snapped, digging into the one good purse she carried to all her best clients. A ten-dollar bill lay just inside, ready for Mel. She stuffed it in the front pocket of the shelter advocate's fleecy jacket. It was the kind of overcoat that was hopelessly unfashionable, but practical in the kind of cold weather the city had lately experienced. The kind of coat she had once owned several like, before she'd gotten her first good charcoal suede and donated the rest to Goodwill. "Feed some unfortunates. Best of luck."

While Melchior made an outraged face and hopped up and down impotently behind them, Blue Eyes shook his head. "Hey hey, now," he complained. "Classy ladies like you don't come down from their east side apartments to slum it with guys like Mel for no reason. You got a question, you ask him." He inclined his head at Mel, now fixing his Burger King crown.

"Mine!" Melchior banged his hand on his chest. "That was supposed to be mine!" She wondered how he'd known. Then again, he probably assumed every stray bill belonged rightfully to him. He stopped his mumbling, however, suddenly alert. "You've got something else though, don't ya?" His nose twitched as he leaned forward. "I can smell it. I got a dog's nose. Plus, I saw it in the stars. Magi. Magician. Where do you think the goddamned word comes from, huh?"

Keely thought Mel was just rambling again in his own odd way; when he suddenly grasped out with both his hands, it seemed to her merely as if he was trying to pull off some showy David Copperfield gesture. She saw the shelter worker react, but couldn't prevent him from striking Mel's left hand with his aluminum crutch. The metallic thwack caused the vagrant to howl in pain. "What are you *doing?*" Keely shouted at Blue Eyes. The idiot!

"Accident!" The man looked sheepish. He bit his lip. "I thought he was going to grab you."

"He's not dangerous like that! If he was, my friend Nadine wouldn't be here every day!" She'd never verbalized that thought, especially to herself, she realized with chagrin. A surge of angry sympathy made her ask the vagrant, "Are you okay?" Melchior by now was nursing his hand under his right arm while digging into his pocket for more M&Ms. He nodded; the hurt probably hadn't been anything more than a knuckle rapping. Still, though! She turned back to Blue Eyes. "Do you do that to people at your shelter?"

"Yes, of course," he snapped back. "Spankings at ten, post-luncheon bruisings, then afternoon tea accompanied by enforced bare-bottomed canings. Listen, I was worried for your—"

"Holy frickin' Hell," Melchior spoke up, his head twitching. "And you want me to go to that place? No way. *No way! Fuggedaboutit!*" While Mel removed his paper crown and began massaging out the crinkles, Keely noticed the blue-eyed man's mouth working silently as he glared at her, obviously angry. Was it wrong that she felt both guilty and gleeful over that expression? The guilt came, of course, from knowing that she'd goaded Blue Eyes into saying something that might prevent the homeless man from seeking the assistance he needed. It had felt grand, though, to get the do-gooder's goat. "You, baby," said Melchior, pointing his injured finger at Keely. "C'mere. C'mere. We got business? Yeah? Like I said, I can smell it on you."

His nod at her right hand coat pocket startled Keely a little. Could he really smell the tiny liquor bottles she'd never given him the day before? He must have heard them clinking, though it was a mystery how he could hear anything through all his wild hair. Keely raised a hand when he had advanced far enough. Even the damp and sour smell of the vapor couldn't obscure Mel's stench. "Not with—" She jerked her head in the direction of the man on crutches.

"Hey, shelter boy," Mel rasped out, following it up with a loogie of phlegm spat into the grating. Keely winced. "The lady don't like gimps."

"That's not—goddamnit!" Keely liked gimps! No, wait.

She was fine with the differently abled! Perfectly fine! That is, she hadn't like, ever dated one, or even in the days she'd had friends, none of them had been disabled, but she was fine! Every time she saw Mel, he was accusing her of something, and she hated it. Keely had only wanted privacy because she didn't want to give Mel liquor in front of a shelter worker. It would be like slipping a nun a sexy book while the Pope watched.

It was too late. The shelter worker had shrugged, twisted his crutches, and hobbled off a few yards without a word. Melchior nodded, gesturing for Keely to reach into her pocket for the miniature twin bottles. He made a snatch for them, but at the last possible second Keely yanked the vodka away. "I have a question first." Melchoir fixated on the Smirnoff. "How did you know about Miss Mercer?"

Because he had known, hadn't he? He'd predicted exactly where she could find the toy fire truck. He had foreseen Keely purchasing it on approval from Mr. Shreves. The magus had to have somehow seen somewhere that when Keely pulled out the antique truck from the depths of its box, tissue paper crackling, Miss Mercer would hold one hand to her cheeks and exclaim, "Oh! Oh my!" before wrapping the other around her trembling, emotional mouth.

Brother Warren had owned just such a toy in his childhood; it had originally belonged to their father. "I don't know how you could have . . . oh my! Oh my!" The trembling had quickly turned into a cascade of emotion as Miss Mercer had turned the truck around and round again, admiring it through a blur of tears and nostalgia. Right then and there in front of her, the old woman had telephoned one of those wonderful, elusive, promised friends to sing Keely's praises. "I don't know how she's done it, the dear thing, but she's found the most perfect present ever!"

The question still remained. *How had he known?*

His voice at first was distant and mystical, drawing her in. "I see things in the stars." Melchoir traced an index finger in the air. Keely looked up; over the pollution of the city lights she could only see a single star. For all she knew, it might have been a satellite. "That's what we astrologer kings do, you goddamned idiot."

"But how . . ." If only he would just tell her! Perfection seemed so simple in air-brushed photographs. What if this was her sole brief encounter with it in real life?

"Listen, whaddaya want from me, tutorials in astrology? I'm the magus, you're the broad who thinks she's better than me, and that's the way it's always going to be, so just fork over the freakin'—" Before he could finish the sentence, she pressed the bottles into his gloved hands. "That's better. You're gonna be coming back, right?"

She didn't think so. "No."

"Oh yeah. You'll be coming back. You wanna know the best place for jewelry steals? No no, don't bother wasting your time at those Park Avenue rip-off artists. There's a place in Alphabet City, Maximillian's, that carries stuff at bargain prices, and there's nothing a rich guy likes more than a bargain if you know what I'm saying. Translates right into under-the-counter bonus shekels a girl doesn't have to report on her 1040."

Okay, it was a little freaky that only that afternoon she'd gotten a call from Tasteful Trinkets—Mr. Armitage of the Upper West Side—to return the five bracelets intended for his mistresses and upgrade them to "something even more tasteful." Perhaps she'd check it out tomorrow, she promised herself, both excited and appalled to be hooked again on Melchior's advice.

With a gap-toothed leer, Mel added, "Yo, yo, don't forget about Tiffany. You're coming back, right?"

"I'm in a hurry," Keely replied. Wild horses and monster

trucks couldn't have dragged that promise from her. What
had he said about Tiffany, anyway? Some guy was with a
girl named Tiffany? Waiting for her? With a guy meant for
her? If he was her guy, why was he dating some bimbo
named Tiffany? If there was one prediction she wished Mel
would get right, it would be one boding well for her love
life. "And seriously, think about the shelter, I'm sure
what's-his-name doesn't really beat anyone." Mel shook his
head firmly, like a child told to eat his Brussels sprouts.
"They'd give you food and a warm place to sleep."

"That would be a pity for you, wannabe. If I left here,
you'd never know how to find me." Over his head, the shop
letters glowed eerily in the red light: ORIENT ARE.

It wasn't until she had taken her leave and stepped out of
the billowing smoke that she heard another voice. "Good
night, Kelly." Blue Eyes stood by the wall, patiently waiting
for her to leave. He leaned heavily on his crutches as if tired
and worn. Keely had actually forgotten about the shelter
worker, even though she'd given him lip service just moments before. She'd actually thought he'd abandoned his
cause and gone back to wherever he'd come from.

"Oh. Good-bye," she said. "I did try to talk him into going with you."

His voice was both disappointed and morose. "Your attempt at a good deed for the day, I suppose?" He loped off
with sudden heated energy.

Was that a slam? "Listen, you. I tried. If I wasn't in a h—"

"I know. I know," she heard from the vapor. "You're in a
hurry. Hurry doesn't always get you places."

Keely opened her mouth, then closed it. Waste of effort,
she told herself. She wouldn't have to see the rude little
man again.

Chapter Six

When Keely was at home evenings, she set her television to the classic movie channel and turned the volume low. She knew most of the plots already—how the Cary Grants met the Katharine Hepburns and how they fought and argued and drove each other mad before finally falling in love by the movie's end. Even without the sound, she loved the black-and-white musicals best, with their colorful backdrops of 1930s swanky nightclubs and sophisticated New Yorkers modeling chic eveningwear. It was a world in which everyone was beautiful and stylish and painfully articulate, where no one ever said *Um* or *You know?* or punctuated their sentences with the ubiquitous *like*, and where romance worked the way it was supposed to.

Inevitably these films would contain a montage indicating the passage of time. Sometimes the romantic couple would tap-dance their way across the television while an invisible hand plucked page after page from the calendar; sometimes the screen would be ablaze with neon-lit names of restaurants and forgotten Manhattan nightclubs that tracked the couple's amorous escapades, or the marquees of out-of-town theaters as the young hoofers inevitably made their journey to a big break on Broadway. Keely's last week and a half felt a lot like one of those montages. A movie of those ten days, though, would have shown her stumbling about with multiple shopping bags in hand, looking up and around her in wonder as store names and street signs flashed overhead: *Barneys. Macy's. Saks Fifth Avenue. Brooks Brothers.*

Perfect Present had paid off. She had actually paid off. Calls had begun to trickle in as early as the next morning from Miss Mercer's circle of well-to-do friends, all of whom were either unable to move about readily or simply didn't have the inclination to brave the crowds and were looking for someone to do some last-minute shopping for them. Most of them were women, and most had a definite idea of the gifts they wanted; it wasn't unusual for Keely to depart those consultations with a long list of objects to be purchased and itemized clothing sizes for the client's relatives. A few of them even uttered the words dearest to Keely's heart—*money is no object.* She could really show off her eye for taste, then. It wasn't that Keely believed that something had to be expensive to be in good taste, but there certainly was something in the notion that working with a good deal of money made it easier to keep the client happy . . . and a happy client meant a fatter bonus. Sale by sale, she was making her way closer to the tasteful photograph in her head of how her life should be.

Then there were the Miss Mercer clones, of course. There were only a few, all of them old women happy to find someone patient and long-suffering enough to indulge their whims. They fussed and pursed their lips and nay-said suggestions even before they left Keely's lips. Before now Keely would have considered abandoning these rich old women—they really were more trouble than they were worth—but now, of course, she had a secret weapon.

Keely had made the first visit back to the old carpeting store secretly, almost stealthily, three evenings after her first. In that short space of time she'd already delighted several new customers with her unerring taste and her eye for a solid bargain, but two of her little old ladies had no solid notions of their own. It was with guilt pangs that she found herself slipping a twenty-dollar bill into her coat pocket next to a shot-sized bottle of Bacardi Gold; it was as if her mind had made itself up without consultation and had begun to propel her feet in Melchior's direction. Did she have mixed feelings about it? Oh hell yes. The orient area rug shop was the last place she wanted to go.

The magus had greeted her both with derision and profanity, but grabbed the libation and went to work. "Tell me about these rich biddies," he asked, when she explained what she wanted. She had given a little summary of both, and was surprised he had actually listened to her with an almost businesslike air, his finger tapping his chin. "Some goddamned showy gift certificates for Geritol candidate the first—all she wants is a name she can recognize and brag about. The second one just needs someone to talk to. That's all women want, talk-talk-talk-talk-talk. Even the Virgin Mary, ay-yi-yi, what a mouth on her. Kidding!" he added when Keely shot him a raised eyebrow. "Buy a few nice things but don't give them to her until you've made chitchat for a half hour or more. She'll love whatever you get. Hey, anyone ever tell you you have a damn fine tuckus?"

Keely's heart had sunk at the suggestion of gift certificates. They were boring and dull and practically an admission of failure. *I couldn't think of anything, so here's a gift certificate.* Mel's insight into the second problem client, though, seemed dead on. The more Mercer-alikes Keely met over the week, the more she was inclined to believe their petulance and fussiness was simply their way to have someone to visit.

The insight was enough to make her take a chance. She purchased the gift certificates the next morning. Her client was so impressed by their practicality that she asked Keely to buy even more. And sure enough, the second client simply wanted someone to pay attention to her; she was so flattered by Keely's notice she accepted the little trinkets Keely had bought for her relatives almost without inspecting them.

Keely walked away that afternoon with several hundred dollars in her purse. *I won't do it again,* she promised herself. She was becoming one of those people the shelter worker guy had pegged her as—an enabler of the homeless, someone who perpetuated their mendicancy and worse than that, their alcoholism. No wonder a simple visit to Melchior felt like a misdemeanor crime.

But she did do it again two days later, when a particularly stubborn male client implied she'd chosen inferior ties for a business trip abroad. Melchior burped and scratched and farted quite loudly before very reasonably giving her the address to a gentleman's haberdasher on Thirty-sixth Street. The day after that he made her stand through a boozy rendition of an ancient Persian song that Keely strongly suspected was nonsense syllables set to a minor version of "There Is a Tavern in the Town" before suggesting aromatherapy oils for an elderly minor Barrymore relative. There was always a price to pay for Melchior's advice, over and above the liquor and the money. By her fifth visit, the itinerant magus ranted for nearly ten minutes about having his astrologer-king powers reduced to catalog shopping for the masses until Keely waved a twenty and got enough of his grudging attention to tackle her list of requests.

She felt cheap, and she felt dirty. But she couldn't deny that Melchior's insights were the real deal. They worked. Her clients were happy. They paid her. She paid him. It was the foundation of a good solid economy, right?

Somehow she didn't want to think about what Blue Eyes might have to say about that theory.

Rat-a-Tat was the new client contributing most to her condo nest egg. "Older than dirt" was how she had described herself over the phone, "and richer than fudge." During their initial interview, Keely in her one good cashmere sweater set and her drab little skirt had felt quite outclassed by Mrs. Gwendolyn Syms, her vintage Chanel couture and her wide-brimmed hat from half a century before. Whenever the woman talked, her long, long fingernails drummed the gleaming surfaces of whatever she laid her hands upon. Mrs. Syms sucked on cigarettes with such force that they were reduced to ash in what seemed a matter of seconds, simultaneously gesticulating with her widespread fingers as she gabbled rapidly, dropping names and places and past events in the same haphazard manner of the White Queen dropping hairpins. "Halston . . . Jackie and Ari . . . Spence and Kate . . . *darling* little soiree in the Hamptons one summer . . ." Keely had imitated to Nadine the day after the meeting. "Of course, Jesus Christ . . . in a stunning robe . . . Balenciaga . . . daiquiris by the kidney-shaped pool . . . stigmata, don't you know."

"Get out of here," Nadine had laughed.

Yet it was true; the woman did speak that way. When

Keely's cell phone vibrated and the caller ID revealed SYMS, G.A., Keely braced herself for a barrage of Rat-a-Tat's mid-century pop-culture references. She wasn't disappointed. "Darling," she heard over the line, "I *do* hope . . . didn't wake you."

"It's nearly eleven o'clock in the morning, Mrs. Syms," Keely replied with a grin. Was that fingernail tapping she could hear in the background?

"Early to bed, easy to rise . . . sweet little *bon mot* . . . Ike . . . summer of '53 . . . but who didn't like Ike, darling?" Listening to Mrs. Syms was a bit like plunging down from the highest height on a roller coaster. You saw the landscape as it whooshed by, but generally the whole thing passed too quickly to pick out more than a few details. "Your sweet gift for my . . . reminded me of a Dior gown . . . sister's daughter Alison's debut . . . fondue was all the rage that year, you have no idea . . . thank you . . . wondered if you could find something similar . . . size twelve, slimming. . . ."

"Mm-hmmm," said Keely, taking notes as best as she could. They'd have to be repeated and corrected afterward. There was no helping that. Between instructions she doodled little daisies on the pad.

"Little gift for . . . was thinking pearls, so sweet on a young . . . you have such a good eye for . . . nothing floral, mind you, but . . . Charles James red number that I had in my twenties . . . gloves, you know . . . not your usual . . . Tiffany's?"

The pen jerked across the paper, marring the daisy's face. "Excuse me?" asked Keely. So thick was the surprise in her throat that she had to clear it with the cell muted.

"I said," repeated Rat-a-Tat with the patience of someone speaking to a dim child, "I know it's not one of the delightful little gifts you purchased for me, but I was wondering if you might return to Tiffany's an unfortunate little something one of my beaux presented me, darling."

In astonishment, Keely looked down at the pad of paper. She'd written the store's name in letters and had traced it over and over, without being aware. She tossed down the pen as if it was possessed.

"Darling, what . . . came over you? You seem . . . *hope* it isn't anything too serious or . . . reminds me of what happened . . . Gloria . . . institutionalized, poor thing . . . delicious boy, Anderson Cooper."

"I'm fine," Keely said. It occurred to her that she rarely had sounded less convincing. "You did say . . . Tiffany's?" Was *that* what Melchior had been telling her since the first time they'd met? She was going to meet someone at Tiffany's? As her heart beat a little faster, she thought back and tried to remember what she'd earlier dismissed as the ramblings of a schizophrenic. She was going to meet *him* at Tiffany's? Him who?

Surely the magus couldn't have meant any romantic interest? It was ridiculous to think Mel had any abilities in that area. But still, he had been uncannily accurate with other. . . .

No. Ridiculous. Utterly mad. Maybe she did need an institution, like poor Gloria, whoever she was. She hoped her cell had padding in a flattering color.

"Beg pardon?" asked Mrs. Syms.

Oh dear. Had she spoken aloud? "I'm sorry," she apologized. "Did I say something?"

Rat-a-tat-a-tat-a-tat. "I don't know what hymns have to do with anything, dear, even if it is Christmas. Oh . . . reminds me . . . *glorious* concert with Leonard and . . . absolute fits, even if he was . . ."

On the TV screen, a young Katharine Hepburn lay down her head on an outstretched arm while she talked, rapt in love, on the telephone. The gesture filled her with longing. Where was her urbane, articulate Cary Grant? Was he waiting for her, foreseen?

"I'll do it," she said suddenly, interrupting Mrs. Syms' recollection midstream. Where had that sudden resolve come from? "I mean," she added, trying to sound less abrupt, "I don't usually do returns on items I haven't purchased, but since you're a favored client . . . When?"

"Why, this afternoon if you've time . . . don't mind? . . . imposition?"

Keely, though, only paid enough attention to pepper the conversation with occasional agreements and grunts. This afternoon. She wouldn't be able to consult Melchior before then. Damn! How in the world would she know what she was getting herself into without him?

Chapter Seven

"Oh, by all that is itemized on my MasterCard!" Nadine hugged herself and twirled around once they were inside the warmth, a move that would have been quite pretty and girlish if Nadine had been wearing an A-line skirt instead of leather. "I have died and gone straight to heaven, and its streets are paved with diamonds. Do you feel it, girlfriend?"

"Two things. First, don't call me *girlfriend*," Keely suggested. "Second, keep your voice down!" She felt something, all right, and it was called surveillance. She'd felt scrutinized since the moment they'd passed between the American flags overhanging the store's large front windows, below the weather-softened figure bearing the weight of a clock on his shoulders who stood above the impressive roman letters reading TIFFANY & CO. Golden light seemed to stream from the high ceilings above them, but there had to be security cameras as well. Keely felt watched by a hundred eyes, in addition to those of the watchful clerks and security guards discreetly standing at attention behind the display cases.

Or perhaps more accurately, a hundred eyes were on Nadine as she jumped up and down excitedly. Keely was probably mere background. "Aren't you at all excited?"

"It's a store," Keely replied in a low, grating voice through a small crack in her teeth. She could have been a ventriloquist. "I've been in plenty of stores. So have you."

"This isn't a store. It's a church. Oh my God, lookie!" Like a toddler freed from its stroller—a toddler wearing oversized black sunglasses and flared Ungaro leather pants—Nadine careened in the direction of a low case featuring a glittering necklace of diamonds so thickly clustered together that nothing held them together seemingly more than the brittle points of light they reflected. Even the modulated, cool clerk took a step back in surprise at her unexpected approach. "Isn't it beautiful?" she asked, her hand flying up to her neck unconsciously. "How much do you think it is? I'm going to ask how much it is."

"You are not." Who did Keely have to be today, Nadine's mother? No wonder that long-suffering woman's hair had been gray at the age of thirty-five. "Calm the hel—*heck*—down already and act like a normal person!"

Keely's grimaces must have had some effect because her friend looked slightly abashed. "Well, I'm sorry to break my stony New York reserve. It's only that I've never been in here before. I always thought it was something that tourists did, you know. Not natives. Now I'm here it's like—" Her eyes grew large and her mouth pulled down in an exaggerated smile. She looked as if Bob Barker had just announced she'd won a new car on *The Price Is Right*. "I feel like Holly Golightly. What was it she said? I feel like nothing very bad could happen to me here." She looked over her shoulder at the protective male clerk and smiled. "My first time," she confided.

The clerk smiled politely. "You don't say," he said, not sounding surprised at all.

Keely grabbed Nadine's elbow and whirled her around. "Remind me why I brought you here."

"Because, you know." Nadine leaned in close and almost giggled. "You need someone to help you spot *him*." Keely didn't say anything. She didn't know how she and Nadine had reached a state of détente over the issue of Melchior; she knew Nadine knew she was visiting him for advice, and she knew Nadine knew she knew . . . No wait. Already she was confused.

Melchior was a big elephant in the middle of the room about which neither cared to comment directly. Now was the closest Nadine had come to admitting she knew about Keely's secret visits to the magus, and Keely wasn't so sure she was ready to address the issue. "Don't be ridiculous," she said, pretending her heart hadn't pounded at the words. Oh, it was silly to believe there was anything to Mel's prophecy, but wasn't it true that she owed herself seeing if there might be . . . something? Some *one?* "I'm here to return a gift. And you can Holly Golightly right back out the door, thank you very much." Nadine looked crestfallen. "Go on."

For a moment, her friend looked ready to fight. Finally, recognizing Keely's resolve of iron, she caved. "Fine." Nadine's neck and back stiffened; she looked over the top of her sunglasses with the same expression Queen Victoria might have employed at her most unamused. "For your sake I'll leave. But when you come back out you're giving me every single detail. And don't pull that back door stunt again, Sneaky Pete." With a pinched-lipped look of regret,

Nadine whirled around so quickly that her flares splayed out. She was on her cell even before the doorman could nod his farewell.

Keely tucked in her smile at the corners in apology for the clerk. His face was civil, though guarded. Keely still had the uneasy feeling that he was poking the tip of his no-doubt expensive and highly polished shoe at some sort of yellow alert toggle to focus all the store's cameras on her. "May I be of assistance?"

"Why yes," she said, stepping forward and trying to assume the confident air she used with her more influential clients. "I have a return. For store credit, of course."

"I see." Why did places like this make her feel like Little Miss Jane Plain from North Dakota, accustomed only to shopping in the local Wal-Mart? She'd learned from both magazines and her own experiences as a personal shopper that good jewelry—really good jewelry—could be found in many establishments. What distinguished Tiffany & Co. from lesser stores was its mystique. The institution managed to be old-fashioned and modern simultaneously; it exuded an aura of wealth and even excess, certainly, but subdued in tone. It was the kind of place one expected to spy a celebrity at any moment, but in which one would never admit to being excited at the spotting.

Maybe Nadine had been right. The Fifth Avenue store really was more like a cathedral than anything else. Although many customers stood about, attended by handsome and well-dressed male and female representatives of Tiffany & Co., their conversations took place in the hushed tones of the confessional. Even as the salesman glided ahead of her, leading her farther into the establishment's depths, every step through the pools of amber-tinged light spilling from the ceiling and the glass cases felt as if she was treading the stations of the cross. Was she supposed to genuflect somewhere? Nadine almost had.

"A return, Mr. Crowley," said her salesman to another, a short man with round glasses nearly invisible on the bridge of his nose. To Keely, it seemed as if the shorter and older Mr. Crowley made certain with his body language to communicate that he was very, very busy on something extremely, extremely important; the way his head twitched at the junior clerk's request reminded Keely of Alice's white rabbit.

"A return? Indeed, indeed," muttered the little man, nodding his head in Keely's direction. It took her but a moment to explain the situation to him. The mere mention of Mrs. Syms' name brought raised eyebrows and a murmur of recognition, followed by the offer of a chair—it was as if she had produced a key to unlock a layer of the merchant's reserve. His praise for Rat-a-Tat was most voluble. Was she not a sophisticated woman? Why, he had attended to her personally for many years. He hoped that Mrs. Syms was not at all dissatisfied with her friend's gift. . . .

The question was her cue to produce the blue box she had carried for the last two hours. Keely could almost feel their eyes studying her purse when she lifted it onto the glass counter. It was one of her best, a cute Kate Spade knockoff that had cost nearly as much as the real thing. Surrounded by so much real luxury she felt that it, as well as her neat professional clothing, might have well all been stamped with the ominous legend MADE IN TAIWAN.

Still, she felt proud of herself for not letting her intimidation show as she opened the blue box and displayed the bracelet lying within, sparkling against the velvet. "Ah," said Mr. Crowley. "Yes. The strawberry bracelet." He used the tip of his pen to lift the links from the box. "Strawberry leaves of eighteen-karat gold interspersed with rubies. A charming piece . . . on someone of, how shall we say, fewer years?" At Keely's raised eyebrows, he set the bracelet back into its box and smiled, eager to correct any wrong impression he might have made. "Do not misunderstand me. Mrs. Syms is a fine woman, but her charms are of a Grecian urn, whose worth is multiplied by its rarity." With a slight bow, he excused himself to fetch the necessary paperwork.

Mr. Crowley could have called her client a ratty old Grecian ashtray for all Keely really cared; the woman gave her good stories to tell Nadine over lunches, but Keely was primarily interested in her contributions to the Lenox Hill condo fund, growing fatter by the day. Well, that was a little harsh—she liked the woman and had gotten a kick out of her, but in the end, Mrs. Syms was merely a client.

While Keely waited for Mr. Crowley to return, she looked around the store with its customers in quiet, discreet clusters. Now that the initial novelty had begun to wear off of being inside one of the city's most swank establishments, she realized she hadn't even seen a potential *him* yet. Surely it wasn't the first clerk? He had struck her as . . . well, more interested in the male customers than he would have been in her. And Mr. Crowley? No vibes there at all. Anyway, he was far from Keely's profile of the ideal guy; the masculine silhouette she pictured greeting her in the hallway of her Lenox Hill home was neither short, nor plump, nor did his hairline begin at his crown. Definitely not.

It depressed Keely that most of the other shoppers that afternoon seemed to be in pairs—young couples, mostly, who enfolded their postures and gazes around each other as they pointed at treasures within the cases. Across the way from her, a swan-necked woman with her blond hair swept into a loose bun looked up and behind her at a slightly older gentleman; he fastened a triple strand of pearls around her neck, smiling. In her mute enjoyment of the white strands, her expression full of love for the man whose hands grazed her nape, the woman was nearly a Renaissance portrait of beauty, all creamy oil paints and high, shiny gloss. A sharp pang of envy stabbed through Keely's chest for the moment the pair shared. The moment should have been hers. Why couldn't it have been hers?

"Surely you're not returning that charming bracelet."

Keely jerked around so suddenly that her purse, box, and strawberry leaves all tumbled to the floor with a racket. "Oh crap," she said, laughing at her overreaction and instantly stooping to the floor. One of her lipsticks was rolling almost out of sight. Every camera in the place must be focused on her. "Sorry. You startled me!"

"Not my intention, believe me." The man who had surprised her knelt down opposite, stopping the lipstick's getaway before he reached for the toppled blue box.

So far she'd only gotten a snap impression of the man, tall and turtlenecked underneath his sports coat. At his apology, however, she looked up and met his eyes. They were impossibly green—the green of Irish mountain valleys in soap commercials. His hair was sandy and boyish and rumpled, scooping into a small wave that peaked at the front. Of all the impossible things, he had an honest-to-God dimple in his chin. "Oh my God," she breathed, utterly bowled over.

He quirked a single eyebrow. She wanted to marry him immediately for that gesture alone. "Are you okay?"

"Yeah. Um, yes, thanks," she said, finding it difficult to break eye contact. Her lipstick-sized tampon case had landed next to his foot among the much less embarrassing stuff; he handed it over without a word. "I um—like I said, you startled me. Are you him?"

"Him?"

Already she'd realized how absolutely idiotic that had sounded. Thrusting away the last of the horrors that had escaped from Pandora's purse, she cleared her throat. "Sorry. Still a little startled, I guess. I meant to say, are you hurt?"

Back on his feet, he stood a good six inches above her. She hadn't expected him to tower. What was it about tall, broad-shouldered men that comforted her? Keely supposed it was because in comparison they made her feel petite. Small. Dainty, even. "Yes," he replied quite seriously, somewhere at the upper ranges of the bass register. "Ever since my unfortunate yak-racing accident in Guatemala I've been unable to stoop without excruciating pains in my hamstrings." Thankfully, she realized almost immediately he was joking; she would have been mortified if she'd actually fallen for it. "In fact, it was my debilitating stooping ailment that caused me to lose the title of Guatemalan Yak Master in the spring of 1994. I remember it well—it was a sunny day in Huehuetenango when I stooped, much as I did just a moment ago, to retrieve a—"

"Okay, okay." Keely laughed, waving her hand. She was slightly embarrassed, not so much at anything she'd said as simply by the fact she was speaking to someone so, so . . . how to describe him? He looked as if he'd stepped out of a *New Yorker*–placed ad for a finer brand of Scotch, or for a company promising early retirement for sound investments. His individual features weren't at all pretty and certainly weren't feminine, but the impression he left was of considerable attractiveness; he looked like he'd been bred from some larger, superior race of men. "It was a stupid question."

"Not at all," said the man. "I'm Neil."

"Keely," she replied, feeling a flush bloom from head to toe. His hand was outstretched, she realized. He was waiting.

His broad, smooth fingers surrounded hers and immediately enclosed them with her warmth. "I'm very fortunate to have met you here today, Keely," he murmured, squeezing.

The gasp she had to suppress was not at the considerable heat he exuded, nor was it at the sincerity of his tone. It was at the realization that once he'd spoken, the anonymous, shadowy silhouette that for years had occupied her imagination now had a face and a name.

Chapter Eight

"I think it's a shame you're returning that bracelet," Neil said. Still holding her hand with one of his own, he scooped the chain from its blue box and draped the links over her wrist. Quite a contrast, the cold of the chain and the warmth of his skin. "It's really quite charming on you."

For a moment she gazed down at the shining gold leaves and berrylike rubies decorating her forearm. The strawberries weren't something she would have chosen for herself. Keely preferred more modern jewelry, with perhaps an heirloom piece or two for variety, but Neil was right. The bracelet really did suit her. "It is pretty," she murmured. Maybe she shouldn't return it, after all.

Hold on for one freakin' second, she realized, letting the chain slide off her wrist. In what universe was the bracelet hers? Foreseen by the mystical forces of generations of astrologer kings or not, this encounter was getting too out of hand. "But you know, I should still return it."

"Oh, I see," he nodded. "Your husband didn't like it?"

"What? No!" Keely once again wished she were one of those people who could blush prettily instead of changing from pasty to roughly the color of eggplant. "I'm not married."

"Your boyfriend, then." Neil sniffed exaggeratedly, his smile playful. "The bum has no taste, obviously."

He was trying to suss out her relationship status! How utterly transparent of him—and yet, how adorable! Her flirtation skills suddenly seemed rusty. In a quick mental scan of all her recent dating experiences, she realized she'd only exercised her powers of endurance, not attraction. "Are you flirting with me?" she asked, realizing the question sounded, well, coquettish.

"I was thinking of it more as a pre-flirtation audition," he replied. "Want to tell me to scram?"

"How about if I just tell you, break a leg?" Oh jeez, she *was* flirting! From what hidden reserve sprung all this banter? To cover up her awkwardness, she began once more to fumble with the bracelet, slipping it back into its box so she could turn her face from the stranger.

He moved in more closely, though. She could feel the warmth of his breath on her neck. "Some guys might take it as encouragement," he murmured, making her dizzy.

Ever since Rat-a-Tat had asked her to come to this store that morning, Keely had felt as if she'd been on some sort of preordained excursion from which it was impossible to escape. No, the feeling went even farther back than that—back to the evening she'd first met the king of the orient area rug store and he'd pronounced her fate. "We certainly wouldn't want to encourage you, would we?" Honestly, those flirty words coming out of her mouth made her sound like some kind of lust bunny. Who actually talked like that outside the movies?

She didn't seem to be driving him away, though. That

was something. "No, we wouldn't want that at all. But see, I've always said a pretty woman should never shop for jewelry on her own. She should always have a man with her so she can have someone to judge its effect."

He leaned the weight of his body onto the counter, creating a casual closeness between them. Keely's immediate impulse was to create some space between them, but after a split-second's consideration, she realized she didn't care to move. "An impartial judge?"

"No," he said, quietly enough that she had to move in to hear him. "A very, very partial one." Without turning, Neil reached out and snapped his fingers. A nearby clerk whose slender, narrow frame and shaved head reminded Keely of a whippet, sprang forward. "The lady may be making an exchange," he announced. "I think we'd like to see . . . yes, that one."

"I'm not—" Keely's brain started firing warning flares. It had been a pleasant little whimsy that Neil thought her wealthy enough to purchase and return a ruby bracelet on caprice. Flattering, really, that a handsome guy could look at her layered bob from the pages of *Vanity Fair* reproduced at her local Supercuts and think it had been done at the hands of a high-class stylist, or that he could take in her carefully selected clothing and her shoes and bag and think that she was as real a deal as he. Neil actually thought she was a Tiffany's woman! Maybe all her self-improvement over the last three years was finally paying off. "Oh, I can't."

Yet Neil and the salesman were already a step ahead of her, and she felt her wrist weighed down. "The round diamonds have an extraordinary clarity," intoned the salesman. A part of Keely's brain registered the sophisticated way in which he gave the adjective seven clipped syllables. *Ex-ta-ra-or-di-na-ry.* "Note how brilliant they are in the light. Eighteen-karat gold and a classic design from one of

Tiffany & Co.'s favorite designers lend this particular piece a classic charm."

"It looks lovely on the lady," breathed Neil. He smiled at Keely then, turning her insides to jelly.

"Indeed, sir, it does."

How much harm could it do to pretend—just for a moment, and more—that the bracelet could really be hers? It might, someday, if Keely kept this forward trajectory. At the rate she was going with her legion of new clients, Lenox Hill might be just the first stop on the way to an address much, much grander. *Oh, everyone relies on Keely and her girls*, she imagined Manhattan's gentry saying. *Her firm is simply the best when it comes to spotting what's perfect.* Soon she wouldn't be getting designer look-alike watches from discount jewelers. She'd be recognized here at Tiffany's, a familiar face, anticipated by all the staff. *Just a little something extra, especially for you*, they'd say, slipping a blue box on top of the pile. *We think you'll enjoy the ex-ta-ra-or-di-na-ry clarity of the diamonds. And thank you, Ms. Boston.* "It really is beautiful," she said, turning her wrist gently and letting the gems sparkle.

"Is there a companion piece? A necklace or earrings?" Neil still held her hand in his palm as he spoke. Keely yearned for him to leave it there for a lifetime.

The whippetlike clerk nodded rapidly. "There is a most beautiful necklace that accompanies the piece, in the same classic—"

"We'll take a look." Keely could scarcely bear to look at Neil, right then. His handsome features wore the same private expression shared by the other young couples around the store, the intimacy she had found herself envying not five minutes before. The irresistible force set into motion the moment the magus first opened his mouth dragged her along with it, shooting ahead into the future. By the look of things, it was the future of which she'd always dreamed.

"No," she found herself saying. The word surprised even herself, but she understood why it had popped out. Everything was happening too quickly, too smoothly. Keely had seen a vision in which she hadn't the slightest bit of control—seductive as it was, it frightened her. Fumbling at the bracelet with trembling fingers, she tried to explain to Neil as sincerely as possible. "I'd just like to return this bracelet, and then I have . . . you know. Things to do. Oh, Mr. Crowley," she said, breathing a sigh of relief at the senior clerk's return. "Is there anything more I need to do to wrap this up?"

The whippet retrieved the bracelet with a faint air of hurt, as if Keely had insulted a chain he'd crafted himself. Neil, on the other hand, just nodded and stepped back for a moment. Was he disappointed? Part of her would have hated that. Another part, though, almost wanted it. Keely's main concern at the moment, however, was preventing Mr. Crowley from uttering Mrs. Syms' name around Neil. She colored deeply as she signed a receipt and handed back over the blue box. Was her pride really so monstrous she couldn't admit that she was not the owner of the strawberry leaf bracelet, nor could have afforded it if she'd wanted?

Apparently so. She completed the transaction with a murmur and a gracious nod from Mr. Crowley. Thankfully, he made not a single mention of her employer. "Nice meeting you," she murmured to Neil. It would feel painful to separate from someone who'd made her feel desirable, but instinct told her to do it quickly, like yanking a bandage from a scab. Neil had glided almost without effort into the masculine silhouette in her dreams, but she hadn't yet done anything to earn those looks of closeness. She couldn't accept them.

"Hey," he called out right before her final turn, just as she hoped he would. "You're like Cinderella, running home before everything's pumpkins and white mice."

Funny that. Keely had felt ready to run out into the street minus one glass slipper. "I really should finish my shopping," she said gently. Was it bad she wanted him to talk her out of it, or at least try?

"Was I coming on too strong? If you say 'too phony,' I'll cry." His regret seemed genuine.

"Too pho—" she tested him. He mimed being struck in the chest by an arrow. "I'm kidding. You're pretty smooth, though."

"Talk to me. I'll only keep you a minute," he promised.

Five minutes later she exited the store in a daze. Ordinarily she would have winced at the subfreezing air and the lightly falling snow, but right then it felt like a splash of fresh water on her pinkened face. Even the sounds of car horns and grinding truck gears and the smell of exhaust invigorated her. She had to look to both sides before spotting Nadine's pants, black and shiny against the piles of white accumulating where building met sidewalk. Keely nodded at the doorman and made her way toward the corner.

"Guess—" she started to say to Nadine's back, and then drew up short.

"And then he suggested I try reflective listening. You know reflective listening?" her friend was saying to someone else. "And I said, 'Mel, I don't think my publisher is into reflective anything,' but his track record was *so good* that I thought I'd give it a whirl. And you know what? It really was a fantastic—" She noticed Keely standing there on the periphery of her vision and smiled. "Hell's bells. You met *him*. I can tell. You're glowing. You have this look. Doesn't she have this look?"

"She definitely has a look all right," Nadine's partner in conversation replied politely. "Who did you meet, Kelly?"

"What are *you* doing here?" The man's identity took a moment to sink in—not because she didn't recognize the shelter worker. How could she not, with his ridiculously red-brown frizzy hair and goatee and crutches? Her brain, however, seemed to have lost the ability to conceive of a world in which he and her best friend could actually be having a conversation.

He shook an enormous can of mixed bills and change. "Help for the homeless, ma'am?"

"Wait a minute." The tip of Nadine's index finger traveled rapidly in both their directions. "You know Duncan?"

"We've met."

"No," said Keely. Their answers overlapped each other. The shelter worker raised his eyebrows. Annoyed, her head bobbed from side to side. "We might have met. But I didn't know his name. Really? Like the doughnuts?" she asked.

She realized instantly how stupid that sounded the minute the words left her mouth. For the first time, she noticed that the man wore a plastic ID with the legend *Duncan Reese: Director, Advent House*. Just desserts for bothering her at every turn. And it wasn't as if he ever got her name right! "No," he replied at last, his face pained. "Like Mr. Hines. Of cake mix fame?"

"Sorry." Mr. Reese, if that was his name, was seriously dulling any excitement Keely had felt upon exiting Tiffany's.

In an effort to get away as quickly as possible, she dug through her purse for a spare five. "That's not necessary," he said in as civilized a tone as possible when he saw what she was doing. Was he trying to shame her for a simple mistake about his name? "You've already given generously."

"Are you turning down money?" she asked, waving the bill in front of his red-painted can. "I thought shelters were always looking for funds."

"Of course. From people who donate with the right motives."

Ouch. So he doubted her sincerity, did he? She was feeling too good to care. "Let's go," she said, rolling her eyes and plucking Nadine's jacket.

"Bye, Kelly," she heard over her shoulder. It was a plaintive sound, almost expressionless, and yet it made her feel cold.

She walked down the street at a furious pace and turned the corner. Snowflakes, drifting lazily between buildings to spread a fresh white layer on the ground, pattered against her face as Keely drew up her scarf around her head. "What's the fuss? You were short with that guy, and he seemed nice. That's not like you. It's like me, but not you," Nadine said in a concerned voice. "What happened in there? You were gone forever."

The glow returned. How should she spring the news? Should she draw it out? Should she tease? "I gave him my number," she heard herself blurting out.

"Oh my God," Nadine drawled in an exaggerated accent. "So was it him? What was he like? I want all the details. Start at the beginning. Oh jeez, I'm so excited! Didn't I tell you that Melchior was the best?"

It was the first time Nadine had spoken the magus' name aloud in days. At the sound of it, Keely stumbled and nearly lost her balance. At the last minute, she felt her foot plunge into icy wetness. In her haste to regain her equilibrium, she had stepped on what she thought was a solid block of ice nestled against the curb, only to have the pretty white crust on the top give way to salty brown slush underneath.

Her shoe wouldn't be ruined, though. She had the sound of a voice, and a name, and a face to paint upon the shadow who had haunted her for years. Not even a muddy foot could ruin her mood now.

Chapter Nine

The right dress: a sheer black overlay atop a separate black slip, slightly ruffled at the cuffs and hem. A V-neck that showed off her prominent collarbone. Inside, a Betsey Johnson label it gave her a warm feeling to know about. Since purchasing it at a steep discount, she'd worn the outfit only once for fear of spills or accidents.

The right hair: Swept back and held down with a pomade that made it shine. Her pale skin and fair hair seemed even more luminous contrasted with the dress' darkness, Keely noted with satisfaction.

The accessories: a colorful velvet Ukrainian scarf, wrapped once around the neck and allowed to dangle over her shoulders. Her expensive-appearing gold watch. A black vintage clutch. Keely was shooting for an image of urban sophistication. Nothing too glitzy. Nothing excessive. Certainly nothing slutty. Someone who knew what she wanted, maybe, and knew how to get it. Oh hell. Why was she so fluttery? Was it because she hoped he liked her?

No, no time to worry about that now. She could be as warm as she wanted over dinner. Concentrate, Keely reminded herself.

The coat: Three-quarter length charcoal suede with a narrow lapel, nipped to show off her waist. She fastened the buttons and pulled the textured fabric tight around her, finally smoothing it down in the mirror and turning in profile to observe how she looked. Hat? No hat. It was cold out, but she'd rather not seem fussy. She slipped her fingers into matching gloves and tugged them down over her wrists. She was ready. Keely took a final look around the apartment, seized the front doorknob in her hand, and yanked it open. At the sight of Duncan Reese on the door's other side, she promptly screamed.

Duncan had been standing outside her doorway at the top of the stairwell, a hand stretched over his forehead and eyes as if he were deep in thought, or the throes of a headache. One of his aluminum canes dangled from his last two fingers. At the door opening and her simultaneous scream, though, he jumped and lurched backward, for a frightened moment Keely feared he might stumble in reverse, topple down the rickety wooden stairs, and break his neck. Instead, he only bumped his head against the opposite wall as he grappled to regain his balance. She winced at the thud.

"What the hell!" she yelled at him. Her first impulse had been to beat him herself with her clutch, but she didn't think of herself as a violent person and as Nadine would have been quick to point out, vintage clutches didn't grow on trees.

"This isn't your business address, is it," said Duncan in a mournful tone.

"No! Are you stalking me?" Should she run back inside and call the police? She didn't think the shelter director seemed like the type to try a full-out assault in the upper hallway of a small apartment building, but you could never tell. On the other hand, how much damage could he do, slow-moving as he was? "What is your *deal*?"

"I thought it was your business address. It's not your business address." She might just change her mind and decide to hit him if he used the words *business address* again. Instead, he weakly proffered a familiar brown-and-white slip of perforated cardstock printed with her home phone number. It had been one of her first attempts at a homemade business card, back in the days before she bit the bullet and had them printed professionally.

"Where did you get this?" She snatched it from his fingers.

"Your friend gave it to me." Duncan sounded apologetic.

"Nadine!" She must have still had them in her purse, damn her. "That doesn't explain why you're here. I deliberately didn't put an address on those."

"Reverse phone lookup," he explained, almost sheepishly. "I'm not a stalker, honest!" At her exasperated look, he rambled on. "Listen, I wanted to know if I could . . . hey, nice apartment."

Keely looked over her shoulder. The door to her little flat had swung all the way open, revealing her living room and its carefully arranged sofas and chairs. She had always thought of it as cramped and confining—a jumble of nice things she'd slowly been purchasing for a better apartment in a better part of the city. For a second, though, she saw it through a stranger's eyes: a comfortable assortment of colors and fabrics, warm and inviting. Only she wasn't planning to invite him in. "I'll be moving soon, so don't bother memorizing my address."

"Seriously? Why would you want to move? This place is

great." He peered around her into the living room once more, then looked around the hallway. Its paneling and trim, distressed but undoubtedly original, had struck Keely as handsome and quirky when she'd moved here a few years before, but she was poised to move on to something sleeker. "Very original. Look at the cool wainscot."

She reached behind her and pulled the door shut, then fumbled with her keys to lock its several deadbolts. Keely refused to turn her back entirely on . . . was it bad that she sometimes thought of him as *the handicapped guy*? She instantly felt a little guilty. "Thank you," she said.

"You're all dressed up."

"You're quite the observant guy, aren't you?" she commented, trying not to sound brusque. "I have a date. Why are you here, again?" She felt a surge of panic. "Did something happen to Mel?"

With anxiety she observed his mouth open, then shut, then open again. At last he said, "No. He's fine. Yes. It's about Mel." Oh. Duncan was here to make more of his socially responsible pronouncements. In her hurried mood, she was ready to agree to anything. Shelters? All for them. Donations? She'd give one. Volunteer work? After the new year. Whatever, so long as she got to the little French café across town on time. Duncan's mouth worked helplessly again. Was he trying to delay her? He hadn't been this incoherent on previous meetings. "I was thinking maybe we could talk about him over lunch, sometime?" he asked, sounding suddenly bashful.

She made a show of looking at her watch. "You know, that'd be reeeeally interesting, but Christmas is a half week away, and then there's New Year's." Which, if all went according to plan, she wouldn't be spending alone. "So not for a couple of weeks. At least." Smiling cordially, she walked past him to the staircase.

"You know, the average street life of a homeless male is twenty years shorter than that of the average population," she heard Duncan stammer out behind her.

"Mel's not going anywhere," she said. Beneath her feet, the stairs creaked like old bones.

"I'm just trying to help. I wish you would too."

She turned on the stairs, annoyed. "Aren't there other homeless in the city you could be saving? Why this one?"

"He's only three blocks from Advent House."

"So it's just proximity? Is it hurting your pride he's eluding you?"

Was that hurt on his face at her question? "No, it's not an issue of pride. It's about . . . it's about this quote: *I am the good shepherd. I know my sheep and my sheep know me, just as the Father knows me and I know the Father, and I lay down my life for the sheep.*" He leaned on his crutches and took a step forward. "And no, I'm not a religious nut. I try to be slightly spiritual, but I'm not denominational. I only always liked that image of the shepherd in the field, searching for the one lost sheep. Isn't that what the holiday season is about?"

Religious talk made Keely uncomfortable. "It's not about shopping?"

"No. Finding things. Like how the shepherds and wise men found the baby Jesus in the cradle. Or how Santa found Rudolph. You know. Won't you guide my sleigh tonight?" Duncan judged Keely's wide-eyed expression. "Oh dear."

Funny. When he'd started quoting scripture, Keely had immediately assumed that Duncan was indeed some sort of religious fanatic. She remembered a painting from her childhood Sunday school room of a morose and wan Christ, somewhat improbably hefting a sheep in his arms as he bore it back to its fold. "I never got that," she said aloud. Why was she even prolonging this conversation when she had a dinner to get to? "I mean, okay, I understand the metaphor and it's all very pretty. No offense to the sheep it-self . . . I'm sure it's a very nice sheep . . . but it's only one stupid sheep out of a whole flock. Why risk life and limb and neglect the rest just for one animal? It doesn't make sense." Her voice rose with impatience. "And listen. Who says that a single sheep isn't happy out there on its own? Maybe it's made its choice. How can someone else decide it needs to be taken back in? It could be having a fine old time. Explain *that* to me."

His strong forearms clutched the grips of his aluminum supports as he stared down at her without a word. Keely had offended him, somehow. Did it matter? She wouldn't see Duncan again. Of course, she'd assumed that before, and look what had happened.

Why didn't he have an answer?

She was going to be late. Keely turned and made her way downstairs. It wasn't until she had crossed the tiled foyer and laid a hand on the front door that she heard his voice calling out, choked. "Kelly." With her mouth twisting wryly—would he *ever* get her name right?—she found him watching her still. "Maybe," he said, his voice echoing through the cavernous front hallway, "just maybe, the sheep doesn't even know how lost it really is." His voice sounded low and sad. "Have a nice date."

She shut the door behind her, perplexed by the entire en-counter. Why had he tracked her down to talk about sheep? Yet there was something about the image of Duncan roaming the cold and snowy streets, shepherd's crook in hand, that gave her the twinge every urbanite felt from time to time, faced with the more unfortunate. How many times had she thought, or heard people she knew say, *Oh, I really should do some volunteer work* or *Maybe I should help out at the soup kitchen on Thanksgiving*? How many times had anything been done about it?

It was almost unseemly, eating a nice dinner after that lecture. "You're distracted," Neil suggested over their sweet and sticky Crêpes Mont-Blanc.

"Mmmm," she agreed, taking a delicate bite of the pastry and ice cream. Then, realizing how inattentive she must sound, she put down her fork, caught his eye, and smiled. Why in the world was she letting some nagging social do-gooder ruin her evening? It had been a perfect first date. Neil's manners were impeccable from the moment he had risen from the table and pulled out her chair, to the way he hadn't even commented on her twenty-minutes plus late-ness, through the way he ordered for her and the way he had kept the conversation flirty, but not at all beleaguering. How was she repaying him? "I'm being dull as dishwater," she said.

"No, not at all. Hey, this time of year is absolutely crazy, don't worry about being a little tired at the end of the day." His grin was so infectious that she found herself sharing in it as she picked up her fork and flaked away more of their shared dessert. "Are you still shopping?"

"Oh, man. Lots," she said, quite truthfully.

"Boy, the shop owners must love to see you coming."

"You have no idea," she volunteered, only remembering at the last minute with a bit of panic that he still didn't know the money she spent belonged to other people.

"I'm just glad you had a spare evening to squeeze me in." Was that his knee against hers, under the table? Indeed it was. Beneath another alpaca turtleneck sweater and the same jacket in which she'd met him, it was impossible to ignore that Neil was one of those guys with a deep chest and Nautilused, Bowflexed thighs; even his knee felt as if it could probably flex a hundred-pound barbell without breaking a sweat.

"Oh, please. It was my pleasure."

"Pleasure enough that I could see you tomorrow night?"

Caught slightly off-guard at the sudden offer, Keely considered. Did she want to? Yes. Hell yes! Did she want to agree immediately? And admit that her social life lately had consisted solely of a best girlfriend, a homeless man, and the liquor salesman who provided her with miniature bottles of booze? "Well—" She pretended to be considering a mental datebook.

"There's a great place I think you'd love in Little India. My treat," he suggested hastily as the waiter arrived bearing a tray boasting a velvet wallet. The folder was hung with a tasseled gold rope, making it look more like an early Christmas gift than the bill it surely must be. "Should I get this?" he asked, taking the wallet and nodding at the waiter.

"If tomorrow's going to be your treat," she said smoothly, "then tonight should be mine."

She'd expected at least a token protest, but Neil handed over the tab with a toothy smile. It was larger than she'd expected . . . apparently Neil had indulged in a few drinks, waiting for her. Still, that was all right. Her fault, after all. She'd had an idea during dessert, mulling over what Duncan had said. Keely summoned the waiter and presented him both with her credit card and a request for a small takeout order. "For a friend," she explained to Neil.

"So thoughtful," he murmured, lifting his glass and downing what was left of his apple martini. "To friends. And thanks for dinner," he added, his eyes meeting hers. "I really enjoyed our time together."

"Me too." She responded with no less than the truth. Keely had enjoyed the evening immensely, though somehow she felt it should have been more than small talk about movies she hadn't seen and parties at summer retreats she hadn't attended, or the finer nightspots around town where she'd never been. Keely had been smart, she felt, not to pre-

NAME:_____

ADDRESS:_____

_____

_____

TELEPHONE:_____

E-MAIL: _____

_____ I want to pay by credit card.

__ Visa _____ __ MasterCard _____ __ Discover

Account Number:_____

Expiration date: _____

SIGNATURE:_____

*Send this form, along with $2.00 shipping
and handling for your FREE books, to:*

Love Spell Romance Book Club
20 Academy Street
Norwalk, CT 06850-4032

*Or fax (must include credit card
information!) to: 610.995.9274.
You can also sign up on the Web
at www.dorchesterpub.com.*

Offer open to residents of the U.S. and
Canada only. Canadian residents, please
call 1.800.481.9191 for pricing information.

tend she'd been to any. Neil certainly gave the impression of running with quite a moneyed crowd.

When she stepped into the cab Neil thoughtfully hailed for her outside the restaurant, she realized she knew all the funny quips Neil had mouthed to entertainment moguls in the Hamptons. She knew where he shopped and what restaurants he liked. Neil was perfect for her, but she knew precious little about him, or where he lived, or what he did for a living, or how he'd grown up. Yet had she been any more honest with him? He still had no clue that she was only a personal shopper and not a Tiffany's girl with a fat checkbook. Why hadn't the date been more *real?*

"Moving too fast," she said, sighing.

"Lady, I'm only going thirty," the cabdriver retorted.

Not to laugh was impossible. The driver must have thought she was crazy, but Keely could live with it. No, *she* was moving too fast. She and Neil had only just been on their first date, for crying out loud. How much could two people learn about each other on a first date? She should be counting her blessings that Neil hadn't turned out a total dud!

He had been great, hadn't he? He'd done all the right things. He'd pulled out her chair and complimented her dress and hair. Well-spoken and dressed, perfect posture . . . Keely loved guys who took care of their appearance. Most importantly, Neil had made Keely feel good. Despite her abstraction, his asking her out had made her feel attractive and worthy of attention. And she was, wasn't she? She'd worked hard the last three years for a perfect evening like that.

The driver agreed to wait two dozen feet down the street; the yellow cab's brake lights cast a red glow over the wet and icy sidewalks. By now, Keely knew the way to the old carpet storefront as well as she knew the women's depart-ments of most of the major department stores. She was almost used to the steam's mossy, slightly urine-tinged odor.

Keely knew better than to be completely complacent on the dark street, even though cars sliced down the street at a regular clip—it was the city, after all. It paid to be wary. Yet she wasn't at all frightened by the shaggy figure rocking back and forth on an overturned paint bucket he was using as a seat. "Melchior?" she asked.

He was in one of his mumbling fits. When she repeated his name, he growled, "I heard you. Go to hell."

"Hey, I brought you some good stuff, buddy." She held up the bag of food from the restaurant: a hefty portion of chicken, a length of French bread, and an apple tart in individual Styrofoam containers. "It's kind of a cold night, and I thought you might like some food." He refused to look at her. She tried to make a joke of it. "Come on, I know magi have to eat."

Her words trailed off when without warning, Mel reached up, tore off his Burger King crown, and tossed it to the ground. "Get the hell away, you high-falutin' stinking know-it-all." Once on his feet, he kicked the paint bucket so that it rebounded against the wall and bounced onto the sidewalk with a hollow, plastic thud. "You don't listen to a single goddamned thing I say. Get the fuck away and take that stink of perfume with you, piece of trash. Fraud. Fraud! Yes, you. Stop looking at me!"

From anyone else she wouldn't have stood having these curses flung her way. This behavior was Mel's random synapses firing, though. Poor guy. "I just wanted to bring you something. Not the usual stuff," she added hastily. She'd not brought any Bacardi or Smirnoff. She stood there, waiting for his thanks. What was she supposed to say now to Duncan's lost sheep? Was she expected to thank him for the cryptic guidelines that in the last two weeks had made her several thousand dollars richer? Was she supposed to thank him for leading her to Neil? Wasn't that why she had come? "Oh, by the way." She tried to keep her tone light. "I've got a last-minute request. One of my clients—"

"I must look like a goddamned slot machine to you," he interrupted, angry. "No more advice. I ain't getting paid enough for this gig. The stars aren't what they used to be." His voice grew louder with every word until it sounded positively thunderous. Against the red light, the shaggy hair, long beard, and bulky layers of clothing stacked high on his shoulders lent him the appearance of a vision of the damned. "Growing dimmer century after century until we can barely see them. The Big Bang, baby. They're flying farther and farther from us with every second and nobody cares. You think it's all Jeanne Dixon and Sydney Omarr. You're a stupid fool."

"It's coq au vin." What a horrifyingly inappropriate thing to say. She sounded as if she was talking to him like a child. "That's not what it sounds like. *Coq* means chicken—"

Melchior's head jerked back; he buried his face in his hands and lowered it down until he was almost nearly doubled over. "So lost," he mourned. "Why can't I find my way?" When she stood there, stock still, he roared through his fingers, *"Go away!"*

"I'll just set this down here." Trying to sound calming, she used two fingers to place the neatly folded bag on the grate in front of him.

"Go away!"

"Maybe I'll stop by tomorrow to see how—"

His roar should have deafened her ears. With a vicious lunge, the magus kicked the paper bag so that it missed Keely by inches as it flew into the air. The Doppler sound of a car horn startled her, followed by a crunch of paper and foam; she didn't need to look into the street to know that her gift was most likely spread out over the road. "Don't be so ungrateful! I'm only trying to—"

"GO AWAY GO AWAY GO AWAY!" Over and over Melchior shouted the words. His head and body thrashed about as if her presence brought him actual physical pain. Keely took one step back, then two, and before a moment had passed she found herself running as fast as she could to the cab, frightened for her life.

"And don't ever come back!" She slammed the door behind her.

The cabdriver had apparently not heard any of the ruckus save for the brief second when his vehicle's door had been opened. As he pulled away from the curb, he leaned over and peered out the side. "Damn, some crazies in this neighborhood tonight," he commented. "You okay?"

Keely nodded and pulled her jacket around her to still the shivers convulsing her spine. She pressed her face against the window. The last glimpse she had of Melchior, right before the building obscured him from sight, was of him holding his hands to the skies, layers of long coats hanging from his arms like robes. His mouth was open, and a column of vapor spilled into the air, curling into a cloud above his twitching, shaking head. The magus was howling angrily at the heavens.

Was heaven even listening?

Chapter Ten

"Don't sweat the small stuff. People change their minds. Roll with the punches." Nadine's advice was as swift and sure as a rapier thrust. Jab, twist, withdraw. She paused both to let her words sink in and to take a long sip of her coffee, black and hot. "Oh my God, you would not believe who I saw in Le Pain Quotidien yesterday. Guess."

"This is not a punch. This is a kick in the gut." Trust Nadine to minimize Keely's conversation and maximize her own!

"Guess! Come on, play the game."

The conversation would get back around to her crisis if she hazarded a random celebrity. "Woody Allen?" She sighed.

"Close! Helena Bonham Carter!" When Keely didn't change expressions, Nadine thwacked her. "Oh come on, you love her. She was wearing these big Jackie O. glasses and reading a newspaper and she looked freakin' *fabulous*."

"Fascinating, Nadine, but forgive me if I don't give a shit." Keely had her friend's attention now; Nadine's eyebrows rose into an upright and locked position. "Sorry. I'm pissed off."

"Because this Hermitage guy wants you to make a return? I told you, it's stupid to get so invested in your clients." The bistro waiter arrived to clear the table of their lunch plates. Nadine, who had precisely four French fries left on her plate, put out a hand to indicate she wasn't done.

How in the world could she explain it? "It's not just a return. It's *five* returns." The jewelry had been one of the first suggestions Melchior had made after the Perfect Present triumph. Old Tasteful Trinkets had declared his most special lady friend would love the lariat necklace with its pendant of multiple diamonds when Keely had purchased it from the Alphabet City jeweler, and that the others would love the various gem-encrusted bracelets she'd selected. He'd loved the prices even more. Keely opened up her purse, lifted the cover off the biggest of the five boxes, and tipped it so Nadine could see. "Mr. Armitage is now a dissatisfied customer who's not going to have anything to give in the morning."

Nadine seemed fascinated. "Really? Was he going to give them to his mistresses tomorrow? All of them?" she wanted to know. "Do they all come over at once for a big mistress party? Or do they arrive in shifts?"

Keely held up a fingertip in Nadine's face. "Point." She made a whooshing noise and mimed it flying right over her friend's head. "Hello. It's Christmas Eve. I failed the guy. I'm not going to be able to find anything before the stores close, and even if I could, it's too late. He's just buying them trips to St. Maarten's or something." She didn't even feel like hitting the shops that afternoon. All her clients were taken care of, at this point; she'd probably just return the jewels the day after Christmas like everyone else.

Nadine seemed unimpressed. "Sweetie, it's a business." Nice advice, but Nadine didn't understand how insulted Keely felt. "How about you come to dinner tomorrow around two?"

"I'm going to feel like a third wheel around you and C.J." If only she could get Neil to make plans for more than one day in advance!

"My mom and her new boyfriend are coming too, so don't worry. You'll be a fifth wheel. Are you seeing that guy, what's-his-name, tonight?"

Was there a note of jealousy in her friend's inquiry? Keely rather thought so. Oh, Nadine had always been telling her to get out and date more often, but now that she was seeing someone, her tone had changed. "Neil," she supplied. "And yes I am. It's getting pretty intense." She waggled her eyebrows playfully.

Nadine was having none of it. "Oh yeah, the mystery man. Still buying his dinners?"

"Oh stop. Only twice." Three times, really, three nights in a row. The first had been their first date, and then the next at the Indian place the night after, when Neil had accidentally left his credit cards at home. It could happen to anyone! Last night, the tab had simply sat between them for so long without either of them reaching for it that finally Keely simply paid up when Neil excused himself to visit the men's room. Nadine didn't need to know though— she'd only make a federal case. Jealousy, pure and simple. In men, Nadine had settled. Keely wouldn't.

"Are you guys—?" Nadine waggled her eyebrows.

"No." Oh, there'd been some light making out after the dates, but where were they supposed to go for more? He'd never volunteered his place, and Keely was afraid to take him to hers, because the minute he stepped through the door he'd know more about her real income than he'd ever want to know. She had to tell him sometime, though. Deceit, even by omission, was making her uncomfortable. Maybe tonight?

Nadine only had one parting shot as she gulped down the last of her fries and collected her coat and purse. "Maybe he'd like a lariat necklace." When she saw Keely's mouth twitch, she grinned and hugged her tight. "Merry Christmas, sweetie. Do whatever makes you happy, okay?"

Happy? What was that? Funny, really, Keely reflected on the cab ride home. She'd spent years with her nose deep in every kind of magazine. She'd clipped coupons and recipes and taken quizzes and read about the love lives of celebrities. She'd learned how to decorate and how to dress, and about who collected what catalog and shopped at which store. Today she felt as if she hadn't learned a damned thing from them.

Using her scarf to clear a patch of vapor from the side window, Keely looked out at the people the cab passed— laughing, happy couples. Families carrying bags as they made their last-minute purchases. Stressed-looking men, mostly single, frantically dashing in and out of storefronts. Many of the street-level windows they passed had been garlanded with wreaths or lights or elaborate Christmas displays heavy on the fireplaces and Santa hats and sparkling, decorated trees. She loved the city in December with its arrays of red and green. It was a time of year when people seemed determined to be happier. Even a new layer of thickly falling snow was doing its best to take the edge off the city's harshness, and to soften and obscure its dirt and grime. So much whiteness, soft and fleecy. Like lamb's wool.

The thought of sheep only made her vaguely restless. The last encounter with Melchior had left her feeling—well, jinxed. After all, he'd sent her running, then within twenty-four hours Mr. Armitage had called with his regrets. Yet other emotions overwhelmed her silly paranoia. She felt sad that her attempt to make his life a little better had been rebuffed. Angry that all that good food had been wasted. Confused over his reaction to her. Mel had called her a fraud, a wannabe, and a fool, if not far worse. What had she done to merit his abuse? Nothing. Absolutely nothing.

Duncan had been right. Melchior needed help. After the holidays, when things had calmed down, she would maybe . . . she didn't know. Do some volunteer work, or something. It was nearly impossible to not feel a twinge of guilt at that unlikely promise to herself. But she'd do something. She owed it to the man who'd single-handedly gotten her through the season.

"Only a week ago I thought I'd be alone for Christmas Eve."

"And now you're not." Something about Neil's voice made her feel surrounded by soft satin sheets. To her ear it sounded incredibly sexy, yet comfortable. Whenever it dropped to a confidential whisper, she felt blushes rising from the most sensitive parts of her spine to lace their way around her neck to her cheeks.

"No, I'm not." He had been waiting for her in front of the Italian restaurant when her cab pulled up, and stood by with a scarf stretched as wide as it could go as she got out and leant over to pay the driver. Afterward, they stood on the sidewalk under the outstretched wrapping, smiling at each other as if they couldn't stop.

"You look fantastic," he said, not taking his eyes from

hers for a second. She said a pretty thank-you. "You hungry?"

"Famished!" she said, then wondered when it was she'd started to talk like Hayley Mills in a sixties Disney movie.

Laughing, they pushed open the wooden outer double doors to Geppetto's and slid across the slick red tile to the next set of doors. Neil tugged on the handle, only to find them locked. "Of all the . . ." he said, rattling the doors until the glass shook.

"They can't be closed, can they?" Keely asked. "On Christmas Eve?" Maybe they could. The most excitement she'd had other years on the twenty-fourth was watching *It's a Wonderful Life* on television with a pan of Jiffy Pop in her lap.

"No, there're people inside."

Neil's repeated assault on the doors had caught the attention of a passing staff member, who in stature and mustache length reminded Keely of the little Italian plumber gamely running up girders in Donkey Kong. From the inside he twisted the lock and poked his head out, though he seemed to have no intention of letting them in. "We're closed," he apologized.

Neil gestured to where a handful of the dozens of tables still had couples lingering over coffee. "But you're still serving."

The little man shook his head. "Kitchen closed at six-thirty. We just have a few stragglers left." Neil looked at Keely; she looked back, her lips pulled into a disappointed point. "Sorry, guys," said the waiter. "It's Christmas Eve. Everyone wants to be with their families."

Neil smiled and shrugged. "No problem. We'll just find somewhere else to go, right?" he asked Keely.

"Sure!" she said. She didn't care if they had Italian or not.

"Good luck with that," said the waiter, retreating behind

the safety of the locked door. "Most places in this area shut down by six if not before. Night, folks. Merry Christmas."

Keely wished he'd have left the door open. The vestibule was freezing. "Okay, so what do we do?" she asked.

Neil's optimistic voice bounced around the small enclosure. "There're lots of restaurants in the area. Let's see what we can find." Keely nodded in agreement. So long as Neil kept his hand on her upper arm, she'd follow him anywhere.

The Italian plumber proved right, however. The upscale Vietnamese eatery next door was also dark and locked, as were the two Asian restaurants within walking distance of Geppetto's, a steak house, and a sandwich shop. Oddly, a gelato store still had its lights on and a bored scooper behind its counter, but walking around in the cold and precipitation hadn't put either of them in a mood for anything resembling the white stuff crunching underfoot. "Okay," Keely said at last. She hadn't at all minded traipsing about in the snow with Neil. On the contrary, it had felt like something of an adventure. The city seemed theirs for the taking, on the increasingly still and silent streets. Her feet were getting cold, however. "We need to make some kind of decision before it's too late. I'm worried about getting stuck without being able to hail a cab."

"I have the ability to hail taxis anywhere. I'm like a yellow checkered David Copperfield." His hair carried fat clusters of snowflakes, while hers felt merely sloppy and soaked. "Do you want me to get one? We could ride around, see if anyplace is open in another part of town."

As they faced each other, he removed his scarf and draped it over her head. She protested, laughing; he would be cold. Yet he proceeded with gentle fingers to knot it under her chin, and then held her by the elbows. "I think everything's going to be closed," she said, looking up into his face, moist from melting snow.

"I don't care where we eat." Once again she felt as if she were naked and sliding between satin sheets, so close to a cat's purr was his voice. "So long as it's with you."

"What if—" she suggested. A lump in her throat nearly kept her from proceeding. She was about to take a fairly big step here. "What if we went back to . . . my place?" Keely tried to read a reaction in his eyes, but found them inscrutable. Hastily she tried to backpedal. "I mean, we could try to order a pizza, or I might have something light I could throw together, like . . ."

"Sssshh," he commanded softly, putting his raised index finger over her mouth.

". . . pasta," she finished softly, the sides of her lips pursing out around the digit's gentle pressure.

Neil waited until she had finished speaking before removing it. "I," he said, dropping words much as Keely imagined him shucking single items of clothing and letting them fall to the floor, "would love . . . to go home . . . with you."

The declaration enveloped her like a sheepskin coat. For a moment, looking into the impossible green of his eyes, she even forgot about how cold it was. The spell was broken only when Neil raised his arm and whistled. As if waiting in the wings to appear, a yellow cab made its slow way over the snow-covered street, its headlights at first barely visible through the falling flakes. "That *was* magic!" she exclaimed.

He held the door open and waited until she was safely in before walking around the taxi to the other side. Keely quickly gave the driver her address. At least the heat inside the car was set at blasting; she would dry out by the time they reached her apartment.

On the other hand, Neil didn't seem to mind, much less

notice, the dampness of her clothes. Scarcely had the door closed behind him and he'd given a friendly nod to the driver, then he snaked his arm behind Keely's back and pulled her close so that her head rested on his shoulder. "I think that this evening will turn out to be pretty special after all," Neil murmured in her ear as he slipped off his glove and stroked her hair from her face.

"I think it just might," she promised him. How much more perfect could this night be? Basking inside the dark hothouse of the cab after running through the streets gave her a glowing feeling inside. Outside the snow was falling so thickly that the passing streetlights looked like distant stars. What did she need to see, though? Her hands could find their way from her lap to his shoulders without the need for light, and his lips had no difficulty finding hers. For several long minutes Keely heard nothing but small noises that told their own story: the sound of their bodies shifting on the cab's vinyl seats. The long metallic ruffle as she released his coat zipper. Soundless thuds as he unbuttoned her suede coat, followed by satisfied moans as they pressed their lips together, as if they were trying to merge into each other. The embarrassed cough of the driver.

Something hard pressed against her back, boring its way into her kidney. Removing her lips from his seemed like actual work, but with a great deal of effort she managed. "I think one of your crutches got loose," she murmured.

"What in the world are you talking about?" Neil's surprise forced her eyes open; it was like surfacing from a wonderful dream to the reality of an alarm blaring at top volume. How in the world could she have confused Neil with Duncan? They were in totally different leagues! If only she could press her cheeks against the windows to cool her flush of embarrassment. Neil, in the meantime, peered outside. "We're on the Queensboro Bridge," he announced. It took Keely a moment to understand that his surprise came from her total lack of it. "I thought we were going to your place."

"I live in Queens," she explained.

"Queens?"

"You know. Opposite of Kings."

It was difficult to read his expression in the dark. "I know what Queens is, silly. I'm sure there are some pretty parts to Queens. I guess I just never imagined you living there." Neil's chin, slightly stubbled, brushed against her neck. His cologne smelled of citrus and the woodsy outdoors. "Now I have a reason to visit, hmmm?"

"Mmm-hmmm!" Keely affirmed, laughing as he chomped on her neck with lip-covered teeth. She was almost afraid to say anything in case another verbal faux pas flew out.

"What's the matter?" Neil asked, stroking her head. "You got distant."

Normally Neil's touch would have tingles waltzing across her skin, but with cold and snow all around, it only made her uncomfortable. The weather might have been painting a storybook Christmas meant to be safely enjoyed on the warm side of a window, but all Keely could think about were the city's lost lambs, and the shepherds who sought them. "Nothing," she said, trying to keep her tone light despite the shadow cast across her mood. "Everything's fine."

By the time the cab's wheels crunched onto her street, Keely was grateful for the camouflaging inches of snow unloosed by the skies; the older buildings around hers looked positively picturesque with several inches of white obscuring their chipped stone stairs and grubby iron rails that wanted a coat of paint. "All this is yours?" exclaimed Neil as they alighted from the cab, his eyes taking in the bulk of the old house. "Impressive. I can see why you'd want to live all the way out here."

Embarrassment fluttered and nested in her stomach. Would now be an appropriate time to tell him she only rented rooms in what amounted to an enormous dilapidation? "Don't get too excited," she warned him.

"Oh, I can see it's a fixer-upper," he commented, as the cab pulled off into the snow-clogged street. He followed her to the front door, where Keely fumbled for her keys. What was Neil going to say to the multiple post boxes inside, warped with corrosion and use? Would he notice the little pile of plaster dust by the staircase? The flaking ceiling above? "But you know, a lot of people go in for that kind of thing, particularly when they've got the money to. . . ."

The smell of old wood rot billowed out as she released the door. "My place is upstairs," she explained, leading him across the foyer and upward. The floorboards crackled and snapped underfoot. Long ago when she'd moved in, Keely had found the commotion a comforting sound, but now every step brought fresh mortification. Keely couldn't bear to look over her shoulder to witness Neil's expression . . . if he had one.

"Here we go." The first door on the left had been battered by decades of previous residents. All the wood scars Keely's eyes had overlooked for years now suddenly seemed vividly highlighted in the flickering light of the upper hallway. Still, Neil said nothing as she unlocked the deadbolts.

"It's just the one room?" he finally asked. Since he'd walked through her door, she'd watched his eyes darting around her home, taking in her furniture, the chenille throws, the pillows, the rugs underfoot—everything to the colorful candles arranged on the grand old mantel. Did she see judgment there? It was hard to tell. "I thought . . ." He fell silent.

"No, there's a kitchen and bedroom . . . listen." Keely set her purse on the table by the door and moved closer, steeling herself. Why hadn't she been truthful from the beginning? "I hope you're not disappointed. We never really talked about, you know, practical things, and . . ." Words seemed to be slipping away from her. "I'm a personal shopper. I'm only . . . I'm planning to move to the Lenox Hill area next month, though."

"I see."

"You're disappointed." In the taxi she'd felt weightless; now every part of her seemed dragged down and bloated by gravity. Keely couldn't read a thing from his expression, and that frightened her.

"No. Oh, hey, no." Neil's tone was back to normal. "You know, I just hadn't thought about what kind of place you might live in. This is great. This is more than great." He grinned and patted his hands together, trying to warm them.

She had to make good. For a moment there, Keely had thought Neil was going to bolt. "Take your coat off. Are you hungry? Should I make something for dinner?" He still stood there, looking around, finally shaking his head. "Or do you want to do . . . something else?" Please, please, she thought, hoping he'd realized she didn't mean watching *It's a Wonderful Life*.

The offer got a response from him. He stopped his nervous hand-patting. His eyes glinted as if he'd like nothing more. "Something else sounds absolutely fantastic."

"I was hoping you'd say that." Keely removed her coat, much relieved, and tossed it carefully over the sofa. The evening was back on track, just as she'd hoped. "Why don't I run to the bedroom and . . . clean up a little. If you'd like, there's wine in the refrigerator, and some glasses in the cupboard over the shelf." *Just please don't notice the roach traps,* she mentally begged.

His head inclined toward hers until their lips met in a slow, sweet kiss. "That sounds wonderful. Why don't you . . . go make things comfy?"

"Take off your coat," she suggested a second time.

"Don't worry about that." He smiled at her and gave her a second kiss, this one fleeting. "Take your time."

The bedroom wasn't that bad of a mess, she decided in her frenzied survey. Thank goodness she wasn't a slob by nature; all she really had to do was clear her chair of the stockings she'd left there, sweep some of the items from her dresser into its top drawer, and then tidy up the pillows. A spritz of perfume on her neck and the back of her knees, a light brushing of her hair, and she was ready. More than ready. Itching for it, in fact.

"Did you uncork a bottle?" she asked, trotting back into the living room in her bare feet. There was no answer. Keely craned her neck to peer down the narrow hallway leading to her even narrower kitchen. "Neil?"

He wasn't in the kitchen. He wasn't in the living room.

"Neil?" she asked, knocking on the half-open door of the bathroom. Surely he wouldn't be, you know, doing his business with the door open? No, the bathroom was deserted. And she knew he wasn't in the bedroom. . . .

Neil had gone. The front door was closed; he'd left her apartment and shut it behind him. Why—?

Because she'd lied to him. The certainty that she'd disappointed Neil made Keely take one uncertain step, then another, then more, until she was racing around in panicked circles in her living room. He'd been polite until the moment she stepped in the bedroom, and then he'd made a polite getaway. Stupid, stupid! Why hadn't she listened to her instincts and . . . she could still make it up to him. She could explain how idiotic she'd been!

"Neil?" she cried as she ran out of the apartment. From below, she heard the faint sound of a latch. Was it the building's front door? Or had it been in her imagination, the sound of Neil abandoning her vision of a perfect life and leaving behind only a faceless shadow in his place? Her feet scraped against the battered wood floor as she skidded to the head of the stairs.

Shoes. A coat. Keys. In her head, Keely itemized the items she needed. She could still catch up with him. Scrambling back to her apartment, she overbalanced on the stoop and nearly tumbled onto the floor. Then she froze.

Sitting on the table, where she'd placed it only a few minutes before, her small handbag gaped wide open. The sight of her bag's contents emptied out onto the chair nearby made her gasp for air. Who—?

Already she knew the answer. He'd left alone her small tin of Altoids and her tissues and all the other things that hadn't mattered, and had gone right for her valuables. Her wallet he'd thrown on the floor; the five twenties she'd folded inside were missing. Keely's thinking, her breath, even her heart slowed; surely the world had spun to a stop. If she walked outside, she'd find snowflakes suspended in mid-air.

Heartbeats passed. At last she was able to turn her head. Her identification lay upon the floor, partly under an occasional table across the room. Keely had always hated that photo of herself, pale and wan, though somewhere in the back of her mind she knew it looked ruddy compared to her trembling, shaking self. She shuffled to pick it up, then froze in place once more. Her mouth opened, but no words emerged. Instead, she only heard a series of grating noises that hurt her ears.

The larger, capacious shoulder bag she'd carried that morning, which had been sitting on her sofa since earlier that afternoon, lay wide open. Someone else, not her, ran toward it and began to dig through its contents; Keely watched dreamily from the ceiling, distant from the noise and the pain and the horror.

One box, two boxes . . . five boxes, all empty.

What was that noise? The nagging, insistent sound dragged her back into her body. Her phone was ringing! Maybe Neil was calling from the corner, ready to explain, ready to say it was all a joke. A dream.

She wrenched her body into action, but not before her answering machine clicked on. "Hello?" She heard a woman's voice through the speaker, familiar and wheedling. "Is this Keely? This is Miss Adeline Mercer. Keely, are you there, dear? Oh, of course you're not. You're probably out having a wonderful, magical Christmas Eve. I'm afraid mine was quite ruined, dear. Brother Warren and I exchanged our gifts this evening, you see, and as it turned out—I don't know how it could have happened, I really don't—it turns out that he already *had* that toy you bought for him." As if in a nightmare, Keely inched closer and closer to the phone until she hovered above it, watching the answering machine tape whirl around and around. Her heart had stopped beating by then. In its place pulsed something cold, dark, and hard. "I'm really quite cross, though I suppose it's partly my own fault. It already sits in one of the display cases in his living room—I showed you photographs of his living room, dear. Perhaps you glimpsed the fire engine in one of them and when you saw it . . . well, I don't believe in casting blame, dear, and perhaps I should have remembered it myself, but—"

Without emotion, Keely lifted the handset two inches up. For a second she heard a tiny, tinny voice from the receiver. "Hello? Hello? Keely, is that—" Then she dropped it back down.

Thousands of dollars of jewelry, gone. Neil, vanished. What in the world . . . *who* in the world had called down disaster upon her?

"Melchior," she whispered. The word fell flatly from her tongue, and vanished into the emptiness of the room.

Chapter Eleven

A crown lay against the wall beyond the steam grate, visible only by one of its paper jewels poking through inches of snow. With two fingers, Keely fished it out. "Mel?" She sounded like a little girl calling for her daddy. "Melchior?"

The vagrant simply wasn't there.

Keely snuffled her runny, frozen nose, wiped her face of its fresh batch of tears, and turned around and around, hoping that Mel would loom up behind her in the same dramatic fashion as the first time they'd met. Nothing. The grate was an oasis of relative comfort, despite the moisture billowing up into the sweatshirt hood covering her head and the freezing Chinooks threatening to flatten her against the building. "Where are you?" As if rebuffed by some invisible wall, her shout stopped at the grating's edge, then vanished into the howl of the wind.

The pain rising in her chest burned like molten lava. Keely reeled back against the plate-glass window and raised her face to heaven, her silent plea for help rewarded only by snowflakes falling onto her face. Cold as she was, each felt like a tiny slap. She had been crying since the moment she'd grabbed a sweatshirt and jacket and run pell-mell out of her apartment. Once again, sobs burst from her, uncontrollable spasms of fear and regret that agonized Keely to her very marrow.

Something had changed here, she noticed once she opened her eyes. Since her last visit, someone had removed the yellowed newspapers from the display window. There was no longer a declaration of ORIENT ARE; they'd scraped away any trace of the old-fashioned painted letters. She followed the window around to the front, where a new felt tip-lettered placard read, HAPPY NOODLE AND SHRIMP! GRAND OPENING 1/6!

Somewhere in the city, the king of Orient Are wandered in the storm without his crown, displaced by a noodle restaurant. Keely slumped against the window, guilt forcing her to agonize. It was all her fault. Everything was her fault. If she'd only helped Melchior instead of using him! If she'd only noticed something was wrong with Neil instead of trying to force him into her life. If only she hadn't been so stupid, spending so much time on an illusion! Where could Mel have gone?

Stepping back onto the sidewalk was a torture. Every step chilled her already-soaked Reeboks and the sharp pangs seemed to set her feet on fire, even as her body trembled from the cold. She'd forgotten gloves, so Keely pulled the cuffs of the sweatshirt out of her jacket arms and clutched them over her fingers as she walked. Three blocks, she told herself. Duncan's shelter was only three blocks away, wasn't that right? Maybe Mel had finally sought refuge.

She doubted it.

The snow made it difficult to tell even on what street she was wandering; it fell so thickly that her vision was restricted to a dozen feet. She was having to constantly wipe flakes from her eyebrows and the apples of her cheeks. Where had everyone disappeared to? The city seemed so empty that for a terrified moment she wondered if the entire population of Manhattan had evaporated from the island. But no, Keely could hear the sounds of a car across the street, and here were a couple approaching, hands clasped. They were well-heeled and in their fifties, the sort of couple she had always secretly envied for their marriage's longevity. "Please," she croaked, holding out Melchior's creased and soggy crown. The man tugged at his wife's hand and moved her to the far side away from Keely, veering away. No, she thought in confusion. They misunderstood! "I'm just looking for a shelter. . . ."

"Harold," she heard the woman say with reproach. For a moment, they stopped mid-course.

Wearing an expression that betrayed resentment, the man dug in his pocket and then gingerly approached. He dropped three dollar bills into her outstretched palm. Keely looked at them numbly, not comprehending. "Don't spend it all on liquor," he commanded, then added, "Merry Christmas," as if he hoped the words stung.

"Merry Christmas!" called out the woman, trying to sound lighthearted. They drifted away into the gray.

The bills made no noise when she crushed them. They had thought she was a homeless person, she marveled. Well, with her wet sweatpants and her raggedy sweatshirt and jacket, her tear-stained face, why should she be surprised? If she'd come across anyone so solitary and down on her luck that night, she would have thought the same. Yet why had the man been so . . . *mean?* He'd only given her three lousy dollar bills—hardly enough to spend on booze if she'd wanted it—and then acted as if she should be *grateful* for it. Well, damn him to hell. She wasn't some scum he could treat like she was scum! She was worth something, damn it. Just because he couldn't tell beneath the clothing and the bedraggledness . . .

Another wave of regret, molten and poisonous, enflamed her lungs. Had she behaved with such off-handed, thoughtless noxiousness to Melchior? She had. Nadine had. Very likely they all had, day after day, week after week. Small wonder the homeless man had abdicated his makeshift kingdom. She hoped he was somewhere warm right now, and safe.

Three blocks. How far had she walked? Surely five times that many, in the last hour. Twice she had managed to find her way back to the old orient area rug store and then set off in a different direction. Now she was totally lost. Even the horizontal faces of the street signs had been covered with snow, as if conspiring to help her lose her way. From time to time she called out Mel's name, but she knew she'd lost hope of finding him. Under the hood her ears were numb; she had been clutching the cuffs of her sweatshirt so tightly that her every finger ached. She was soaked to the knees. Somewhere in her rambling the crown had come undone. It streamed behind her like a ribbon, flapping wildly as she forced herself to take step after step in the brutal tempest.

If this had been a movie, Keely thought bitterly as she trudged forward, by now an angel would have appeared to show her a vision of how much worse the world would be without her. Some kindly Samaritan would have stepped in to lend a kindly hand. In a movie, Melchior himself would have shown up, transformed, happy, healed—yet she knew it wouldn't happen. Maybe she was no George Bailey. Maybe the disappointments of the night and the disappointments yet to come were no more than she deserved.

One of the storm's dramatic cross-street whirlwinds caught her off-guard. She stumbled. The Burger King crown flew from her fingers. It was gone before she could even turn her head, vanished into the night, and with it disappeared all her glossy magazine dreams. All she wanted from life was warmth and refuge and kindness. Why had she even come out in this tempest? She must be crazy. What if she never found the shelter? What if she never found a subway station? What if she did, and found it closed? She had no idea of the time. Despair began to chill her more thoroughly than the frostbite she was certain she soon would be suffering. At least frostbite only affected her extremities—the despair penetrating her from the inside felt as if it would never thaw.

A harsh laugh astonished her. It was her own. "Oh, don't be such a drama queen," she muttered to herself. She had a little money in her pocket, plus three dollars more. All she had to do was find someplace where she could make a phone call, and she could be in a cab on the way home. If she swallowed a little of her pride, she could probably even call Nadine and have herself fished out of this mess. Her new intention invigorated her slightly. She lifted her head to see where she might go.

It was dark in every direction save one; in the block ahead Keely could barely make out a light suspended in midair. Forcing herself to put one foot in front of the other was more effort than it should have been, but she trudged forward until her confused eyes made out a star, blazing through the storm. No, it was a lighted sign hanging over the sidewalk, in the shape of a symmetrical, pointy-rayed sun. She drew nearer, blinking away the sting until she could see that someone had fixed duct tape in the center of the sign; she could make out the words *Sunshine Bakery* around the tape's edges.

Light shone around the blinds in the window. She banged at the door. "Hello?" she called. Someone had to answer. They *had* to. "Hello?"

After what seemed like long minutes, a small eye-level hatch set into the door opened. A thick-faced woman looked out and twitched her mouth as she took in Keely's disheveled appearance. "I'm real sorry, hon," she said in a deep voice, "but you know curfew's at eight. It's after eleven."

Without comprehension, Keely stared at her. "Curfew?" she repeated numbly. The woman had to let her in. She would batter the door down with her fists if worse came to worst.

"Honey, you look like you know the routine. We break the rules for one of you and suddenly everyone wants to stay out in the streets late. Christmas or no, shelter curfew is eight o'clock." At the word *shelter,* Keely felt a small jolt. She looked around wildly for a sign in the shopfront, but the window was obscured by snow. "Like I said, I'm real sorry, hon. If you hold on I'll call and see if you can get in at the—"

Already the woman was shutting the little door on her. "No!" Keely yelled. The noise rebounded around the small alcove, catching them both by surprise. "Is this Advent House? Is Duncan here?"

"Honey—"

"Duncan. Duncan Reese. I'm looking for Duncan Reese. Tell him it's Keely. No, I mean, tell him it's *Kelly*." The woman's expression had already been undecided, but at

Keely's uncertainty over her own name, she looked positively suspicious. The little door shut. For the first time in hours, Keely's stomach came to life, squirming in anticipation. Had the woman gone to fetch Duncan? Was Duncan even there this late? Over and over, she muttered a silent prayer that was as simple and basic as they came: *Please please please please please.*

Keely was leaning on the door with her forearms, forehead against her cold hands when it opened. "Whoa," said a familiar reedy voice. She had never been so glad to hear the clatter of aluminum. "Brianne, can you get me a blanket? And a wheelchair?"

"I'm okay," she murmured, trying to regain her balance. Duncan's warm hand on her frozen face felt like a branding iron, but she was too weak to protest.

"I *told* her about curfew," said the disapproving Brianne.

"I know she looks like hell, but she's a personal friend of mine," Keely heard Duncan say. She smiled at that, though it made her face ache. Personal friend. She had a personal friend. The sudden increase in temperature made her feel quite drunk. "Can you walk to my office, Kelly? Are you able to do that? Can you walk for me?"

Her legs were stiff and numb, but she could walk for him. The next few minutes were a blur of motion and noise as Keely found herself slowly maneuvered onto a sofa and covered with a blanket. Someone removed her soaking jacket and sweatshirt; someone else brought her coffee, hot and black. Duncan was there throughout it all, sitting on the floor with his legs splayed out, massaging the life back into her sore and frozen feet with his wonderful hands. His attention hurt; it felt as if he jabbed her with little icy daggers. "That's just a sign of the life coming back to them. You're very lucky," he scolded once she was warm enough to complain.

He gave a damn. Keely couldn't help it. A few hot tears made a getaway down her cheeks. "Hey, don't cry! Am I really hurting you?" he asked, struggling to pull himself up on the sofa beside her, and then lurching to his feet.

"No. I've just had a really bad evening," she said, trying to wipe away the rogue tears.

"You're fortunate you're not seriously hurt."

Keely completely forgot the miseries of her body as she studied Duncan crossing the office without crutches. One of his legs, she now saw, was several inches shorter than the other; from its unbending, rigid position, it appeared to be fused at the knee. He hopped on his better leg and limped until he reached his desk and the aluminum crutches that lay against them, and finally sat down at the chair with his hand on the phone. "Is there anyone I can call for you?" She shook her head, ashamed for staring. From above, the floor suddenly began reverberating with the muffled sounds of an out-of-tune piano playing the strains of "Hark the Herald Angels Sing." Duncan looked at the ceiling and grinned. "Normally we'd be long into lights-out by now, but what the heck. It's Christmas."

"I didn't know you could . . . you know. Get around without crutches." Duncan assumed a defensive expression she recognized with sympathy; it had been the same she had worn when the couple had given her a handout, not an hour before. "No, seriously, that's great."

He cleared his throat, looking at the floor. "I lost a wrestling match with an SUV a year and a half ago. I was told I wouldn't walk again, but . . ." He shrugged. "I lost a financial job. Couldn't handle the high pressure anymore. So I took over this place. With its own high pressures." He nestled the crutches under his arms, leaned forward until he was upright, and maneuvered back to the sofa. "Now. How about you tell me why you ended up here tonight?" When her lower lip trembled, and she once more started to tear up, embarrassed at the thought of admitting how far off the rails her life had gone this evening, Duncan reached out and put his hand on hers. His blue eyes were kind—so kind and gentle and understanding.

What had she ever done to deserve his warmth, this cup of coffee, his look of kindness? The simplest things overwhelmed her. Bit by bit she spilled out her story—how she had swapped money and booze for advice from Melchior, how Neil had run away, the loss of the jewelry, Miss Mercer's call, her wanderings in the snow—and through it all he held her hand and listened. Neither condescension nor judgment clouded his eyes. She talked all the way through a half-dozen Christmas carols on the tuneless piano above, grateful for the blanket, the hot liquid, and for the way he squeezed her fingers while she talked.

Only when she was done did he speak. "I don't understand why you went looking for Mel," he said at last.

"I don't know. I thought that if I made it up to him, everything would—" What? Fall back into place? Give her a happy ending? She saw him shaking his head. "I know. It was stupid. But when he wasn't there, I panicked for him."

"There are a few things we can do." Duncan sounded brisk and businesslike. "We can have the staff call area hospitals and precincts and shelters to see if there's anyone answering to his description. But Kelly, it might turn up a blank. Melchior might not even be his name. He might be back this week or the next or next summer, but there's a very good chance we'll never know where he went. It's just how this culture works. You know that, right? Don't hate me if we don't find him."

She nodded, biting her lip at his words. "I don't hate you anyway. And it's Keely," she said, voice trembling.

"I know your name," he said softly. Why didn't that confession surprise her? Without warning, he grinned as broadly as a kid on a schoolyard playground, totally disarming her. "We'll call around, okay? Now, about your other problems. The minute you're feeling better, you and I are going to get a cab to your place, where we're calling the police."

She hung her head. "I'm such a dope. I should've done that before I ran out of the house."

"You were emotional."

"I was stupid. I wasn't myself." she tried explaining to him, wanting him not to think badly of her. "I'm usually so careful. I think things through. I don't go out of my head!"

"Everyone needs to go out of their head once in a while," he murmured. "You just chose a really, really cold way to go about it."

Keely couldn't help herself. His frankness was so genuine that she closed the space between them and settled a kiss on his lips. His goatee tickled her chin; he smelled like hot coffee. "Oh, crap," she said, once she opened her eyes again. "I'm sorry."

She was ready with a hundred explanations, but Duncan's eyes shone as he said, "I'm not."

The admission warmed her. With every passing moment Keely could feel herself coming back to life. Overhead, the piano player switched to "Joy to the World." She thought for a moment before she spoke again. "Oh, man. I am just royally screwed by this jewelry thing." She rubbed her forehead. "I mean, I've got insurance. Apartment and business, both. I should be covered, right?"

"See? It's not that bad."

"But it'll take weeks for the insurance to settle, and I know Mr. Armitage isn't going to want to wait that long for his refund. I'll get reimbursed eventually, but I'll have to—" It would take nearly all the nest egg she'd saved for three years to pay him back what that jewelry cost. Good-bye, Lenox Hill. Hello for life, Queens. The taste in her mouth turned acrid, though her lips still smelled of coffee. "I guess I won't be moving next month."

She'd expected sympathy, but she only got, "Now, that I don't understand at all." Duncan's tone was brisk. "Why in the world would you want to move out of that great apartment into some soulless building? I'd kill for a place like yours. I mean, okay, the stairs are a little tough, but I managed."

It was exactly the tonic she needed. Although her regret was still there, Duncan's candor once more took away its sting. "Well," she admitted, "it was going to be a squeeze. I was barely going to be able to afford it." Keely thought of the day she'd moved into the Queens apartment, so much younger and optimistic than she was now. Yet she'd built her business from that apartment. It had served her well. "Queens isn't a bad place, I guess." Not at all.

"There you go," he said, squeezing her arm. A silence fell between them. Keely had dreaded the moment when they might run out of things to say. To her surprise, the quiet wasn't at all awkward. "Kelly," he said at last, "I'm going to sound incredibly eighth grade saying this, but I really like you. I'm sorry that Neil—" He couldn't bring himself to finish the sentence.

"Neil was a prick. And a thief."

"The first time I saw you—" Duncan blurted out, then stopped. Embarrassed, he ran a hand through his hair and stroked his goatee. "You looked like someone playing dress-up. No, don't get mad," he begged, though anger was the last thing on Keely's mind. How often had she felt as if she were tramping around in costumes? "Anyone can look at you and see determination. Professionalism. But when I saw you, I thought, *she's worth seeing*. So when I heard Mel telling you about Tiffany's—"

"It wasn't by chance you were there, handing out pamphlets," she suggested. "You were waiting for me." Had she always suspected?

"Hah! I was there three afternoons before you showed up. Not that it was a bad thing. So," he said, shrugging, "if you think that's stalker-y, I really apologize."

"No." She shook her head. "It's not. Well, maybe a little. But not in a bad way." Keely was relieved when he laughed along with her, his eyes flashing, his head hung with a little shame. "When I found . . . this place tonight . . . I was so worried you wouldn't be here," she confessed.

"Where else would I have been?" He seemed genuinely puzzled. "I'm here 24/7, it feels like."

"Home," she suggested. "With, you know, someone special." He shook his head. The tender way he held her glance for that long moment warmed her inside and out. "Or out looking for Melchior. The shepherd looking for his lost lamb." Overhead, the nameless piano player started a slow, quiet rendition of "Silent Night." A few of the shelter inhabitants joined in, muffled and distant.

"Keely," he said. She looked up, surprised to hear her correct name. "The lost lamb I worried about? She came looking for me tonight."

"Oh." The declaration moved her beyond words. Could she abandon that long-held glossy ideal to which she'd clung for years? Oh yes, easily—it had vanished into the night with Melchior's Burger King crown. She liked Duncan. Was it mere settling to hope she might see him again after this night? Not in the least. She'd settle for no one less. "I'm nowhere near perfect," she warned him.

"Well s'yeah!" he joked heartily. "I might limp like crazy, but I'm not blind! Besides," he added, more serious, "I'm not perfect either. Not by a long shot."

She nodded. "Weird," she said, oddly giddy. "But this is the first time I've ever been happy to hear someone admit it."

"Be warned that if I have my way, you'll be doing a lot more volunteering," he said, fixing her with a comical look of mock seriousness.

Keely was warm now, and merely damp instead of soaking. She stood and tested her feet. "I'd like that," she promised. She wanted to start anew. Needed it. "How about right now?" she asked, handing the shelter director his crutches and pointing to the ceiling. "Let's join in."

She was pleased to see how thoroughly she'd surprised Duncan; he wore astonishment on his face like a mask. "Huh? I thought we were getting you home. It's a little late—I mean, there's nothing that needs doing now. They'll probably sing carols a while more, then watch some old Christmas movie on the tube."

"I love old movies! And I'm in the mood for carols. Christmas Eve's the night for carols. Come on!"

When she and Duncan finally strode into the gathering room at the back of the shelter, where dozens of people huddled in sleeping bags bathed in a blue-and-white glow, they were still side by side. "I'm really sorry," he apologized, red-faced and worried. "Walking with me is an exercise in patience."

Keely looked around the room and the people within. They were all part of the flock, safe for the night, blessed not to have to wander alone and lost. "Don't be sorry," she told him, simply glad to be there. "For once, I'm in no hurry at all."

Jingle This!

by Stephanie Rowe

To my family, for giving me so many wonderful Christmases, no matter what crises were going on in my life at the time.

Thanks to my wonderful agent, Michelle Grajkowski, for being the inspiration behind the scene in Tiffany's. Payback will be mine!

And thanks to my fantastic editor, Kate Seaver, who will one day win the NYC marathon.

And for Josh, for being my NYC tour guide and photographer last Christmas. I love you!

Chapter One

If you want true love, buy a dog.
—Angie Miller

Angie Miller eyed the fake mini Christmas tree on the corner of her desk.

I wonder if it's fire retardant.

Anything holiday related didn't deserve to live.

She pulled open her desk drawer and rummaged through it to find the lighter she kept for office birthday parties. She searched past a toothbrush, toothpaste, an emergency stash of tampons, and her Christmas CD's until she found her lighter.

Damned thing had a snowman on it.

After she burned the tree, she'd have to find a hammer and smash the lighter too.

She grabbed the tree, shook it over the trash can to free its shiny aluminum balls, then held the lighter up to a branch.

To think she'd been so excited for this holiday season. *Hah.*

The tree smoked and emanated a nasty smell that sort of reminded her of burnt microwave popcorn.

But no flame. Figured. She couldn't even successfully destroy all evidence of the holiday season. Nothing was going right for her.

"Angie! What is that god-awful smell?" Her friend Heidi Oliver flung the door open, irritatingly festive in a full-fledged elf costume complete with green felt shoes with bells on the toes. Her gaze caught the lighter flame trying to ignite the tip of one of the branches. "What are you doing?"

"What does it look like I'm doing? Trying to burn this thing. Not working so well." She eyed her friend's pointed hat. "Nice outfit. Is it flammable?"

"Don't even think about setting me on fire." Heidi grabbed the tree out of her hand and set it on the corner of the desk, annoyingly out of reach. "Since when are you in a bad mood on the first Monday after Thanksgiving? This is your primo season." She gestured to the walls, which were decorated with tinsel, lights, and snowflakes. "You could get run over by a car during the Christmas season and still be in a fabulous mood. So what's up with the pyromania?"

Angie sighed and held up her left hand. "This."

Heidi frowned. "What's wrong with your hand?"

"It's empty."

"Right . . . and your point is?"

Nothing like friends to forget the most important day of your life. Or utter lack thereof. "Don't you remember? The private Thanksgiving celebration with Roger, instead of a crazy affair with my family? Specially orchestrated by Roger so we could be alone on the holiday?"

"Ohh . . . right . . ." Heidi slid into the chair opposite Angie's desk, her bells jangling cheerfully. "So, I'm guessing the one-year anniversary of the day you guys started dating didn't culminate in a proposal of marriage, huh? Or does he want you to foot the bill for the ring? Yeah, that's probably it. With the company not doing so well and everything, he'd probably want you to pay for it. Modern man and all."

"You can stop pretending to like him. He dumped me." *He dumped me.* Just saying the words hurt like hell.

Heidi blinked. "He dumped you? As in, broke up? As in, I'm no longer going to woo you in hopes that the Miller inheritance will wind up in my bank account once I marry you?"

"Don't hide your feelings. Tell me how you really feel." Heidi loved to expound on her favorite topic: why Roger wasn't good enough for Angie.

"This is great!" Obviously, her sarcasm was lost on Heidi, who jumped to her feet and started doing the Snoopy dance. "Now you can really enjoy the holiday season! Imagine if you'd gotten yourself wedded to that slow-brained, penny-pinching, sponging dimwit? Christmas came early for you!"

Funny how she wasn't feeling the real strong female-bonding thing right now. "You better watch it. When we get back together you're going to have to make up for insulting the man I love."

Heidi stopped her spontaneous jig and her stupid bells mercifully quieted down. "You wouldn't dare."

"Dare? What does this have to do with daring?"

"You know I've been hoping for this day for an entire year. If you take back this gift, then you aren't a true friend." Heidi folded her arms across her chest and jutted her chin out in an impressive display of pouting.

"You're the one who isn't a true friend. Can't you see I'm devastated?" Understatement of the millennium. "I love Roger. We belong together." Angie felt the burn of tears at the back of her eyes. Bastard. How dare he make her cry? She lifted her chin. "Can you hand me the tree again? I really need to vent." She picked up the lighter. "I'll pretend it's Roger. That should make you happy."

Heidi grabbed the tree and cradled it to her glittery red vest. "No chance. Hand over the lighter or I'm turning you in."

"To who?"

"The authorities. Granted, I'm all for torturing Roger, but if you end up burning down this office, then I'll be out of a job, and I won't be able to pay for all my new clothes for the holiday parties and my honeymoon. You wouldn't do that to me, would you?" Heidi flopped down in the chair again. "So, I'm thinking of going to Tiffany's and making a list of the items I like, so Quin will know what to buy me for a wedding present. Do you think that's tasteless? I mean, I know he's going to buy me jewelry, so there's nothing wrong with giving him a little guidance, is there? He is a guy, after all. They usually aren't born with a natural sense of fashion."

"How did you know that talking about your upcoming wedding would be exactly what I needed to make me forget that I just got dumped by the man I thought was going to propose?" Angie shoved her chair back from her desk and started yanking decorations off her walls. "You must be a genius."

"Hey there, missy." Heidi jumped up and grabbed Angie's wrist before she could really gather some good momentum in the holiday destruction effort. "How can you let some schmuck destroy your joy in your favorite season and your excitement about your best friend's wedding? Ten years from now, you'll look back and be so angry at yourself for letting some loser ruin your holiday." Her rouged elfin cheeks seemed to wink and grin, the complete antithesis of the total misery pervading Angie's body and soul.

"He's not a loser."

" 'Course he is. If he wasn't a loser, he wouldn't have dumped you, right?"

Angie almost grinned. "Not a bad line of logic, Heidi."

"See? I *am* a genius." Her eyes still sparkling, Heidi leaned forward. "Don't mean to pressure you, but what time are you going to have your story done? I need to copyedit it and get it posted online by five o'clock today. You may technically have a midnight deadline, but with me as your copy editor, I'm saying five o'clock. No way am I staying that late."

The story. The mere thought of it made Angie want to drop her forehead to her desk. Hard. And repeatedly.

"Well?" Heidi looked at her expectantly.

"You really think I'm going to be able to write a daily serial about love and the Christmas season after I just got dumped? When I pitched this project in October, I thought I'd be celebrating my own holiday engagement, so it would be the perfect complement. I can't write about everyone else's love now." Not when every holiday reminder was like a club to the head, reminding her of the sewer her love life had become. Ever since she and Roger fell in love over the holiday season, every twinkling light made her think of him. Now that she hated him, she didn't really want to be thinking of him all the time.

If she was going to successfully deny that it was the holiday season, she couldn't easily write a series of stories about how the holidays renewed the love of various couples.

Heidi snorted. "Gah. Could you sound more pathetic? You have a job to do, my friend, so do what you must. You know this entire company is depending on whether we impress this client or not. My future, no, *all* of our futures are in your hands."

"So *you* write the damn thing."

"Can't. I'm a copy editor, not a writer." Heidi popped out of her chair. "So, there's a vastly expensive party lunch to kick off the Christmas season today. The big boss is hoping to bring in lots of holiday business."

"Yeah, sure. I'll be there." Seeing as how "the big boss" was also the loser who'd dumped her four days ago, it was quite likely she would get lost on the way to the conference room and not quite manage to find the holiday party.

Heidi leaned forward and set her hands on the table. "Angie."

"What?"

"Roger isn't good enough for you. Don't sweat the breakup."

Even knowing that her friend meant well wasn't quite enough to make Angie feel like listening to her pop psychology. "I'll have the article for you by three. Is that enough time?"

"Barely. Don't be late." Heidi grinned. "Love you, hon. Try to enjoy the Christmas season, okay? You'll feel better."

"Sure." Angie managed to keep herself vertical until Heidi had shut the door behind her, then she laid down on the floor, propped her feet up against the wall, crossed her arms over her face and closed her eyes.

How was she supposed to write a story about love, romance, and the holiday season every day for the next twenty-five days?

And to think she had once thought this assignment would renew her enjoyment in her job.

Fat chance of that.

The door swung open again, and Heidi gently kicked her in the butt. "Hey, pathetic creature."

"What?"

"I'm going to Tiffany's at ten to make my list. Want to come? Maybe it'll give you inspiration for your story."

She opened her eyes and looked up at her friend, who was looming over her. "I can see up your elf skirt."

"Sweet. I'll remember that when I see Quin. Maybe it'll lead to some good foreplay." Heidi wiggled her hips. "Think that'll work? Sexy enough for ya?"

Angie groaned and closed her eyes. "I can't deal with you."

"Great. So I'll be by at ten."

"I can't go. I have to write my story." About love and the holiday season. For her boss. Who dumped her. *I hate my job.*

"You'll still be lying here on the floor at ten. Checking out Tiffany's will be great to help you focus on your client, who, after all, is trying to beef up their department store jewelry counter so they can outsell Tiffany's this season. What better research than sussing out the competition?"

"Go away."

"No. Not 'til you promise to come."

So nice to know she had her own personal stalker. "Are you going to wear that elf outfit in public?"

"Of course. It's the Christmas season. Want me to get one for you so we can be twins?"

Angie opened her eyes and glared at her friend.

"Okay, so maybe not today. I'll see you at ten." Heidi left the door open behind her, no doubt trying to shame Angie into getting off the floor.

Heartless fiend. Next time she was going to pick her friends better.

* * *

By Tuesday morning at eleven, it was all Kyle Black could do to keep himself from racing out of his office, grabbing his partner by the neck, and demanding that he hand over the company before he destroyed it. Instead, he strolled casually down the hall, stopped in the kitchen to refill his coffee, then continued down to where his friend Roger Lockhardt had his overly plush and not-at-all deserved office.

Kyle nudged the door open with his toe to find Roger doing pushups. "Roger, we need to talk."

"In a sec. This is my last set."

It rankled him to see Roger working on his body when his company was teetering on the edge of ruin. Hard to believe they'd been best friends in college. Kyle found very little to admire about the guy now, knowledge that would have come in handy *before* he'd agreed to give Roger half of the company they started together. Roger had ponied up the dough, Kyle had invested the brains.

Though Roger was decently smart, ever since he'd started dating Angie Miller a year ago he'd been only half committed to the company, running off on a moment's notice to do couple things instead of working until the early hours of the morning to get things done. No small company would survive with nine-to-five leaders. Not only was Roger working half-time, but he was still making decisions as if he had full information. Kyle had cleaned up more than a couple messes as a result of Roger playing the dutiful boyfriend to Angie.

Angie Miller and her cute little dimples were the sole cause of Roger's abdication of his responsibilities as a leader of the company.

Made Kyle damn pleased he hadn't followed through on his attraction to Angie two years ago when they'd been working on a project together. Instead, he'd gone for Angie's sister, Sheila, a hot tamale who could keep a man entertained but who was too independent to cramp his style.

Yep, he'd always be grateful to Angie for introducing him to her sister before he'd made the move on Angie herself. Not that the thing with Sheila had lasted more than six months, but by the time he was free, Angie had her hooks in Roger, and Kyle could no longer be tempted.

Roger finished his pushups, then hopped to his feet, sporting yet another brand-new designer suit. Were the funds for that coming from the company coffers? "What's up?"

"Got a call from Swift Department Stores." Kyle wasn't in the mood for preamble.

Roger stared at him blankly.

"Our new client."

"Oh . . . the jewelry one?"

Kyle ground his teeth. "Yes." *What? Were you being dragged around by Angie for the entire Thanksgiving weekend and completely forgot everything you know about the company?*

"Well, what's up? And talk fast. I have to go buy flowers."

"Angie feeling blue?" Kyle had never bought a woman flowers in his life. Too insincere. He wasn't interested in romance and love, so why pretend?

"Hot date tonight." Roger wiggled his brows. "My new woman. Been waiting for weeks to make it official and tonight finally . . ."

"New woman? What about Angie?" Was it possible? Had Roger finally seen the light?

Roger shrugged. "Broke it off."

"Wow." Kyle had to sit down for that one. "You and Angie are over?"

"Yep."

Hallelujah. It was about bloody time. "Decided you needed your space? Planning to spend a little more time at work?" This was great. With Roger rededicated to the business, they actually had a fighting chance.

"No way. I said I have a new woman, and I mean it." He grinned. "She's too hot to leave alone. I gotta be there to keep her cool, if you know what I mean."

"So, you went from Mr. Married Guy to dating a sex fiend?"

"Yep. Never realized what I was missing. I had one hell of a weekend after I dumped Angie." He wiggled his brows as he picked up his coat. "I gotta hit the road. Spruce up the pad for some hot lovin' tonight."

"Wait a sec!" Sex talk or not, Roger wasn't going anywhere. "We have a work crisis! You can't go home and do interior decorating."

"What's the crisis?" Roger shrugged on his coat and threw his monogrammed silk scarf around his neck.

On the plus side, if Roger was no longer drooling over Angie, it certainly made his bad news less dicey. "Angie messed up."

"What'd she do?"

"She screwed up the first story for Swift. They want to pull out." Merely voicing the words was enough to make him break out in a sweat. If they failed to land Swift as a client, they might be doomed, especially without commitment from Roger.

Roger frowned. "Do we care if they pull out?"

"Yes, we care!" Kyle caught himself and lowered his voice to a more reasonable level. "We really need Swift for a client. This daily serial is a test, and if we fail, we don't get 'em. And we need them. Big time." He narrowed his eyes at Roger, who was now inspecting his suit for stains or stray threads or something. "Roger, the company isn't doing very well. We need this client."

"Then get the client." Roger fingered his tie. "Does this tie match? I want to make a good impression. Should I go buy another one, you think? I'm no good with ties. Angie always picked my ties."

"Maybe you should ask Angie if it matches. I'm sure she'd be delighted to help you dress for your new woman." As loyal as Angie was, somehow Kyle doubted she'd be feeling too kindly toward Roger. Good. About time they broke up. Hopefully this new flame would burn out in about twelve hours and Kyle could reclaim Roger for the company. "You need to take Angie off the client. Bring in one of the other folks from Creative." Kyle suddenly closed the loop as to Angie's sudden inability to produce a palatable story. "Apparently, with her state of mind after the breakup, she's not in the mood to write about love." *Nice timing, Roger.*

And that was putting it kindly. The "love story" she'd written was a horrid tale about adulterous spouses, emotional devastation, and psychological terror. Not exactly the kind of touchy-feely sentiment that would lure men into buying diamonds for their beloveds.

Roger was already shaking his head. "No way. Can't interfere."

"Why not?"

"Sexual harassment. She was sleeping with the boss, and then I dump her and take away the best assignment in the company? Nope. Too dicey. You'll have to figure out how to get her to write better."

Kyle felt a boot in his gut. "Me? I have to figure it out? I'm not in Creative. I'm a business guy."

"Yeah, but I can't exactly coach her, can I?" Roger cursed. "This sexual harassment thing sure is inconvenient, isn't it? Probably should've thought of that before I slept with her."

"Roger, you have to deal with her."

"Nope." Roger flung his overcoat over his shoulders. "I gotta go buy a new tie. This doesn't match."

Kyle grabbed his arm as Roger tried to burn by him. "Roger! Would you focus for a second? This is the company's future we're talking about here. Angie has to get it together by the time she submits her story for tonight. You're the head of Creative. Edit her stuff, or better yet, write it yourself. You can't go run off and buy ties while the company crashes and burns."

Roger grinned and slugged Kyle on the shoulder. "Sure I can. That's why you're my partner. I pay the bills, you save the day. It's worked so far, right?"

"But it's not working now."

"Then you're not doing your job, are you?"

Because you're mucking it up. "Why don't you get back together with her, at least through the holidays? Keep her happy long enough to write twenty-five stories about true love and the holiday season."

Roger snorted. "Not a chance. I'm not giving up my social life for New Age Marketing. Fix it."

Kyle felt like smashing his head into the wall. Or Roger's. Yes, it would definitely be better to do the damage to Roger instead of himself. "Look, that's fine if you don't want to put this company first, but if that's the case, you need to get out."

Roger rolled his eyes. "Not this BS again. I'm not selling my half of the company to you, so forget it."

"If you don't, you might find yourself with a valueless asset in six weeks."

"You won't let that happen."

In another life, he might find his partner's utter confidence a good thing. As it was, he was half-inclined to step back and let the company fail, just to get out. Except he never would. This company has been his dream, his vision. The only reason he'd brought Roger in was for the funding, and he wasn't going to give up on it. Roger knew him too well. "Fine. I'll talk to Angie."

"Good luck. She nearly stabbed me with the turkey fork when I broke up with her. She's a bit volatile."

Great. That's all he needed, to have to deal with some brokenhearted woman with violent tendencies. He wasn't the touchy-feely type who could sweet-talk her into happiness. "Thanks for the warning. I'll wear my bulletproof vest when I meet with her."

"Good plan. I'll see ya." Roger socked Kyle in the arm again, then ducked out the door in search of a tie.

Yeesh. As if the day would ever come when he'd cut out of work to buy a friggin' tie to impress a woman. Roger had gone soft, and he was heading the company toward certain doom.

Unless Kyle could stop it. And the task started with Angie Miller.

Chapter Two

*The larger the diamond you buy for your true love, the
more useful it will be for grinding into his forehead when
he announces he is leaving you.*
—Angie Miller

Angie stared at the computer screen.

December second.

Twenty-four stories to go.

She'd never make it.

For the twentieth time in the last hour, she growled at
herself for such negative thoughts. She *was* going to make
it. She was a brilliant writer. No broken heart was going to
stop her from writing brilliant prose.

"Um, Angie?" Heidi stuck her head in the door, wearing
a Santa hat and a fake beard. "Got a sec?"

"Sure, unless you're going to wax poetic about the great
elfin sex you and Quin had last night. Not really in the

mood for that." Not that she was ever really in the mood for that conversation. Heidi and Quin's sex life far eclipsed any interesting stories she'd ever had to tell about herself and Roger. And now that she had no sex life at all to compare? Even worse.

"Actually, Quin had to work late last night. Didn't even see my elf outfit." Heidi walked in and stood, her arms folded loosely across her chest, then hanging by her sides, then across her chest again.

"What's wrong with you?" Angie leaned back in her chair.

"Um . . . your story."

"What about it?"

"Well, you know how you finished it so late that we skipped the copyediting stage and you just went ahead and posted it without me reading it?"

"Yeah." That had been a nightmare. Angie hadn't even started typing until five o'clock. As it was, she'd barely made the midnight post time, though that may have been due to the three-hour nap she took on her floor from seven to ten o'clock. Ruined her silk blouse with all the drool.

From now on, she was pretending the deadline was five o'clock, not midnight. How was she supposed to find a way to find joy in the holiday season again if she was stuck at work every night and had to miss all the holiday parties and everything else potentially fun?

"Did you even read it when you finished?"

"Read what?" At Heidi's raised eyebrow, Angie turned on her brain and focused on work. "Oh, right. My story. Of course I read it. Why? Were there typos?" That would be appalling if she'd posted a story with stupid mistakes. She prided herself on turning out only the highest quality work. If the breakup had made her so depressed she couldn't even catch some lousy typos . . . that would be unforgivable. The one thing she still had was her writing talent. If she let some guy interfere with that . . .

Heidi rolled her eyes and tossed a printout on Angie's desk. "Read it again. From the point of view of the client, looking for a tale of love."

A firm rap sounded from the door before Angie could grab the document. Angie looked up to find Kyle Black standing in her doorway.

Kyle Black.

In a pair of black slacks, a pale blue shirt, and a nifty tie. Looking urban and rugged at the same time. Had the guy's shoulders gotten even broader since the last time she'd gawked at him in the break room? Almost two years since she'd met him and he still made her stomach do all sorts of weird jigs. Still sent her pulse into overdrive.

Heidi cleared her throat, and Angie realized she'd been gaping again. She quickly snapped her mouth shut and picked up the article Heidi had dropped on her desk, though she couldn't begin to concentrate on the words.

"Hi, Kyle," Heidi giggled.

Oh, great. Could Heidi sound more amused? With that lilt to Heidi's voice, Kyle would have to be an idiot not to realize that Angie had spent hours extolling Kyle's virtues to Heidi. Note that those hours were in the past, before he'd started shacking up with her sister. Once that had happened? Forget it. He'd been wiped from her heart. No one would be allowed to break her heart twice. "Looking dapper as usual," Heidi said.

Kyle raised an eyebrow in Heidi's direction, and Angie couldn't help but sneak a peek to see if he checked out Heidi's ample bosom peeking out from under her bushy, white Santa beard.

Heidi was truly the only woman Angie knew who could wear anything on the planet, including a Santa outfit, and look so hot that even the most proper, old, or asexual men couldn't help but check her out.

Except Kyle apparently. He was looking at the beard, not the boobs.

Point for Kyle. Probably because Heidi was engaged. As hot and heavy as Kyle had been with Angie's sister and as much as Angie thrived on gossip about what a jerk he was—not that there was nearly enough negative gossip to satisfy her—he'd never been linked with a woman who was already taken. So nice to know the playboy heartbreaker had morals.

"You look . . . nice," he said to Heidi.

"Thanks. It's my Santa outfit." Heidi glanced at Angie, probably to make sure Angie was still vertical. "Can I help you with anything, Kyle?"

"Nope. I'm here to see Angie."

Me? He's here to see me? Since when had he remembered she existed, let alone had a need to see her?

Oh sure, there'd been a time when she'd thought he'd noticed her. The first five months she'd been at New Age Marketing they'd worked on a project for a footwear company. Lots of late nights at the office, and even some at his condo. Private jokes, pizza delivery . . . she'd fallen hard for Kyle, and she'd been so certain he'd fallen, too, but was too shy to make a move.

Which was why she'd recruited her sister to help out. The plan had been for Sheila to join Angie and Kyle at dinner. Sheila was supposed to assess the situation and then create a plan to make Kyle throw Angie to the floor and make mad, passionate love to her.

Only it was Sheila he'd ended up with by dessert, leaving

Angie to rebound into the arms of Roger. Ever since, Angie had made sure to stay off Kyle's projects and keep out of his way. It had taken Roger's undying devotion to finally chase Kyle from her heart.

And he had. Roger had been completely and utterly devoted to her, putting Angie in front of work, family, and friends. He'd constantly surprised her with flowers, chocolates, cute stuffed animals—anything he thought would make her smile. It was exactly the ego-boosting dedication that her broken heart had needed to mend. Which was why she'd been so blown away by his breaking up with her. From dedicated, devoted lover to ex-boyfriend? It made no sense, and she'd been utterly unprepared to be dumped, hence the misery.

And despite her confusion and depression, now that she no longer had Roger playing downfield blocker, her body was reacting to the sight of Kyle as if those two years hadn't elapsed.

She hated her hormones. Total traitors. The last thing she needed was to fall for yet another guy who didn't want her. First Kyle, then Roger, and now Kyle again? Was she really that stupid? No. Definitely not. She folded her arms across her chest and tried to think evil thoughts about Kyle. "What do you want to talk to me about?"

"The story you wrote for Swift. The one that you posted last night."

She'd barely begun to relax—impersonal discussions about her good work she could handle—when Heidi cursed. Angie snapped her gaze to Heidi. "What's wrong with my article?"

"I didn't copyedit it," Heidi said to Kyle. "She submitted it without going through me. I never would have let it through."

"Excuse me. What's wrong with my article?" Surely, they were overreacting to a few typos. Granted, she was quite appalled that she'd managed to let something slip by her, but still! Was that cause for swearing?

"You're dismissed," Kyle said to Heidi.

"I'm fired? But I didn't even see the article!" Heidi wailed. "I need this job!"

Kyle grimaced and looked like he wanted to be anywhere but in the room. "I didn't mean fired. I meant, you can leave. I need to talk to Angie alone."

Heidi's distress vanished immediately, and she shrugged. "Oh. Well. Okay, then. See you guys around."

Alone? He wanted to see her alone? The last man who'd wanted to spend alone time with her had dumped her and broken her heart. But seeing as how Kyle had already broken her heart when he'd chosen her sister, he couldn't exactly do that again, could he? So technically, she was immune from his heart-breaking power now.

Excellent.

She smiled and watched him shut the door of her office. It was a good thing she was immune or she might be feeling a little bit dizzy from being locked in a room with Kyle Black.

But seeing as how she was immune to anything and everything Kyle, she wasn't feeling dizzy and was, in fact, completely relaxed. "To what do I owe this visit? I think it's the first time you've ever ventured this low down the totem pole at work." Damn it. That made it sound like she kept track of how close he came to her office. "I mean, that's what I've heard. You know, from people. Personally, I'm too busy to keep track of your whereabouts." Gee, that sounded a whole lot better. It was amazing to think she actually made a living from her ability to manipulate the English language.

Kyle looked wary, and moved to the back of her office, which wasn't actually very far. Despite shtupping the big boss for the last several years, she still had the smallest office in the entire company. That had been to protect her from allegations of favoritism, which had seemed logical at the time, but seeing as how she was the best copywriter in the entire office by a long shot, it seemed rather stupid actually.

She pulled out a sticky and made a note to talk to Roger about getting a bigger office. Or maybe she'd e-mail him. If she actually spoke to him, she might accidentally stab him with a letter opener, and that might get people talking. How could he have made her feel like a treasured prize for the last year, only to dump her without any warning?

"Angie, about your story."

A sense of calm settled over her. As crazy as the rest of her life might become, her work always gave her a sense of pride and togetherness. It was the one place she was always queen. "It was good, huh?"

He gestured to the printout on her desk. "May I?"

"Sure." His hand came within eighteen inches of her when he went for the printout. Very annoying to realize he still made her stomach jiggle. Beast. Probably just aftershocks from the devastating breakup of only a few days ago. Kyle had been a crush that had quickly ended. Nothing more.

She'd had to endure his relationship with her sister for almost six months. If she hadn't started dating Roger that Thanksgiving, it would have been far worse. A year ago on Thanksgiving, she'd given her heart to Roger, making for the most magical holiday season ever.

And now? She had the holidays to look forward to.

Alone, with nothing but memories of the man who was supposed to love her.

Angie scowled. *Stop thinking about him.* Work. Think about work. That was a good thing to think about. Her writing always made her feel better.

"Mind if I read you a few excerpts?" Kyle perched on the edge of her client chair, as if ready to spring away at a moment's notice.

"Sure." She settled back. It was always therapeutic to hear her own prose. Sometimes she amazed herself with what she came up with.

He started reading. " 'Love is an illusion specifically designed to lure you into a sense of complacency so your purported true love can destroy you emotionally.' " He looked up. "How is that supposed to make a man want to buy a diamond for his woman?"

"Well . . ." She hadn't really written that, had she?

"And how about this: 'During the hour the author spent with Max and Ethel discussing how the holidays rekindle their love, the author noted that Max checked out female passersby six times when he thought Ethel wasn't looking. Obviously, their love is an illusion and it's just a matter of time until one or both of them is going to wake up alone and devastated.' "

"Are you sure you're reading my article? I'm quite positive I wouldn't have written that." But a black gloom was beginning to settle around her.

"And the moral of your story? 'In closing, the author would like to point out that even fifty-six years of marriage cannot be relied on. If you want to keep your spouse from leaving you, buy a couple pieces of expensive jewelry and try to bribe them into staying around. I can't promise it'll keep you from ending up alone, but at least you tried, right?' " He set it down. "What the hell?"

"Let me see that." She snatched the paper from his hands and scanned it. Yes, that was her name on the byline, and that was the couple she'd interviewed . . . but how had it come out like that? It was like some evil creature had invaded her brain and made that drivel occur. "Umm . . ."

"It's awful."

Awful? She didn't write awful. Writing was the one thing she could always count on. "It's not that bad." Not *that* bad. Even "not bad" was unacceptable! What was wrong with her?

Don't panic. There had to be a reasonable explanation for this. Someone had hacked into Swift's website and rewritten her story. Yes, that must be it, because there was no way she would have screwed up so badly.

Kyle ran his hand through his hair and paced her office. Which meant he took one step in either direction before turning around. Needless to say, he gave that up quickly. "Listen, Angie, I heard that Roger dumped you."

Tears immediately sprang to alertness before Angie even knew they were coming. Bastard. How dare he drop that on her without warning? "Which is none of your business." Oh, great comeback.

"It's my business when it affects your work." He planted his hands on her desk and leaned forward.

Why did he have to smell so good? Way more sophisticated and classy than Roger ever did. Roger had a tendency to overdo the cologne. The more the better was his philosophy. Not so with Kyle. There was just the slightest hint, as if it was left over from yesterday, clinging to his skin with a caressing gentleness and . . . Wait a sec. "You think my breakup with Roger affected my writing?"

He lifted a brow. "You think there's another reason for what you wrote?"

Damn. Was he right? Had she actually let Roger take

away her one talent? Totally unacceptable. She was ending that fiasco now.

"From now on, every story goes through me before it goes to copyediting or anywhere else," Kyle said.

"What?" How dare he treat her like some neophyte incapable of self-editing? "That article was a one-time mistake. An aberration. You can be certain it won't happen again, and I don't need you checking up on me."

"If today's article is great, then I won't have to make any corrections, right?"

"Trust me, you won't." She was going to write the best damn story about this miserable holiday season and the destructive nature of perceived love. People everywhere would swoon and then rush off to Swift to buy tons of jewelry to celebrate the mind-destroying, hateful, stupid love in their lives.

"What is post time?" Kyle asked.

"Midnight. But I get it done by five so I don't get stuck at the office." That would be all she needed, to be stuck at work while Roger was off celebrating the holidays.

"Then have it in my in box by noon so I have time to edit it."

"Noon?" She looked at her watch. "It's almost eleven."

"It's five minutes after ten."

So he was already starting with his over-picky corrections? This was going to be trouble.

He set the article on her desk. "I want the first draft in my in box by noon. And make it happy, cheerful, and full of the Christmas spirit. Got it?"

And to think she'd cried for three days when he'd shared a cab home with her sister that night. Hah. Who had time for arrogant, controlling, domineering men? "You're seriously going to review all my work?"

"I'll read it, then bring it down, and we'll discuss the changes I want made. And the process will continue until you get it right. Any questions?"

"Yeah. Why can't you trust me? Give me one more chance before launching into the micromanaging thing, which really isn't all that popular with employees, in case you haven't read any 'how to manage so your employees don't hate you' books lately."

"I can't trust you because New Age's future is resting heavily on whether we get Swift as a client. They called me this morning and said they were canceling the contract for the rest of the season."

Oh my God. Swift was canceling the contract because her story was so horrible? A hard lump formed in her stomach. How could she have written something that awful?

"I talked them into giving us one more chance, which means tomorrow's article better be the best thing you've ever written. And that means *happy*. Feel-good. Inspiring. Waxing poetic about love and the holidays. Got it?"

Like this pep talk was going to put her in the right mood for that kind of story. "Maybe you should have someone else do it, instead of me." Even as the words came out of her mouth, she wanted to grab at the air and shove them back inside. This assignment was hers! She'd earned it by writing great copy for the last two years, and she deserved to see it through.

"Nope. It's yours."

Phew. No more emotional reactions permitted.

He gritted his teeth. "Tell you what. I'll be back in at one o'clock to go over what you've done so far. See if you're on the right track."

See if she was on the right track? Could he be more insulting?

Besides, she didn't want Kyle in her office. It was her space, her personal oasis. Heart-breaking, domineering men weren't allowed to contaminate it. "Why don't I just e-mail it to you? It's much more efficient."

"Nope. I'll be back." He pulled the door open. "Three hours."

And then he was gone.

Well, physically gone. His aura was still hovering in her office. She decided to ignore it as she turned back to her computer. She'd show him. He'd be down on his knees, begging forgiveness for ever doubting her talent. And while he was down there, he'd also apologize for making.the biggest mistake of his life when he'd passed her over in favor of her slutty sister with the artificially augmented breasts.

Angie paused to doodle a picture of Kyle genuflecting at her feet, tears rolling down his face. Threw in a bubble with her denying him forgiveness and condemning him to a life of being constantly corrected on everything he ever did.

Then she threw in a picture of Roger pinned under the legs of her desk.

She tacked the picture up on her bulletin board for inspiration.

There. Feeling much better now. More than ready to create a marvelous story of passion, laughter, and everlasting love.

Chapter Three

*Nothing ruins a holiday season more than seeing your
lecherous true love salivating over some ho. Protect
yourself by keeping title to the diamond. He leaves, you get
the goods.*
—Angie Miller

Two and a half hours later, Angie's mood had seriously declined. She'd gone through her files on couples she'd already interviewed, and no one was inspiring. But it wasn't because she was bitter or anything, as Kyle would probably accuse her of. It was simply because she hadn't chosen her subjects well.

She scowled at her folders. Was that really the reason? Surely there was electricity somewhere in those files. She didn't have time to interview anyone else in the next half hour, so she'd better find a way to make magic out of nothing.

That's what they paid her for, right? Her talent with the written word.

She sat up and randomly picked one of the files from an interview she'd done last week while life was still good. How annoying that she'd drawn little candy canes in the margins.

It wasn't just that she'd been dumped. It was just that last Christmas season had been when she and Roger had fallen in love. Since then, everything Christmas had brought back a memory of that special time. The first time he'd held her hand when they'd been watching the Macy's windows. Their first kiss at Central Park with snow falling. The first time he'd told her he loved her, when she'd bought that silly flashing Santa hat from the street vendor near Rockefeller Center. The picture they'd taken with the Grinch on the street corner.

Memories everywhere. Everywhere! Serving as constant reminders that the first and only man she'd ever truly loved had broken her heart on the very night she'd thought he was going to give her a diamond ring and declare his true love for all eternity.

She stared glumly at the notes in front of her, getting increasingly annoyed. What a jerk. Timing the breakup to ruin her Christmas and render her incapable of writing a good story? How dare he steal her joy and her talent?

Okay, so maybe Kyle had been right that her bad story was the result of her breakup with Roger. Now that she recognized it, she was going to overcome it. Time for an immediate rebound. From now on she was going to enjoy this stupid holiday season and write uplifting stories about love.

And she was going to be happy, even if she had to staple a perpetual smile on her face.

Angie turned to the computer and began typing, after

shooting off a quick e-mail to Kyle asking for an extension to five o'clock and a promise that it would be perfect.

At precisely five o'clock, she handed her masterpiece to Kyle. Best work she'd ever done, and in one short afternoon. She'd been truly inspired by her anger toward Roger. Obviously, it was the sign of a genius to be facing such difficult times and still be able to rise above them.

She settled back in her chair and waited for the apologies.

Kyle read for about ten minutes, then he picked up her pen and started writing.

And writing.

And writing.

With each stroke of the glittery red pen she'd gotten for signing Christmas cards, she felt lower and lower.

By the time he looked up, she was nothing but a muddy puddle on the floor of her office.

"Maybe you should put on some cheerful music when you write," he suggested. "I have some CD's you could borrow."

He could have told her she sucked.

He could have shaken his head and declared her useless.

He could have taken her off the assignment.

But instead he'd offered her music.

It was too much.

Criticism she could have handled, but sympathy? Kindness? Music? She was going to cry.

Damn it.

She really hated crying in public.

Kyle had no idea what to say when the tears welled up in Angie's eyes. "Um . . . sorry, I didn't mean to upset you."

She waved him off and stood. "This always happens when I chop onions."

"Onions? You aren't chopping onions."

"No, but I will be in about a half hour. I have to go to my mom's for the Miller holiday party. It's the anticipation that's getting to me." She pushed by him, her thigh brushing against his leg. "You remember the party, don't you? If I recall, you came to one the year you were dating Sheila."

And you were wearing that red silk dress that made you look like an angel in devil's clothes. "I don't recall. It was a long time ago." He suddenly realized that she was shrugging on her overcoat. "Where are you going?"

"To the party." She pulled a red hat over her head. "I need a new hat, don't you think? Black maybe. None of this red crap. Too much like Christmas." Then she scowled. "I mean, I need a new hat that's even more festive than this one! Maybe I'll stop and pick up a Santa cap on the way. Maybe go shopping with Heidi next time she supplements her holiday outfit arsenal. Because I *am* excited about the holiday season, damn it!"

"Angie!"

She yanked her green fuzzy mittens over her hands. "Stupid green too. Do I always look so ridiculous at the holiday season? I need to buy some that have snowmen on them, don't you think? This putrid green simply isn't holiday enough for someone who loves this stupid season as much as I do."

"You can't leave. We need to work on this."

She sighed and patted his cheek. Heat immediately cascaded through him, and he snapped away from her touch.

She glared at him, then yanked the marked-up document out of his hand and displayed it with a flourish. "Since you have such a clear idea of what needs to be done, I'll let you do the editing, so it's up to your standards. Much more efficient than trying to mold me into something I so obviously am not capable of at the moment." She tossed it on her desk. "Good luck."

"I can't do it without you."

"Well, you better, because I need some serious infusion of holiday spirit. The best way I know how to get that is to hang out with my family. So I'm outta here."

And then she walked out and shut the door behind her.

If it weren't for her tears, he'd march right out there and haul her cute little fanny back into the office to work.

But the fact was, it was obvious Angie was suffering right now. She was super talented. An asset. So he'd cut her a break. This one time. Let her enjoy her holiday party. Maybe the old, talented Angie would be back tomorrow.

She better be, because he had no idea how to help a woman get back on her feet. Sensitive and doting weren't his forte.

Angie flung her arm around Heidi's shoulders. "I'm so glad you could come at the last minute."

Heidi grinned and honked her red Rudolph prosthetic nose. "I wouldn't miss the Miller holiday launch party for anything." She eyed Angie. "Are you going to be in trouble for walking out on Kyle? He's not exactly known to be a softie when it comes to the company."

Angie frowned. Now that Heidi mentioned it, he had been pretty placid when she'd walked out. Wonder what that was about? "Probably glad to get rid of me so he could rewrite my piece."

How insulting. A finance guy could write a better story than she could? She'd sunk to a new low, heretofore previously reserved only for people she pitied. Well, she wasn't going to feel sorry for herself. She was going to have fun with Heidi and her family and grapple her way back to her old self. "So where's Quin?"

A tiny bit of the sparkle left Heidi's eyes. "He had to work tonight."

"Again? What's with the hours?"

"I don't know." Heidi paused at the top of the steps leading into the Miller's condo. "Do you think it's something I should worry about? I mean, I don't want to marry a guy like Kyle who works 24/7." Then she shifted. "You don't think he's having second thoughts and avoiding me, do you?"

"No way!" Angie grabbed Heidi's shoulders and shook her lightly. "You two are a perfect match. True love forever. It's totally natural to be getting nervous a month before the wedding. He loves you, you love him, all is good. Right?"

Heidi relaxed and grinned. "I'm being stupid, aren't I?"

"No, just human." Angie draped her arm around Heidi as they walked inside. "You saw how Roger dumped me when things got serious, so you're naturally extrapolating Roger's horridness to the entire male gender, and that's totally understandable. Wrong, but understandable. Quin isn't Roger, so you're fine."

"Man, how can you be so mellow? I'd have thought you'd be totally bitter after the Roger thing."

"I am, but I'm fighting it. That's why we're here. We are going to have a great time tonight and enjoy the holiday season kick-off. No talking about men anymore. Deal?"

"Deal."

What would she ever do without Heidi? Die a miserable and lonely death, no doubt. "When we get to the condo, you walk in first. They think I'm not coming, so it'll be a surprise."

Heidi raised a brow. "Why do they think you're not coming?"

Angie grimaced as she put her key in the lock to the entrance of the building. "Because I thought I'd be working on that online story until midnight, but since I dumped it on Kyle, I'm free." She hesitated. "Plus, I haven't told them Roger and I broke up. My family will be so bummed, because they love Roger. I don't want to deal with it. We'll just say he's working tonight."

Heidi rolled her eyes. "I love your family, but they really missed the boat on that one. When they start telling you what a great catch you lost, I'll rattle off all his faults." She tucked her arm through Angie's. "But not tonight, I promise."

They reached the door to the apartment, which was propped open for partygoers' easy access. Angie felt a rousing sense of relief as she followed Heidi inside. This was what the holidays were about. Family. So what if she was single? They would still love her and support her. She could skip all the parties she and Roger had attended last holiday season and stick with her family. Maybe she'd even tell them tonight after all. Tonight would be a cleansing night for her, and tomorrow she'd be the genius writer of seasons past.

See? She could rebound.

"Hi, all," Heidi said. "I'm here!"

Angie heard the shouts of greeting from her family, and felt a warm snuggle settling in her chest. She was so glad she'd come tonight. Far better than sitting in her office being lambasted by Kyle the autocrat.

She grinned and popped her head around Heidi's shoulder. "Surprise! I made it!"

All the faces in the room froze. Glasses that had been raised in toast to Heidi suspended in midair, and a total silence fell over the room. A look of shocked horror seemed to be on every face turned in Angie's direction.

For a long moment, Angie stared back, waiting for someone to shout "Just kidding."

No one did.

So she carefully wiped the sleeve of her jacket across her nose. Ran her tongue over her teeth to eliminate food that might be stuck. Checked the buttons on her blouse for indecent exposure. Still no one spoke. What the hell was wrong with her? "Hello? Anyone?"

"I thought you weren't coming." Angie's mom finally spoke up, her face still as horrified as before.

"Thanks for making me feel welcome. Cheers to all of you. Happy holidays and all that jazz." Maybe they were horrified by the look of devastation in her eyes. Yes, that was it. Shocked because they'd expected to see her dance in with her usual holiday ebullience. As family, they were so perceptive they immediately noticed their beloved Angie was carrying a heavy emotional burden.

God, she loved them.

"So, anyone want more eggnog?" The sound of her sister's voice emanating from the kitchen sent the room into a frenzy. Her dad nearly threw his eggnog to the floor as he vaulted over the coffee table and sprinted for the kitchen while the rest of the crew erupted into hyper exclamations. Her cousin Maxine grabbed Angie's arm and hauled her off to the den, muttering something about a Christmas tree.

"No freakin' way!" Heidi's shocked exclamation had Angie whirling around to see what was going on.

She made the about-face just in time to see Roger remove his hand from her sister's waist, courtesy of her dad yanking him away. Sheila stood there with a tray of eggnog, looking surprised to see Angie there.

Heidi grabbed her Rudolph nose and hurled it at Roger. "You are a *pig*."

Angie just stared. At Roger, who was looking sheepish in a brand-new tie, and her sister, whose cleavage was barely contained in an outfit that was hardly appropriate for a family holiday party. The smug look on Sheila's face left no doubt as to the nature of her relationship with Roger. None at all.

Angie was going to be sick.

The room was totally silent; the only movement was Heidi retrieving her nose from the floor. "Since it hit Roger, I have to go disinfect it before I can put it back on my face," she announced.

Someone cleared his throat. "Um, Angie? Can I talk to you?"

Angie spun to her left to find Kyle standing in the doorway, looking more than a little uncomfortable. "Did you know too? And what are you doing here? Came by to observe my fall of shame?"

He glanced around the silent room. "Um . . . I need your help with the article. I didn't mean to disturb anything but I can't do it without you."

Come to think of it, he did look a little disheveled, and his tie was askew.

His gaze landed on Roger and Sheila, and Angie saw him stiffen. He looked at Roger. "This is your new woman? Sheila?" His voice was cold, his eyes flashing.

Sheila flipped Kyle a smile. "Now, Kyle, don't be getting all possessive. We broke up eons ago. I'm not yours."

Oh, crap. That was why Kyle looked upset? Because he still loved Sheila? Great. The only two men she'd ever thought twice about were in love with her sister.

"Kiss him."

Angie glanced over her shoulder to find Heidi whispering in her ear. "What?"

"Kiss Kyle. Show everyone you don't care because you're already shacking up with your sister's ex."

"I can't kiss Kyle." Just the thought of it was enough to make her heart race.

"He won't stop you. Look how pissed he is. Do it." Heidi elbowed her in the back. "Just do it."

Her mom trilled a fake, nervous laugh. "Well, I guess it's good that it's out in the open." She turned to Angie. "We thought you would be too upset, so we decided not to tell you for a while."

Angie frowned. "How long have you known?"

"Awhile."

Whoa. Awhile? Her boyfriend had been having liaisons with her sister and her whole family had known about it? The entire clan had been waiting for Roger to drop the bomb five days ago? No wonder her mom hadn't tried to talk her into attending tonight when she'd declined.

Heidi whispered in her ear. "If you have any pride, you will march over there and lay one on Kyle right now."

She saw Kyle glance over at her. Had he heard what Heidi had said? Totally embarrassing. He lifted a brow.

What was that about? Could he read her mind and know she was dissecting his mouth piece by piece, wondering what it would be like to have his lips on hers?

His gaze still tight on hers, he walked toward her. Oh my gosh. Was he going to kiss her? Take Heidi's advice and kiss her into oblivion?

Angie's heart began really hammering, and she lifted her chin and met his gaze as he approached. *Kiss me, you big hunk. I'm all the woman you'll ever need.*

He stopped right in front of her, then lowered his head.

Yes! Take that Roger and Sheila! Kyle wants me!

"We need to work on that article," he said.

Angie opened her eyes. "What?"

"The article. We need to work." He shot her an apologetic smile. "Sorry."

"Sorry?" For not kissing her and saving her reputation? There was no forgiving that.

Kyle tucked his hand under her arm and turned to the still silent room. "Angie and I have work to do. Sorry to cut short the festivities, but it looks like you all will have a fine time without us." He began directing her out of the condo. "Happy Holidays to everyone. The condo looks gorgeous as usual, Mrs. Miller."

Okay, so he wasn't throwing her on the ground for a good shagging in front of everyone, but he *was* giving her a totally legit excuse for leaving. No one could say that she'd snuck out with tears streaming down her face. "Can't we do it in the morning, Kyle? I'd really like to stay."

He shot her a look like she was totally insane, and she almost grinned. If he bought it, then maybe other people would to. Then she'd be the talk of the holiday season, how she was faced with the betrayal of her longtime love, and she hadn't even batted an eye. How she'd even wanted to blow off work to hang out and bask in the good fortune of two people so dear to her.

She shot Heidi a glance, and Heidi pointed to the eggnog and gave her a thumbs-up. So good to know Heidi was going to put something nasty in the punch. A true friend.

Angie released a resigned sigh. "Well, if I must go . . . I know the entire company is relying on the success of this project that I'm working on, right Kyle?"

"About time you realized that," he muttered as he pulled her through the open door. "Have a nice evening, everyone."

Angie waved cheerfully and let Kyle haul her out the door and down the hall.

A low murmuring of conversation erupted the moment they were out of sight of the party.

They were talking about her.

Talk about good humor fading fast.

* * *

Kyle punched the elevator button and watched Angie warily. So much for his hope that an evening with her family would cheer her up. *Roger, you bastard.* "You okay?"

She was leaning against the wall, fiddling with her mittens. "Did you know? About them?"

"No."

She looked up, vulnerability stark in her eyes. "Really? You didn't?"

Damn Roger. How was he supposed to get Angie to write something good about love now? "Angie, I swear I didn't know."

"Oh." The elevator door opened, and they stepped inside. "So, are you mad?"

He watched the numbers flick by. "About what?"

"Roger dating Sheila."

"Yes."

"Because you love her."

Kyle cursed and glanced at her. "I'm mad because he screwed you over. I don't care about Sheila."

She looked up from picking the fuzz off her coat and studied him. "Why do you care what he does to me?"

He caught himself before he mentioned the articles for Swift. Somehow, he doubted that was what she needed to hear tonight. But he had to think of something to distract her from Roger. His brief tangle with trying to write the article had convinced him that there was no way he could do it without Angie. He had to find a way to bring her back into the fold. "Have you had dinner?"

She eyed him warily. "No."

"Let's do a working dinner. It'll be good to get out of the office." He frantically searched his brain for a fun place that would get her mind off the night. Someplace that would cheer her up. "What are you in the mood for?"

"Murder."

He grinned at the matter-of-fact tone in her voice. "Not on the menu for tonight. How about we get take-out and go to Rockefeller Center? We can watch people skate while we work. Check out the Christmas tree."

The elevator hit the ground floor. "I hate Rockefeller Center. Reminds me of bastards."

"Then you'll have to get a new association for it, because that's where we're going." The only solution was to throw her in the middle of the holiday season and get her out of this funk. Make her forget about Roger. Who knows? Maybe she could even find some other guy out there to fall for, get her through the holiday season.

He scowled as he hailed a cab. Or maybe not. Another guy might be more than her psyche could bear. Probably best if she stayed single. For the good of the company.

Chapter Four

Stuck in a volatile relationship? Diamonds soothe and cajole, and might even get your teenager to stop swearing.
—Angie Miller

"Angie!"

She snapped out of her fantasy of Roger getting run over by Santa's sleigh and some rogue reindeer and looked at Kyle. "What?"

"Did you hear anything I just said?"

"No."

He looked so aggravated it was almost cute. Should she clue him in that she was a hopeless cause? They'd been arguing over her story for an hour, and she knew there was no way she could give him what she wanted.

But it was the couple she'd interviewed, not her inability to perform. Surely if she found an inspirational couple, that would jettison her back to her usual level of performance.

"Angie, we've been here for an hour. What can I do to help you focus?"

Ravage me with wild, passionate sex for forty-eight hours straight. Whoa. Where had that thought come from?

Rebound sex.

When faced with public humiliation and betrayal, it was a natural tendency to want to revert to something safe and familiar. Lord only knew that her attraction to Kyle was familiar. Sure, she'd suppressed it when she'd been dating Roger, even though she was totally over Kyle. But now that she was single and sniffing his aftershave?

Rebound sex on the brain.

Kyle shot her a wary look, and she was suddenly certain he knew exactly what she'd just been thinking. Perhaps having a poker face wasn't her forte. Or maybe he was a mind reader.

Damn.

That would be totally inconvenient.

Or maybe not. Maybe if he knew she was salivating for the touch of his skin against hers that would be enough to overcome his residual desire for her sister.

Sheila.

Okay, there went the happy, gooey feeling that the thought of Kyle and sex had brought on. Wonder if Heidi had successfully contaminated the punch?

A loud shrieking caught her attention, and she looked around. A teenaged couple was screaming at each other. The girl threw her skate at the boy and only his quick duck kept him from being sliced open. "Now, this is what I'm talking about."

She grabbed her glitter pen and notepad out of Kyle's hand and jogged across the asphalt. "Excuse me! Excuse me!"

"Angie!" Kyle grabbed her arm, but she shrugged him

off and plopped herself down on the bench between the arguing couple.

"Hi, guys."

They ignored her and kept shouting at each other. Nice creative use of obscenities. "So, you're saying that love increases creativity. Good to know." She pulled out her notebook and started writing.

"Angie, what are you doing?" Kyle was standing in front of her, shouting to be heard over the screaming teenagers.

"Getting inspiration. Have a seat." She moved over, giving the girl a shove. "Make some room for my boss." She lowered her voice to a conspiratorial whisper. "He's hot, isn't he? I'm totally having sex fantasies about him."

The girl stopped shouting at her boyfriend long enough to stick her pierced tongue out at Angie and flip her off.

"Mmm . . . good point. Nonverbal communication is the key to a successful relationship." Angie patted the bench next to her. "Sit, Kyle. Watch genius at work."

"I'm afraid I'm going to be watching you get beat up." He glanced warily at the boy, who was brandishing a skate guard like a baseball bat. "Um, Angie, wouldn't it be better to do this from afar?"

"And lose the emotion of the moment? Not at all." She turned to the girl. "So, did he cheat on you? Check out another girl? Get your sister knocked up? Why are you yelling at him?"

"None of your business, bitch." The girl directed a hostile glare at her, and Angie noted none of her six eyebrow rings were holiday related. Obviously not in the festive spirit.

"Fine." She turned to the boy, who had stopped yelling at his girlfriend and was now glowering at Angie. "So, what's the problem? She flirt with one of your friends? Shtup the math teacher in the shower?"

"Angie!" Kyle plonked himself down between her and the guy. "You're going to get yourself killed!" He scowled at the kid, who backed up a hair.

Was that cute or what? Kyle was protecting her. If she didn't know it was merely for her story-telling talent, she might even get all soppy and lovey about it. But as it was, two years ago she'd made the mistake of misinterpreting his interest. There'd be no making that mistake again.

"So, since you guys aren't yelling anymore, want to talk about what the holiday season means for your relationship? Really beefs up the hostility, huh?" Angie waggled her glitter pen while the two kids stared at her. "I hear you. Christmas sucks. So, um, do they make those nose rings in holiday colors to match your hair?"

The boy touched his green hair. "It's puke color, not Christmas."

"Right. I should have realized that." Angie elbowed Kyle. "Guess I'm not the only one struggling to get into the holiday spirit, huh?"

Kyle ignored her in favor of removing a small pocket knife from the fist of the boy.

At the sight of the knife, Angie faltered, then plowed on. "So, were you going to use that on your girlfriend? I'm all for making loved ones suffer, but don't you think that's taking it a little far?" Angie shook her head while Kyle pocketed the weapon. "I mean, death is pretty permanent."

The girl swore at the boy, obviously not impressed with the knife thing. Actually, she seemed to be swearing at Kyle for stealing the knife. "Look at that, Kyle. Loyal until the end. I suppose I should be impressed." She waved her hands to silence the raging obscenities. "So, listen, girlfriend, I have a question for you."

The girl told her what she could do with the question. Interesting option.

"Anyway, if Rambo here were to buy you diamonds for Christmas, would you dig that?"

The girl blinked. "What kind of diamonds?"

Ah-ha. An entire sentence without any curse words. See what diamonds could do? Clean society right up, they would. "Whatever you want. Earrings. Nose ring. Nipple ring."

"Big diamonds?"

"If you want them. Size isn't always what's important you know." Always good to be a little inflammatory and see what kind of interesting response you can get.

The boy sniggered and elbowed Kyle. "Big is always better, man, don't you know?"

Kyle muttered something and looked like he was in pain.

"So, anyway, is that a yes? Diamonds kick butt and all that?" Always gotta bring the interviewees back around to the story.

The girl shrugged. "He can buy me diamonds if he wants."

"I don't want," Rambo said. "But I got other big stuff for you if you want it."

She leered at him and waggled her pierced tongue at him. "I'll take it."

Ah-ha. The mere mention of diamonds had turned two raving, cursing lunatics into snuggle bunnies. "So, diamonds would keep you guys happy together. Is that what you're saying? Despite the screaming and the fights and the incipient violence?"

The girl ignored Angie. "Want to ditch this place?"

"Yeah." The kid shoved off Kyle and stood, grabbed the girl by the wrist, and hauled her to her feet, where he proceeded to suck face with her for a good long time. By the time his hands made it up the front of the girl's coat, Angie decided it was time to move on.

"Well, that about does it, don't you think, Kyle?" She stood and patted the kids on their shoulders. "Thanks for the interview. Happy Holidays." They ignored her in favor of more public displays of affection. "Great. See you guys around."

She'd made it only about twenty feet when Kyle's hand closed around her arm and he pulled her to a stop. "Angie . . ."

Damn it. She was not in the mood to take crap from him. So she slapped a mittened hand over his mouth and scowled at him. "If you can't say something nice, then say nothing at all. Got it?" She was feeling inspired, and she certainly didn't need Kyle lecturing her on the inappropriateness of her subjects.

His dark eyes met hers, and she realized how silly he looked with a fuzzy green mitten clamped over half his face. Not exactly the refined businessman he liked to project at work. She grinned. "You almost look human right now."

His eyes flashed, and he closed his hand around her wrist and removed her hand from his mouth. "You could have gotten yourself killed."

Kyle fingered the knife in his pocket and felt a cold chill go through him. He'd been chilled to the bone ever since he saw that knife in the kid's hand.

That was why he'd sat down next to Angie. To stay between her and the boy. With her expensive coat and leather boots, she exuded enough money to make it worthwhile for a kid like that to make a move for her purse.

Angie rolled her eyes. "There's about a gazillion people around. He wasn't going to do anything to me. Glad you got the knife though. Not sure what was up with that."

"He was going to mug you." Damn. Why couldn't he stop thinking about that? His only interest in Angie was making sure she wrote a good story. So why did he feel so worried about her? "Did you want to get mugged? Think it would make Roger feel bad for ditching you?"

She stared at him, and he regretted his words.

"Face it, Angie. Roger's never going to feel bad. He's a jerk, and you deserve better."

He felt like a heel. She just stared at him. Probably shouldn't even have brought it up. From now on, he'd practice avoidance and pretend Roger didn't exist.

"I thought you hated me. Why do you care who I date?"

Whoa. Wasn't prepared for that statement. He tucked his hand under her arm and guided her back to their table. "I don't care who you date."

She studied him. "Then what's with the Roger remark?"

"It's interfering with your writing." He really did feel like Roger wasn't good enough for her, but wasn't sure why he cared. It felt like it ran a lot deeper than her writing.

Angie's lips tightened. "Right. It's all about the work. Forgot that for a sec." She turned away. "Won't make that mistake again."

"What mistake?"

"We lost our table." Angie changed the subject.

Their table had been taken over by a rowdy party in their early twenties, who had at least stacked Kyle and Angie's papers neatly on the corner of the table. Kyle retrieved them, only to find Angie already leaving by the time he returned. "Angie, wait up."

She glanced over her shoulder. "I'm going to go write now."

What was up with the niggling in his gut? There was vulnerability and resistance in Angie's eyes that he didn't understand. It felt so familiar, like something he'd seen in them two years ago.

He clearly remembered his relationship with Angie before he'd started dating Sheila. They'd been close, and he'd nearly broken his rule about getting involved with someone at work. Not to mention, his resistance to a woman who would want more from him that he was willing to give. You didn't dabble with Angie. Sheila was for dabbling, which was all he'd wanted at the time.

But he wasn't interested in revisiting the relationship they'd had before Sheila. He hadn't thought much about it for ages, but now that Angie was single again, those memories kept cropping up. *Focus on work.* "Are you going to write about that couple?"

"Yeah."

She said nothing else, and neither did he. He wasn't in the mood to discuss their past relationship, and all he could think about was Angie with that pocket knife sticking out of her back.

He grabbed her arm and didn't let go until they were inside the lobby of his condo building.

"Um, Kyle?"

"What?" He punched the elevator button.

"Why are we here?"

She fixed her eyes on him, and he realized they were wide and wary. And so blue. He'd forgotten how blue. "Because I have remote access to the network from home. Figured you could write your story from here."

The elevator opened, and he stepped inside. Angie remained in the foyer. "And why would it be better for me to write here than in the office?"

Kyle punched the door open button. How was he supposed to answer that? Tell her that he figured maybe a change of scenery would help? That she'd probably had her share of action with Roger in her little office, and he thought it would be appropriate to get her some place where she didn't think of it. So she'd be able to stay positive and write an inspirational story about love.

The fact that they'd had some fun times working late in his condo? Mere coincidence. Or maybe, he was hoping she'd rediscover some of that levity, for the sake of her work.

"Kyle?"

"Because it's closer than going all the way back to the office. It's almost ten, and we don't exactly have a lot of spare time to get this thing posted online." Sounded lame even to him.

To his surprise, Angie cursed and jumped in the elevator. "Almost ten? I had no idea." She pulled out her notebook and started reading on the ride up, muttering to herself.

That was a good sign. At least she was trying to write something, even if she was no good at it. Scratch that. She was good, just not appropriately inspired. So maybe if he inspired her . . .

The elevator door opened, and he held it while Angie stepped into the hallway.

Yep. That was what he'd do. Set up an inspirational mood. Love, romance, and some hot loving, along with some holiday music. She'd write brilliantly, Swift would be impressed and hand over all their business to New Age Marketing, then Roger would sell the company so he would have more time to woo Sheila, and everything would be great.

Angie could feel the nervous anticipation race through her as Kyle opened the door. What was her problem? It wasn't as if he'd invited her there to take advantage of her. It was work only. So what if she remembered many nights of bonding in this very apartment? It had all been a façade anyway. Yeah, while she was falling in love with him, he'd been scanning for a new hot chick to date.

So what? She was smarter now. She knew where she stood with him, and she'd be too smart to interpret anything as more than work oriented. He was trying to get Swift as a client, and she was the key, so he was investing in her. Nothing else.

Chill out, Angie.

She followed him inside. "Looks the same. Nice."

And it was. A very spacious and roomy loft. Sure, it was a bit plain, but it had black, modern furniture, a sweet kitchenette, and even a little dining area off to the right. The bedroom was clearly visible behind a couple of Japanese folding screens, and the bed hadn't been made since he last slept in it.

She could envision him, stretched out in those silver sheets that barely covered his waist, just as she'd envisioned so many times in the past. Never came to fruition, though. *Remember?*

"So, the computer is over here."

"Right. The computer." She followed him to the desk set up right next to the bedroom area and sat down at the computer. As if she could concentrate with his bed only feet from her. Sure, she hated him because he'd broken her heart and canoodled with her sister, but feelings of total infatuation and lust weren't that quick to dissipate, especially when she was sitting there inhaling his scent as he leaned over her and cleaned his files off the desk. And talk about memories. She could still remember the time they'd cooked popcorn and stayed up until two in the morning watching a Meg Ryan marathon on television.

She'd thought any man who could watch Meg Ryan for hours was her perfect match.

Well, everyone makes completely asinine assumptions, don't they?

"Go ahead and get to work. Don't worry about me."

Don't worry about him. Hah. She was in the condo of the sexiest man she'd ever met and she was supposed to pretend she was in her office?

"Less than two hours."

Damn. Okay, she could concentrate. She'd better. It wasn't as if he cared about the fact she could take a diving leap to her left and land on his bed without touching the ground first.

Besides, she needed to prove to herself that she was completely capable of writing brilliant prose even when her social life was a disaster.

She opened her notebook, then looked up when the first chords of "Deck the Halls" shattered the room's silence. Kyle shot her a sneaky grin, then turned on the Christmas tree lights that he'd strung through the rafters of the loft. "Getting in the mood yet?"

The mood she was getting into with Kyle walking around his loft in his sock feet and looking mischievous wasn't exactly the Christmas one.

"Hang on." He pulled open a cabinet, took out a tin, and brought it over to her. It was red with a painted Christmas scene on the top. "My mom makes me Christmas cookies every year. Take your pick." He opened the container and set it down on the desk. Candy canes, Christmas trees, little Santas, all meticulously decorated.

"Your mom must love you to make all this for you."

He turned red. "I help."

Well, that was a new one. "You help your mom decorate Christmas cookies?"

"Yeah."

"Not exactly the autocratic financial wizard image you project at work."

He looked surprised. "You think I'm autocratic?"

"Everyone does. Because you are." She gestured to the computer. "You've been bossing me around all day."

"But that's because . . ." he paused. "Sorry."

Sorry? He apologized to her? Since when was he the type to apologize for being focused on work.

"So, you in the holiday spirit yet?" he asked.

She sighed. "Kyle, I appreciate the effort, but I've got to do this on my own. A few reminders of Christmas aren't going to snap me back in place."

He held up his finger. "Hang on." He disappeared into his bedroom, where she could see him riffling through a wardrobe. He let out a triumphant grunt, then re-emerged, holding a headband that had antlers sprouting out of it. "Here. Wear these. Got 'em at a White Elephant party last year."

She eyed them. "I think you should wear them. How am I supposed to respond to them if they're on my own head and I can't see them?"

He narrowed his eyes. "You serious?"

"Sure." She didn't believe for a minute he was going to put them on his head.

"Fine." He yanked them on. "You better be inspired."

He looked so ridiculous with the antlers bouncing around, with the headband totally askew on his head that Angie couldn't help but grin. "You're crooked. Come here."

He obediently squatted in front of her so she could reach his head. "I'm at your mercy. Be quick with it. It's torture for me."

She laughed and tucked the ends of the headband behind his ears. "It goes behind your ears, and then you need to free the antlers so they bounce." She fluffed his hair around the headband. "There. You look fabulous." She suddenly realized that his hands were on her thighs for balance. "Um . . ."

"So, you're in the Christmas mood now?" His voice was husky, and he seemed to have developed a deep fascination with her lips.

"Getting there."

"What about love? Romance? You feeling that yet?"

"That would be a no." Sex maybe. She might be feeling that. Love? Bah. Love was for idiots.

He twisted a strand of her hair around his index finger. "It's my job to inspire you."

Her mouth felt dry. "Is that right?" *Remember, he's only motivated by work. This isn't real.*

"Mmm." He shifted onto his knees so his face was almost level with hers. "You think a kiss might inspire you?"

She tried to swallow. "Depends on who it was from. Rudolph, yes."

"Me."

Brain melt. "You want to kiss me?"

"No. But I'd do it for the company."

"You really do know how to make a girl swoon. Do you give lessons on sweet-talking?" She shoved at his chest. "Forget it. A kiss for Roger's company isn't exactly going to put me in the mood to be all lovey and romantic."

"Damn it. It's not for Roger!"

Before she could react to the anger in his words, he grabbed her face and kissed her.

Chapter Five

There's nothing like some good tongue action to make the holiday season brighten right up. Who needs diamonds?
—Angie Miller

The instant his lips touched hers, she was toast. Everything miserable and hateful and depressing vanished from her body, replaced with a warmth that started in her belly and slowly spread to every nerve in her body.

She grabbed the front of his shirt, holding on tight to feelings she didn't ever want to leave. *Kyle is kissing me.* Her body was trembling, her heart pounding. *Kyle is kissing me.* Never stop.

He broke the kiss long before she was ready. "Ready to write the article yet?" His voice was hoarse as he let his hands slip to her waist.

"No. Not yet. I'm still feeling rather bitter and hostile," she said. "I think we should try again. For the sake of the article."

"For the article." This time when he kissed her, it wasn't

soft or soothing. It was hot and demanding, invading her defenses and leaving her exposed and vulnerable.

And she loved it. It was nothing like the kisses she'd shared with Roger. This was something deeper. It was everything she'd always thought a kiss from Kyle would be, and then some.

She heard a noise echo from the back of her throat, and Kyle responded by deepening the kiss.

I'm down with that. The antler headband took a dive as she ran her hands through his hair. A worthwhile sacrifice.

His hands were all over her. Back, waist, ribs, breasts. Was that about the article too?

But damn, it felt good. Just another minute . . . and wow, she was losing her balance. Better wrap her legs around Kyle's waist to make sure she'd didn't fall and hurt herself.

Something crashed to the floor. Her heart, maybe? Because for one that was so thoroughly broken, it was certainly pounding in her chest like nobody's business. And . . .

Kyle broke the kiss. "That was my laptop."

Lap? Sure. She'd climb onto his lap.

She opened her eyes to find Kyle peering past her hip at the floor, his hands still in very interesting places on her fanny. She leaned over and looked down. "That was your computer that fell?"

He glanced at her. "That's what I said."

Oh, right. Laptop. Never had a kiss that made her forget the English language before. She cleared her throat and realized her hands had somehow worked themselves under his shirt, where she was massaging his bare chest.

"So—" He moved his hands from her rear to a more neutral place on her hips. *No! Come back!* "—about the article."

"Yeah." With supreme effort, she managed to extract her hands from his garments. "I think I could write it now."

Yeah, if she was supposed to write the screenplay for a porno flick.

"Great." He looked like he was going to kiss her again, but before she could yell an affirmative response, he pulled back and stood. "I'll . . . um . . . pour some eggnog."

"Coffee would be better. I could use some caffeine." She felt the headband on her ankle, so she grabbed it and held it up. "Your crown."

He stuck it on his head, crookedly again, then shot her a cocky grin. "Coffee coming up."

She decided not to offer to fix the headband again. Last time that had led to something she wasn't equipped to deal with. Yes, she knew it had been only for the sake of her story. But it was really hard to keep remembering that. Best not to get involved at all.

Next time he tried to kiss her for inspiration, she was going to kick him in the kneecap.

By ten o'clock the next morning, Kyle was on his way down the hall for his third cup of morning coffee. He'd stayed up with Angie working on her article until almost two, then taken a cab back to her place to make sure she got there safely. By the time he got back home, it had been after three.

Not that it mattered. He'd spent the rest of the night lying in bed thinking about kissing her.

What was his problem? Getting involved with Angie Miller was bad news from all angles. Roger's ex, Sheila's sister . . . not to mention the fact she worked for him. Plus, she was dangerous. He'd seen how she'd stolen Roger away from the company. No way was he willing to sacrifice his company for a woman. He was staying out of Angie's clutches, even if her lips were soft and she smelled like peaches.

He cleared his throat and frowned. His job was far more enduring than any relationship with a woman, regardless of whether her kisses did make him a little bit crazy. That's why he'd never given in to his urge to kiss her before, why he'd taken up with her sister. Because he knew what he could give a woman, and it was far less than what Angie would demand or deserved.

Women like Sheila were his style. They fit his life. A little action, no demands.

"Kyle!"

He turned to find Roger jogging down the hall toward him. He tensed, wondering what Roger would do if he knew he had kissed Angie. Even though Roger had dumped her, the code mandated that the ex would stay off limits for a certain period of time, if not forever. "Morning."

"I wanted to thank you for last night."

"For?" Surely he couldn't know about the kiss.

"For dragging Angie out of the Miller Christmas party. That could have been quite the scene. Probably would have started throwing wineglasses at me if she'd stayed around."

Kyle tensed. "I think you're overestimating your allure. Angie seemed fine after we left."

"Yeah, right. I read yesterday's article. You weren't kidding. Didn't realize I'd broken her heart that badly. Think she's hopeless? You still think maybe I should take her back for the rest of the month?"

"No! I don't think taking her back is the solution," Kyle snapped. He took a breath and forced himself to relax. "Did you read today's story? Much better." After that kiss, he and Angie had had fun taking that screaming couple's episode and turning it into a colorful love story about the power of diamonds. It hadn't quite been the sappy slant that he knew Swift was hoping for, but it was a hell of a lot better than the first story she'd written.

No call had come from Swift this morning telling him they were ending the deal, so he figured they were still skating by.

"If you change your mind, let me know. I'm sure I could put Sheila on hold for a few weeks."

"No. I have it under control." He flexed his fingers and considered tossing Roger down the elevator shaft.

Roger clapped him on the shoulder. "See? I knew you could handle her." He frowned. "Hey, you aren't mad about Sheila, are you?"

"She's all yours."

"Well, right, I know that. But are you mad? Because you know, you wouldn't be getting her back even if I wasn't in the picture."

"I don't want her."

"Yeah, well, I understand how you feel. I'd be bent out of shape, too, if you started dating one of my exes."

"Trust me. I don't want Sheila." Sure, she'd seemed like a good answer at one time, but now? When he saw her in that skin-tight dress at the party last night, he'd felt nothing. Until he'd seen the look of total humiliation on Angie's face. Then he'd felt something for Sheila, and it hadn't been complimentary.

"That's the right attitude." Roger glanced over his shoulder to check for eavesdroppers. "You know how Sheila and Angie's dad is in the Christmas musical every year?"

Yes, he recalled accompanying Sheila to that event, while Angie hung on Roger's arm. "Yeah."

"Well, opening night is Friday. I'm going to take Sheila, so will you keep Angie occupied? I don't want it to get weird for me and Sheila, you know?"

"God forbid you feel uncomfortable."

"Exactly! Give Angie some extra work or something."

"How about if I take her back to my place and keep her occupied?" He had no intention of doing that, but he wanted to know what Roger's response would be. Because if Roger didn't care, then, well . . .

Roger was in his face in an instant, his eyes glittery and black. "Don't touch her."

"Why not?"

"Because she's mine."

"You dumped her."

"Doesn't matter. You want the company, you keep your hands off Angie."

Good to know Roger had ego and control issues. "I wasn't going to do anything. I was merely curious, seeing as how you're dating my ex and all."

Roger shrugged. "It's different."

Indeed. Maybe because Angie was a great person and Sheila was shallow and self-serving?

"And I'm bringing Sheila to the company Christmas party in a few weeks. Deal with Angie on that one too."

Kyle stilled. "Sheila's coming to the New Age holiday party?"

"Yeah. She's got this sexy red dress I've been dying to see her wear."

"Angie works for this company. She deserves to be able to go to it."

Roger narrowed his eyes. "It's for her own good. You saw the article she wrote. The woman can't live without me."

For the first in his life, Kyle wanted to hit his friend. "I think she can handle it." *You're not that much of a loss, and I'll make sure she realizes it.*

Roger shrugged. "Your funeral if it makes her unable to write anything decent."

"Kyle?" his admin hollered down the hall. "Swift is on the phone for you."

Swift? Were they calling to complain about the story? If

so, he wasn't going to tell Angie. She needed support, not more things bringing her down. Somehow, he'd find a way to protect her.

Heidi had her feet tucked up under her as she munched on sushi for their late morning snack in Angie's office. "Good call to blow off work this morning. What's up?"

Angie nibbled on some seaweed. "So, um, what happened at my parents' after I left last night?"

"Oh, right. Totally weird. After you left, everyone just resumed conversation like nothing had happened. Freaky."

She paused. "Are you kidding? No one said anything?" She'd been so certain her mom would call her first thing this morning to explain. No call.

"Nope." Heidi took a sip of her Diet Coke. "Your mom's really a good cook, you know? Those shrimp hors d'oeuvres were really good. I was totally bummed Quin couldn't make it."

"Heidi! Stop talking about the food! My entire family betrayed me and no one cared?"

"Nope. Wouldn't worry about it though."

"Why not?" Seemed to her that being excommunicated by the family was sort of a big deal.

"Because you got to kiss Kyle."

She knew she shouldn't have told Heidi about that. "I told you. He was trying to inspire me."

"Yeah, I'll bet. When Quin inspires me like that, we wind up sweaty and . . ."

"Thanks for the visual." Like she hadn't had her share of hot and sweaty dreams last night.

Heidi sat up and leaned closer. "I do have a question for you."

"What's that?" If Heidi asked her about birth control, Angie was going to kick her out of the office. One kiss didn't mean sex was around the corner.

"Do you know what you're doing?"

Angie frowned. "About what?"

"Kyle. When you talk about him kissing you, there's that same glow in your eyes as there was when you first met him. Remember what happened then?"

"Of course I remember. I'm not falling for him again."

"Are you sure? He didn't even kiss you last time and it still took you ages to recover."

"The kiss was to inspire me. For the article. I know it, so don't worry about me." She'd been reminding herself all morning, but she couldn't help but wonder if this time it was different. He'd never kissed her before. He wouldn't kiss her and not mean it, would he?

Only if he made it very clear it was purely for the company. Which he had.

And that was fine. She didn't need a man right now anyway. She had some healing to do, and she had to do it on her own. Speaking of that . . . "Did you read today's story?"

Heidi nodded. "It was a lot better than your first one. Didn't even sound like you wanted to kill every happy person in the world." She lifted a brow. "It read like you were having fun while you wrote it."

Angie sighed with satisfaction and leaned back in her chair. "I knew it was better. See? Roger can't destroy me."

"Or maybe it's Kyle who's healing you. Trade one man for another."

She sat up. Impossible. She wasn't the type who needed a man in her life to be able to write good stuff. "No way."

Heidi furrowed her brow. "Maybe men are your muse. Roger's been your muse for the last year, and then when you didn't have one, you couldn't write. Kyle gives you a hot kiss and voila, you're back." She shook her head. "I thought you weren't getting attached to Kyle. He's not a relationship kind of guy."

"You're wrong. I don't need a man to heal, especially not Kyle." Needing a man in that way made her way too vulnerable and dependent. It was unacceptable, and she was going to prove it by keeping her distance from Kyle and still writing great stories.

"Well, maybe we need to find another way to inspire you. You need romance and sex on the brain? We can talk sex. That'll get you going, without the burden of involving a man. We'll get some wine and some chocolate and spend the night at my place talking sex. Quin is working late this week, so he won't be by. What do you think? Alcohol and sex sound good to you?"

"Must you talk about that kind of thing in the workplace?" Kyle was standing in the door, his hands on his hips, the corner of his mouth quirking.

Heidi was unapologetic. "I'm trying to inspire Angie for her smut stories. What better way than to talk sex? Want to join us? Got any good sex stories?"

The flash of surprise on his face was gone so quickly Angie would have missed it if she wasn't gawking at him and the heavy outline of whiskers on his face. Someone hadn't shaved this morning, and she'd be damned if that wasn't a very good look for him.

"Plenty of good sex. No stories," he said.

Plenty of good sex? With who? Sheila? Other sluts?

"Well, I suppose that's admirable in a man. No kiss and tell," Heidi said.

"And Angie isn't writing smut stories. They're about love, romance, and the passionate commitment between a man and a woman."

How could she not fall for a man who talked like that?

Maybe he'd dated her slutty sister, but that was a while ago. Obviously, the man had depth.

Heidi raised her brow at Angie, then stood. "Well, I suppose you want Angie to yourself so you can inspire her. Seemed to work for today's story."

Kyle raised his eyebrow and looked at Angie.

Totally busted.

Heidi walked over to him and eyed him. "Just so you know, if you break her heart again, I'll come after you."

Heidi!

"All this sex talk has gotten me in the mood. I'm going to go call Quin." Heidi picked up the container of sushi and walked out. "See y'all later."

She shut the door firmly behind her.

An awkward silence fell over the room, no doubt due to the residual sexual talk hovering in the air. "So . . . um . . ." Should she tell him she'd been up all night replaying that kiss in her mind? That she was way too vulnerable when it came to him and she'd decided that they needed to get some space between them?

"Break your heart? Again?"

"She's been sniffing glue again. Don't mind her. What do you want?" *Look at those lips. The same ones that had kissed her last night.*

"What did she mean, 'again'?"

"She was being a dork. Trying to make more of our kiss last night than it was. You know Heidi, always the matchmaker." She had to change the subject fast, because he was looking mighty interested in this topic. "So, any feedback on the story? It was good, huh?"

She saw the shift in his facial expression. From soft and personal to businesslike and impersonal. Her fault. She was the one who had changed the subject, hadn't she? "Swift called," he said.

Hmm . . . he didn't have that happy, glowing look about him. "And?"

"They weren't happy with the story."

Angie felt her spirits drop. "Why not?"

"Too irreverent, and teenagers don't buy diamonds." He rubbed his forehead. "I should have realized it was all wrong, but I got caught up in . . . the kiss. Lost my focus."

"Caught up? Did I distract you? Keep you from doing your job?" Angie sat up quickly. He'd gotten caught up in the kiss? Did that mean it had meant more to him than merely inspiration for her story? Had he felt his soul crash and soar like she had?

"I should never have let that happen. Never lose sight of the client." He eyed her. "No more of that kind of inspiration."

Wait a sec. Was he resenting her for distracting him? Like she was some she-devil temptation? "You're the one who kissed me!"

"I know. And I was wrong."

So that's how it was? He'd been tempted, and it was wrong. Fine. She didn't like him anyway. She folded her arms across her chest. "For your information, my article was great."

"But it was wrong for the client." He dropped to the chair across from her. "Listen, Angie. You have the talent, but you've got to get it together mentally. I want sappy, romantic love."

Angie ground her teeth. "Fine. You want sap? I'll give you sap. Now get out of my office so I can work."

He looked startled by her venom. Good. It was about time someone in her life noticed that she could actually feel pain. "Don't take it personally, Angie. It's just about the job."

"Believe me, I'm well aware of that. And that kiss last night was only to humor you. I didn't even want to kiss you."

He lifted his brow, and she wondered how bright the neon "Liar" sign was on her forehead. "So, when's your next interview?" he asked.

Dropping the subject. A good idea. She was on board with that. No need to discuss his lips on hers any longer. "I don't have anything scheduled. I was going to go out at lunch and see what struck my fancy."

"Like you did with the teenagers?"

"Yes."

"I'll go with you."

She scowled. "I'm perfectly capable of interviewing on my own."

Kyle leaned forward, his face intense. "Angie, you're hurting, which is human. But it's better if you admit it and accept that you need help to get this assignment right. Because I'm going to help." A muscle ticked in his cheek. "And I'm not going to get distracted this time. The articles *will* be right. Every one of them."

"You're going to be leaning over my shoulder for the next month?"

"Yes."

Did that stink or what? Ten minutes ago, jingle bells would have been jangling in her belly at the thought of Kyle snuggled up next to her while she typed. She would have been thinking of all the possibilities. But now? It was obvious that he was all about the company. Last night, he hadn't been lying when he'd said the kiss was to inspire her.

Inspire her. Hah! She didn't need a man to inspire her. She was going to find a muse on her own and prove to everyone that she was just fine

Chapter Six

Mink coats and limousines not enough to convince her you love her? Give her a couple glittery diamonds, and she'll stop complaining about your long hours at the office.
—Angie Miller, the uninspired

"How about them?" Kyle pointed to a gray-haired couple sporting expensive coats climbing out of a limo. "They look happy."

"They're too rich. No one will respond to them."

"People who spend a lot of money on diamonds aren't usually on welfare. Remember your audience."

If he corrected her one more time about the damn story, she was going to push him under the feet of those carriage horses she'd spent the morning stalking. She'd thought that there'd be happy couples going for romantic rides around the city, but apparently that activity was more popular in the evening than at eleven o'clock in the morning on a cloudy day. Besides, the three couples she actually considered approaching had all been vetoed by Kyle.

"Plus, they aren't holding hands, and he didn't even look back to make sure she didn't trip on the curb," she added.

He looked at her. "Holding hands is a sign of romance?"

"Of course it is. Those little touches are unnecessary, but you do them because you can't keep your hands off each other. Nothing sexual, just caring." She noticed then that Kyle's hand was on her elbow, supporting her. "Like the way you're holding my arm."

He let go immediately. "Not everyone expresses true love by touching. Let's go talk to them and see."

Angie rolled her eyes when he grabbed her arm again and propelled her across the sidewalk to the couple. They'd probably have her and Kyle arrested for stalking, not that Kyle seemed to care.

When they stopped next to the couple, Angie noticed that Kyle didn't let go of her arm. Because he was afraid she'd bolt or because deep down inside he was passionately in love with her? It would be fun if it was the latter. Then she could reject him and walk away with her pride intact.

"Good afternoon," he said, his voice smooth as silk. With his black overcoat, polished shoes, and leather gloves, he certainly fit into the world he was pursuing. "I hate to bother you, but if you have a moment, I'd love to talk to you."

The gentleman gave Kyle the once-over, then nodded his approval. "May I help you?"

Kyle pinched her arm. Fine. "Hi, my name is Angie Miller. I have to do an interview on true love. Want to be interviewed?"

The woman smiled, but the man gave Angie an odd look. Couldn't be because of her flippant tone, could it? "What is it for?"

"The Internet."

Kyle interrupted with a poetic description of the website and of romance and the holidays. By the time he finished, she was ready to melt at his feet. What kind of man could talk about love like that?

Obviously only a putz. No one she would want.

Kyle had the man and woman so enraptured, they offered to buy him lunch so he could interview them. Yeah, she'd buy him lunch, too, if he directed that poetry in her direction. What happened to the shallow boob-chaser who'd dated her sister? If he kept this up, he was going to really mess with her plans to stay immune to him.

Angie pressed her hands to her forehead and stared at the computer screen. *I can't do this for one more minute. I am going to lose my mind.* "I need coffee."

Kyle didn't even move away from his perch over her left shoulder. He just held up a full cup of coffee and kept reading the screen.

"Right. Forgot." So she'd gotten back from a coffee break only two minutes ago. Didn't mean she was ready to sit back down at this computer and face her total inability to write. She'd lost her muse, and now that she'd accepted that the kiss with Kyle had meant nothing, she couldn't even get back to the level of the story she'd written about the teenagers. Five stories she'd battled through this week, only to have Kyle practically rewrite each one. Took countless drafts to get something decent enough that Swift didn't cancel the contract. Her writing, being edited by a finance guy. Not only being edited, but actually being made better by a finance guy. She sucked, and she didn't want to face herself anymore. "I have to go to the bathroom."

"You just went."

"Since when do I have to justify my bodily urges to you?"

He slanted a look in her direction.

"Not those bodily urges. I don't have those anymore. You're too much of a pain in the ass to get me all excited anymore," she grumbled. "And to think I wasted all that time having a crush on you. How stupid was that?"

He shifted to his right so he could look at her. "What?"

"I said I was stupid."

"No. Not that. You had a crush on me?" He looked shocked, but at least he had the good grace not to look nauseated by that fact.

"I *did*. Not anymore." She took the coffee out of his hand, barely noticing when her fingers touched his. Guess that was what a week of being harangued could do to sexual attraction. Wither it up into nothingness. "Listen. I know it's only six o'clock, but it's Saturday and I'm fried. Can we just call in sick and scrap the posting for tomorrow?"

He was still gawking at her.

"What?" She pushed at his jaw to direct his gaze back to the computer screen. "Quit staring at me."

"You had a crush on me while I was dating Sheila?"

Like she needed to be reminded of that. "Only because I was immature and stupid."

"And while you were dating Roger?"

"Well, what do you expect? Obviously Roger isn't a good enough catch to keep any woman truly content, right? You were merely a convenient scapegoat. I would have had a crush on anyone who ignored me as thoroughly as you did. Want what you can't have and all that jazz." So good to realize after the fact that bringing up the past crush wasn't the best idea. Even if she was over him, it was still a little embarrassing, especially with the way he was gaping at her like she'd sprouted two heads. Besides, when he was this close to her, she couldn't exactly ignore how good he smelled. Like soap, a bit of aftershave and something else she couldn't place.

"Why don't you have a crush on me anymore?"

She ignored him. "You think the first sentence is too boring? Doesn't really grab me."

"Why don't you have a crush on me anymore?"

She sighed and looked at him. "Because you're a pain in the butt. You're autocratic, overbearing, and you're haunting me. And you're making me rehash these damn stories until they're dead and flat, and on top of that, you made me miss my dad's opening night last night to work. Oh, sure, I know, it's all about the company, but you are way too obsessed about this company for my taste."

He looked startled, but this felt too good to stop. She faced him and kept going. "You think Roger's an idiot because he doesn't take this company as seriously as you do, but I personally would rather be with a man who actually took time to have some fun in life, who didn't moan for weeks if one client muttered a word of dissatisfaction."

"You prefer a man who will put you first?"

"Well of course! What woman wouldn't? No, what person wouldn't? Do you think anyone really wants the person they love to put other things first?"

"I'd understand if work came first."

"Then all the crap you've been spouting all week about true love has been a lie? Something you saw a documentary on when you were flipping through the channels and it got stuck on the Oxygen network?" And to think she'd actually gotten weak-kneed at some of his descriptions about how emotional and loving these stories were supposed to be.

"How could I be lying? I wasn't talking about myself. I was talking about the focus of the story." He frowned.

"That's fine for other people for love to come first, but that's not my gig."

"And you wonder why I don't have a crush on you anymore." She turned her back on him. "Go away and leave me alone so I can write drivel in peace."

Kyle felt like he'd been clubbed in the side of the head. She'd had a crush on him?

A crush.

On him.

"What about all those glares you gave me whenever I showed up anywhere with your sister?" he asked.

"Your imagination." She didn't even look at him. Just kept typing.

"And you've given me those looks at work too."

"That's because I'm representing the masses, who resent you being an autocrat."

"Oh, so now no one at work likes me?"

She shrugged and kept typing. "It's not a matter of liking you. It's a matter of not liking working for you." She slanted a look at him. "Don't take it personally, Kyle. It's just about work."

He stared at her.

She grinned.

He grinned back. "Touché, huh?" Did she have a nice smile or what? He realized he hadn't seen it much. Was he really driving her too hard? "I'm not really overly obsessed with New Age, am I? I mean, people know I value them, don't they?" Sure, he worked hard, but always thought he was fair and a good boss. Prided himself on it, actually. A company was nothing without happy, motivated employees. "I don't work people too hard."

She lifted a brow. "Then why are we at work on a Saturday evening?"

"Because we have a story due." The words were out of his mouth before he could stop them. But what was wrong with that? They had a deadline. It wasn't optional.

"Okay, Kyle." Angie leaned back in her chair and folded her arms across her chest. "What's wrong with my writing?"

"It's flat."

"Right. And your editing makes it flatter."

"I'm trying." He wasn't a writer, though Lord knew he'd been trying all week.

"I'm trying, too, despite what you may think. However, I've concluded that being handcuffed to my desk isn't going to fix the problem. You know what will?"

"What?" He thought of the kiss they'd shared, and the story she'd written immediately after. More of that? For the company, he could make the sacrifice.

"Getting out of here and enjoying myself. Finding a reason to be happy." She put a finger over his mouth when he started to speak. "Not forever. Just for a few hours. Time spent outside with sane people, not looking for my next victims. You need to release me. Now."

He wrapped his hand around hers and removed it from his lips, contemplating for a moment what she'd do if he took her hand and kissed each fingertip one by one . . .

"So? Can I go?" She picked up her purse and looked at him expectantly.

"So eager to be spared my company?"

"Yes."

"Thanks. Didn't need my ego anyway."

She snorted. "Give me a break. A herd of elephants couldn't damage that thing."

He frowned. So, she thought he was a pain in the butt, too obsessed with work, a bad manager, and he had a big ego? What kind of image had he been presenting? That wasn't who he was . . . was it? "Fine. You want to go out? Let's go."

"With you?" Her eyes widened, and she looked almost panicked. "I meant for me to go alone."

"Maybe I need to get out of here too." Yeah, maybe he didn't want to be at work. It was Saturday evening, after all. "What do you want to do?" *Get inspired at my condo?*

He cursed immediately. What kind of thought was that? Since the kiss, he'd been in complete control around Angie. Hadn't trailed his fingers over her arm when she'd been leaning across him to get something from the other side of the desk. Never kissed her earlobe when her snowman earrings had caught his eye. And certainly had refrained from giving her a backrub when she'd complained about sitting too long. So why in the hell had he thought about escorting her back to his condo and taking that kiss to the next level?

"I was thinking Christmas shopping. Need to buy Roger some arsenic."

"He's not worth the money." Why did she care so much about Roger? Didn't she know that he simply wasn't worth it? "Though it would probably give me the company if you killed him, so maybe it's not such a bad idea . . ."

"You and your precious company. I told you—you have a one-track mind."

"No, I don't." He pushed back from her desk and took her hand to pull her to her feet. "Let's go Christmas shopping."

She eyed him. "I really wasn't planning on having you join me."

"Why not? What if you run into an interview candidate?"

Her mouth opened to protest, so he quickly moved on. "Besides, you're so anti-Christmas these days that you'll probably last for one store, kick a Santa in the nuts, and then bail for home. I'm going along to make sure you have some fun." All in the name of the story. That's what it was all about. Just business. He had a professional interest in making sure she lightened up enough to write something truly phenomenal because the twaddle they were creating now was flat and wouldn't get them a contract.

It was all about work.

She was staring at him. "You're seriously going to let me go shopping?"

"Sure. You're right. We're not making these stories any better with this approach. Let's go. I have shopping to do as well."

"I hate shopping. Hate it." Angie squeezed through the crowd of people lining the aisles of Macy's. "I'm going to do Internet shopping from now on." *Must get out. Must find freedom.* She barely dodged a handbag being thrown from a mother to her teenage daughter, who was circling the side-lines. "Either that or abandon present-giving altogether. It's kind of a commercial proposition, anyway, isn't it?"

"Except diamonds. That's not commercial." He had his hand on her lower back and was providing a buffer between her and the crowds. "Diamonds are about love and every-thing pure."

She rolled her eyes. "Do you ever forget about work?"

"According to you, never." He guided her toward an exit. "Let's go to Tiffany's and scope out the competition. Maybe you'll get inspired."

"I went to Tiffany's with Heidi last week. It's just jewelry."

"Ah, but you didn't go with me and get my unique perspective." They reached the sidewalk, but it wasn't any less crowded. The line to walk by the store window displays was all the way around the corner, and a Salvation Army volunteer was standing on the corner ringing his bell.

Kyle dumped something in the bucket as they walked by, then he stopped. "I forgot. I need to get my mom a nightgown." He turned to go back to Macy's. "Come on."

"No way. I'm not risking my life for those crowds again."

He grinned, walked over to her, slung his arm around her neck to anchor her to his side, then started back into the store. "I'll protect you, my fair maiden."

Okay, so being smashed up against Kyle might be sufficient justification to brave the crowds again. She sighed as she let him clear a path for them. What was she doing?

She was falling for him again, that's what she was doing.

She'd been so removed from him this week, trying hard to blow him up into an autocratic workaholic hated by the world. Had even convinced herself of that. Yet it had taken only a few minutes of being out of the office and seeing his dimples to make her feet start tap-dancing to songs of love.

No, not love.

Lust.

No way would she love him.

"Okay, here we go." He stopped next to a rack of flannel nightgowns. "Navy blue. Size extra large. Perfect."

Angie grabbed his hand as he went for the item. "Not so fast."

He lifted his brow. "You don't like it? It's conservative, practical. Perfect for my mom."

"Is she married?"

He frowned. "Yeah, to her second husband. Why? I'm not getting him the nightgown." He grinned at his own joke.

"Well, maybe you should."

"He's not a cross-dresser. I don't think he'd want it."

"Not the flannel one." Angie strolled over toward the other side of the lingerie section, where lace, silk, and spaghetti straps were in abundance. "He might, however, enjoy something from here." She picked up a pale blue nightie with a lace bodice and held it up. "This is what you should get your mom." She turned to show it to him, only to find him still standing at the flannel nightgowns, a look of horror on his face.

She waved it at him, and he shook his head and turned back to the rack.

And he thought he knew all about romance. "Just because she's your mom doesn't mean she doesn't like being sexy. And your stepdad, I'm sure, would appreciate a little heat in the bedroom just as much as you do."

"Stop it!" He backed up. "My mother is not wearing that."

Angie started laughing as she walked across the store to where Kyle was hiding. "If I was in your bed, would you rather I was wearing this flannel nightgown—" She held up the item in question. "—or this sexy little number?" It really wasn't even that sexy. Demure, with a little bit of naughtiness mixed in.

Kyle's eyes went black. "You? I'd take you naked."

She swallowed, her mouth suddenly dry. *Stay focused.* "Before you got me naked. Flannel or silk?"

His gaze was so intense she felt like he could see right through her clothes to the matching black lace panties and bra she'd put on this morning to try to get in the romance mood. "Silk." His voice was husky, deep. It sent chills down her spine.

She took a deep breath. "Well, then, that's what we should get for your mom. She's a woman like I am, and your stepdad is a man like you."

"I'm not thinking about my mom." But it wasn't a protest. It was an arrogant statement that said very clearly who he *was* thinking about.

She lifted her chin and took a step toward him. "You couldn't even begin to imagine what I'd be like in your bed, so don't bother guessing."

His hands snaked out and grabbed her waist, hauling her up against him before she could step away. "Tell me." His lips were hovering over hers, his breath mingling with hers.

Oh, Lordy. She was in way over her head. "Words can't do it justice. I'd have to show you."

"Then show me."

Show him? Yeah, that would be a real hardship. She trailed her finger over his lips, and tried to remember how he'd broken her heart before. "Sorry. I already resolved that I wouldn't allow you to inspire me anymore."

"I'm not talking about inspiring anyone."

Oh, wow. Was this about them? About the heat burning up the air between them? Not about work or her stories? Did he want her the way she wanted him, pure and simple? Not that there was anything simple about the feelings racing through her.

Don't kiss him, Angie.

"I can't kiss you," she whispered. The finger she'd been trailing over his lips was suddenly in his mouth, caught in a suckling whirlwind of moist heat. "Um . . ."

"You're the one who brought it up." His voice was hoarse, tight, his tongue winding around her fingertips.

"Brought what up?" How could he speak with her fingers in his mouth? He must do that a lot—suck on women's fingers. An expert.

"You. Me. My bed. Nakedness," he said.

She'd never been ravaged by an expert lover before. With the stories Heidi told about Quin, Angie was well aware that she'd been missing out. Maybe that was why she couldn't write the romance stories for Swift. Because she hadn't truly experienced mind-numbing lovemaking.

Perhaps in the name of research . . .

Chapter Seven

*Shopping for diamonds? A way to find out what really
makes your true love tick.*
—Angie Miller, somewhat less anti-diamond

One quick kiss. Just to assess whether he was truly an expert. And to prove it was lust, not love, that was making her nipples snap to attention. *You can do it, Angie.*

She let the nightgowns drop to the floor, mashed her hands into the front of his jacket, and tugged him down toward her.

He came.

And when his lips caught hers, there was no doubt about the fire racing through her body.

She pressed her body against his, trying to squeeze every last inch of contact into the kiss. More kiss, more tongue.

This was it. Kyle was what she wanted. It didn't matter if he was going to break her heart, or if she was falling too soon into the arms of another man before she'd proven she didn't need a male muse to write. All that mattered was him.

"Excuse me. Are you going to be buying one of those?"

Argh! Was it any wonder she'd always hated salespeople? Did it look like she needed a commission-based piranha assisting her right now?

But Kyle broke the kiss and dropped his hands from her body. Angie growled and glared at the saleswoman with her precious beige suit and her overly cheerful smile. Not so sure she was enjoying her first moment of sexual frustration.

Kyle muttered something and retrieved the garments from the floor, giving Angie a moment to take a deep breath and let her blood stop bubbling. By the time he was handing the flannel nightgown to the saleswoman, Angie had regained control of her brain. "No, he's buying this one." She put the silk one into the saleswoman's hand. "You know men. Think their moms aren't sexual beings."

The saleswoman's plastered smile faltered slightly, but recovered nicely. "All women love to feel sexy."

"Exactly." She stepped on Kyle's toe when he started to protest and distracted him with a glaring contest long enough for the saleswoman to march over to her register and start ringing him up.

Kyle handed over his credit card. "You know I'm going to return this tomorrow."

"Don't. Your mom will love it, and she'll feel great that you think of her as a young, sexy woman."

"She's my mother. I've never thought of her as sexy."

"You know what I mean." She shoved at his chest. Mmm . . . what a nice chest. Would love to spend a few minutes licking every inch of it. "Don't you want to make your mom feel happy?"

"Not at the expense of me being able to sleep at night." He took the bag from the saleswoman. "My turn now."

His turn? For what? Doing some chest-licking? *There's a dressing room over to the right. I'd be happy to rip off my clothes for you . . .*

"We're going to Tiffany's." He shot her a look. "Why do you look so unhappy?"

"I thought you were going to proposition me."

His eyebrows shot up as he held the door for her. "You did?"

"Well, sure. Your tongue seemed pretty happy in my mouth." Did she sound pouty? It was all the saleswoman's fault. And to think they'd given her a sale. She realized Kyle wasn't walking next to her anymore. She turned around to find him standing in the doorway of Macy's, an appealing look of lust and confusion on his face.

Apparently, he was still adjusting to the notion that he wanted her. That it wasn't just to make sure she wrote a good story. She wasn't foolish enough to think he wanted her, as in, to love and cherish forever. But raw animal sex was definitely on his brain at the moment.

Wow. She'd never had raw animal sex before. Heidi would be so jealous.

She walked back and tucked her arm in his. "Let's go to Tiffany's. I promise not to scare you with anymore sex talk." *For at least ten minutes.*

Angie decided not to make conversation on the way to Tiffany's. Force him to think about that hot kiss, and the notion of her, naked, in his bed.

By the time they got to Tiffany's, Angie's blood pressure had returned to normal and her brain was functioning again. Enough to realize that having sex with Kyle would be a very bad idea.

Because she'd fallen for him again. One hundred percent. She was practically in love. He was barely in lust. Perfect recipe for splattered heart number two. He'd already proven he was quite the talent at turning her heart into mincemeat.

Making love to him would be too much for her to deal with, at least when he got up in the morning and sent her on her merry way.

Besides, she had too much pride. No prostituting herself for a heartless man. Plus, she still needed to find her muse, and it wasn't going to be a man.

So there it was. An extensive list of reasons not to have sex with Kyle.

Thank heavens for that saleswoman interrupting them before they dropped to the carpet and consummated their dysfunctional relationship right there in Macy's.

Moment over. Time to focus on jewelry. Diamonds. Work.

She stepped inside and scanned the store. Display cases everywhere. Customers oozing wealth. The residual feelings of contentment over her excellent decision not to go for a roll in the hay with Kyle were replaced by a sensation of yuck.

Not that jewelry was a bad thing, but it was the bane of her existence right now, and it wasn't as if some hot lover was going to surprise her with a light blue box on the twenty-fifth. Nope, not in the mood to be shopping at Tiffany's. She'd have to find her muse somewhere else. "Okay, I've seen enough. Ready to go?"

"No." Kyle took her arm and walked her farther into the store. "Look at those pine boughs. They must be twenty feet long."

She gave a cursory glance upward. "Yeah, I guess." There was no safe place to look. Couples were everywhere, men in their overcoats, buying gifts for their wives, or girlfriends, or mistresses. Or to appease their wives who just found out about their girlfriends. See? Diamonds weren't about true love. They were about enabling people to get away with bad things because they'd be forgiven if they put a rock on someone's finger. Or on their ears. Or around their neck.

Nice attitude, Angie. Yeesh. No wonder she couldn't write a good story. It really would behoove her to get it together, huh?

Sex with Kyle might help her regain her delight in the holiday season and all things romantic.

Until he dumped her.

Yeah, not such a good choice.

"And check out the Christmas tree in the corner. How tall do you think that is?"

She dragged her eyes to the corner. The tree was actually gorgeous, if she was in the frame of mind to appreciate such things. No. She *was* in the mood to appreciate the holidays, and if she had to superglue garland to her forehead to remind herself of that fact, then she would. "I'd say that beautifully decorated tree, such a wonderful statement of the fabulous holiday season, is ten feet tall."

"No way. That thing has to be at least fifteen feet." Kyle threw his arm around her shoulder and guided her into the store, peering at the first display case on the right. "Look at that diamond. Love the setting."

She glanced at him. "Do you have any idea what you're talking about?" *Shrug his arm off your shoulder, Angie.*

No. I like it there.

Too bad. You already made that decision, didn't you?

"Of course I know what I'm talking about," Kyle said. "Bought five engagement rings already. I'm an expert."

She just about fell off her chair, or she would have if she'd been sitting on one. "You've been engaged five times?"

"No."

"Then . . . ?"

"I lied. Wanted to see if you were paying attention." He didn't even crack a smile, his gaze intent in the case. "You were, apparently."

"Yeah, yeah."

"So, are you two looking for an engagement ring?" A saleswoman in a very expensive suit and perfectly coifed auburn hair materialized before them.

Kyle answered before Angie could decline. "We're looking for the perfect diamond, that says everlasting love."

"Kyle . . ."

He shushed her. "No, my love. I want you to have it. No more arguing about it."

His love? Just like that, all her immunity to his charm shot to hell. Maybe it was because she'd had repeated dreams in which he'd used that exact endearment while telling her he'd made a mistake in dating her sister. Or in the aftermath of their lovemaking. *"Angie, my love, I want to make love to you every night for the rest of my life. I can't live without you."*

The saleswoman nodded. "What price range are you looking in?"

"Fifty thousand. Maybe a little more if it's perfect." Kyle dropped the numbers like he was talking about the price of milk, and the saleswoman bought it. She nearly tripped over herself sprinting to another cabinet for a display that would be "more to their liking."

While the saleswoman was off hunting and no doubt wiping the drool off her chin, Angie elbowed Kyle. "What are you doing?"

"Research. Let's find out what kind of love fifty grand will buy us." He tucked a stray hair behind her ear. "I think we look like a fifty-grand-ring kind of couple, don't you? You're gorgeous as usual, with impeccable taste in clothes."

He thinks I'm gorgeous?

Kyle rubbed his jaw. "I should have gotten my hair cut, don't you think? I'm a little shaggy for a big bucks kind of guy." He licked his hand and slicked his hair down, which made no difference at all, and Angie couldn't help but laugh at how ridiculous he looked trying to primp for the saleswoman. "Don't laugh. You could use a little help too."

He pulled a monogrammed handkerchief out of his pocket, pretended to spit on it and then rubbed her cheek. "Just have a little bit of food stuck here."

She laughed and punched him lightly on the arm. "What's your problem?"

"Ah-ha. A smile. Didn't think you owned any of those." He slung his arm around her shoulders and hauled her up against him as the saleswoman returned with several trays. "What do you think, sweetheart?"

He's trying to make you laugh so you'll write a good story. He doesn't actually enjoy your company.

And the arm around her shoulders? His hard body pressed against her side? Part of the game. He wasn't feeling all sorts of weird zing-zings shooting up and down his body.

Impervious jerk.

Or maybe his ruminations on the walk over had led him to the conclusion that he would only be complete as a man if he kidnapped her for some all-night loving.

Huh.

Unfortunate that his decision was too late, after she'd already concluded that there were too many reasons not to shag him.

"So, here are some options you might like. All of these are specifically designed for Tiffany's, so you'll never see any other ring like them."

Angie grabbed Kyle's hand, which was on her shoulder, and threaded her fingers through his. Might as well play the game, since this was only for work purposes, right? Maybe pretending to buy a diamond with the love of her life *would* get her back on track. Her muse could be the act of *pretending* to be in love, instead of actually needing to rely on a man. "Mmm . . . those diamonds are kinda small." Kyle tightened his grip over hers. How was she supposed to concentrate now?

"Lovey, I want you to be happy." Kyle looked up. "Do you have anything with larger stones?"

The saleswoman nodded and popped another tray right up. "I thought you might say that. These will be much more to your liking, I think."

If Kyle hadn't had her wedged against him, she was quite sure she would have dropped to the carpet laughing hysterically at the size of the jewels in those rings. She'd have to lift weights just to heft them around!

"So, which one speaks true love to you?" Kyle asked the saleswoman.

"True love?" The saleswoman picked up the one with the largest stone and held it up. "This one."

"Why?"

The saleswoman glanced at Angie. "Um . . . because . . . the setting."

"What about it?" This was fun, making the saleswoman squirm. Fun. She hadn't thought about fun in quite sometime. Novel idea. "What specifically about that setting says everlasting love more than this one?" She picked up another ring that, to her untrained eye, looked pretty darn similar, except the diamond was smaller.

The woman peered at the ring Angie was holding, then at the ring in her hand. "Well, they both declare love. That's what diamonds do. They are about love. They last forever, like love."

Angie snorted. "Since when does love last forever? I mean, sure, sometimes, but not always."

Kyle took the ring from the saleswoman and slipped it on Angie's ring finger. The one she'd scrubbed up nice and clean on Thanksgiving, thinking she'd be modeling a diamond on it. So she was a few days off with the timing, had the wrong guy, and had underestimated the cost by about two zeros. She still had a ring on her finger, didn't she? So life was just as she'd expected.

When Kyle brought her hand to his lips and kissed the ring, her flippant attitude abandoned her. Her knees wobbled, and the flashing holiday lights started making her head spin. *Get it together, Angie. This is only a game.*

Must.

Remember.

Broken.

Heart.

Kyle wrapped his hand around hers and studied the ring. "I think it says true love because the sapphires go all the way around, like a circle that can never end. The diamond in the middle is our hearts, intertwined so closely they look like one." He trailed his finger over the platinum band. "And each engraving on the band represents all the little hardships we've faced in life that have brought us closer. Together, they create beauty because they deepen our relationship and give our love the power and strength to last forever. And the diamond itself is as clear and pure as our love." He looked up. "Close your mouth, love. You're gaping again."

Angie snapped her mouth shut. What in the hell was that all about? What kind of man had that kind of insight? And how dare he show it to her? One night with that kind of a man was worth all the broken hearts in the world.

"Well, my, my, that was beautiful." The saleswoman was actually flushed.

Hey! He's with me! "You can see why I picked him, can't you?" Angie said.

"Oh yes. What a romantic." She held Angie's hand and inspected the ring. "If I had the money, I'd buy this ring out from under you. My heart is still pounding from that description." She locked her baby blues on Kyle. "You are such a catch. Truly."

Come to think of it, Ms. Sophisticated Saleswoman wasn't wearing a ring of her own. *Mine. Mine. Mine.* Angie leaned closer against Kyle . . . a poor decision, as she got a whiff of him that mixed with the romantic thoughts still dancing through her brain. It was a volatile combination that made her desperate for another kiss like the one she'd had at Macy's

Take me. I'm yours.

Kyle slipped the ring off her hand, and she had to stomp on her own foot to keep from following it over the counter. He winked at the saleswoman. "Maybe I'll be back later to get it."

She giggled and winked back. "Of course. Maybe I'll set it aside in case you do."

Oh, puhleeze. *Don't be flirting with my man.*

Oh my God. What was she thinking? He wasn't her man and he wasn't buying her a rock the size of New York either.

His arm still over her shoulders, Kyle bid adieu to the saleswoman and then turned Angie away. "So, you still think diamonds aren't about love?"

She eyed him, using amazing self-control to keep from leaning into him and sucking all his maleness into her body before he could steal it away. "I think you should be writing the stories."

He grinned. "I was just having some fun."

"Seriously, I've never heard a man get all lovey-dovey like that. Do you write poetry too? Sing love songs?"

His cheeks flushed a faint pink. "No. I was just goofing around to make you smile."

"Ah-ha! Mr. Autocrat is getting embarrassed." Well, that was no good. She didn't need to add that he was appealingly human to the list of his other attributes. "That's why you're helping me with these stories. Not because of Swift but because you love to wax poetic about all those emotional things but you're too much of a guy to admit it."

"Hey, look at that. A wedding." Kyle pointed across the room, but Angie didn't even look.

"A completely transparent attempt to change the subject." His arm was still around her and casually she rested her head against it. "That's why you and Sheila didn't work out, isn't it? Because she's cold and heartless and wouldn't know love if it smacked her in the head and knocked her into a coma for a few weeks." She frowned, not much liking thinking about Kyle and Sheila in love. "But really, deep down inside, you're a one woman kind of guy."

Oh dear, she was getting sucked off her no-sex-with-Kyle pedestal. She certainly hadn't stayed there very long, had she? What happened to willpower? Independence? Conviction?

"Seriously, it's a wedding." He pointed toward the

Christmas tree, where a bride and groom posed while cameras snapped.

Excellent. She'd focus on the wedding. On getting another couple to interview. Work was a much safer topic. "It's not a wedding. It's a Tiffany's photo shoot. There are . . ." She quickly counted. "A giant camera and a light person. And a makeup person. It's totally a photo shoot for the store."

"I imagine many wedding photographers have a light person who works with them."

"And the photographer is wearing faded jeans and an old jacket." Mmm . . . now that she took a look at the photographer, he wasn't half bad. Sort of liked the blond streaks in his hair. And his battered boots? The antithesis of everything Tiffany's. Perhaps he would be a good distraction from her miserable social life.

"Why does it matter what he's wearing?"

"Because a wedding photographer would be dressed up. He'd never show up looking like he just came in from the desert." If she sidled up to him and flashed him a little thigh, maybe he'd take a break from his photo shoot and ravage her for a while. And then Kyle would get jealous and beat him up and declare his love for her. Yes. She definitely needed to go over there and strike up a conversation . . . not to make Kyle jealous, but because she was not going to succumb to her attraction to Kyle. What better way to get over him than to seduce another man?

"His name's Luke."

Angie spun to find the flirty saleswoman leaning over her shoulder whispering. "What?"

"The photographer. His name's Luke. Quite a looker, isn't he?"

As if she was going to succeed in driving Angie into the

arms of another man so she could get her grappling hooks into Kyle. "I have no idea what you're talking about." She took Kyle's arm and snuggled close, boxing out the woman.

Still focused on the wedding couple, Kyle was thankfully oblivious to her embarrassing show of possessiveness. He shook his head. "Look at the way the groom is gazing into the bride's eyes. That's not two models. It's true love."

"You're soft. Still have mush brain from that story you made up for the saleswoman." She craned her head to get a better look at the couple. The photographer glanced up, a quirky smile on his face. Was that smile for her? Could he sense her womanly virtues from this distance? And if he could, why couldn't Kyle sense them when he was only two inches away from her? *Focus, Angie.* "As I said, you should be writing the stories, with all the romance you see in everything."

He shot her a sharp look. "I'm only doing it for the story."

"Don't believe you. You're a sensitive guy who's trying to hide it." Good thing she didn't like sensitive guys. She liked men like Roger who were too emotionally stunted to commit. They were where it was at.

Kyle scowled. "I'm not. It's just about the story."

"Then why are you seeing love when it's just a couple of models?"

He glared at her. "You're the one who's overly cynical and wouldn't believe a couple who'd been married for seventy-five years actually had a good thing going."

"What?" Angie posted her hands on her hips. "I'm just a realist. It's obvious that couple is a fake. What's cynical about that?"

Kyle eyed her for a long moment, a thoughtful look on his face.

"What do you want?" She shifted, a warm heat settling deep inside her.

"Let's make a bet," he said.

A bet, huh? That led to all sorts of interesting possibilities. A bet to how long they could kiss before one of them passed out? A bet about how long it would take for her to get his clothes off? "What kind of bet?"

Chapter Eight

Who needs diamonds when he has a sense of humor?
Or . . . um . . . gift wrap those diamonds in a sense of
humor and she'll be yours forever.
—Angie Miller, the tempted

"A bet as to whether those two are actually a couple," Kyle said.

Well, that wasn't the kind of bet she'd had in mind. No sex involved at all. "That's your bet?" She tried not to be unduly obvious with her disappointment.

He nodded. "If I'm right, then you have to tell me about the first time you truly fell in love. You have to relive it, so you remember that feeling." He cleared his throat. "Because maybe that will help you get in the right mind-set to write a great romantic story."

She blinked. "No way." That was much too personal for her, especially since she couldn't stop combining the L word and Kyle's name. Couldn't really think of any other guys at the moment.

"So you think you'll lose?" he challenged.

"No."

"Then take the bet."

"What if I win?"

He rubbed his chin. "What do you want?"

Hot, bad-girl sex with you. She immediately sent her hormones to the corner for a time-out. "I want you to write the next story. I want to see you evoke tender emotions of love and devotion with the written word. And then I'll edit it."

He looked pained. "I don't write about love."

"Afraid you'll lose?"

He studied the couple again, then shook his head. "It's a deal." He held out his hand.

Damn. Had to do that skin-touching thing again. If he kept up with all these torturous things, she was going to throw herself at him by the end of the night. Calling her sweet names, espousing romance and love so her heart turned over, putting his arm around her and now, bare skin to bare skin. She could only imagine how warm his hand would be against the rest of her bare skin.

"So, go ask them," he said. "Find out if they're actually a couple."

"What? I'm not going to go interrupt them."

"Fine. We'll go up there and eavesdrop. Maybe we'll be able to figure it out." He started walking toward the couple. "But if they turn out to be a real couple, we're going to interview them for our next story."

"Why doesn't that little suggestion surprise me? You're like a bloodhound on the hunt for romance." She laughed when he shot her an evil glare. Being dubbed a romance king apparently wasn't manly. Good to know. She'd be sure to call him that regularly from now on.

She was still grinning when he cruised to a stop a few

feet from the photo shoot. "Let's pretend we're admiring the tree," he said.

The man was a total kook, she realized as she started vocalizing her admiration for the tree. And weirdly enough, she was having fun.

She took note of the star on the top and launched into a long dissertation on its credits while she turned her gaze to the couple. The "groom" had his hand on the "bride's" arm and was leaning forward and whispering something in her ear that made her laugh. Very cozy.

But no attendants. If this was a wedding, shouldn't the rest of the bridal party be there? And look at the size of that camera. Way too much for a simple wedding.

Then again, the rock on her hand was enormous. Anyone who could afford a diamond that was bigger than the bride's palm probably pulled out all the stops.

She suddenly realized the camera had stopped whirring and the couple was staring at her with annoyed glares. Even the hot photographer was looking at her, his mouth quirked in that same amused grin. Crap. She was totally bagged for gawking. And how had she ended up only about eighteen inches from the couple?

It was Kyle's fault. When she'd been looking up at the tree, he'd had her hand on her back pushing her forward.

She quickly spun to her left to pick up her conversation with Kyle and pretend she hadn't been staring . . . but he was gone. She was alone, practically in the middle of the photo shoot.

"Excuse me, ma'am, but if you're done shopping, it would be best if you left." A security guard appeared by her shoulder and took her arm.

"But I was just talking to my friend . . ."

"And what friend would that be?" He began steering her toward the door.

Angie looked wildly around, and that's when she saw Kyle. Over by the elevators laughing his damn ass off. He'd abandoned her on purpose! Bastard!

"You see," the security guard said, "here at Tiffany's, we take special care of our customers, which includes protecting them from paparazzi."

"But I don't have a camera!"

The look on the security guard's face said it all. "You were working your way closer and closer. Too close." He reached the revolving door. "I think it's best if you find somewhere else to shop from now on. Merry Christmas."

"But . . ."

Kyle appeared behind the security guard, still laughing. He caught her in his path and pushed them both out the revolving door. "Your face was priceless," he said in her ear as he pushed the door open.

"You are so dead." She wanted to be mad, she really did, but seeing Kyle laughing was too contagious. His eyes were sparkling, and his dimples were working overtime. "You're a jerk."

"And you're laughing."

"I am not." She burst free of his arms when the door released them, and she started marching up the sidewalk, shoving her way through the throngs of people.

"You are. I can see the corner of your mouth curving up." He fell in beside her, his eyes still twinkling. "Admit it. That was funny."

She eyed him. Okay, so it was funny. "Why'd you do that?"

"To lighten you up. Show you that the holidays can be fun." He slung his arm around her shoulders and hauled her against him, then kissed the top of her head. "Didn't expect the security guard though. I just wanted you to turn around and see I wasn't there. That was priceless."

"Yeah, yeah." She finally grinned. "You're busted though. It's not a real wedding."

"Really? Didn't hear the security guard say that."

"Well, he said they were customers, which certainly doesn't sound like how you'd describe a bride and groom—"

"To Tiffany's, everyone is a customer. I think it's still undecided, at best."

Damn. "So, you want to go back and ask?"

He laughed. "Not a chance. I don't have time to bail you out of jail for being a stalker."

Did he have a nice laugh or what? She was quite sure she'd never heard him laugh at work, or even when he was dating Sheila. Not a laugh like this one. It was so deep, like it was reverberating from deep inside him. And pure. And genuine. Not a fake, polite laugh. The real thing.

She could get used to that laugh.

"So, I think we both win. I'll write the story, you have to tell me about the first time you fell in love."

Her euphoria faded. "How about, since it's a draw, neither of us has to do anything?"

"Nope. I want to hear your story. I want to hear what makes Angie swoon for a man." He pulled out his phone. "I'll order take-out from an Italian place near my building. We'll head up there and get this thing written and posted by midnight. And then you have to start talking." He tapped his phone softly against her cheek. "And it has to be an upbeat story."

"Why?"

"Because you're pretty when you smile."

Oh, damn.

"Okay, so I was wrong. Your talent is all in the spoken word." Angie was ensconced on Kyle's couch, a printout of his story in her hands. Could she feel more content? His place was cozy, and the camaraderie quotient had been high.

And she had managed to keep herself from disrobing and then straddling him while he sat at the computer. For now. She wasn't making any promises as the night went on and she'd had another glass of wine.

"It's not that bad." The couch sank under his weight as he sat down next to her.

"Did you even try?" The couch felt a little cramped with him on it. Perhaps she should sit on his lap to make more room.

"Sure." His shoulder brushed against hers as he leaned over to look at her notes. A sign he was trying to seduce her? "Did you even leave one word I wrote?"

She pointed. "The."

"Well, it's because I didn't have anything to work with. It wasn't as if my neighbor was in the mood to wax poetic on the elevator ride up. If you hadn't gotten thrown out of the store, we could have gotten a real couple to interview."

"The couple wasn't real." Did he smell good or what? Mmm . . .

"Maybe they were." He pulled the paper out of her hand. "So I wrote the story. You pay up. Tell me the story about the first time you fell in love. Truly in love."

You mean tonight? With you? Because that's my only story. "But we haven't finished the story."

"We have time."

She held up her watch. "It's eleven-thirty. Since when do you put a work deadline at risk?" Now that she mentioned it, it was sort of odd. Was he starting to fall for her?

No! Don't think like that! It was that kind of hopeful thinking that had burned her before.

He frowned, then took the printout out of her hand and walked back to the computer.

Victory.

But it felt like she'd lost, sending him back to work. She liked this side of him. Which was why he should go back to work. No need to get her heart broken again.

Nineteen hours since he'd sent Angie home from his condo without grabbing her and kissing her. He'd taken her home in a cab and escorted her to her door, and then walked away. No kiss.

And he'd never regretted any decision more.

At the same time, he'd never been more grateful for a show of willpower.

Because he wanted her.

And because he couldn't afford her. Couldn't afford to put his relationship with Roger at risk until Roger had sold him the company. Couldn't dally with a woman like Angie, who would demand all of his soul.

Now it was seven o'clock in the evening, and he was sitting alone at his desk, as he had all day. Keeping a wide berth around Angie's office. Couldn't risk being alone in that broom closet with her, not when he was still thinking about that kiss in Macy's.

He hadn't made it down to her office to talk about today's story, which had been quite a big improvement over the others. There'd even been a hint of raciness beneath the surface, which he was sure Swift would appreciate. Lord knew, he sure as hell did.

Yeah, he'd had fun with her. Fun shopping, fun kissing, fun that had made him forget she was Sheila's sister and Roger's ex. Fun that had made him forget his priority, which was work. When she'd pointed that out last night, he realized he'd gotten sucked in too far. Dallying with Angie was too dicey, with the company's future at stake.

She wasn't anything like he'd expected. None of Sheila's cold, calculating ways. None of the selfish woman he'd somehow imagined. Angie was genuine, expressive in her emotions and without guile.

And damn cute too.

Sure she was a little serious, but what could be expected? She'd been hanging around with Roger for the last year, hardly the kind of experience that would make one light-hearted and cheerful.

He scowled and e-mailed his latest revisions to Angie. Okay, fine, he could admit it. He was getting tempted. Which was why he was staying where he was.

Or maybe he'd pull himself off the case entirely, for the company's good. He obviously wasn't inspiring Angie to greatness in her writing, though today's story gave him some hope. He'd definitely sensed a changing of tone in her work. Was she beginning to recover from Roger?

He'd like to think it had something to do with the fun they had last night.

Or not.

He didn't want to think about the fun. What kind of bet had that been? Trying to corner Angie into telling him about how she had loved some other guy? Yeah, that would have made his night, hearing about her and Roger.

"Okay, so what's your problem?"

He looked up as Angie flopped down in one of the chairs in his office. She was wearing a long black skirt with a slit up the side. Modest, yet hinting at what was beneath. Her maroon v-neck sweater cupped her breasts almost accidentally, as if she hadn't intended to wear something that admitted she was a woman.

"You're staring at my breasts."

Cursing, he looked up and met her gaze, his gut lurching when he saw the heat lurking beneath the surprise.

"Since when do you stare at my breasts? I've never seen you do that."

Um . . . there simply wasn't an acceptable answer to that question. "Um . . ."

"I'm completely offended." But her tone belied her words. There was a trill under the surface that caught him off guard.

Was she feeling the same things he was?

"So, what are you doing up here?" Best to change the subject. Wasn't quite sure about his footing.

"I was sitting at my desk feeling unappreciated, so I figured I'd come up here and have you gawk at my body for a while. I feel much better now. Thanks."

"Damn it. I'm sorry! What else do you want me to say?" He felt his cheeks growing hot. Nice.

"Enjoying your payback for Tiffany's yesterday? Feeling a little embarrassed? Excellent." She grinned and looked damn cute. "So, I also came up here because I want to know what's up with the long-distance harassment today?"

"You mean, e-mail?"

"Yeah."

There was a sparkle in her eyes that hadn't been there before their shopping excursion yesterday. Residual effect of their evening?

Not sure what he thought of that.

"So, did you decide I had cooties or something?" She tilted her head. "You know, it's bad enough when you're harassing me in person, but by e-mail, it's worse. Makes it inhuman. Destroy me to my face or not at all."

She didn't look that destroyed. In fact, she looked awesome.

"Want to go to a party tonight?" Damn it. How had that made it out of his mouth? He didn't want to go to a party with her. He wanted her to go back downstairs to her office and stay on the other side of the e-mail so he didn't have to look at her.

She looked startled. "What kind of party?"

He flicked an invitation that was sitting on his desk. "Swift is having a Christmas party tonight. Come with me. It's formal though. Do you have anything to wear?"

Angie picked up the invite and read it. "I'm the one working on their assignment and they invite *you*? The finance guy?"

"Um . . ." Not so much sparkle in her eye anymore. More like evil flashes. Like the old Angie who used to shoot him those glares whenever she saw him.

She threw the invite on the table. "I'm the one who's been busting my butt for them, and they invite you? What's up with that?"

He sat up, feeling much more comfortable with her hostility than with smoldering sexuality. "I'm sure they invited me instead of you because I'm the one who negotiated the deal."

"That's wrong. They should honor the laborers. The little people."

"Well, don't glare at me like that. I invited you, didn't I?" Good thing too. He'd hate to have been her victim if she found out after the fact. "So, you coming or what?"

"Yes, I'll go. They need to meet the goddess who's been busting her ass for them. Do you realize how many Christmas parties I've missed so I could work on their stories?" She stood. "Let's go."

"After you finish that story."

"Yeah, I know. Give me ten minutes."

"Don't rush it," he shouted after her disappearing figure.

Her only response was the thudding of her feet as she ran down the stairs to the lower level, leaving Kyle alone to ruminate over what he'd just done.

Invited Angie to a party? And how did that further his goal of keeping his distance from Angie? He thought of the dancing that was sure to be at the party.

Dancing with Angie.

Tonight was going to be one hell of a test for his resolve.

Chapter Nine

*Holiday parties: the true test of your relationship. Up your
odds of survival by giving her a diamond before you hit
the dance floor.*
—Angie Miller

When Angie opened the door to let him into her apartment,
he knew without a doubt that this had been the worst idea of
his entire life. Absolute worst. Even worse than going into
business with Roger as a partner.

Angie was wearing a slinky black dress with tiny little
straps and a low-cut front. It caressed her in all the right
places, left just enough to the imagination.

She was breathtaking.

"What?" She shifted under his gaze. "What are you staring at?"

"I'm wishing you still had a crush on me."

Her cheeks flamed a slow red that traveled down her
lovely neck to her chest. "Shut up."

He decided to obey her command. Didn't trust the next words out of his mouth. Instead, he took her coat from her hands and held it up for her, dropping it over her shoulders without touching one inch of that luxurious bare skin. How the hell was he supposed to stand back while other men gawked at her this evening?

Not sure, but he'd better figure it out fast because he had no claim to her. Didn't want one either.

He let the coat settle on her shoulders, then pulled her hair out from under the collar, letting his fingers trail over the silken strands.

Angie turned slightly. "See my earrings? Aren't you proud?" She was wearing Christmas trees made of emeralds, rubies, and diamonds. "Total Christmas spirit."

But he couldn't think about the holidays. He was too busy noticing how long and elegant her neck was. He dropped a kiss on it. Just a quick one. One that didn't mean anything. "Did some beau get you those earrings?"

She was staring at him. "I pilfered them from Heidi. Quin bought them for her last year."

"Quin?" Did he care?

"Her fiancé. They're getting married on New Year's." She sounded out of breath, and she hadn't moved away from him. His hands were still in her hair, her back against him, his lips inches from her neck. "I hated her for a while. You know, wasn't in the mood to hear about fiancé type things for a while."

"Why not?" Oh, what the hell. One little kiss couldn't hurt, could it? He brushed his lips over her neck again, and felt her tense under his hands.

"Because I was depressed after being dumped." She sighed and tilted her head a tiny bit.

"By Roger?"

"Who?"

"Roger. Getting dumped by him?" Her slip-up was encouraging. Maybe she was ready to start writing some great stories. *That's right, Kyle. Keep it focused on work.*

"Oh, right. Roger."

"You look gorgeous tonight."

She turned around so she was facing him, her eyes sparkling. "Really? You weren't staring at my breasts, so I figured I hadn't impressed you."

"Were you trying to impress me?" He gently took the edges of her coat in his hands and tugged.

She took a step forward. "I just wanted to try to embarrass you again. You're cute when you blush."

"I don't blush." He pulled again, and she didn't resist, moving even nearer to him.

"And I suppose you also don't gawk at women's breasts." She was so close he could almost taste her lips.

"Not women's. Yours only." He brushed his lips over hers, and she didn't draw back.

"So you admit it?" She put her hands on his coat.

"Never. I admit nothing." He kissed her then, not lightly. He wanted her, and he kissed her hard.

When her mouth parted under his and she met his tongue with equal ardor, he felt like he was where he should be, where he'd been searching for his entire life. He let his hands slip off her coat to her waist. Silky material danced under his fingers, so thin he could feel the heat from her body caressing his fingers. Each rib, her belly button, the curve of her breasts.

Her arms went around his neck and pulled him closer, her body pressing against his like she'd been wanting him for as long as he had, as if she, too, was unable to rationalize herself out of the kiss.

He cupped her bottom, crushing her against him while his tongue sought out hers. He couldn't stop. Didn't want to stop. He wanted all of her, not just her body. Her mind, her soul, every part of her existence.

The thought shocked him, and he broke the kiss. He rested his forehead against hers, and her breathlessness nearly drove him back to her mouth. "Angie."

"What?"

"I want to make love to you."

She pulled back and looked at him. "Seriously?"

"No, I thought I'd risk sexual harassment charges by propositioning one of my staff. So, what do you think? Are you going to sue me?"

She grinned and socked him softly in the gut. "Maybe. Depends on whether you're a good lover or not."

He felt his gut tighten. "I don't want to pressure you."

"I've already decided that I'm not going to sleep with you. It would be a huge mistake for me." She took a deep breath.

He traced his finger over her jaw. "Maybe we can think about it at the party. See what we think when we get home."

"I'm not going to change my mind." She punctuated her statement by kissing him again.

"Too bad. I'd love to take advantage of you." He cupped her breasts, flicked his thumbs over her nipples.

She made a small sound. "If I changed my mind, which I won't, I would be the one taking advantage of you. Women's lib, you know."

"Hey, I'm all about equality." He buttoned her coat, pausing to give her a long kiss when he got to the top button. "You sure we need to think about it?"

"I have to go give Swift hell for not sending me an invite," she said. "And I don't need to think about it. The answer is no."

"Or maybe you don't need to make a decision now." He held the door for her, then closed it behind them.

He would not think about what he was doing. He wasn't going to think about Roger or the company or Sheila or anything else. Tonight was about Angie and him, and nothing else mattered.

It was the best cab ride she'd ever had. Never had she been kissed quite as thoroughly and deliciously.

And to think she'd actually talked herself out of her crush on Kyle. And then she'd tried to convince herself she didn't love him? Big mistake. The man was better than she'd ever imagined. He made her feel special, desired, appreciated. Loved.

The cab pulled up in front of the posh restaurant Swift had taken over for the evening. There were bouncers checking invites, and Angie felt a bit decadent being waved inside with the rest of the special people.

Or maybe she felt decadent because she was on Kyle's arm, and he was whispering little somethings in her ear about what he wanted to do to her when they got back to her apartment. "You think you can change my mind?"

"That's my goal." He delivered her coat to a man in a red jacket, then offered her his arm. "Shall we mingle?"

"Sure." As she floated along on his arm, she realized that she was truly enjoying herself in a way she hadn't for a very long time. Not just since Roger had dumped her, but before then. He hadn't made her feel this special in a long time. Or maybe ever. Kyle had a special touch that had worked its way firmly into her heart.

She stumbled, and Kyle caught her. "You okay?"

"Yes, fine." How had he gotten into her heart? That was

totally a high risk activity she didn't condone. Especially since he was so clear in his goal to seduce her tonight. What did that mean? Did it mean he'd fallen for her, too, or was it more about inspiring her to write better stories?

It couldn't be the latter. He wouldn't do that. A hot kiss was one thing, but making love?

No, he had to mean it.

This was the same thing she'd done to herself when she'd first met him, reading too much into his actions. Why couldn't she just demand to know whether he was falling in love with her?

Because even if he was, he wasn't ready to admit it.

So where did that leave her?

Kyle cursed under his breath and tried to turn them to the right.

Angie felt his tension. "What's wrong?"

"Nothing."

But Angie followed his gaze to find Roger and Sheila bearing down on them. Sheila was wearing a gorgeous black shimmery dress that positively oozed sex, and Roger was wearing a tux and looking more than a little annoyed.

How much hotter was Kyle than Roger? Ridiculous to think she had been broken up over that pathetic creature.

Roger and Sheila cruised to a stop in front of them. Roger narrowed his eyes at Kyle. "What are you two doing here?"

"Angie's working on their project, so it made sense." Kyle dropped her hand from his arm and took a step away.

Ouch. Apparently, Kyle couldn't bear to let Roger think they were together. Not that they were *together*, but they were sort of together. It couldn't have been clearer if he'd taken out an ad in the *New York Times*: I value my job more than Angie Miller.

Roger tightened his lips. "Listen, Sheila and I are together. We don't want to make you two uncomfortable, so maybe it's better if you both leave."

Whoa. She'd forgotten about the Kyle-had-picked-Sheila-over-her thing. How could she have misplaced that little nugget? That's why her heart had been chopped up in the first place. Twice. Once by each of them. And from the way Sheila was eyeing Kyle, Angie wouldn't be surprised if Sheila set Roger down in the corner and wrapped her legs around Kyle.

This was why she wasn't going to sleep with him.

"Give me a break, Roger. Neither of us care about you guys." Kyle put his hand on Angie's lower back. "We're going to go dance, and we'll stay out of your way. Have a good evening."

She allowed Kyle to direct her only because it was an excuse to get away from Roger and Sheila. But once they got to the floor, she tried to pull away.

"You're going to let them bother you?" Kyle slipped his arms around her and pulled her close. "They aren't worth it."

Angie kept her body tense. "It's not them that upset me. It's you. Thanks for the reminder that work is more important than me."

Kyle frowned. "Why do you say that?"

"Because Roger came over and gave you that possessive-male-glare-thingy, and you let go of me. That's why I'm not going to sleep with you. Because you'll put New Age or Sheila or something before me and break my heart again."

Kyle stopped dancing and stared at her.

And stared.

And stared.

"Stop looking at me!"

He shook his head once, then kissed her. Not some

brotherly thing on the forehead. The bad-girl-sex kind of kiss. The kind that made heat pool inside her instantly, and work its way downward. The kind of kiss that no one at the party would be able to misinterpret.

Even Roger or Sheila.

She pulled back and studied him. "You know what you just did?"

"Sure do." He kissed her nose, and his eyes were as dark as she'd ever seen them. "Let's go introduce you to the person at Swift who signed you on. And then let's go back to your place and make love until we can't walk."

What woman could say no to that?

She shut her apartment door behind Kyle, then leaned against it. Could her heart be pounding any louder?

Kyle faced her, his hands in his overcoat pockets. He said nothing. Just waited.

For her. He was waiting for her to make the first move To say yes, she wanted to make love to him.

"I want to." It came out a whisper.

He didn't move. "But?"

Ah, he knew her too well. Yet another reason to love him Which was yet another reason to fear him. "I'm afraid."

He smiled. "So am I."

She took a deep breath. "Kyle."

"What?" He took two steps forward until he was directly in front of her.

"Um . . ."

He began unbuttoning her coat. One button at a time, hi gaze never leaving her face. "What is it, Angie?"

"I can't remember."

The back of his right hand grazed her breast as he fin

ished unbuttoning her coat. She was suddenly lightheaded. "I want to make love to you, Angie."

Oh, hell. Sometimes a girl had to take a risk. What was a broken heart, anyway? She'd survived last time, right?

There was no going back.

Chapter Ten

Sometimes, even a big-ass diamond isn't going to save you if you really screw up.
—Angie Miller

First thing on the agenda? Engage in detailed study on how he tasted. Angie let Kyle remove her coat while she embarked on her thorough research, which he seemed most happy to oblige her with. He tasted like champagne and chocolate—had they had champagne at the party?

Too hard to remember things that long ago when she had to spend her energy trying to recall how to keep her legs from buckling while his hands explored her zipper.

Interesting. She could tell him what would happen to her dress once he unzipped it and flipped the straps off her shoulders. But who was she to interfere with the joy of finding things out for himself?

Especially since she really wanted to get that coat off

him. Wonder if she could keep kissing him while getting his coat off?

Yes! Success!

Oh, wow. Cold air on her body. He'd obviously finished his research. Excitement trilled through her, and she faltered. Was she really going through with this? .

Yes.

"No fair! You're still dressed." She unbuttoned his shirt. No. She pulled his shirt open and managed to tear off three of the buttons. "I've always wanted to do that."

Kyle was busy nibbling on her collarbone. How could he be nibbling on that when her breasts were fully exposed? She nudged him while she tried to pull his shirt off his shoulders. "Hey."

"You taste like vanilla."

Ah . . . so her scented body lotion did have a flavor. Interesting to note. "How come you gape at my breasts when they're covered, but you ignore them when they're yours for the taking?"

"Oh, I'll get to them."

The promise in those words had her hands trembling. "How about now? Why don't you get to them now?"

He picked her up instead, and she obligingly wrapped her legs around his waist. Note to self: the skin on her inner thigh was very happy with the feeling of his bare skin against it. Must make an effort to indulge more often.

Oh, wow. He'd skipped the breasts. Straight to her bottom. Hadn't she worn a pair of underwear tonight? Where was it? Because his fingers were definitely doing skin-to-skin kneading.

"Where's the bedroom?"

"Here." The bedroom was like twenty feet away. How was she supposed to keep her breasts waiting that long?

Oh, sure, her bottom was getting its due, but it wasn't enough. His hands should be everywhere, his lips . . . okay fine. So they were doing pretty well on the earlobe suckling.

"On the floor?"

"It's carpeted."

"Rug burn's a killer." He kept walking, and sucking, and kneading. Okay, so maybe this trip wouldn't be such a long one. Definitely a good way to pass the time.

He set her on the bed. Was it her bed? Not sure. It was soft and squishy, but she couldn't be bothered to look at what she was sitting on. Not with her first view of his chest. She traced his nipples with her thumbs, then tugged at his pants. "Too many clothes."

"Wouldn't want to disappoint you." He showed his agreeable nature by removing all his clothes in record time.

She feasted her eyes on parts of him previously hidden, then blinked. "Whoa. I'm not thinking this is going to be a successful endeavor." It was quite apparent he was enjoying himself and ready to do anything she requested, but hello! Would he fit?

He gave a smoky grin that had her insides demanding a chance to prove nothing was impossible. "Then we'll have to spend some time making sure you're ready."

Oh yes! Spend some time!

"Black lace panties, fishnet stockings, and black high heels." He lifted her foot to his chest and kissed her toes. "Quite the sexy combo."

One finger trailed down her inner thigh while he slipped her shoes off.

Then he wound her stockings down her hips, over her thighs, knees, calves, ankles, heels, arches, toes. He followed their path with his lips, and suddenly every drop of heat in her body had pooled just north of where his left hand was.

Oh, hello. Breasts, meet Kyle's tongue. Tongue, these are my breasts. Obviously you guys are going to get along just fine.

"This what you were wanting?"

"Yes." She almost giggled at how trembly her voice was. But what did she expect with that kind of sexy voice emanating from the vicinity of her very alert nipples?

But since his mouth was otherwise occupied in an excellent way, perhaps she'd have to find something else to do. Let's see. Pinch nipples for a moment. Trail fingers over stomach. Feel arrogant when Kyle's body twitches.

Nice abs. When she was coherent, she'd have to check those out.

Hmm . . . the road seemed to continue. Where might it lead? Let's see . . .

"Angie!" He croaked out a guttural groan, and his body jerked above her.

"You like that? I could do it again. Or what about this? If I did that . . ."

He grabbed her hand. "I'm not made of stone, love. Wait a few minutes on that."

Love? He'd called her love? Fresh heat surged through her that could never be coaxed by mere physical touch. *I love you too, Kyle!*

Ack! What was that? When had she decided to admit her feelings? That was stupid, dangerous and . . .

Wow. That was a much better place for his tongue than her nipples, which weren't feeling so lonely, as his very talented hands were keeping them comfortable.

From now on, she was a big advocate of multitasking.

A foil packet dropped on her chest. "Want to help?"

"Is it jumbo sized? Because that's what we're going to need." She grabbed the packet and tore it open. Okay, so she loved him. She loved him!

Exhilaration and liberation rushed through her, and she knew she'd never been in a more perfect place. He was everything she wanted, and he was hers.

She had to have the man she loved, now. She pushed Kyle onto his back, then settled on his thighs while she took care of the condom. Who'd have guessed she'd never done that before? Obviously, he inspired her to great things.

He grabbed her hips and pulled her toward him.

She shifted. "No, that's wrong. To the right. Oh, there we go . . ."

Kyle groaned and as if in a dream she heard someone shout. Who was in her bedroom with them? Wow. Not that it mattered. "Okay, so I was wrong. Seems a good fit."

"A perfect one." He settled her in place and began moving under her. And then his hands decided to help with the cause. "Let yourself go, love."

Love again? Love? Love? She heard someone screaming the word, and then Kyle shouted her name, and then every muscle in her body spontaneously burst.

Love. He'd called her love.

Twice.

She was never going to be the same.

Angie reread the story she'd written. It was unbelievable. Incredible. The best she'd ever written. She and Kyle had stopped at Starbucks on the way to work and interviewed a darling young couple who were holding hands while burning their tongues on lattes. They'd been married for two years, and were so in love it was palpable.

Just like how she felt about Kyle.

They'd been two hours late for work this morning, because they'd hadn't quite made it out of bed when the alarm went off. It had been just as amazing as the first time, and he'd called her "love" three more times.

Oh yes. He loved her. And soon he'd realize it. And her life would be perfect.

Her door flung open, and Heidi stuck her head in. "You busy?"

"Come, on in." She couldn't wait to tell Heidi. Or maybe not. Heidi would lecture her for making a mistake, for setting herself up to be burned again. Maybe it would be better to wait until she had proof of Kyle's love. Not that she needed proof for herself, but it would make Heidi feel better.

Heidi shut the door then sat down, and Angie realized her friend's eyes were all red and puffy. "What's wrong?"

"Quin."

"Is he hurt?" Angie's heart sank. "What happened?"

"I think I'm going to call off the wedding."

"Why?" So, he was okay. Relief poured through her. Wedding jitters she could help with.

"Because he loves work more than me."

Angie frowned. "Since when?"

"He hasn't made it to one party this entire season. He's always at work. We haven't had sex in three weeks!"

Probably not a good time to tell Heidi why she'd been late to work. "You know he loves you. He's just busy."

"Is he? Or is it something else? Like he's had second thoughts and doesn't know how to tell me, so he's just avoiding me?" Heidi pulled the collar off her Mrs. Claus outfit and blew her nose. "Will you talk to him?"

"Me?"

"Yes. Find out. If he doesn't love me, I can't hear it from

him. You have to tell me. Go talk to him." Heidi pointed to the phone. "Call him right now and set up lunch for today."

"Right." Anything for her friend. Angie quickly dialed and made an appointment. She set the phone down. "Wednesday."

"Wednesday? But it's Monday! I can't wait for two whole days, wondering if my life is going to fall apart and be ripped to shreds." Heidi's voice escalated to a wail that had the windows trembling.

Distraction was in order. "I had sex with Kyle."

The wail stopped abruptly. "You did?"

"Several times." Not quite sure exactly how many. Hard to do math when her body was a mass of sexual exhaustion.

Heidi tossed the collar in the trash. "I knew there was a reason you wrote such an incredible story today. So, tell me all about it."

Angie frowned. "That's not why I wrote a good story."

"Of course it is. Kyle's your new muse."

"My professional success doesn't depend on a man."

Heidi rolled her eyes. "Oh, come on. You came into your own when you started dating Roger . . ."

"Because I learned how to write, not because I was dating him."

". . . And then when you were single, you sucked—pardon my French—and now that you're with Kyle, you're even more brilliant than before."

Angie felt a tinge of panic tighten in her chest. Was she really dependent on a man for success at her craft? That made her pathetic, and so dependent. So frightfully and terrifyingly dependent.

Like there wasn't enough at risk already with her heart. Her professional future was also in Kyle's hands? "No. You're wrong. You must be."

"Am I?"

* * *

Kyle smiled to himself. What a weekend.

And he didn't regret a single minute of it. Had no idea what would happen next, but he was going to make dinner for Angie tonight at his place. Where it would go after that?

Didn't know.

But he was going to find out.

A light knock sounded on his door. Kyle looked up to find Roger standing in his office. His face was all twisted, and there was a twitch in his cheek.

Oh, hell. Forgot about Roger.

Kyle leaned back in his chair, clasped his hands behind his head, and tried to look relaxed. "What's up?"

"Make a choice. Now."

He almost flinched. *Don't make me do it.* "What choice?"

"The company or Angie."

Kyle's hands balled into fists. "She's not yours to claim. You're with Sheila."

"The company or Angie."

"Why does it matter to you?"

Roger's face twisted even more. "Did you hear me? I don't want this damned company anymore. I'm bored, and I want to get out. You can have it, but only if you leave Angie alone."

Kyle slowly sat up. "You're serious? You'll sell me your half of the company?"

"Yes. If you walk away from Angie."

The company. His. If he'd give up Angie.

A week ago, no problem.

Today? He couldn't do it. But there might be a loophole. "When do you want to close the deal?"

"February 10. Gives us almost two months to negotiate the details and get the paperwork drawn up."

So all he had to do was cool things with Angie until February 10. Once he had the company, then there would be nothing Roger could do. In two months, he could have everything he wanted.

Because he did want Angie. He knew that now. "It's a deal."

Roger walked over and shook his hand. "I'll make the call and get things moving. Good choice."

Kyle barely waited until Roger was out of sight, then sprinted down the stairs to Angie's office. The company was his! And after February 10, he and Angie could be together. No more risks.

He flung the door open, to find Heidi in Angie's office wearing a Mrs. Claus outfit. He stifled his shout of victory that had been for Angie's ears only. "Heidi, can you give us a moment?"

She beamed at him. "You bet." She nodded at Angie. "Don't forget lunch on Wednesday."

"I won't."

Kyle waited until Heidi was through the door, then he slammed it shut, vaulted over the desk, and pulled Angie into his arms.

A long, wet kiss later, he was ready to push everything off her desk and show her how spontaneous he could be. As soon as he owned the company, he was ordering locks put on all the office doors. "Guess what?"

She was laughing, her eyes dancing. "What?"

"Roger is going to sell me New Age! It's going to be mine!"

"No way! That's awesome!" She flung her arms around him and gave him a hug like he'd never had. Her ebullient response struck him deep inside his gut. She was so excited, for him, because she knew how much it meant to him. She understood him. And it felt good. Really good.

"So, after February, we can be together all the time and don't have to worry about anything."

She tensed and pulled back. "What do you mean, after February?"

Anyone else, he'd worry about. But not Angie. She'd understand. "Roger said I had to choose between you and the company. If I agreed to stay away from you, I could have the company."

Her face became cold. "And you agreed?"

"No, it's not like that." He grabbed her hands and pressed them to his chest. "I agreed, but once I own the company, he won't be able to do anything about it. So we'll just lay low for a couple months." He grinned. "I can think of plenty of things we can do behind closed doors." Then his elation dimmed slightly, extinguished by the look on Angie's face. "Angie?"

"No, thank you." She pulled out his grasp and walked to the door. "You can leave now. For good." She opened the door and stood there.

"But, Angie, it's just temporary. You know how much New Age means to me."

"Unfortunately, I do. I'd forgotten. But I remember now." She grabbed her purse and coat off the door. "If you won't leave, I will. And don't follow me." She walked out and slammed the door behind her.

Should he follow her? Or let her take time alone? He had no idea what to do, and a rising sense of panic threatened to overwhelm him. It was the first time he'd ever cared when a woman had walked out on him, and he had no idea what he was supposed to do.

He was going after her. He couldn't let her walk out, and

if that wasn't the right thing to do, then too bad. No way could he lose her.

He jumped around the desk and sprinted to the door. When he yanked it open, Roger was standing there.

"Roger."

"What are you doing in Angie's office?"

"I told her about our deal." A deal he wasn't feeling so sure about anymore.

"No wonder she looked pissed. Excellent." Roger clapped a hand on his shoulder. "Let's go to lunch and talk the details of the transfer."

Kyle glanced down the hall, but there was no sign of Angie. It was only until February. He could make it work. He had to. He'd find Angie later and get her to understand.

He had no idea how, but he knew he had to.

Chapter Eleven

Diamonds. Sigh.
—Angie Miller, the converted

The next afternoon Angie walked into Heidi's office and sat down. "Well?"

Heidi folded her hands across the desk. "It's bad."

"I knew it." Angie sighed. "I rewrote that story eight times already. It doesn't work at all."

"No."

"What happened? I was finally back." Angie groaned and buried her face in the reindeer blanket draped over Heidi's chair. "My article was so good. How can I revert again to horrible drivel?"

"You have a fight with Kyle?"

Angie was silent. *That can't be it.*

"Angie?"

"I told him I never wanted to see him again." What was up with the tears in her eyes? Didn't they know that she'd done the right thing? Stupid emotions, always thinking they know better than the brain.

"Why?"

"Roger told him that if he stayed away from me, he'd sell him New Age." That still burned her up. Where was the love?

"And he agreed?" Heidi sounded so shocked, Angie decided to pull the blanket off her head and actually face her friend.

"Yes."

"Even after the great sex?"

"Must not have been that great." No, it had been! No way could she have felt that kind of connection if he hadn't. But maybe that wasn't enough for him. Maybe he could never put a woman before work. "But I'm glad to find it out now." *Be strong, Angie.* "He's already called me six times since then, and sent me forty e-mails."

"Has he changed his mind?"

"No, but he apologized and hopes I can understand."

"Forget that."

"I know." She sighed. He'd seemed so perfect. And now he was willing to barter his woman for personal gain? "So I guess I'll go back and rewrite again."

"Find a new muse."

"I don't need a muse."

Heidi raised an eyebrow. "Well, you need something. Maybe you should start writing while under the influence of mind-altering drugs. That might help."

Angie stood. "I'll figure this out."

"Don't forget lunch on Wednesday," Heidi said.

Right. Lunch. Both their lives were falling apart. "Want to come over tonight? We'll rent movies, eat cookie dough, and drink wine. Like the old days when we both were too smart to get bogged down with men?"

Heidi grinned. "That'll be great."

Yeah, great. That's exactly how she wanted to spend her evening, instead of spending it wrapped in Kyle's arms.

Get over it, Angie.

Angie stared glumly at Quin over dessert. Three days. Three stories. All of them were terrible.

Was Heidi right? Was she incapable of writing well without a man? Impossible. Unacceptable. There had to be somewhere else to find inspiration.

"So, why did you invite me to lunch?"

She propped her chin up on her hand. "Because Heidi thinks you don't want to get married and she's working herself into a frenzy."

Quin looked shocked. "What? She said that? Why does she think that?"

"Because you've been too busy to spend any of the holiday season with her. Missed parties, no sex in three weeks." She almost laughed at Quin's horrified expression. "What? You think women don't talk about sex?"

"But I've been working."

"And therein lies the problem. She thinks you put work before her, and she can't decide if it's because you're a workaholic who will ignore her once you get married, or whether you're obsessing about work as an excuse not to spend time with her."

She stopped suddenly. She could say those exact same things about Kyle. Had the deal with Roger been an excuse because he changed his mind, or simply evidence of what he was like? Not that it made a difference. She'd come second, and that's what mattered.

"That's not true! I love her!" Quin shoved back his chair and ran his hands through his dark hair. "I didn't even realize. I was trying to get everything finished so we could take off a month for our honeymoon."

"A month? She said you're going for a week."

He shook his head. "It's a surprise. I already cleared it with her boss. We're going to Australia for three weeks, after our week in the Bahamas, which she knows about."

Well, phooey. Tears in her eyes again? She was turning into a total sap. "That's the sweetest thing I've ever heard."

One corner of his mouth curved up. "I thought it was a good idea, but apparently it's not working. I don't want to tell her now, so what do I do to make her feel better?"

Angie pursed her lips. "Did she ever give you her Tiffany's list?"

"Her what?"

"I went with her to Tiffany's, where she made of list of the items she loved. She said you were planning to give her jewelry for a wedding present, so she was going to give you some direction."

"I was going to give her jewelry. I was thinking of a pair of diamond studs. Should I go get them now?" He stood. "I'll go now and give them to her early."

"Sit down, stud." Angie waved him down. "She doesn't want diamond studs. I went to the store with her, so if you want, I can go with you and show you some of the stuff she liked."

"Would you?" He looked so grateful she almost felt heroic.

"Of course. Let's go." How could she not support that kind of love? Quin working overtime to give his love a monthlong honeymoon. Heidi was so lucky.

Thursday morning, Angie was sitting at her desk when Heidi burst into her office, wearing a jumpsuit with jingle bells sewn all over it. "Angie! You wrote about me and

Quin!" Heidi's eyes were glowing, and her cheeks were flushed. "It's the most beautiful story ever written by anybody about anything!"

Contentment swelled inside Angie. "You liked it?"

"Liked it? I started blubbering like a fool in my office when I read it!" Heidi ran around the desk and bent over Angie. "Look at the diamond pendant he gave me. With the two little diamonds flanking it. It's exactly like I wanted, but even more!"

Angie smiled. She done good.

Heidi flung her arms around Angie. "You are the best friend ever!"

Angie hugged her back. "So, I guess you're my muse."

"I guess so! You can write stories like that about me anytime." Heidi released her and danced back around the desk. "You know what I want you to give us for our wedding?"

Oops. Hadn't even thought about a wedding gift. "What?"

"I want you to print the story you wrote about us, sign it, and frame it."

"You're kidding." What was up with that? Tears again?

"Oh yes. It's so wonderful, I want my children to read it when they get old enough so they can realize how much Quin and I love each other." She fingered her pendant. "It's a masterpiece, Angie. You should submit it to journalism contests."

Angie sighed, a big fat sigh of contentment. She'd found her muse on her own without a man. It had simply taken a truly inspirational story. "Maybe I will!"

Her phone rang then, and Heidi sprang to the door. "You can take that call. I'm going to go read that story again. Love you, Angie!"

Angie was still grinning when she picked up the phone. "Angie Miller. Can I help you?"

"Is this the Angie Miller who wrote the story on the Swift website about Quin and Heidi?" a male voice asked.

Angie frowned. "Yes."

"Excellent. My name is Ken Oaks, and I am in charge of the website for Tiffany & Co. I was alerted to your story today by a colleague, and it's fabulous."

"Thanks." Wow. She'd known it was good, but this was something else entirely.

"We have been thinking about doing something like this for a long time, and this put us over the edge. We'd like you to come work for us and be in charge of creating and writing human interest stories for our website. It's a brilliant idea, and your talent is obvious."

Whoa. Leave New Age? Never have to see Kyle or Roger again? Evolve into her own independent woman? It was one thing to refuse to return Kyle's phone calls, knowing he was upstairs. But if she left New Age, she'd never run into Kyle again. She pursed her lips and knew she couldn't do it. She couldn't give up hope on him yet.

Her door burst open and Kyle stormed into her office. "You can't keep avoiding me," he announced. "I'm not going to let you go that easily."

"Hang on a sec, please, Mr. Oaks." She covered the mouthpiece with her hand. "Are you going to tell Roger that you love me and won't let me go for the company?"

Kyle scowled. "We can work this out, Angie. It's only for a few weeks."

"So that's a no?"

"Angie!"

Decision made. She uncovered the mouthpiece. "Mr. Oaks, I would love to work for you at Tiffany & Co. Assuming we can work out the salary, I accept the offer."

"Excellent! I'll e-mail you a written offer of terms, and

you can let me know what you think. Fabulous. We'll get you on board right away."

They exchanged mutual congratulations, and Angie hung up the phone. She felt great. Excited. Exhilarated. She was her own woman and needed no man for her muse or even her job. She leaned back in her chair and eyed Kyle. "I just accepted a job at Tiffany's. They loved today's story so much they made me an offer."

Kyle felt his heart sink. "You accepted another job? You aren't going to work here anymore?"

"Yes, and no."

"But how could you do that? I thought we had something! You're going to throw it away because you're mad at me?" His gut hurt, his chest burned. He felt like he was going to be sick. "That's ridiculous!"

"Don't ever call me ridiculous!" Angie jumped to her feet and shoved him in the chest. "I've loved you for two years, and you chose my sister over me. And then I fall in love with you again, and you choose your company over me. Do you need to make it any more clear that you don't return my feelings? Forget it, Kyle! I'm not going to let you break my heart again!" She was dry-eyed and her voice was rock solid. "I deserve a man who will love me like I love him, and that doesn't mean being bartered off for financial gain!"

He felt like he was falling off a cliff. "You loved me? Before I started dating Sheila?"

"Of course I did! How could I not? We had so much fun together, and I thought you were too shy to make a move, that you really were falling for me too. Hah!"

Kyle thought back to those times with Angie, and how

tempted he'd felt, and how relieved he'd been when Sheila appeared. He hadn't been ready for Angie then. "I think I loved you then too."

She laughed, a cold and bitter laugh. "And you showed it by taking my sister to bed?"

"And I love you now."

"Then I would hate to be a girlfriend you didn't love, if this is how you treat me." She tried to whirl away, but he caught her arm.

"Angie. I love you. I'm ready for you."

Her eyes were flashing. "It's too late, Kyle. I need more."

They stood there in silence for a long moment, and Kyle realized he'd lost her. Driven her away by a stupid decision. The company would never make him happy the way Angie would.

He couldn't let her walk away. It was that simple. "Come here."

"No."

He grabbed her hand and walked out of her office, dragging her with him. "Kyle! Let go of me."

"No."

"Why? Where are you taking me?"

He refused to respond to any more of her questions. Up the flight of stairs, down the hall to Roger's office. He shoved open the door. Roger was practicing his putting.

Kyle stepped in front of Roger's ball, pulled Angie against him, and kissed her. Gave her the deepest, hottest kiss he was capable of delivering. He didn't stop until she was sagging against him.

Then he nodded at them both and walked out.

"I'm not selling you the company!" Roger shouted after him.

"I know." He continued walking, hoping, waiting. *Please come after me, Angie.* He didn't know what else to do.

He'd put everything out there for her. If she knew him like he thought she did, she would understand. And she'd forgive him.

He walked into his office and shut the door and waited.

And waited.

And waited.

Finally, he sat down at his desk and let his head drop to his hands. Too late. He'd been too late.

"Kyle?"

He snapped his head up to find Angie standing in front of him, her eyes soft. His throat tightened, and he felt like he couldn't breathe. "Angie?"

"I love you."

The world opened for him. "I love you, too."

"I'm still taking the job at Tiffany's. I need my independence."

"I can respect that."

She nodded. "And you aren't my muse."

He frowned. "Okay . . ."

"And you have to kiss me like that at least five times a day."

He grinned and held out his hands. "I can live with that."

"All right then." She let him pull her onto his lap. "Let's start now. For practice."

For practice.

The phone woke up Kyle at one o'clock the next morning. Angie was sprawled across him, her hair tickling his chin, her new ring sparkling on her left hand.

He sighed with immense satisfaction, knowing that everything was right in his world.

When the phone shrilled again, Angie jerked, so Kyle grabbed the phone before it could wake her. "Hello?"

"Kyle? Roger. Did I wake you?"

"Yeah." He kissed her hair. "Angie and I are engaged."

Roger was quiet for a moment. "Congratulations."

"Thanks. We're very happy." Angie stirred and lifted her head.

"Who is it?" she whispered.

When he said Roger, she smiled and began nibbling his right nipple.

"Rog, I gotta go." He shifted so he had better access to her. "I'll talk to you tomorrow."

"Wait! I'll still sell you the company!"

Kyle brought the phone back to his ear. "What?"

"I don't want the damn thing. Take it."

"You serious?" He didn't realize how tightly he was holding Angie until she elbowed him in the stomach to get him to loosen his grip. "You'll sell?"

"Yeah. Let's close it soon. I have other things I want to try. Meet tomorrow morning at eight to go over it?"

Kyle brought Angie's fingers to his lips. "Let's make it ten. I think I'm sleeping in tomorrow. I have a new fiancée who comes first."

"Fine. Ten. See you then."

Kyle hung up the phone and grinned at Angie. "Have I told you how much I love you?"

"He's selling you the company anyway?"

"Yep."

She smiled. "That's awesome."

"Not as awesome as this." He kissed her ring. "This is what really counts."

"And they say you can't teach an old dog new tricks."

"I'm not old." He pushed her onto her back and kissed her thoroughly. "But if you want to teach me any more new tricks, I'd be game for it."

A mischievous light came into her eyes. "Well, I had this one inspiration . . ."